HIS CONVENIENT
ROYAL BRIDE

CARA COLTER

A FORTUNATE
ARRANGEMENT

NANCY ROBARDS THOMPSON

MILLS & BOON

First Published in Great Britain 2019
by Mills & Boon, an imprint of HarperCollinsPublishers,
1 London Bridge Street, London, SE1 9GF

His Convenient Royal Bride © 2019 Cara Colter
A Fortunate Arrangement © 2019 Harlequin Books S.A.

Special thanks and acknowledgement to Nancy Robards Thompson for her contribution to the Fortunes of Texas: The Lost Fortunes continuity.

ISBN: 978-0-263-27235-2

0519

MIX
Paper from
responsible sources

FSC
www.fsc.org   **FSC™ C007454**

This book is produced from independently certified FSC™
paper to ensure responsible forest management.

For more information visit: www.harpercollins.co.uk/green

Printed and bound in Spain
by CPI, Barcelona

HIS CONVENIENT ROYAL BRIDE

CARA COLTER

To all my brave friends entering civic politics—Bill, Debbie, Ellen, Karen—intent on changing the world for the better in their own way, with their own gifts.

CHAPTER ONE

"Look, Maddie, it's them."

"Sorry, who?" Maddie asked, distracted. The Black Kettle Café opened for the day in—her eyes flew to the clock—thirty minutes.

She checked inventory. The glass-encased shelves were lined with an abundance of scones, in six different flavors. The scones were her idea. She felt her stomach knot with familiar anxiety. What if it was too early to put out so many? Should she have waited for the weekend concert crowds? What if she had spent all that money on something that wouldn't sell? Wouldn't it have been better to chip away at some of the overdue bills?

And then there was the ever-present voice of self-doubt. *What kind of an idiot thought scones could save a business?* And deeper yet, *Was there any point in saving a business in a town that was probably going to die, despite her best efforts?*

"Those awesomely attractive men I told you about. A perfect ten on the ooh-la-la scale. Both of them. Don't you think that's unusual? Two perfect tens together?"

Maddie bit her lip in exasperation. The weight of the whole world felt as if it was resting on her not-big-enough shoulders, and her young helper was rating every male she saw on an ooh-la-la scale? Sophie probably wouldn't be nearly as excited about the awesome attractiveness of the visitors, if she knew Maddie was worried about how the café was going to pay her wages!

It was Sophie's first day working the coffee shop in the remote town of Mountain Bend, Oregon. Sophie, just out of high school, was the summer help and she was easily distracted and resisted direction. She had not wanted to put on an apron this morning, because it "hid her outfit."

Though technically Maddie was the café manager, there were several problems with reprimanding her. Sophie was the owner's niece. And she and Maddie had grown up practically next door to each other in the small village. Maddie felt almost as if they were sisters—older and younger.

"What men?" Maddie asked reluctantly.

"I told you! I saw them last night. They're driving the sports car. A Lambo in Mountain Bend. Can you believe it?"

Maddie had no idea what a Lambo was and, unless it was fueled by scones, she didn't really care.

"They're jaw-dropping," Sophie decided dreamily. "I like the big one. He's got a certain formidable look about him, doesn't he? Like he might be a cop. He wasn't driving, though. The other one was driving. They're right outside the door. For heaven's sake, quit scowling at me and look!"

Against her better judgment, Maddie followed Sophie's gaze out the large, plate glass window. The quaint main street—and all her troubles—faded into nothing. Maddie was not aware of the loveliness of overflowing flower baskets, or that the stone-fronted buildings were, like the house she had inherited, showing signs of disrepair.

Maddie was aware, suddenly and intensely, of only *him*. Some energy, some power, shivered around him, and it dimmed even the extraordinary morning light that lit the lush green forest that carpeted the steep hills that embraced Mountain Bend.

The day's menu was posted, and two men were studying it. It was true, the bigger of them was memorable—large, muscled, redheaded, with a thick beard that matched his hair. The man was definitely a throwback to some kind of Gaelic warrior.

But regardless of his obvious power, he was not the one who had made the entire world fade into nothingness for Maddie.

It was the man who was with him. A full head shorter than his companion—which still would have made him just a hair under six feet tall—the other man radiated power and presence, a kind of rare self-confidence that said this man owned the earth and he knew it.

Tall and well built, he was stunningly gorgeous. His thick, neatly trimmed hair was as rich and chocolaty as devil's food cake. He had high cheekbones, a straight nose, a chin with a faint—and delicious—hint of a cleft in it. He glanced away from the menu, through the window and straight at Maddie.

Her thought was to duck, as if when he saw her, he would know there was something weak melting within her, like an ice-cream cone that had toppled onto hot pavement. But she found herself unable to move, in the grip of a dark enchantment. All her sensations intensified as his gaze met hers. His eyes were deep blue, ocean water shot through with sapphires. A hint of pure fire sparked in their endless depths.

She was shocked by the reappearance of a demon within her. But there it was: pure, undiluted, primal attraction to a gorgeous man. Good grief! How many times did a woman have to learn life's most unpleasant lessons?

There was no one riding in to the rescue.

Though maybe this was the sad truth: in times of stress, there was no drug more potent than an extraordinarily attractive man, the fantasy that someone would come along and provide respite from the onerous challenges of daily life.

And since there was no arguing the stressfulness of

these times—Past Due notices stacking up like a deck of
cards in the café office—Maddie indulged the feeling of
unexpected magic whispering into her life.

Her eyes dropped to the full, sinfully sensual curl of
a firm bottom lip, and she felt the most delightful shiver
of, well, longing. To be transported to the place that a kiss
from lips like those could take you.

That was not real. A place of weakness, she reminded
herself, annoyed by her lapse. Fairy tales did not exist. She
had found that out the hard way. Maddie gave herself a determined mental shake. It was the strain of her life that was
making this small diversion seem so all encompassing.

If this was a test, she was as ready for it now as she
would ever be.

"Go let them in," she said to Sophie.

Sophie gave her a startled look—they never opened
early—and then dashed for the door, divesting herself of
that hated apron on the way, and pulling the ribbon from
her hair. Sophie's romantic schoolgirl notions could be
forgiven—she *was* just a schoolgirl—but Maddie was
twenty-four.

She had lost both her parents. She had lived and worked
in New York City. She had suffered a heartbreaking betrayal from a man she had thought she would marry. She
had come home to find the café and her town struggling.
Really, all these events—the awareness that life could
turn bad on a hair—should be more than enough to make
her jaundiced forever.

Despite being jaundiced forever, Maddie found her
hand going to her hair, light brown and short, with the
faintest regret. She had cut it in the interest of being practical, particularly now that her dreams were all business
based, but still it shocked her every time she looked in the
mirror. The shorter cut had encouraged waves to tighten

into corkscrews. Coupled with her small frame, instead of achieving the practical professional look she had aimed for, Maddie felt she looked as if she was auditioning for the part of a waif in a musical.

"Good morning, gentlemen," Sophie sang as she opened the door.

Maddie felt a hint of envy at Sophie's easy vivaciousness, her delight in the potential for excitement. She could warn her, of course, that the path was fraught with danger and betrayal, but Sophie wouldn't listen. Who believed, in the flush of youthful enthusiasm, such things could happen to them?

Hadn't she known, in her heart, her parents would not have approved of the supersuave Derek? Hadn't people tried to tell Maddie that her fiancé might not be worthy of her? Including the friend who had—

"Welcome to the Black Kettle, the coffee shop that won the People's Choice award for Mountain Bend."

This was news to Maddie, but Sophie had decided she would take marketing when she saved up enough money for college. She obviously was testing her skills and looked pleased with the result.

Because the men, if they had been debating whether to stop in, suddenly had no choice.

"Thank you," the darker, younger one said, moving by Sophie first.

His voice was deep and velvet edged, as confident as everything else about him. In those two words, Maddie detected a delightful accent. Maddie felt the air change in the room as soon as he entered, something electrical and charged coming through the door with him.

Electricity is dangerous, she told herself primly. *Not to mention expensive.*

"Good morning," Sophie said, beaming at his larger

companion and batting her thick lashes at him. The man barely glanced at Sophie.

Instead, he surveyed the coffee shop, tension in his body and the set of his jaw, as if he was scanning for danger.

In a just-opening coffee shop in Mountain Bend?

For a reason, she could not put her finger on, Maddie thought that the men did not quite seem equals, the younger man effortlessly the leader between them.

"We aren't usually open yet," Sophie said to the bigger man's back. "But you looked like a couple of hungry guys."

"Thank you," the other said, his pleasantness making up for his friend's remoteness. "That's very kind. We are hungry. It would be dinnertime where we are from."

That accent, Maddie decided, could melt bones. Plus, there was something about him, a deep graciousness, that went with beautifully manicured hands, the perfect haircut, the fresh-shaven face. Despite the khakis and sport shirt, this was not your ordinary *let's check out the hiking and fishing* type of man who spent a week with his guy friends in the mountainous Oregon village.

"Have a seat anywhere," Sophie invited them. "We don't offer dinner—we're just a day café. We close at three o'clock. But we have a great breakfast. I'll bring menus. Unless you want to look at the display case?"

"Menus, thank you." Again, it was the younger one who spoke.

Sophie nearly tripped over herself in her eagerness to get the men menus as they took a table by the window. Maddie ordered herself to get busy. Still, even as she filled cream pitchers, she was aware of that man, reluctantly feeling as if she had been given an irresistible reprieve from the worries that crowded her waking moments.

"So, in what exciting part of the world is it dinnertime

right now?" Sophie was back. She hugged the menus to herself instead of giving them out.

The big man looked at her, irritated at Sophie's question. His look clearly said, *Mind your own business.*

"Scotland," the other said, flashing Sophie an easy smile.

Maddie felt her heart dip at, not just the perfect teeth, but the natural sexiness in that smile, a heat that continued to his eyes, making the sapphire in them more intense.

"I thought so," Sophie said sagely, as if she was a world expert on dialects. "I detected a certain *Braveheart* in the accent. Your car is dreamy. I'm Sophie. And you are?"

Maddie put down the cream. "Sophie, if I could see you?" Obviously, she was going to have to give a lecture on being a little more professional. Dreamy car and introductions, indeed.

"In a sec," Sophie called.

"I'm Ward," the younger man, the one with the amazing presence, said easily.

The other said nothing.

"Lancaster," Ward filled in for him, giving him a look that might have suggested he be friendlier.

"Lancaster, are you by chance a policeman?"

Both men's eyebrows shot up.

Really, Maddie needed to step in, to stop this inquisition of customers, to take this opportunity to brief Sophie on professionalism, yes, even here in Mountain Bend. But if Sophie found out what Lancaster did, wouldn't it follow that Ward might volunteer what he did, as well?

There was something about him that was so intriguing, some power and mystery in the way he carried and conducted himself, that he had made Maddie aware there was a whole world out there that did not involve baking scones, fretting about bills, or watching helplessly as your world fell apart and your hometown declined around you.

Ridiculous to feel as if hope shimmered in the air around a complete stranger.

Because wasn't hope, after all, the most dangerous thing of all?

That, Maddie told herself, was the only thing she needed to know about the man who had entered the little main street coffee shop.

Not that he was a reprieve from a life that had gone heavy with worries.

No, that he was the exact opposite. That all her worries would intensify if she followed this lilting melody humming to life in the base of her being—the one that coincided with his appearance—to where it wanted to go.

She touched the gold chain on her neck. It was a pendant made with a gold nugget that her father had found a long time ago and given to her mother. Touching the pendant usually had the effect of grounding her. Sometimes, Maddie even imagined her father's voice when she touched it.

What would he say, right now, if he were here and saw her in such a ridiculous state over a man she had only just laid eyes on, to whom she had not even spoken a single word?

Something, she was sure, practical and homespun. *Whoa, girl, go easy.*

But she did not hear her father's voice, not even in her imagination. Instead, the pendant seemed to glow warm under her fingertips.

CHAPTER TWO

"LANCASTER DOES HAVE a military background, to be sure. What would you recommend from the menu?" It was Ward who spoke, his tone easy, but for the first time it seemed he would like to close the conversation with the young waitress

"Does Scotland have an army?" Sophie asked, non-plussed. "I wouldn't have thought—"

"Sophie, would you please give those gentlemen their menus, and then I need to talk to you for a minute?"

Ward turned and smiled at her and his smile was charismatic and sympathetic, as if he entirely got that training young employees was a little like trying to train an overly enthusiastic puppy.

Sophie surrendered the menus in slow motion. "What brings you to Mountain Bend?"

"We've come from a few days' holiday in California," Ward answered. "We're finishing up our stay in America with the Ritz concert."

The Ritz were a world-renowned band. Kettle's nephew, Sophie's cousin, was the drummer. It had been Kettle's idea for the band to officially open the summer season with a huge outdoor concert tomorrow night.

The hope was, once they had sampled the pristine charms of Mountain Bend, the throngs of people who had purchased tickets for the concert would return. Plan vacations here. Buy some of the empty miner's houses for summer cottages. Spend money on coffee and groceries and gas. Save the town.

It was a long shot, at best, but Maddie baked a back supply of scones, and printed off dozens of business cards, just in case.

"Well, the locals know the best sights," Sophie declared. "I'd be happy to show you around."

"Sophie!"

"After work," Sophie amended reluctantly.

Lancaster handed her his menu and folded his massive arms over his chest. "I'll have the Bend-in-the-Road."

"I think you'd prefer the Mountain Man," Sophie said sweetly.

"Could I see you for a moment?" Maddie called sternly and urgently.

Sophie ignored her. "Or maybe a few scones? That would make you feel right at home, wouldn't it?"

"If I wanted to feel at home," Lancaster said coolly, "I would have stayed there. And it's pronounced scone, as in gone, not scone, as in cone."

"I love a man who knows his scones," Sophie said, not insulted.

"I want the Bend-in-the-Road. I'm pretty sure I cannot get an edible scone in Mountain Bend, Oregon."

Maddie was pretty sure he was given a little nudge under the table with the other's foot.

"They happen to be the most delicious scones in the world," Sophie said loyally. "Maddie could have had a shop in New York someday, but—"

This was going seriously off the rails!

"Sophie!" Maddie called again, before it developed into an argument or a tell-all about Maddie's broken dreams and bad boyfriend.

Still, she could not help but be annoyed. You couldn't

get a good scone in Mountain Bend? That was a challenge if she had ever heard one!

Sophie gave her a disgruntled look, and the customers a reluctant one. "Sorry," she said. "Duty calls."

But then, before duty asked too much of Sophie, she leaned both elbows on the table, put her chin on her hands and blinked at Lancaster.

"So, do you ever wear a kilt?" she purred.

The big man looked stunned. After an initial moment of shocked silence, Ward threw back his head and laughed. If he'd been gorgeous before, it was now evident that had just been the warm-up. His laughter was pure, exquisitely masculine, entirely sexy.

Danger, Maddie reminded herself firmly.

Before Lancaster could answer, Sophie giggled, straightened up from the table and headed over to Maddie.

"What do you think?" she asked in a happy undertone. "Match, game and set to me?"

What she thought was that she envied Sophie's relative innocence. The younger woman thought you could play at this game with no one getting hurt. Both those men had a masculine potency about them that spoke of experience.

No doubt both of them had a string of broken hearts in their pasts. She didn't care if the assessment was completely unfair. It was better safe than sorry, and Sophie was a naive small-town girl.

Just as she herself had been when she met Derek. Maddie felt, again, protective of the younger woman.

"This is not how you interact with customers," she said, firmly. "You do not flirt with them. These shenanigans will end now."

"Shenanigans?" Sophie asked.

"A kilt?" Maddie demanded in an undertone.

"Don't say you don't want to know the answer," Sophie

said, grinning impishly, unintimidated by the neighbor she had known her whole life.

Maddie made to deny it. Her mouth opened. But her gaze, of its own accord, slid back to Ward. His strong, tanned legs were tucked under the table. A kilt? Good grief! She could feel herself beginning to blush!

Sophie laughed knowingly.

"Look," Maddie said, pulling herself together, "you're being way too inquisitive. They're customers. They're here for breakfast, not to exchange life stories. And they're not Americans. They won't appreciate your friendliness."

Sophie pursed her lips together, miffed at the reprimand, as Maddie had known she would be.

"Or apparently your scones," she said, pronouncing it as *gone* rather than *cone* as Maddie always had. Then she flounced through the swinging doors into the kitchen and gave Kettle the order.

"We ain't open yet." This declaration was followed by a string of cusswords used creatively and representing a long military history. "I don't make exceptions. And that includes the apron. And tie your hair back. We have standards." He put enough curse words between *have* and *standards* to impress a sailor.

Sure enough, Kettle himself stomped through the kitchen door. Despite the scowl on his grizzled face, Maddie felt a rush of affection.

Kettle had been her father's best friend, there for her and her mother when her father had been killed in a logging accident. He'd been there for her again as her mother, heartbroken, had followed on her father's heels way too quickly, leaving Maddie an orphan at eighteen.

Maddie's fiancé, Derek, had not gotten it when she had felt compelled to return to Mountain Bend after Kettle's accident, to manage the café. This was the code she had been raised with: you did right by the people who had done right by you.

So Kettle's stomp was a good thing. He was nearly back to his normal self after he had fallen off the restaurant roof while shoveling snow in the winter and had a complicated break to his hip that had required several surgeries.

Kettle had spent a military career he would not talk about with Delta Force before returning to Mountain Bend. Now he skidded to a halt, surveyed the two men with a certain bemused expression, and then turned back to the kitchen in time to intercept Sophie, who was coming out behind him.

"Maddie," he said gruffly, "you handle them customers. Sophie, you can help me in the kitchen for now."

Sophie looked as if she planned to protest, but she knew better than to argue with her uncle, especially her first day of working for him. She cast one last longing look at the table before reluctantly obeying and going back into the kitchen.

"I trust you to be sensible," Kettle told Maddie in an undertone. In other words, he trusted she'd outgrown the kind of shenanigans that got small-town girls, like her and Sophie, in all kinds of trouble.

Yes, she thought with a sigh, she was the sensible one *now*.

"I'm sure you won't be imagining anyone in kilts, or any other romantic nonsense, either."

So, he had heard something of that. She hoped she wasn't blushing, again, but Kettle wasn't looking at her, but watching their first guests of the day with narrowed eyes.

"What did they say they're doing here?" he asked quietly.

"The Ritz concert."

"The big one's security. Written all over him. Maybe doing an assessment before the band arrives."

"What about the other one?" Maddie asked, keeping her tone casual.

"Well, that's the odd part."

"In what way?"

"He looks like the principal, to me."

"The what?"

"Never mind. My old life creeps up on me, sometimes. I'm sure they are exactly what they say they are."

But he didn't sound sure at all.

"Like a school principal?" Maddie asked, unwilling, for some reason, to let it go.

Kettle snorted. "Does he look like a school principal to you?"

Maddie looked at him one more time, that subtle aura of power and confidence. "No," she admitted.

"Exactly. Someone who travels with a close protection specialist. Interesting."

Interesting enough to make Kettle stop from tossing them out before regular opening hours. He had definitely recognized something that had automatically given them his respect—generally hard earned—but that had also made him cautious about exposing his man-crazy niece to them.

"A close protection specialist?"

"A bodyguard in civilian terms. Never mind. I'm being silly." Kettle shook his head and went back to the kitchen muttering, "Ah, once a warrior."

The ancient coffeemaker let out a loud hiss, announcing the coffee was ready, and Maddie went and grabbed the pot.

She popped her head in the kitchen door. "Sophie, can you hand me some mugs from the dishwasher?"

Sophie brought over the mugs. "I know what their car looks like," she said in a hushed tone as she handed Maddie two thick crockery-style coffee mugs. "I'll bet they're staying at the Cottages. I'm going to go look as soon as I'm done with work."

She already was planning to thwart Kettle's plan to protect her!

"You will not," Maddie said.

Feeling uncomfortably in the middle of something, Maddie started to take the mugs and the pot over to the window table. Then she paused and picked up two scones from the display and set them on a plate.

"Coffee?" she asked. She set down the scones. "Complimentary. The grill isn't quite heated yet. Breakfast will be a few minutes."

While Lancaster eyed the scones with deep suspicion, and even prodded one with his finger, it was Ward who answered, and again she had a sense of him being in a leadership position.

Did he do something that warranted a bodyguard? It seemed a little far-fetched for Mountain Bend. Poor Kettle just hadn't been himself since he fell off that roof.

"Thank you. I'm Ward and this is Lancaster. And you are?"

She actually blushed, but kept her tone deliberately cool. "It's Sophie's first day. I hope she didn't give you the impression it's some kind of American tradition for staff at restaurants to introduce themselves to customers."

"It isn't? Lancaster, didn't we have that happen before? In Los Angeles? That fellow. Franklin! He definitely introduced himself. *Hi, I'm Franklin, and I'll be your server tonight.*"

"You're right," she conceded. "It is protocol at some of the big chains. But here in Mountain Bend, not so much."

"Thank you for clarifying that," Ward said. "I find learning another country's customs a bit like learning a new language. There's lots of room for innocent error. But now you have us at a disadvantage. You know our names, but we are none the wiser."

She frowned. She was aware of *needing* to keep distance between her and this powerfully attractive sample of manliness. Still, she could not see a way out of it. Asking him to call her Miss Nelson would be way too stilted.

"Madeline," she said, and it sounded stilted anyway and somehow unfriendly. "Maddie," she amended in an attempt to soften it a bit.

"Maddie."

Just as she had feared, her name coming off his lips in that sensual accent was as if he had touched the nape of her neck with his fingertips.

"I can't help but notice your pendant. It's extraordinary." He reached up, and for a moment they both froze, anticipation in the air between them.

Then he touched it, ever so lightly. The pendant suddenly felt hot, almost as though there would be a scorch mark on her neck where it rested.

Maddie shivered, from the bottom of her toes to the top of her head.

CHAPTER THREE

"BEAUTIFUL," WARD SAID SOFTLY. He withdrew his hand, his amazing sapphire eyes intent on her face.

The pronouncement could mean the pendant. But it could also mean—

"A gold nugget?" he asked her.

Obviously, he meant the pendant! Maddie had to pull herself together! Good grief. She felt as though she was trembling.

"Y-y-yes, my father found it and had it made into this piece."

"Lovely," he said, and again, it felt as if he might be commenting on more than the pendant. "My name's a diminutive, too. Short for Edward."

Did Lancaster shake his head, ever so slightly?

Ward changed tack so effortlessly that Maddie wondered if she had imagined that slight shake of head.

"Do you live up to it?" Ward asked in that sexy brogue. He took a sip of the freshly poured coffee and his laughing eyes met hers over the rim of the cup.

"Excuse me?"

"Your name? Are you mad?"

She wondered if, in her attempts to remain professional, she had ended up looking cranky! That was the thing to remember about men like this. Even simple things were complicated around them. She tried to relax her features as she realized he was deliberately trying to tease some of the stiffness from her.

She remembered Kettle's confidence that she would be sensible. But not stiff and uninviting, even if it was self-protective. And suddenly she didn't feel like living up to Kettle's stodgy expectation of her.

"Mad, angry or mad, crazy?" Maddie asked him, returning his smile tentatively. It was an indicator of how serious everything in her life had become that she considered engaging in this banter and returning his smile living dangerously.

"Obviously, neither," he said, saluting her with his coffee cup.

Was he flirting? With her? That certainly upped the chances of the mad, crazy. Especially if she engaged with him. Of course, she wouldn't engage!

Or any other romantic nonsense. Though she suddenly felt a need not just to defy Kettle's impressions of her, but to have a moment of lightness.

"And do you live up to your name?" she asked him.

He raised an eyebrow at her.

"Do you ward?"

"Ward, protect?" he asked her. "Or ward, admit to the hospital?"

They shared a small ripple of laughter, that appreciation that comes when you come across someone who thinks somewhat the same way you do. Their eyes met, and a spark, like an ember escaped from a bonfire, leaped between them.

Maddie reminded herself that one spark, even that small, could burn down a whole forest. She'd had her moment, Maddie told herself, clinging to the sensibility Kettle was relying on her for.

"Ward off pesky waitresses, I hope," Lancaster said darkly, and then before she could take it personally, "Where's your friend?"

"Her uncle needed her in the kitchen."

"Locked her up," Lancaster muttered with approval. He took a scone off the plate and scowled at it. "Is this a flavor?"

"Yes, it has a hint of orange in it."

"There's no flavors in scones," Lancaster said firmly. "Do you have cream?"

"Cream? For the coffee? Of course. I'll go get it."

"No, for the scones. Cornish cream?"

"Sorry, I—"

"Too much to hope for." He took a gigantic bite. And then, to Maddie's satisfaction, he sighed and closed his eyes. "That's good. Even without cream. Try it," he insisted to Ward.

Ward picked up the other scone and took a bite. Even that small gesture spoke of refinement. There was that ultrasexy smile again. "You owe somebody an apology," he told Lancaster. "Not only edible, but possibly the best scone this side of the Atlantic."

"Any side of the Atlantic." Lancaster finished the scone in two bites and eyed Ward's hungrily.

"Who made these?" Ward asked, polishing it off.

"I did."

"You did not. You've got to have a Celt hiding in that kitchen." Again, Ward was teasing her, as if he sensed she took life altogether too seriously.

Maybe it was weakness to engage, and to want to engage, but what the heck? The men would eat their breakfast and be gone. They might come back, or she might see them in the street and wave, but it was hardly posting banns at the local church. After the concert tomorrow night, they would disappear, never to be seen again.

Unless they bought one of the old miner's cottages. Unless they fell in love with Mountain Bend.

She did not want to be thinking of falling in love, in any of its many guises, anywhere in the vicinity of the very appealing Ward!

"It's an old family recipe," Maddie supplied. "My grandmother was English. And she pronounced it scone, as in cone."

"Two strikes," Lancaster muttered.

"Both entirely forgivable," Ward said. "Do you think I could bother you for another for my hungry friend?"

Maddie brought back a plate of scones and Ward asked, "So it was you who was going to have a shop in New York City?"

"If I was, it was a long way in the future. Anyway, New York City is in my past now." She needed to move on. She had just lectured Sophie about professionalism. There was no fraternizing with the customers!

She stood there, paralyzed.

"We visited briefly, before we went to California," Ward volunteered. "This seems preferable to me, the little piece of America everyone knows exists, but that is hard to find. I work in community-based economies. I'd be interested to learn more about your town."

She cocked her head at him. His intelligence and genuine interest was pulling at her. He was definitely a man she would love to sit down and have a conversation with.

And of course she was not going to give in to that temptation!

"I'd love to talk to you," she said, and unfortunately, she meant it. "Maybe we'll get together sometime."

That part she did not mean at all!

"Can I get you something else?" she said quickly, a reminder to all involved what kind of relationship this was.

"Tea would be wonderful."

She brought tea and more scones to their table, but thankfully it was opening time, so she could not linger. There was a surprising number of people coming into the café. The town appeared to be benefiting already from people arriving for tomorrow's concert.

Was it possible this was going to work?

She didn't have time to contemplate it for long. Her life became a whirlwind as Sophie remained in the kitchen. Kettle delivered the two men breakfast, but Maddie did not interact with them again until it was time to take their money at the till.

"You know how to make tea, too," Ward said. "That's a rare gift in this country!"

A small thing, not worthy of a blush, and yet there she was, blushing over tea! Or maybe it was the fact that his hand had brushed hers, and she had felt the jolt of his pure presence, the same way she had when his finger had rested, ever so briefly, on the pendant at her neck.

"That English granny again," she said.

"Somehow the last thing I think of when I look at you is an English granny," he said, his voice a sexy rasp. Then he looked faintly taken aback, as if he had said something wildly inappropriate. He recovered quickly, though.

"I hope we do have a chance to talk about your town's transition," Ward said. He said it as if he was talking to someone whose opinion he would respect. She glanced at him. Small talk.

"Me, too," she said with bright insincerity. "Enjoy your stay here."

Then she snapped the cash register shut and whirled away from them, feeling somehow as if she had escaped some unknowable danger.

Why would such a feeling, the feeling of a near miss on a road named Catastrophe, be tinged with regret?

* * *

"That was a good breakfast," Lancaster said, as they exited the coffee shop. "You've got to give it to Yanks. They know how to eat. The scones were a surprise of the best possible sort."

"Are you saying barracks food doesn't appeal?"

"No, Your Highness."

Both men looked around, but no one was within hearing.

"Sorry, sir, lifetime habits are hard to break."

They came to the car and Ward regarded it appreciatively. "Do you want to drive, Major Lancaster?" He glanced around. "You're right about lifetime habits."

"I was hoping for an opportunity. Where to?"

"I feel, after California and New York, I just need to stretch my legs and have some space. What about those hot pools we heard about?"

"The hotel clerk told us they were in the middle of the wilderness," Lancaster said, appalled.

"That part of America interests me."

"I think this is bear country," Lancaster said doubtfully, the quandary written on his face. How to keep the Prince safest?

"I'm prepared to live dangerously."

"I was afraid of that." Lancaster looked less than pleased, for he was a man born into the station of guarding the royal family of the Isle of Havenhurst, and he sniffed out—and avoided—situations that might place the Prince in danger, but he also knew an order when he heard it.

"The cover story went well," Ward said as they left Mountain Bend and took a rough road that began to twist up the mountain through thick forest.

Lancaster was silent.

"Didn't you think so?"

"The old guy didn't buy it."

"What old guy?"

"He came out of the kitchen for a minute and gave us a good look over. Limping. Ex-military."

"How can you tell that?"

Lancaster shrugged. "There are ways to tell. But it works both ways. I think he could tell a bit about us, too."

Ward contemplated the fact he had not registered the man coming out of the kitchen. Of course, it was Lancaster's job to notice who was around them, and Ward was confident Lancaster was probably better at his job than just about anybody in the world. But still, Ward suspected the woman, Maddie, had something to do with the fact he had not noticed the man come out of the kitchen.

There was something about her that engaged him, especially after coming from California, where the women he met all seemed very outgoing, very tall, very tanned, wrinkle-free and white-blond.

In contrast he had found Maddie's beauty was understated and natural, as refreshing as a cool breeze on a warm day. She was lovely, with those kissed-by-the-sun curls springing around her head, her delicate features, the perfect bow of puffy lips, hazel eyes that looked green one moment and doe brown the next. Despite the faintest hint of freckles, unlike her California counterparts, her skin had been porcelain pale, as if, despite being surrounded by the outdoors, she did not get outside much. And there had been faint shadows of what—weariness? worry?—under those remarkable eyes.

In their short encounter Ward had found her both delightfully interesting and intriguingly attractive, and at the same time a painful reminder of the kind of woman and kind of life he would never have.

"I'm not concerned. Yet," Lancaster said. "But I wouldn't be telling anyone else your name is Edward."

"Havenhurst is probably the least known kingdom in the entire North Atlantic, a little speck in the ocean, two hundred kilometers from the North Channel. Even the Scots, who are the most culturally linked to us, barely know who we are. So, few people know who I am."

Ward's publicity-averse family employed a small army to fend off the pursuit of royalty-crazed tabloids, and though the odd picture or story about him emerged, he was mostly an unknown.

Lancaster looked unconvinced.

"I'm off the radar," Ward assured him.

"Best to keep it that way. I think your California friend, Miss O'Brian, would have loved to have milked your status for a bit of publicity."

Ward gave Lancaster a look. "Did you give her a talking-to?"

Lancaster lifted a huge shoulder. "Laid out a few ground rules, aye."

The road had ended. Lancaster turned off the car, and they got out. They removed day packs from the trunk and hoisted them onto shoulders.

Hours later, they returned to the car. They had hiked all day, but they had not succeeded in finding the hot pool.

"The more we didn't find them, the more I was homesick for a dip," Ward said. "Maybe we should take that young waitress up on her offer to show us the sights, after all."

"Huh. With a chaperone, maybe."

"Perhaps Maddie could join us, too."

"I don't think that's a good idea," Lancaster offered.

Ward shot Lancaster a look. Had he guessed there

was something about the gamine scone enchantress that had piqued his interest? But no, the scowl said something else entirely.

"Because the young Sophie may have been a bit smitten with you?"

Lancaster scowled. "Emphasis on *young*. There's bound to be a slipup. Questions asked that can't be answered. The cover story won't stand up to close scrutiny."

Ward reminded himself it was Lancaster's job to think like this, to be on the alert for potential threats and possible dangers, real and imagined.

But he realized wanting Maddie and Sophie to join them wasn't just about finding the hot pools. Maddie, with her curls and her tentative smile, had made him long for something he knew he could not have. Or maybe he could, not forever, but for a few moments in time. Maybe these last few final days of anonymity could give him one chance to see what it was like to have fun with an ordinary girl in an ordinary world. He felt a need to articulate it.

"Please don't deprive me of this opportunity to do a few normal things, Lancaster. Yes, I want to drive a car like this one. But I want to laugh with a pretty lass. Dance at a concert. This may be the only opportunity I ever get to experience a normal life."

A normal life. They got back in the car and Ward took the driver's seat this time. Their small island home did not lend itself to a vehicle like this. In truth, he rarely drove himself anywhere. He put the car in gear and enjoyed the surge of power as he pressed down the gas. Lancaster made an unflattering grab for a bar above his door, but Edward soon found his groove and drove the car as quickly as the poor road would allow.

"I understand, Your Highness," Lancaster said. "This

is really your only taste of freedom. In a few weeks you'll
be a married man."

"I've never had freedom," Ward said quietly, "married
or not. Just the same, I've reached a decision. I've decided
not to marry Princess Aida."

CHAPTER FOUR

"BUT...BUT YOUR marriage is expected," Lancaster stammered, after a long silence.

"I've always understood that service comes before self, and that certain sacrifices would be expected of me."

"Princess Aida is a beautiful woman, sir, hardly a sacrifice."

"She doesn't love me."

"Love?" Lancaster shot him a distressed look. "What does that have to do with it?"

Love. Ward had never had an expectation of it in his life. His father, the King, had not loved his mother, nor she him. Their public lives had been orchestrated to be civil; privately they had been cold and distant to one another.

Ward himself had been sent away to a private school when he was six. So *love* was a nebulous thing to him. He had not experienced it, nor had any expectation of it.

Edward thought of Aida with affection, like one would think of a little sister. When she had come to him and told him she *loved* someone else, he had felt a shocking sense of envy for what was shining in her eyes.

And he'd felt the difficulty of what he needed to do. His nation wanted one thing. His family demanded one thing. His conscience commanded another. He could not be the one to kill the light that had shone from Aida when she talked about Drew Mooretown, the man on her personal guard that she now loved.

"The sacrifice would have been hers, if we married,"

Edward said slowly. "I've no notions of love. We've both known, since we were children, what was expected of us and what the benefit to both of our nations is. Like me, she'll do what's required of her, but, Lancaster, she loves another. I cannot do this to her."

"You're a good man," Lancaster said with a sigh, and Prince Edward Alexander the Fourth knew he had been paid the highest of compliments from one who rarely gave them. He could only hope it was true. "But it's not going to be as easy to get out of it as you think. Your father—"

"Would force it, I know."

"I don't relish the thought of marching you down the aisle with a sword at your back." Lancaster was only partly kidding. "What are you going to do? I've known this whole trip something was deeply troubling you. It seems impossible to get out of it. Unless you're thinking of not going back?"

"Rest easy, Lancaster. You don't have to feel a divided loyalty between your duty to your King and your duty to me. There will be no having to think of a way to wrestle me back to my kingdom. I have always known my destiny is there, and I embrace that. I love my work on economic development, bringing the island new ideas and prosperity, acting as a liaison with the people. I love listening to their ideas and concerns, involving them in the future of our island. I love Havenhurst."

"Then what?"

"I have to set Aida free. And I think there's only one way to do that where unbearable pressure wouldn't be brought on her."

"Which is?"

"I have to marry someone else. Before we return."

"Within days, in other words?"

"Yes."

"A kind of pretend marriage?"

"Yes, just long enough to enable Aida to go off and marry her chap without the indignation of two kingdoms being heaped on her."

"Being heaped on you, instead."

"I have broad shoulders. After it has all died down, a quiet annulment could be arranged."

Lancaster was silent but then spoke. "But you would have to marry genuinely, eventually. Marriage is expected."

Yes, it was expected that Edward would marry, and that out of that marriage would come that all-important heir to the royal legacy.

Not expected: that he would ever know the kind of love he had seen shining in Aida's face when she had confessed to him that she had met another.

Not expected: a longing for this thing his position would probably keep him from ever knowing.

Not expected: that a man the world would see as having absolutely everything—wealth and power beyond the dreams of most mortals—would feel this odd emptiness. A sense of missing something that had increased every day they had explored America, been normal, been free of Havenhurst.

"Perhaps I won't marry at all."

"That sounds a lonely life."

"Will you marry again, Lancaster?" Ward asked softly, remembering the man Lancaster used to be, a man who had radiated a kind of faith in the goodness of life.

"I don't think so," Lancaster said, looking off into the distance. "A man's heart can only take so much."

Lancaster's wife and young baby had been killed in a cottage fire. Lancaster had been away at a training program off-island when it had happened. The whole island had mourned the loss of his family, and five years later, Lancaster still carried an aura of deep mourning about him.

Mourning, mingled with a kind of steadfast, put-one-foot-in-front-of-the-other strength.

"No, I won't marry again," he said. "Not while there are streams that need fishing. But you…you'll be expected to find a wife."

There was the weight of all those expectations again.

"My position makes it more difficult to find a partner, not less."

Lancaster snorted. "Once you are seen as available, women will be throwing themselves at you, Your Highness."

"Not at me," Ward said, and could hear the weariness in his own voice. "At the fantasy of being a princess. At the role they think I play. At their impossible romantic ideas. The reality is so different. The obligations that go with the title would place an unfair burden on someone not brought up in it."

"There is the little issue of an heir," Lancaster reminded him. "You will be King."

"My sister is married, and they have dear, sweet Anne. Perhaps one day she will reign."

"She's a girl!"

"The times are changing, Lancaster."

Lancaster looked dubious about that, at least in the context of Havenhurst. "You've given this some thought."

"I have, indeed."

"How do you find someone to play the role of a pretend princess? It's not as if you can put an ad in the personal section of the newspaper. *Prince in search of bride.*"

"I've asked Sea O'Brian."

They had just spent several days with Sea at her villa in California. Ward had met the actress at a party, a long time ago, on a yacht in the Mediterranean. He had not developed a taste for such things, but he and the famous actress had kept in touch.

Lancaster was silent.

"You don't approve?"

"It's not my place to approve or disapprove of your choices, sir."

"My thought was that she was an actress already. She could play it like a role. And the publicity would certainly benefit her career. I'd like whoever takes this on to benefit in some way. I think the deception of a nation—not to mention my father and mother—is a great deal to ask of an individual."

Again, Lancaster was silent, but his brows had lowered and he was looking straight ahead with such fierce concentration that it could only mean disapproval. They had known each other so long and spent so much time together there was an unbreakable bond between them, almost as if they were brothers.

"I'm interested in your thoughts."

Lancaster took a deep breath. "As you say, sir, she's an actress. There always seems to be lots of drama unfolding around her. I overheard her talking to her press secretary about alerting a tabloid to your presence at her villa and had to head her off."

Ward had not been aware of any of this, an indication of how well Lancaster did his job, and how seriously he took it.

"I don't imagine Sea O'Brian is easy to *head off*," he said mildly.

"Correct," Lancaster said.

"How did you manage it?"

"I took her cell phone hostage," Lancaster admitted reluctantly. "Her *life*, as she told me. She'd been snapping pictures of you when you weren't aware. Anyway, all this leads me to believe that trying to extricate yourself from the situation could get very complicated."

"True," Ward conceded.

"The people won't like her," Lancaster said, his voice low. "They'll see her as glib and superficial. She's not of the earth."

This was a highest form of praise in Havenhurst: he or she is of the earth.

There was a grave silence between the two men, and when Lancaster spoke, his tone was faintly lighter.

"Perhaps you could consider that lass from the café this morning. Think of the scones!" Lancaster crowed. Now that they were alone, he pronounced it *skoons* in the language of their island kingdom.

Both men laughed.

"I think there is far less danger of damage hiring an actress to play the role of my wife than to involve an ordinary girl living her ordinary life," Ward said firmly.

He had found a way to save Aida, without hurting anyone else, or his island kingdom. He was satisfied with his choice. The truth was a woman like Maddie, from the little time he had spent with her, deserved things he could not give.

Love, for one.

That was a topic he knew nothing about. Nothing. Love would be for him, as it had been for his parents, the great unknown. His parents had done precisely what he would do—they had sacrificed any chance of personal happiness for what they saw as the good of Havenhurst.

And he would do the same. Love was not part of his duty, nor his destiny, and he had known those truths forever. He had made a decision to save Aida from this same lonely fate, and that was good enough.

Even though Ward had decided the scone enchantress

was not marriage material—she might already be married for all he knew—he had a feeling that if he wanted to glimpse normal, to feel it and be it for these few days of freedom remaining to him, she could show him that. It would be even better if she had a husband or a boyfriend. They could give him a glimpse of that tantalizing thing called *normal* together.

"Why don't we go see if Maddie and Sophie are willing to show us the pool?" Ward suggested after a moment.

"I still don't think it's a good idea."

"Maddie might even have—what do they call it here? A significant other! Who could come with us."

Lancaster cast him a long look and finally, reluctantly, nodded.

"We're just getting ready to close," Maddie said when the bell rang over the door. She was exhausted. The day had been frantically busy, visitors already thronging the town for tomorrow's concert. She would not be attending the concert. She preferred a warm bath and a good book.

She glanced up and froze.

It was the two men from this morning, Ward and Lancaster.

"Are there scones left?" Lancaster asked without preamble.

"Is that panic I hear in your voice?" Ward asked. He smiled at Maddie. "It takes a lot to panic him. Please tell him you have scones left. Hello, by the way. Nice to see you again."

He said it as if he really meant it.

"You, too," she said, and then wished she hadn't, because she really meant it, too, only she probably really meant it way more than he really meant it.

"If we've dispensed with the social niceties?" Lancaster prodded.

Exactly! Social niceties. Meaningless. Not that she wanted them to have meaning. She was done with that kind of thing. The thrill of a handsome man. The excitement of getting to know someone. The feeling of being close. The tingle of hands touching. That incredible sensation of being alive.

She was done with it—but she was aware she longed for it, too. She had told herself she remained in Mountain Bend, after Derek's betrayal, because she was needed here.

But couldn't that be a way of hiding?

And now, what she was hiding from appeared to have found her. It was like a chocolate addict giving up bonbons. It was all well and good until someone waved one under your nose.

"Do any scones remain?" Lancaster asked plaintively.

See? She was already drifting off, contemplating the many missed pleasures of bonbons. She drew herself up short.

"Unfortunately, no," she said. "We've had crowds. Once I added the Cornish cream, I couldn't keep up with the demand."

"You said you didn't have any!"

"You're making the poor man swoon," Ward pointed out good-naturedly.

She dared not look at him. If he was smiling, and she knew he was—she could tell by the added lilt in his voice—she might be the one swooning!

"I looked up some recipes. It's really just whipped cream, but done until it's very nearly butter, yes?"

"Will you marry me?" Lancaster asked. "And if not me, him?"

Despite her vow not to look, she cast a startled glance

at Ward, thinking he would be laughing uproariously. Why did Ward not seem to think that was funny?

"Anyway, we sold out, but I have some in the freezer I could get for you."

"Perhaps a dozen? And as much cream as you're willing to part with."

"You'll get fat," a voice behind him said. "They're made with pure butter. And then whipped cream, too? Your arteries won't thank you. It's a disgraceful way to treat a beautiful body."

Lancaster whirled and glared at Sophie. "I'll thank you not to comment on my arteries. My body is not your business, either."

"We could change that," Sophie purred.

"We couldn't," Lancaster snapped firmly, much to Maddie's relief. What was Sophie doing, talking to a virtual stranger like that?

"Mountain Bend is a beautiful place," Ward said conversationally to Maddie as she returned with frozen scones and packed them in a box. "Our part of the world has some beautiful places, to be sure, but nothing quite this untamed. Sophie mentioned the best sights were known by the locals. Would you say that's true?"

Maddie nodded, feeling oddly wary.

"Do you think maybe you could show us some? When you're all wrapped up here? You and the delightful Miss Sophie?"

Maddie felt herself freeze. Did Ward like Sophie? Well, who could blame him? And why did she care? It felt like this treacherous attraction she felt for him had to be quelled immediately. But still, Maddie looked over her shoulder at him, and he was smirking at Lancaster with a certain devilment in his smile. He turned back to her and winked.

Winked!

Immediately, she ordered herself to say no to this. She was not up to a man who could make such a simple thing as a playful wink seem sexy. But somehow that simple word stuck in her throat and would not come out.

"Lancaster and I spent the day trying to find a hot pool," Ward said, "and despite having a map we did not turn it up."

"Honeymoon Hot Springs," Sophie said, excited as a puppy who had been shown a toy. "How did you hear about those? It's Mountain Bend's best-kept secret."

"Someone at our hotel told us."

That was unusual, but he *was* charming. He probably just had to smile to get poor old Adele, who worked the front desk at the Cottages, to want immediately to impress him with all the secrets the locals guarded from outsiders. Even now, when they were desperately trying to attract tourists, Honeymoon Hot Springs was rarely mentioned. The name said it all—it was so special to people here. A favorite place for wedding proposals, romantic interludes, honeymoon nights. It was a place couples went for privacy. It was absolutely the wrong place to go with a man you felt the slightest attraction to!

"Naturally, we'd want your, uh, significant other, to come, as well," Ward said.

"She doesn't have one!" Sophie said, like someone in possession of a piece of juicy gossip they couldn't wait to share. "Her fiancé was the world's biggest jerk."

Maddie gave Sophie a look that could kill.

"Well, he was," Sophie said, somehow missing the look entirely. "She came home to look after Kettle, and guess what he did? With her best friend?"

Maddie was mortified. She stared at Sophie in shocked horror. They all stood there in embarrassed distress.

Too late, Sophie became aware of her gaffe. She turned stricken eyes to Maddie. "I didn't mean to—"

"Not to worry," Maddie said brightly. "I'm sorry, no. Local people don't like outsiders going there. I have things to do. Thank you for your interest, but I can't. I—"

"Of course, we'll show you," Sophie said, stubbornly, recovering way too quickly from divulging other people's private lives. She was obviously as thrilled by the men's interest in that secret place with its reputation for romantic enchantment, as Maddie was not.

"Sophie," she said. "It's—"

But Sophie cut her off with a toss of her thick black hair. "I will, if she won't."

There! Sophie had managed to make her sound like a terrible stick-in-the-mud. Had she become a terrible stick-in-the-mud? A person thrown over for another who could not get over it? She thought of her life since she'd returned to Mountain Bend. Work and worry.

She turned stiffly and handed the box of scones to Lancaster. "If there's anything else?" Yes, she recognized it. The voice of a stick-in-the-mud, a woman whose broken heart would no doubt lead her to spinsterhood.

It was what Kettle loved about her, she reminded herself!

But then, ever so naturally, Ward laid his hand across Maddie's wrist. His hand was warm and dry and his touch was firm. But more, his touch transmitted something of his power. She could feel the jolt of his substantial and seductive energy surge up the whole length of her arm.

It occurred to Maddie he was not a man accustomed to people saying no to him, which made it all the more imperative that she do exactly that!

"Please say yes," Ward said softly.

CHAPTER FIVE

MADDIE YANKED HER wrist out from under Ward's hand and resisted an impulse to rub it where it tingled.

Say no, she ordered herself.

Now she was pretty sure he was insisting out of pity. On the other hand, Sophie was going to do whatever she pleased, no matter how ill-advised it was. And playing with fire was ill-advised. Taking a man you barely knew to a place with a name like Honeymoon Hot Springs was playing with fire! Joining the excursion would not be the least bit sensible, which was Kettle's expectation of Maddie.

Really? Maddie thought this was a very bad idea. They did not know these two men. Of course they seemed charming, but you couldn't know these things from a short conversation. She watched true crime shows! And Honeymoon Hot Springs was a long way off the beaten track.

She cast a glance at the two men. It was a poor argument. Ward has asked if her *significant other* would like to join them. Besides, both men radiated decency, a kind of bone-deep honor.

The real reason she was reluctant was because she did not see the point of encouraging Sophie to get in any deeper with Lancaster. He was leaving; she was staying. And the same went for getting to know Ward any better. The hot springs, themselves, invited a kind of instant intimacy. Bathing suits! The romantic setting.

The whole idea had emotional catastrophe written all

over it. But she could tell Sophie was set on going, and she was not about to let her go alone, particularly since there would be bathing suits involved! Chaperoning Sophie might be the more *sensible* way of looking at it!

Besides, hadn't Maddie played it safe her whole life? Said no to every adventure? Scuttled away from every perceived danger? Had it, in any way, protected her from what life had planned?

It had not.

Besides, now, thanks to Sophie, she had to correct the impression that she was hiding away in Mountain Bend nursing a broken heart.

Which had enough elements of truth to it, that it suddenly felt imperative to make that correction.

Feeling as if she was standing on the rock ledge that jutted out way, way above Honeymoon Hot Springs, with that pool of deep turquoise steaming water far, far below, Maddie closed her eyes. *Jump?* Or walk away without ever knowing what adventure might have unfolded?

Maybe it wouldn't even be an adventure, just an ordinary excursion, getting to know someone a little better, saying, *See? I'm not broken.* Couldn't she just have fun? Wasn't it her who was attaching seriousness to the whole encounter that it did not need to have?

She had never jumped off that rock ledge, as some of the bolder people had done. It was time to take a chance, wasn't it?

"Okay," she said. "Yes."

Sophie whooped with surprised delight.

And Maddie noticed the exhaustion she had been feeling, just minutes ago, seemed to have evaporated.

"I'll have to go home and put on a bathing suit," Maddie said.

"A bathing suit?" Sophie said. "Usually we—"

Maddie gave her a look that could have stripped paint. "I don't know what you usually do, Sophie, but you won't be doing it today."

She sounded like a miffed schoolteacher. She turned back to the men. "Can we meet back here in an hour?"

Somehow, now that she had acted like a miffed school-teacher, if felt imperative that she not *look* like one, like a stodgy chaperone, old and humorless before her time, there to spoil everyone's fun.

"Perfect."

As he was going out the door, Lancaster turned back to her. *Thank you*, he mouthed. Maddie was not sure if he meant for the scones, for her agreement to accompany them to the falls, or for her setting out dress restrictions.

Picking an outfit proved more difficult than she had imagined. The bathing suit was not a problem—she had only two, both black, one-piece and equally matronly.

But what to wear over top? Honeymoon Hot Springs was not exactly a walk in the park, but a hike with some steep and rocky terrain to traverse.

Aware of the ticking of the clock—what had made her say they would meet in an hour—Maddie showered and dressed. Several times. She finally settled on a pair of shorts, longer than the ones that Sophie was wearing today, but that still showed off the length of her legs. She put a blue plaid shirt over her bathing suit and knotted it at the waist. The outfit was completed with sturdy hiking shoes.

She put some product in her hair and scrunched up her curls, and then she added large hoop earrings that made her short hair look like she had actually planned the cut as an act of supreme self-confidence, not sheared it off because it was convenient and because she no longer cared to be attractive!

After debating a moment—the hot springs did not really lend themselves to makeup—Maddie dusted her nose with a bit of makeup to hide her freckles and then added some waterproof mascara and just a touch of shadow. She used a color that made her eyes appear more green than brown. One thing about the hair, she decided, giving herself one more quick once-over in the mirror before she headed out the door, was it made her eyes look huge. In fact, she was pleased to see she looked quite pretty. She realized, surprised, she had just enjoyed the rituals of being feminine again. She felt as if she was going on a date. Was she going on a date?

Her hand went to the pendant on her neck, as it so often did when she was uncertain. What would her father think of her going to the hot springs with a stranger? Surely, he wouldn't approve?

But when she closed her eyes and pictured him, he was smiling. *Life is so short*, he said. *Don't be afraid to be bold.*

Maddie opened her eyes, and looked at herself one more time. Maybe there was just a hint of her father's boldness in her.

Every bit of the extra time she had taken felt worth it when she saw Ward's eyes light up with appreciation when they met again in front of the café.

Seeing Sophie's outfit—even shorter shorts than earlier in the day and a crocheted cover-up over a very colorful but skimpy bikini top—Maddie thought she and Sophie should ride in the back of the car together.

But Ward opened the front door of the vehicle for her and nodded at the scowling Lancaster to get in the back with Sophie. Lancaster looked less than pleased about the arrangement and turned so he faced out the window.

As they roared up the mountain road, Maddie relaxed

her need to be in control. In fact, it reminded Maddie of those carefree days of being a teenager. Not the car, of course, but the *feeling*. Bold. Embracing the everyday adventures that were offered.

The trailhead was not visible from the road, especially at this time of year, with the shrubs leafed in. Behind the leafy shrubs, the beginning of the trails was marked with a single wooden post with no markings on it. There were colorful rings around the bottom of it, and Maddie slid a blue one up to the top and hung it on a nail there.

"What does that mean?" Ward asked, curious.

"It will alert others to the fact there are people in the pools, but it's blue, so it means anyone is welcome, and that certain—"

She cast Sophie a meaningful look, which Sophie ignored.

"Certain conventions will be respected. The pink ring would mean someone is in there who wants privacy, and the yellow would mean others are welcome but whoever is in there is without a bathing suit."

She blushed when she said it.

"I think it may be fortuitous that Lancaster and I didn't find our way earlier," Ward said with a smile.

"You may be right," Maddie agreed, returning his smile.

Within a few minutes of being on the trail to the hot pools, Maddie wondered how she could have possibly envisioned catastrophe of any kind. A well-beaten dirt trail, wide enough for two people to walk abreast, wound its way through the shady groves of old-growth forest. The light filtered, green and gold, through the thick canopy, and she could smell the heady perfume of pine and cedar needles being crushed underfoot, and the headier perfume of Ward: clean, male, earthy.

"I'm not sure how we missed this when we looked earlier," Ward said. "I may have to surrender my Boy Scout badge in woodsmanship."

"They have Boy Scouts in Scotland?" Maddie asked. Did he hesitate ever so slightly before he answered? No, she must have imagined it.

"Aye," he said, "and they wear kilts."

"They don't!"

"Scout's honor," he said, and they laughed easily together. Given her resistance to coming in the first place, it was terrible to be so glad that she had!

It had been a long time—way too long—since she had done anything just for fun. The walk to the pools, like the drive, reminded her of more-carefree days. The forest was a soothing, serene place.

Lancaster, carrying the huge picnic basket as effortlessly as if it was a doll's purse, strode up ahead, with Sophie having to skip along to keep up with him. This did not stop her breathless chatter from drifting back to them.

"I'm worried she's giving him entirely the wrong impression," Maddie confided in Ward. "She's acting as if she's far more worldly than she is."

"Don't worry," Ward said easily. "You will never meet a man with more honor than Lancaster. He sees her as a foolish young girl with a crush. He would never take advantage."

"Oh? Also Scout's honor?" Maddie asked.

"Something like that."

Again, she felt he was ever so deftly sidestepping something. But what? She chided herself for being way too serious, as always.

She was going to ask him a bit about where he came from and what he did for a living, but he beat her to it.

"Tell me a little about your town," he said.

This seemed like safe ground, conversationally.

"You said you know a little bit already."

"A little," he agreed.

"That transition you mentioned this morning? From resource based to tourist and ecology is not much more than a pipe dream at the moment. Many of the old-timers here resist the idea of tourists, even if it could save the town, and that's a big if. They see it as unspoiled around here. And they're protective of that. I think they'd rather let the town die a natural death than see a paved path into these springs, or a hotel sitting at the trailhead."

"That's understandable. What happened to the economy?"

"By the time I was born, the mine, the town's biggest employer had already shut down. There was still logging and a bit of trapping. They were dangerous, dirty professions—my dad was killed in a logging accident."

"I'm sorry," he said, with such genuine sympathy she felt an unexpected prick behind her eyelids. "I can see the pendant must have extra meaning for you. How old were you?"

"Sixteen."

He made a sound at the back of his throat, sympathetic and distressed, a man who wanted to protect others from the tragedies of life.

"The work in Mountain Bend attracted hardworking honest people who invested in the town. But now everyone's kind of watching helplessly as the town disintegrates a little more every year, and the only things they own, their houses and businesses, are becoming a little more worthless.

"There is a big hope that the Ritz concert will bring people here who wouldn't normally come. That they'll see what a special place it is and snap up some of the empty houses. If they did, businesses like the Black Kettle would be more viable, even if we could just have a summer season.

"I'm hoping the scones will take off. If people liked them enough, they might be willing to place online orders, though the logistics of shipping from here I haven't quite worked out. If we could attract a few people here who could work online..."

Her voice drifted away. She suddenly felt as if she was talking too much, almost chattering, but there was something about Ward—an intent way of listening—that made that so easy to do.

"Why does a young woman come back to a town with so few prospects?" he asked. "This morning Sophie suggested you had worked in New York."

She sighed. She had tried to give herself over to being carefree, but maybe it was impossible to be carefree when you carried burdens like she did.

She was already sorry she had confided so much, but she couldn't take it back, and it felt somehow good to share what was going on with the town, as if a burden she had carried silently was lightened. Why not go for broke? There was something about Ward that inspired confidences. And there was something in her, alone with all of this for so long, that she felt almost compelled to unburden. Maybe there was something about Ward being a near stranger, someone she would likely not see again, a safe person to share with.

"Kettle fell off his roof last year shoveling snow. I can't believe he was up there. He's in his sixties, for Pete's sake. He broke his hip. He needed help. Not that he asked for it."

"You gave up your aspirations to help him?"

"*Aspirations* might be a little grandiose. I was a clerk at a bank, baking a few scones on the side, which my friends were willing to pay for. But I came back to look after the Black Kettle. I'd worked my way up starting as a teenager there. I knew the ropes and no one else was available."

They walked silently for a while, and then he said, "So you were repaying a favor by coming back?"

"Not at all," she said quickly. "It's not a balance sheet. It's loving people. It's doing what needs to be done."

"Will you go back to your old life when Kettle is fully recovered?"

Sophie had already revealed her old life was a disaster, but she wasn't going to pursue that with a complete stranger. She had already talked way too much.

"This is my life now," Maddie said, determined and cheerful. "Kettle didn't have great medical coverage. I don't know how he's managing to keep the café open, but as long as he does, I'll help him in any way I can. We all have a great deal riding on the concert."

"You're so young to be carrying the worries of the world," he said softly. "Look, you're getting a little worry knot right here." He stopped and touched her forehead.

His finger pressed gently into her brow. She felt herself leaning into it. The weakness that overcame her was swift.

This was always her problem. When she most needed to be strong, she was not! But she would not fail herself this time.

Maddie stepped back from him and away from the odd comfort of the physical connection between them. "You caught me on a bad day," she said crisply. "I usually don't confide my life story to strangers."

"I'm glad you did. Sometimes, just to tell someone, can make your troubles seem smaller, aye?"

"Yes," she agreed, but grouchily. What would he know about it? This self-possessed man did not look as if he would have a problem in the world!

He regarded her thoughtfully. It seemed as if he could see her lonely nights, and her fret-filled days. Maddie had the uncomfortable feeling her heartbreak was an open book.

"Perhaps," he suggested, "you could leave them now? Your troubles. Just for this moment. Just for this beautiful spring afternoon. Here. Hang them on the branch of this tree."

It was silly. But also endearing. He took imaginary worries from around her neck, as if they were leis, his fingertips tickling briefly on that sensitive skin—touch number three—and hung them carefully on a low-hanging branch of the tree.

"You can pick them up again on your way out."

Ridiculously, she felt lighter! His casual contacts were making her feel as if she had been drinking champagne. But beneath the kind of tingling awareness of him, she felt wariness. He was very smooth. The kind of man who could make a woman believe in dreams again. And really, wasn't that the scariest thing of all?

"It's going to be okay," he said. "It always is."

He said this with utter confidence. Again, she felt the wariness of wanting to trust him. He was a man you could believe in. He was a man who could make you believe such a thing, even when the world, her world, had presented her with a great deal of evidence to the contrary.

But for this moment, with this powerful, self-assured man at her side in a forest that had stood strong for a thousand years, that had survived fires and storms and endless winters and the black hearts of greedy men, it felt as if maybe, just maybe she could believe it.

For one second, she put her wariness away and allowed herself to believe that everything would be okay.

CHAPTER SIX

WARD STOOD VERY STILL as Maddie searched his face, looking, he knew, for a truth she could hold on to. That everything would be all right.

She had no way of knowing that, as a prince, he often had the power and the resources to make everything right, and so when her shoulders dropped ever so slightly, and her forehead relaxed and a light came on in the deep green pools of her soulful eyes, he felt gratified.

She trusted *him*. Not the Prince of Havenhurst, but *him*. It was a first for him, to be trusted not for his influence and status—for what he could do for someone—but for something she saw in him. Ward felt some deep pleasure unfurl within him.

Of course, it was complicated. The very fact that she had no idea who he really was probably negated the heady trust he saw shining in her mossy eyes.

But he shook that off, and he took an imaginary necklace of worries from his own neck and hung it on the branch beside hers.

"You have worries?" she said.

"Aye, everyone has worries."

"And what are yours?"

It was a simple question. It occurred to him he had never confided his worries to anyone, except maybe ever so casually, every now and then, to Lancaster. What she was offering was different. And dangerous.

He backed swiftly away from the sanctuary he saw in

her eyes. They were strangers. He was going to enjoy a day of reprieve from his true identity. End of story.

He tapped the branch. "I've left them here. Today isn't a good day for worries of any kind. Perhaps when I pick them back up, I'll share them with you."

This, of course, was a lie. Still, hanging up his worries did not feel like a lie. It felt as if he had also hung up the remaining threads of who he was. Today, he was just an ordinary man. It felt like a gift.

For this brief moment in time—Prince Edward Alexander of Havenhurst—could be normal, experience normal, delight in normal. No one was watching his every move; the mantle of duty had been removed.

And he suspected Maddie needed *normal* as much as he did at this point in her life. Could they just be two ordinary people, enjoying each other, and these moments they had been given, before surrendering to the rigors and demands of the lives that would call them back?

They came to a part of the trail that narrowed, and they had to scramble over some rocks. Like an ordinary guy he went up first, and then he held out his hand to her. She hesitated, but then, her eyes never leaving his face, she took it.

Her hand felt small in his. And surprisingly strong. He helped her up over the rocks. She let go swiftly, as soon as the obstacles had been overcome.

Oddly, he missed the sensation of her hand in his. Perhaps because, as a prince, this was one of the things he had not experienced often: casual physical contact with other people, and particularly not pretty people!

To him, everything felt more intense than it had even moments previously. He drank it in with all the appreciation of a person who knew how relentlessly the clock ticked, as if he had been told he had days left to live.

They smelled the familiar earthy mineral smell of the pools before they arrived. Still, he was not prepared for the grotto when the forest opened up to it. It was breathtaking, like a mystical paradise. The growth was almost tropical, the steaming pools surrounded by lush greenness and ferns.

"It's like this even in the wintertime," Maddie told him. "The pools heat the air around them, allowing tropical plants to grow."

They had entered at the upper end by the highest of the three pools. Each pool was connected to the one beneath it by a small waterfall. The pools, where they were visible through thick shrouds of rising steam, were amazing colors, jade green and deep turquoise swirling into indigo blue.

"This top pool is the smallest and the hottest. Each pool gets progressively larger and cooler."

"And do you like it hot or cool, Miss Maddie?"

The words were out before he could stop them. Another first, an ordinary man flirting lightly with an ordinary girl. He had made her blush. But also, her eyes darkened with sudden and unexpected heat.

Stand down, he ordered himself. There was danger in uncharted territory. And that should not feel nearly as enticing as it did.

Maddie stared at Ward. What made a man so sure of himself? It was aggravating. That kind of confidence was just plain off-putting.

Or so she tried to tell herself, a flimsy defense against what she was feeling. Which was what?

Attraction.

"I prefer the water cool," she said primly.

And then she was annoyed with herself. It was a little harmless flirting! She had hung up her worries, and hopefully with them, that little voice that was constantly chiding and trying to see the future. Ward was here until tomorrow night after the concert. She didn't always have to be the serious one, she didn't always have to try and ferret out future disaster in a little harmless flirting and she did not have to live by the mantra *doom is imminent.*

"I like it hot," he said.

"Well, I'm going to start in the cool pool. It's not for the faint of heart. You do what you want."

He lifted an eyebrow at her. "Are you questioning my manliness?"

Good grief, no. "Yes," she said. And then added, "Bok-bok-bok."

"Are you calling me a chicken?" He looked so genuinely aggrieved that she found herself laughing.

She could just have fun. For once in her life she could just give herself over to having fun. She could listen to the voice of her father, suggesting she be bold.

"If that's a challenge, I'll beat you into the water."

"No, you won't." She took off running, unbuttoning her shirt as she went. She looked ahead, but could hear him pounding up the path behind her. She tried to struggle out of her shorts while still running. He caught up to her, but when he surged by her, she caught his shirt in her fist and nearly fell over as her shorts tangled around her legs. He pulled his shirt over his head and she found herself holding it. The broadness and utter male beauty of his naked back nearly made her lose her focus. But no, she stepped out of her shoes and shorts and raced after him. He stopped at the edge of the pool and sloughed off his own shorts and shoes.

For a moment, she froze, drinking in the sculpted perfection of his body, the broadness of his back and neck, the muscled strength of his naked thighs. She wasn't entirely sure those were swim trunks!

He froze, too, staring at her. And then he smiled ever so slightly. It occurred to Maddie he was hypnotizing her with his gorgeousness on purpose to win the challenge!

He broke her gaze and jumped.

"Oh, no you don't!" Maddie came out of her trance and made one final grab for him. Instead of evading her, he reached back and captured her hand and pulled her into the pool right after him.

The water was freezing! His hand felt as if it was sizzling where it was touching hers.

"I think I like it hot, after all," she said, breaking his grip, and thinking that his hot hand in the cold water was frighteningly sensual.

"Bok-bok-bok!"

"Oh!" She cupped her hands and sent a mighty splash into his face. "I'm not! Take that!"

"Be careful, Maddie," he said in warning. "You shouldn't start things you can't finish."

How true was that? Still, she couldn't resist splashing him again, this time swiping her whole forearm on the top of the water, sending a wave of the freezing water over top of him.

"Lion versus gazelle," he said wickedly, and reached for her.

Maddie glanced at the bank. There was no way she could get to it and scramble up it without him catching her.

He twirled an imaginary mustache and laughed villainously.

She threw herself away, swam with all her might, dived under the water and came up to find him right on her heels. She tried to back away, but she was laughing so hard she was choking on the mineral-laden water. She couldn't put much distance between them.

He splashed her with such force her nose filled up with water, and then while she was sputtering, swam away. But she quickly went after him, backed him against some rocks and unleashed a flurry of water at him. They went back and forth like that, filling the pools with the sounds of their shouting and laughter.

She recognized her defenses tumbling, one by one. She recognized she *needed* this, probably more than she knew. A giving over to playfulness, letting the lightness of her spirit rise to meet the lightness of his.

When the pool was too cold to stand a minute longer, they chased each other up the slope and jumped into the warmer one, and then into the one above that. Tired, and literally played out, they finally floated side by side in the hottest pool.

Finally, they found Sophie and Lancaster on a warm rock above the pools.

Lancaster was fully clothed. Sophie was sunning herself in a very skimpy bathing suit, while Lancaster pointedly ignored her.

"I'm glad someone is having fun," Sophie said snippily.

"You're not having fun?" Ward asked her.

"He didn't even get wet," Sophie sulked. "He seems to think he's the lifeguard."

Lancaster cast her a narrow-eyed glance, stood up and wordlessly left them. Moments later he was perched on a rock high above them that jutted out over the hottest pool. Somewhere along the way, he had lost most of his clothing.

Lancaster turned his back to them and spread his arms wide. It was obvious what he planned to do. The bravest— or the most reckless—of Mountain Bend boys sometimes jumped from that high outreach, but no one ever dived from it.

Like Ward, Lancaster seemed to be a man 100 percent positive of his own strength and his place in the world. He launched himself, backward, soaring up before starting to fall back toward the pool. He twisted in the air, arms tucked in close, legs straight, before slicing cleanly into the water. Moments later, he surfaced, shaking water droplets from his hair, laughing.

"He could have been killed," Sophie said, furious.

"Ah, that man could dive into a cup of water," Ward reassured her. "Where we come from we cut our teeth on this. In fact, I think I'll join him."

Soon, Ward was on the same perch Lancaster had been on earlier. Maddie suddenly understood Sophie's frightened fury. She had lived here all her life and never seen anyone dive into the pools like this. She, herself, had never even taken the terrifying jump from that place.

Ward turned his back to them, showing them the perfect curve of his spine, the broadness at the top of it and the slenderness at the bottom. He stood on his tiptoes and his calf muscles rippled.

Maddie wanted to object, too.

But the beauty of what unfolded stopped her. He launched himself backward, somersaulting one complete time before cutting cleanly into the water.

The men dived and dived and dived, each outdoing the other's previous dive.

Maddie was entranced, and she was pretty sure, despite all the shrieking, Sophie was as entranced as she was.

She felt as if they were doing the age-old dance—men showing women their strength and prowess, impressing them with it, making some hunger burn like a flame in their bellies. It had been a long time since she had been involved in this particular dance, and never really in this way. The men's strength was raw and easy, magnificent to behold.

Still, Maddie recognized her fascination was deeper than appreciation of the male form. It was with the boldness of it, the freedom and the faith one had to feel to throw themselves into the air like that, to trust the water would catch them.

Finally, as the light leached from the sky, the men stopped diving. They came and toweled off, laughter and power shimmering in the air around them.

"Can you teach me how to do that?" Maddie asked, when the men joined them. She was envious with how alive they seemed. She wanted, in that moment, as much as she had ever wanted anything, to taste the power and joy that shimmered in the air around them.

Don't be afraid to be bold.

But both men appeared very uncomfortable with her boldness. They regarded her silently.

"What?" Maddie demanded.

"It's too dangerous," Lancaster said.

"I'm afraid time has run out, anyway. Look at the light." Ward couldn't hide his relief, and Maddie couldn't help but feel he was protecting her, which made her feel quite nice, instead of properly outraged.

Besides, he was right. It was too dark now.

And maybe she was just a little relieved, too. What she had asked was scary. And besides, she already felt way too much attraction to Ward. Inviting further interaction might be more dangerous than the diving.

They sat on the blanket they had brought and ate the picnic that had been packed. It was nearly dark by the time they were done. The tension over her request dissipated, and Maddie and Ward talked lightly of the different interpretations of the sport of football, the worst food they had ever eaten and the best, their favorite music and movies. Sophie sulked silently as Lancaster sat slightly apart from them, aloof.

The night air was getting chilly, and Maddie was relieved that Sophie wasn't nearly as sophisticated as she wanted everybody to believe, not as desperate to get Lancaster's attention as Maddie had been concerned about. Like Maddie, she ducked behind a shrub to change back into dry clothes.

As they prepared to leave the grotto, Lancaster put himself in the lead.

"I should probably go first," Maddie said, "I know the way better."

Ward laughed, low in his throat.

"Women don't dive? Or lead the way?" Maddie asked, genuinely annoyed now. Somehow, after the light conversation earlier, the prickliness felt much safer.

"Humor me," Lancaster said, as if this was not even open to discussion. "I'll try not to lead you off any cliffs."

"I do not need two big strong guys to lead me through the woods!" Maddie said. "I grew up in these mountains."

"What if we meet a bear?" Lancaster asked her.

"How would you be better able to handle that than me?" Maddie challenged.

"I'm capable of tearing out his throat with my bare hands. Are you?"

For a moment they were all silent.

Maddie watched as Lancaster's eyes flicked to Ward. She remembered what Kettle had said, that he thought Lancaster was a close protection specialist. And hadn't Sophie noticed something, too? *He thinks he's the lifeguard.* And at supper, sitting apart from them, not engaging with them. She tried to think. Had he been watchful?

Something shivered along Maddie's awareness. These men really were not who they said they were.

What did they say they're doing here? Kettle had asked.

Maddie gave herself a little shake and acquiesced to Lancaster's desire to be in the lead. None of it mattered. Tomorrow her life would be back to normal. *Normal* had become a highly overrated experience. There was no need to read deep dark secrets into this. The men obviously came from a more traditional culture. There was no sense trying to fix that, or change it, in this one-off encounter with them.

In the darkness, she could see Ward watching her. He smiled and when she stumbled over a root on the dark path and nearly fell, he reached for her hand and steadied her.

Just as well, then, she wasn't in the lead. She could feel the quiet strength in him. His ingrained instinct to protect her. Maybe a man's traditional need to lead and protect wasn't such a bad thing! Maddie took a deep breath and squeezed Ward's hand and then let it go before it felt too nice to hold it.

Still, she recognized, once again, she was being way too serious, and she didn't want to spoil what remained of this experience.

Even in the dark, they both recognized the branch of the tree where they had hung their worries. They paused and looked at the branch, and then at each other.

Without saying a word, they both moved by it, and the laughter blossomed naturally between them.

"I do not see anything funny," Sophie said, obviously in a very poor humor indeed.

They finally stumbled through the darkness to the car. Ward drove down the tricky mountain road in the dark, and asked directions to Maddie's house. He stopped in front.

"Is this one of the original miner's cottages you talked about earlier?"

She nodded, flattered that he listened so carefully, and she turned and looked at her house through his eyes. Her home was tiny, but adorable, with its yellow painted front porch and shutters and its deep mauve siding. Flower boxes bloomed cheerfully under the windows. The houses on either side of it were not quite so well loved. One had a For Sale sign that had been hanging so long one of its hooks had rotted away, and it hung crookedly.

"I live just down the street. I'll get out here, too," Sophie said. Lancaster got out and opened her door for her. She tossed her hair and marched by him with her nose in the air. He raised a brow at Maddie and shrugged.

Ward stood looking down at Maddie. Her heart began to pound. Did he feel the same as her? That there would only be one magical way that would be suitable to end such a magical day?

He took a step back from her.

She took a step back from him.

"Will you be at the concert?" he asked, finally, breaking the silence between them.

"I don't have a ticket." She didn't want to admit that she had refused a free ticket from Sophie, whose cousin had supplied her with several. The other tickets had been priced right out of her range. She had realized she had become the person who always said no instead of yes. She had said no to a free concert ticket to the Ritz, preferring to stay in the safety of her home, with her book and her bath, where she controlled everything, where nothing surprising ever happened.

"I'll find you a ticket," he said. "Please come with me."

"I have to think about it," Maddie stammered. Yes, she did. She had to think. She had to think carefully. She had such a powerful attraction to this man. Why torment herself, getting in deeper, when it could not go anywhere?

Not that she wanted things to go anywhere! She had learned her lessons!

"I wouldn't go to the concert with you if you were the last man on earth," Sophie shouted over her shoulder at Lancaster.

"I hate to break it to you, lass, but you weren't asked," Lancaster called after her.

"Sparks," Ward noted, his eyes unrelenting on her own turned-up face.

"Fire danger high," Maddie returned huskily.

And then they stared at each other. Because it seemed as if they could be talking about Sophie and Lancaster.

But they both knew they weren't.

Which was all the more reason to say no.

She willed herself to say no. She had to say no. What was going to happen after the concert when he left for good? She would have had this little taste of excitement, that little tingle of anticipation, that tiny expectation of something out of the ordinary happening. And when that was gone? Wouldn't life seem like it was without light? Without meaning? Without hope?

Had her life become like that? And if it had, wasn't it up to her to fix it? Wasn't that the whole lesson of Derek? *You are responsible for your own life. Your own happiness. Do not count on other people. Particularly handsome, charming, make-you-weak-in-the-knees people.*

Say no! It was going to be worse if she allowed their lives to tangle for yet one more day. So the sensible answer to his invitation was no. The only answer.

But she could not say it.

Why not, just this once, allow life to surprise her? Why not see where it all went? If it went nowhere at all, she would have had a great night at an outdoor concert. Surely, that had to be preferable to sitting at home?

"If you find a ticket," she said.

But she would probably find herself sitting at home, regardless. The tickets had been sold out for weeks. He wasn't going to find one. Or was he? He looked like the kind of man who pulled the impossible out of thin air routinely.

Ward grinned at her, as if he had a ticket already!

CHAPTER SEVEN

MADDIE HAD THOUGHT Ward would show up at the Black Kettle sometime during the day, at least to tell her they had not been successful in getting the ticket. But he did not. She was aware that, despite the fact she had been telling herself all day it was better if she didn't go, as each hour passed she was more disappointed.

Not that there was much time for any kind of introspection: the Black Kettle was absolutely packed all day long.

Then just before closing, an envelope was delivered to her by a courier. A courier in Mountain Bend! It held a single ticket to the concert, and a note.

I'll pick you up. Eight o'clock.

Just before Ward arrived to pick her up, Maddie had an attack of nerves so bad, she thought she wouldn't be able to go to the concert. He was leaving, for heaven's sake. This was not going anywhere. He didn't even live in the same country.

Her head knew all of that. But when she touched the pendant on her neck, Maddie was intensely aware her heart was singing a different tune. Her heart was telling her she had not felt so alive, ever.

Not even the initial excitement of New York had made her feel like this. Not Derek. Not the thought of starting her own baking business. Nothing.

She realized part of her had been shut down since the

second blow to her life: her mother leaving her, just as her father had. But no, that wasn't it. Not precisely. After the death of her mother, there had been a wild time when she was grief stricken, looking for release from all that pain, looking for love…

Pregnant. She had a pregnancy scare by some beautiful boy who had made her heart do *exactly* what Ward was doing to it now. That boy hadn't even known her name.

She remembered those terrifying days of being so alone with the shame and guilt and remorse, playing out her whole frightening future as a single mom, wondering how she could live with the disappointment of everyone who expected her to be the sensible one.

It had turned out to be a false alarm. But she had never really trusted herself since then, as if she, and she alone, knew there was a wild girl inside of her who simply could not be trusted when a certain man looked at her a certain way.

Derek had not been that man. Had she chosen him precisely because he did not make her lose that precious control? Had he sensed something in her holding back? Was that why he had turned to her friend?

But Ward made her feel that way: on fire with life, reckless.

If he had given her a cell phone number, she would call him now and plead illness. But he had not.

Maddie went and looked at herself in the mirror. She had deliberately chosen an outfit that was conservative, not in any way sexy. She wore jeans, and a T-shirt; she had put a casual blazer over the top because spring nights in the mountains were notoriously cool.

It was an outfit that said she was a decent girl who did not chase strange men around hot pools. An outfit that said, *I know you're leaving, I don't have to impress you. I won't do anything I'll regret.*

But despite the conservative, if contrived, *I don't care* look, she saw something in her eyes that made her a different woman than she had been yesterday morning.

Really, she looked as though she had been kissed! If she looked like this after an innocent afternoon of chasing around the pools, what was she going to look like— be like—when he did kiss her?

Was he going to kiss her?

Of course he was going to kiss her! She had seen it in his eyes as surely as she was feeling it stirring in her own soul. Passion. Hunger. And then he was going to leave, she reminded herself. He might even promise to stay in touch, but he wouldn't. They lived in different worlds.

In other words, she had nothing to lose. She didn't have to care what kind of impression she made on him. She didn't have to be the sensible one. It was a one-night thing.

In light of her dawning realization of complete freedom, the outfit suddenly felt all wrong. Feeling emboldened, Maddie went and changed clothes.

She had a dress that she had always worn over tights. It was a sleeveless shimmering aquamarine with a band of embroidery embellishing the deep V of the neck. It was extremely short, but wearing it as a dress instead of a top made her feel fun and flirty and bold and daring.

"I have great legs!" she told herself, twirling in front of the mirror. She burst out laughing and hugged herself. How long since she had felt exhilaration like this?

She was the wallflower who had been unexpectedly invited to the prom, and she wanted to make the most of her moment. She was ready to be seen differently. She felt young and excited. She felt as if—for the first time in a long time, or maybe even the first time ever—she wanted to be memorable. She wanted to be sexy.

Ward was going to leave. But that didn't mean she couldn't be a brand-new person! In fact, it gave her the complete liberty to be a brand-new person!

The doorbell rang. Maddie's confidence fled.

Don't answer it, she begged herself. But that other part of her ran her fingers through her curls, so they sprang even more wildly about her head, and that other part of her put a dab of lip gloss on, and that other part of her sprayed perfume in the air and then walked through it.

She touched the pendant, hoping for some sensible advice. Instead, she remembered how wildly her father had loved her mother, how impetuously. Her father used to sing to her mother, his arms wrapped around her waist, his chin resting on her shoulder.

Good grief! She was going to a concert! Maddie went and opened the door.

We should have picked up those worries, she thought. Worries kept people sensible.

The way Ward looked did not make her feel sensible. He was wearing dark glasses, which he removed to look at her. Whiskers had darkened his face; his eyes were as navy blue as midnight. He wore jeans, the dark denim creased and very navy blue, like his eyes. They clung to the large muscles of his thighs. He had on a button-down casual shirt and a leather jacket. He was wearing a dark fedora, which one in a million men might be able pull off. He was that one man. He looked like he could model for the cover of *GQ*!

Despite her effort at being conservative, his gaze took her in and was loaded with a subtle male appreciation that left her feeling breathless.

Charmingly, he handed her the cutest little posy of

wildflowers and she buried her nose in it, so he wouldn't see what was in her eyes, which was sure to be longing. For his strength, and his closeness, and his lips, and the scrape of those whiskers across the tender skin of her face.

He was a stranger. She didn't think it would be a good idea to let this newfound sense of liberty get out of hand.

Her eyes drifted over Ward's shoulder, and she saw Lancaster waited at the vehicle. *Lancaster,* she thought with relief. *Chaperone.*

But then, for a chaperoned lady, she had the wildest thought. *We're going to kiss good-night. When he brings me home, should I invite him in for a hot chocolate? A glass of wine? Could that be misinterpreted? Could she trust herself, in the privacy of her own home, not to want to taste him, touch him?*

Maddie took a jacket from the coat closet. Thankfully, spring nights in the mountains could be chilly and the coat covered most of the outfit she now realized was way too skimpy.

CHAPTER EIGHT

THE ATMOSPHERE AT the concert was electric. Though the outdoor amphitheater had bleachers built into the hills that surrounded the stage area, everyone was standing. The band came out, and from the first note it was obvious the acoustics were going to be unbelievable. The crowd went wild. There was no warm-up time. In seconds, everyone was dancing and singing along.

Maddie felt something in her let loose, some inhibition she had carried her whole life—except for one regrettable moment when she had paid dearly for it—let go. This time, she told herself, she was safe. This time, there would be no price to pay for just being herself.

Within minutes, she had the jacket off. The music was so loud it felt as if it was inside of her. She had the best time. She danced with Ward. She danced with strangers—aware she was still dancing for Ward. Then she danced with Ward again. She had never felt quite so confident, so on fire with life.

Only Lancaster seemed immune to the music and the energy, tense and grim. At the intermission they—or, more accurately, Lancaster—pushed their way through the crowds, and they found the refreshment booth.

As they waited in line, a whisper began to go through the crowd.

"A prince? Where? That's ridiculous."

Maddie glanced around. She didn't see anything or anybody who looked like a prince. She noticed that Ward, who had taken off his dark glasses, took them out of his jacket pocket and slid them back on.

"It's him, I tell you. I saw a pic of him on Entertainment World. *He was at Sea O'Brian's villa in California."*

"Yes, you're right. I remember…"

Maddie was craning her neck like everyone else to see what was going on. But then she noticed Lancaster and a shiver went up and down her spine. He looked grim. Every muscle in his body was tensed, as if for battle. His hand was resting ever so lightly on his hip. Her eyes widened as she saw there was a bulge there. Was Lancaster carrying a weapon? But why?

And why had Ward put those glasses back on? It was dark out.

"Move," he breathed tersely in her ear. Lancaster went into action with such swiftness that it was stunning. He blocked Ward's body, and hers, with his own. He plowed through the crowd, like a ship cutting a wake that she and Ward walked in. The crowd parted without protest in front of his formidable form. Ward's hand found hers, but there was nothing romantic about it. There was urgency in his touch.

"What is going on?"

"Follow Lancaster," he ordered her sternly. "No questions. Not right now."

"It is him," somebody screamed, holding up a picture on their phone for all to see. "It's Prince Edward of Havenhurst."

Suddenly, it seemed everyone had a phone out. And all of them were aimed at Ward. People were gaping at him. Women looked starstruck. People were starting to shout his name. Maddie wanted to laugh. It was an error, obviously, a bad case of mistaken identity. Maybe the desire to laugh was a form of hysteria—it felt as if her world was tilting crazily.

Except she could tell from the sudden closed look on Ward's face it was not a mistake. She could tell from the way Lancaster had gone into battle mode.

Lancaster, the close protection specialist, was parting the crowds with a look. He had not yet had to use physical force; his warrior countenance was enough.

Prince?

She felt something catch in her throat, as they pushed through the crowds. Why the pretense? Why hadn't he told her?

She slipped her hand out of his.

"I can explain," he said.

Hadn't she heard that before? Hadn't that been Derek's exact phrase when she'd found him with her best friend when she'd decided to surprise him by coming to New York for the weekend?

The answers were coming from the rising swell in the crowd around her.

"A real prince?"

"I'm Googling it—yes, a real prince!"

"Havenhurst. It's in the North Atlantic."

"Edward Alexander the Fourth."

Everyone who was not taking pictures on their phones seemed to be looking up facts about Havenhurst and its Prince.

Pieces seemed to fall into place with stunning clarity for Maddie: she had *known* these men weren't who they said they were. Kettle had actually told her Lancaster was a bodyguard! So there had been plenty of moments when she could have come to her senses and what had she done?

She had pooh-poohed her own instincts. She had chosen to believe in fairy tales—ironic since it appeared Ward was a prince!

No wonder, at the pools, Lancaster had remained aloof to the playful atmosphere. Sophie would be happy to know it had nothing to do with her! He'd been at work. He had not relaxed until Ward was out of the pools. Even then, he had undressed away from them. Probably because he was concealing that very weapon his hand was resting close to now! When Ward decided to follow his lead and dive, Lancaster dived with him. Not showing off at all. Doing his job. Taking the lead that dark night out of the pools, because it was his job, if a bear materialized, to put his body between it and his Prince.

Now Lancaster had a look of fierce determination on his face, searching for a way to get Ward out of the crush of a crowd that now knew he was no ordinary man.

Lancaster shoved Ward toward a temporary security fence that had been erected around the concert area. He had seen a door concealed in it that Maddie had not seen. It opened under a shove from his shoulder, and he stood, his back braced against it as Maddie and Ward passed through. Lancaster stood for a moment, eyeing the crowd—daring them—and then he turned and went out the door and closed it behind himself. He found a piece of rock and wedged it under the jamb.

It seemed suddenly very dark and very silent. But it lasted only seconds. Another door in the fence, several yards down, opened and people began to spill out.

The Google-fueled chatter started again.

"He's engaged."

Maddie felt something in her freeze.

"To a real princess."

"It's like a fairy tale."

But for Maddie, it was not like a fairy tale, at all, but like the return of a familiar nightmare.

Lancaster put his arm around Ward's shoulder and they bolted toward the parking lot. Ward reached for her hand, but she evaded his grasp. The crowd surged by her in hot pursuit of his celebrity.

Now she turned quickly and pushed her way against the crowds.

She heard her name called, once, desperately.

"Maddie!" It was Ward. No, *Edward*.

She turned and walked backward. She did something she had never done, in her entire life.

She presented Edward Alexander the Fourth, Prince of Havenhurst, engaged to a real live princess, with her middle finger.

With some satisfaction, she registered the distress on his face and the shock on Lancaster's. Apparently, it wasn't protocol to present the Prince with your middle finger!

She walked home, taking a well-known trail through the forest, feeling sick to her stomach, remembering *everything*. He had teased her about her name that first day at work. She had thought he was flirting with her. But no, he was accustomed to people being uncomfortable with his status. He was used to putting people who were intimidated by him at ease. From teasing her about a Celt being in the kitchen, to complimenting her scones and tea, it was all part of that graciousness of being born to an elevated position in life.

No wonder he was so good at listening intently. No wonder he was so sure of himself.

They weren't from Scotland. That's why he'd hesitated when she asked if there were Boy Scouts in Scotland.

As she walked home, Maddie was aware of a change in herself.

She didn't feel victimized. She didn't feel sad. She didn't feel as if she was going to break down and cry.

No, she felt as angry as she had ever felt in her entire life.

Ward watched helplessly as the waves and waves of people separated him from Maddie. He could see the fury in the set of her shoulders and the stiffness of her spine.

He had to get to her.

"Let her go," Lancaster said roughly when he saw Ward's intent. "The mob was so focused on you they didn't figure out she was with you. It won't do her any good if they do."

He was right, plus Maddie was moving swiftly, putting more and more people between him and her with every determined footstep that she took. It was obvious there would be no getting to her now.

They got to the car and Lancaster shoved him in unceremoniously, got in the driver's seat, and they left the crowd behind them.

"That was one of the worst moments of my life," Lancaster said, after a moment.

No lecture, of course, though Lancaster had been adamant the whole trip in general, and the concert in particular, had the potential to become security nightmares.

Ward thought of Maddie's stricken look when she first realized the depth of his lie to her. He looked out the window. He had betrayed her trust, something he was sure, given Sophie's revelations that day in the café, that she did not give easily.

"And mine," he said softly, "and mine."

"Do you want me to find her?"

"Of course."

"Let's just find a different car, first. This one is highly recognizable." But for all Lancaster's amazing skill, this time it was not enough. Though they patrolled every street of Mountain Bend, and drove by her house several times, they did not see Maddie Nelson.

Ward's phone buzzed in his pocket. Unreasonably, he hoped it was Maddie, though he knew he had not given her the number.

But it wasn't Maddie. It was Sea O'Brian.

Telling him, breathless with excitement, that she had to cancel her engagement to him. She'd been offered the lead role in an upcoming television series. Which could give her flagging career a better shot in the arm? Playing princess on some remote island, or taking the role?

She had taken the role.

Ward slipped his phone back into his pocket.

Lancaster cast him a glance. "Sir? Everything all right?"

Wearily, Ward explained what had just happened. The silence stretched between them as they drove every street in Mountain Bend looking for Maddie.

Finally, one last drive past her house, the lights were on, and Ward saw a shadow move on one of the closed drapes of the front window. He felt both relief that she had made it home safely, and trepidation that he had to talk to her. He had to set things straight. Though, so far, his efforts to make things right with women were not unfolding all that well.

"I'm going in," he said.

"Sir, we know she's safe. She seemed, er, a little angry when we left her. Maybe a cooling-off period is in order?"

A little angry might be the understatement of the century. Ward was certain he had never seen a woman angrier than Maddie had just been, walking, backward, away from him, making a gesture that represented all of her barely restrained fury.

He didn't want a cooling-off period. He wanted to tackle this right now. He was astonished by the fact he felt faintly thrilled when he considered confronting that fury.

He opened the door of the car and stepped out.

CHAPTER NINE

"GO AWAY," MADDIE called in the direction of her front door.

Ward's arrival was nothing like the ones in fairy tales. He hadn't ridden up on a white charger; there were no trumpets blowing. If he pounded her door much harder, it was going to break loose from the frame!

She had been home over an hour. She was in her pajamas, sipping tea and looking at a book, though she found herself unable to comprehend the words. For once in her life, the book was not providing the escape she had always looked to books for. Even in the most difficult circumstances a book could carry her away. But not tonight.

She was in her nicest pajamas having tea out of her good china. The book had been chosen to make her look sophisticated in her reading material. All of that probably meant she had both expected his arrival and intended to let him in. Sooner or later.

"Maddie, please talk to me."

"Is that a royal decree?" Still, she could feel the weakness, as it had been from the first time he had pleaded with her to go to the hot pools with him.

Please say yes. Please come with me. There was something about the way Ward said *please* that disarmed her, that had disarmed her from the beginning, that had made her say yes to taking him to the hot pools and yes to the concert, when she should have been saying no.

She should have been protecting herself against this

very thing that was now unfolding. Unwanted drama in her life. Uncalled-for complications. Betrayals and lies.

The weakness could be lack of food, Maddie told herself. She'd been too excited before the concert to eat, and now, even though she was hungry, food did not appeal.

The pounding came on the door again. She would not have him thinking she was hiding. That she was cowering behind her door, afraid of him, or crying her heart out.

And so she got up deliberately, set down her teacup and her book. She must have got up too quickly because she felt woozy. She took a breath, steadied herself and went to the door. She threw it open, and then folded her arms across her chest and planted her legs firmly, determined not to let him see she actually felt both emotionally and physically weak at the moment.

His arm, raised to bash her door again, fell to his side. It was really unfair that he looked so charming. Since he was a prince. And since this wasn't any kind of a fairy tale with a happily-ever-after in the script.

Okay, so he looked very tired. And slightly disheveled in a very unprincely way. In a way that made her want to run her fingers through his mussed hair and smooth it back into place, as if he, somehow, was the one in need of sympathy here!

Buck up, Maddie told herself. Ward had deliberately withheld information about himself. He had pretended to be someone he was not. He had been toying with her when he was engaged to someone else.

"Unconscionable," Maddie greeted him without preamble.

"I agree," he said.

Maddie did not want him to be agreeable! She didn't want to look at him; she didn't want to fall into the pools of his eyes one more time. So she looked past him. Over his shoulder, she saw the "normal" guy persona had been abandoned. The Lambo was gone, replaced with something black, shiny, solid.

Probably bulletproof.

"What do you want?" she demanded, hardening her heart to the look on his face, the intensity of the way he looked at her, the almost-electrical ripple it caused to surge inside of her.

"To explain."

"What's to explain? You lied to me. You did it deliberately and you did it often. You didn't tell me who you really were, and you were flirting with me while you were engaged to someone else! Scout's honor?"

"You have a right to be angry."

"Thank you, Your Royal Princeship. Are you giving me permission to feel mad? Mad as in Maddie? Should I curtsy now?" She glared at him. "Are you smiling?"

"I'm trying not to. It's just that—"

"Just that what?"

"No one has ever spoken to me that way. Not in my whole life."

"Being given the finger must have been a novelty for you, then, too."

"Indeed it was."

"If you start laughing, I'll kill you." Did she actually feel something softening toward him? No, she simply wasn't feeling well. *Buck up*, she reminded herself.

"Lancaster won't allow it. My killing."

"Yes, I've figured out Mr. Lancaster's role in things."

"Major, actually."

"Well, Major Lancaster is a long way away, Prince Whatever-your-real-name-is." She squinted through the darkness at where Lancaster waited, arms folded across his chest, rear rested against the door of the car, looking up and down the street. Watching. "He's looking the wrong direction for the danger. It's right in front of you."

"Indeed it is," he said, and even though his tone was solemn, his lips twitched.

"Oh!" she said, and stepped back from the door. "Come in. Let's get it over with."

He stepped over the threshold. Pure power rode into her tiny cottage with him. She wondered how humble it looked through his eyes. She decided she didn't care.

She gestured at the sofa. "Sit. Spit it out. I'm not offering tea."

He took the sofa. She stood across from him, arms still folded. But he had an air of command about him, and she knew he wouldn't say what he had to say until she sat down. With a sigh of long-suffering she flounced onto the chair across from him, picked up her now-cold tea and took a long sip, just to reinforce she was not offering him one.

"First, let me tell you why I didn't reveal my identity," he said, quietly.

She actually wanted to hear about the *real* Princess first, but she bit her tongue. Why appear like a jealous shrew? He had never promised her anything. The fact that he was here possibly meant he had a shred of integrity, though, really? She did not feel inclined to give him the benefit of the doubt.

All the playfulness was gone from him. "Havenhurst is my life. It's a very tiny island kingdom in the North Atlantic, with a Celtic culture. We have a population of about a million people. My duty is to those people. That duty comes before everything.

"Our main industries, in the past, have been logging and mining. Those are, as you know, limited resources. They both were managed poorly and petered out, leaving the island economically depressed and in a desperate situation."

Despite herself, Maddie found she was interested. This *was* like Mountain Bend. She needed to know if the story was going to have a happy ending.

"People were leaving the island in hope of work elsewhere. It was a truly grim situation. The island was now losing its most valuable resource—people. It was becoming a place of ghosts."

Again, the very same future Mountain Bend was facing. Despite herself, she could feel herself leaning toward him, interested. "What happened?"

"We have an abundance of hot springs on the island, so we are slowly reviving our economy with tourism and export of some of our mineral waters, which claim health benefits. I have taken on the economy as my main responsibility. But I have others. One is an expectation of a marriage that will bring benefit to our island. And that's part of what brought me to America.

"I wanted to sample normal. That's why I didn't tell you who I was."

Maddie grudgingly accepted that explanation. She could see that a man might not want to print *Prince* on his business card, that he might want to be liked for himself, but the engagement part?

"I'm supposed to be married soon."

His announcement was joyless.

"Yes, I couldn't help but hear that from the googling throngs."

"Yes, but you heard it was Aida. The other part of my trip here is that I came to ask someone else to marry me. Have you heard of Sea O'Brian?"

"The actress?"

"Yes."

It was a stark reminder of the rarified circles he moved in. It was a stark reminder of yet more treachery!

"Are you telling me you have two fiancées?" Maddie breathed.

"Um—"

"You cad! You've been flirting with me for two days!"

He was smiling again.

"Stop it! I'm dead serious."

"I know. But as I say, I've never been shrieked at before. It's, er, refreshing."

"Shrieked?" she inquired dangerously. "I did not shriek."

"I'm sorry. Let me think of another way to put it." He was silent for an insultingly long time. "Squealed at?"

"Oh!"

He frowned. "Yelped at?"

"I think you have to leave now."

"Just a few more moments of your time."

"Humph. This had better be good."

"Marriages, in my family, and on my island are not love matches, Maddie. It was decided when I was a child that one day I would marry Princess Aida Montego of the island that neighbors ours. Wynfield is our biggest ally and trading partner. This isn't a choice. It's a business decision, made by our fathers. Contracts were signed a very long time ago."

"But what about love?" she asked, aghast despite herself. "Oh!" she clapped her hand over her mouth. "That's where Sea O'Brian comes in, isn't it? You love her."

No reason to feel sad! The man was a cad.

"No," he said, "I don't love her. And she's just told me no, in any case."

She ordered herself not to feel relieved. That made him a worse cad, didn't it?

"Though," he continued, "to be sure, love plays a part in this story, but not Sea's part. Aida met a young man. She loves him madly. And he her. She would still do what is expected of her. She would marry me, even as she loves another. She really would have no choice, and we were both raised with the notion we were not to expect personal happiness."

"Not to expect personal happiness?" Maddie asked. On the other hand, maybe it was a good thing. The pursuit of happiness could lead to very poor decisions, as she well knew. Maybe his family was onto something!

"When you are born into a royal family," Ward said, "it is drummed into you from birth—service before self."

"I don't know what to say. Despite the fact I can see the practicality of it—an expectation of happiness can cause no end of problems, after all—I'm appalled for you, and I'm appalled for that poor girl."

"If I returned from America married," Ward said softly, "then she would be free. One of us, at least, could have some chance at personal happiness."

Maddie's mouth fell open.

"I reached an agreement with Sea to play the role of my wife," he said. "To set Aida free. Now, unfortunately, Sea has been made a better offer, and I am back at square one."

Despite herself, Maddie found the story—and his honor, his interest in giving Aida a life he had not asked or expected for himself—brought tears to her eyes. She saw in front of her a man who had everything: title, wealth, power. And yet he had no expectation of the greatest richness of them all, love.

"But now what?" she asked him, her anger completely gone.

"I'm not sure."

"People cannot be forced to marry one another in this day and age. It's archaic."

"Ah, yes. *Archaic.* That is probably as good a word as any to describe Havenhurst."

"You have to get out of this," Maddie said vehemently, "Not just to save Aida, but to save yourself."

"I agree. But I don't know anyone else who would be willing to return to Havenhurst as my wife. I'd have to know something of their character." He paused. He frowned. He stared at her. "Unless—"

He was looking at her so intently, her heart began to pound. She wiped her sweating palms on her pajamas.

"What?" she stammered.

"What if my meeting you was not mere coincidence, but chance meeting opportunity? What if it was whatever people called these stunning moments in time when the seemingly absurd, the impossible, manifests into destiny?"

Maddie stared at him. She felt light-headed. She really should have had some crackers with her tea.

"What are you saying?" she whispered.

He cocked his head at her. That smile tickled the gorgeous sensuous curve of his bottom lip.

"I'm asking you if you would consider being my wife."

CHAPTER TEN

WARD WATCHED AS Maddie tried to absorb what he had just said. He didn't blame her. He was stunned that he had said it himself. He watched the blood drain from her face. She reached for her tea, as though a sip would steady her, but her hand was shaking.

And then the teacup slid from her hand, spilling tea all over her and landing on the floor with a clatter. He leaped to his feet, afraid she had burned herself.

But before he could close the distance between them, her eyes got a glazed look in them, rolled back in her head, and she went completely limp, as though there were not a bone in her entire body. He reached her, just as her body crumpled from her chair.

Ward slid his hands under her and caught her before she hit the floor. He cradled her, one arm at the bend in her knees, the other around her shoulders.

"Maddie?" he called softly. Her eyes fluttered, but didn't open. He hefted her against his chest and took the seat she had been on, feeling her warmth seep into him.

He looked down into her face. How had she become so familiar in such a short period of time? The faint freckles, the scattering of hair, the delicacy of feature?

Maddie looked so pale and so frail. It was as if her every vulnerability was open to him. Why had he done this to her? Why had he invited her to participate in a deception? It was all wrong, and she was the wrong person for it.

Still, it was done. He had asked. She was sensible. She would say no.

He thought he should get a damp cloth, or call Lancaster, who was more adept at first aid than he was, but instead, he did something he was not sure he had ever done.

Except maybe once, when he had decided not to marry Aida.

He listened to his heart, and he dropped his lips to the smoothness of her brow.

Her eyes fluttered open.

And at first, she smiled, as if she had been having the best of dreams.

But then, she struggled against him. "What on earth?"

"You fainted. Shush, don't struggle like that. Just relax for a moment. Regain yourself."

She followed the instruction in that she quit struggling, but she was stiff in his arms, a frown on her face as she gazed up at him.

"I did not faint," she decided. "I'm not the fainting type."

"Well, I did not poison your tea, so unless you have another theory?"

Her frown deepened. She rubbed at her forehead. "Did you kiss me?"

He decided silence might be the best defense!

"Oh," she said, brightening. "I get it. It's a dream. Kissed by a prince and all that rot."

"I think the rot part might be a little strong," he said, pretending insult.

"So, it's not a dream. I have a real live prince in my house. Don't get the idea I swooned for you. I haven't eaten properly today," she said defensively.

"It had nothing to do with me asking you to marry me?"

Her eyes went very round. "Nothing," she whispered.

"A business arrangement," he said softly.

Did she look disappointed? Had he led her to believe something else? That it would be real?

Would she have gone for that?

Ward realized he could not allow himself to think of that: of Maddie forever his. Of waking in the mornings to those green eyes and that small smile, of being treated like a normal man. Of being told to go sod himself when that was what he needed to hear. Of chasing each other, the way they had chased through the hot pools.

Of possessing her in every way a man possessed his wife.

No, he could not go there. This woman, who had suffered so many losses—parents, fiancé, career—deserved something he could not give her.

A family. A normal, wholesome all-American family.

But what he could give her, a tender gift to her, was a way out of the challenges she was facing now. He was in a position to make sure the benefits of marrying him outweighed her reservations and overcame her anger.

"A business arrangement," she said, her tone wooden.

"I can make it worth your while, Maddie, well worth your while."

"I can't."

"Why?"

"It's just wrong. It's deceitful, for one thing. For another, think of the poor example it sets for someone like Sophie. You marry a man you just met? Because he's a prince? Because he can solve your problems and give you things?"

He decided now would probably not be the safest time to tell her that her voice had become a little shrill again.

"I think you should give it some thought."

She seemed to realize she was still in his arms. This

time, when she struggled, he let her go. She found her feet, a trifle unsteadily, but still folded her arms over her chest and planted her legs apart, a posture intended to show strength even if she still looked pale and shaky.

"I'll do no such thing," she said.

"It's more than evident the whole town is struggling, including the Black Kettle."

"And?"

"Please sit down before you go down again. Maddie, I can help. I can show you some of our mineral water exports. Not to mention what your newfound notoriety could do for tourism. Mountain Bend, home of an American princess."

He found he could not take his eyes off her. She was adorably cute when she was fuming like that. Had he thought this through properly? Wasn't the cute factor going to make the arrangement he had just suggested more complicated?

Maybe not. She had called him a liar. A cad. And a sneak. She had called his kisses "rot." Another man, a saner man, might be withdrawing his offer and heading for the door.

But he did not feel sane. Not at all.

He felt as if he was a man who had waited his whole life for this moment: honesty. Someone who was strong enough to be completely straightforward with him. Funny, that honor would come wrapped in such a fragile-looking little package. He suspected Maddie was hiding strength she did not even know about.

"I thought the concert would save him," she said, her voice hollow, "and help Mountain Bend."

"I think it's a case of too little, too late. No business can be saved on the strength of one night's success. You would need to look at becoming a regular concert venue.

Which is a possibility. I could have my business team look into it."

Maddie looked stricken. He could see tears behind her eyes. Her loyalty and her ability to love, coupled with that honesty, made her both a good choice, and a very, very complicated one for him.

But the choice was not his alone. He had given her the facts, as he knew them. Now he had to trust her to make the decision that would be best for her.

He hoped it would also be the one that was best for him.

"I didn't tell you my assessment of the town to make you feel threatened," he said. He closed the distance between them and caught a tear as it slid down her cheek.

She slapped his hand away and moved back from him. She rubbed furiously at her eyes.

"Really? I'll be out of a job soon, Sophie's college dreams will be up in smoke and Kettle will be out on the street, and you didn't intend for me to feel threatened?"

"I didn't create any of that situation," he pointed out. "I'm offering a way out of it. But the choice is yours. Marry me. Be my wife for one year, three hundred and sixty-five days. I'll come back in the morning. You can let me know your final decision."

She looked as if she planned to let him know her final decision right now! And in the shrill voice, too.

But then she stopped herself. She just looked tired and pale and Ward thought the decent thing to do would be to say he would look after things no matter what she decided.

But something stopped him from saying that, too.

They both needed time to think, obviously.

"Come back early," she said. "Before I start work."

"All right." If she said no, she would just go to work as if it was an ordinary day. Even though she knew what the future held. There was a kind of bravery in that, he supposed.

He realized he did not want her to say no and that there was bravery in saying yes, too.

"Can I help you?" he asked. "Get to bed?"

Her eyes widened as if he had propositioned her. Ward realized seeing her bedroom might not be a good idea.

"Get something to eat?" he said hastily.

"No." Her voice was proud. "Please, go."

"Can I call Sophie to come be with you?"

"Please, just go."

He took one more look at her face, and then went and quietly let himself out the door. He had an unusual moment of self-doubt. What had he just done? He had held out a carrot to her, that given her love and loyalty, he did not think she was going to be able to refuse.

This was how he'd been raised: get what you want. Use whatever means it takes to get it. He had borne witness to his father's ability to be ruthless on many, many occasions.

Was he just like him?

No, because his father would be gleeful at the kind of predicament he had just put Maddie in.

She would have trouble saying no.

But Ward didn't feel gleeful. Not at all. He felt like the cad she had accused him of being.

So he would save Aida. And he would save himself from marriage, an institution he did not think he had any capacity for, given what he came from.

But at what price to Maddie?

"I'm not going to hurt her," he promised himself, standing on her front porch for a moment, watching the stars stud the skies over mountains that looked as if they were a silhouette cut from black paper and stuck against the sky. Why should he feel bad about saving everything she cared about?

"She's going to come out of this better than ever. She's going to be able to do what she most wants to do—save her world and everyone in it."

And if all of that was true, why did he feel as rotten as she had said his kiss was? Why did he wonder if, in the event she said yes, if she would walk toward him with all the enthusiasm of a prisoner being led to the gallows?

Lancaster hoisted himself off the car as he approached. He lifted an eyebrow in question.

"I asked her to marry me."

Lancaster looked stunned. "And?"

Ward said nothing.

"She said no?" Lancaster breathed with disbelief.

"Let's just say she didn't say yes. And you needn't look so pleased about it."

"My apologies, sir," Lancaster said insincerely.

"Spit it out," Ward said, then realized he had inadvertently used the same phrase she had used on him.

"She's strong and feisty, and honest and real. She's making you feel things you never felt before. It's all good."

"Unless I go home without a bride."

"I suspect your engagement to Princess Aida is over now, no matter what."

"You're so right," Ward said, and felt the relief sweep through him.

"But it's a good idea to bring home a bride. Insurance for Aida. If you called off the engagement, and her relationship with someone else came to light too soon, people would sense the truth. It would improve your popularity. But not hers."

"I don't want to hurt Aida. It has always been my intention to protect her. But I don't want Maddie to inadvertently end up hurt, either."

"Maddie's a good deal stronger than she looks, and she's good for you," Lancaster decided, looking at him shrewdly. "I hope she says yes."

"You've just an eye on the scones," Ward said, trying for a light note, but he was aware that was what he hoped for, too.

"I doubt if a princess would be baking scones for the likes of me," Lancaster said wistfully.

"I doubt if you could stop her," Ward disagreed.

"Yeah, she's that. Just a nice girl."

"Not all nice. She gave me the middle finger salute."

Lancaster laughed. "Ah, well, a little naughty mixed in with the nice could be a good thing. All sugar is a bit too sweet. You need a little spice."

"The middle finger," Ward mused. "I've never been on the receiving end of that before."

"You wanted to experience a bit of normal," Lancaster reminded him, wryly. "Not that the middle finger means what most people think it means."

"It doesn't?"

"No, in the old days the middle finger was the most important one on an archer's hand. If he was captured, it was cut off. And so when he won a battle, or eluded capture, he would extend his middle finger to the enemy to show *I will fight again*."

"I don't think she meant it that way," Ward said, drily. "Sod off, plain and simple."

"And yet to fight you again may be the way of her destiny."

"You're not leaning toward domestic bliss if she says yes?"

"What would the fun in that be?" Lancaster growled.

"Despite the scones, I don't see Maddie as traditional, the way our women are. But I like it, and I think it will be good for you. Once the initial shock is over, I don't think she's going to be cowed by the fact you're a prince."

Ward thought of the spark in Maddie's eyes when she unabashedly yelled at him, but, if she said yes, he was probably going to miss the sparks flying as part of a union with Maddie. Regrettably.

"It's not as if it's real, Lancaster."

"Aye, that's what you say."

"You sound doubtful."

"Just wondering, how do you keep it from getting real with a girl like that?"

"With great effort," Ward said. If she said yes, wouldn't that be the most important part of this exercise? Protecting her?

Lancaster was silent, he made no effort to get in the car. Ward realized he was faintly preoccupied.

"Something else on your mind?"

"Would you wait for me for a few minutes?" Lancaster said, glancing up the street.

"You'll leave me without your protection?" Ward asked drily, following Lancaster's gaze. "Is that Sophie's house?"

Lancaster looked torn. "I have to say something to her."

"Yes, you do," Ward agreed softly, and watched the big man lope away from him and knock softly on the door. It opened and he slipped inside, and it closed behind him.

Ward stood back and breathed in the crisp mountain air, the silence, the sense of being alone he had so rarely experienced. He was aware of freedom, the exhilaration of somehow being in control of his own fate, no matter what Maddie's answer was.

CHAPTER ELEVEN

MADDIE AWOKE IN the morning, aware of a shift in herself. It was the first time in a long time she had awoken without the feeling of dread in the bottom of her belly. Given the magnitude of the decision she had been asked to make, that seemed extraordinary.

She had thought she would have trouble sleeping, but instead, she had slept like a baby and awoken knowing her answer.

Oddly, it was not just about saving Kettle's business, Sophie's education and possibly, the town.

It was something more, a part of her she had been unaware she had.

There was in her a deep craving for adventure. A need for the unexpected. An embracing of this surprise life had offered her. She had not even touched her talisman, her pendant, seeking an answer, or reassurance, or a remembered voice to guide her. This had to be her answer, and hers alone.

Yesterday, she had been an ordinary girl, struggling with ordinary issues.

And today, that had all changed. Since the death of her father, Maddie had been so aware how life could change—for the worse—in a second, in the blink of an eye. That lesson had been reinforced, in the worst possible way, by Derek stepping out with a woman she counted amongst her best friends!

But this morning, she was aware it could change in the blink of an eye in other directions.

So she was going to say yes. Today, she was going to say yes to marrying a prince. She was going to marry a man who was a stranger. And one who had lied to her.

She was going to participate with him in the telling of an even larger lie. But there was a larger good here: both her town and the people she loved were going to benefit from this, as was a stranger named Aida. It was a wild adventure in saying yes instead of her customary no. So it was crazy to feel as calm as she did, as if she was marching toward that very thing he had mentioned last night: destiny.

She chose a simple summer dress, longer than the one she had worn yesterday, Indian cotton, pale yellow, buttoned down the front, belted at the waist, the skirt full and sensual as it swished around her legs.

She had no sooner tried to do something with her curls when she heard the soft tap at the door.

Taking a deep breath, she walked through her house to her door and answered it.

Ward stood there. He looked a different man. He was in a beautifully cut suit, a pristine white shirt, a navy blue silk tie knotted at his throat. He was freshly shaven, and he looked exactly what he was: wealthy, powerful, privileged. A prince.

It was as far from Maddie's own working-class background as you could get.

She contemplated, for the first time ever, the word *commoner*. Doubt attacked her, coming from all sides.

This was supremely dumb. It was hasty. It was fraught with emotional peril. Their arrangement was based on a lie. They were going to try and fool a whole nation.

In about five seconds, her mind chattered, rapid-fire, going through all one thousand reasons this was not a good idea in about five seconds.

But even as her mind chattered, there was a calmer place inside her. It regarded him deeply. It looked into his eyes and found something there she could both trust and hang on to in a world that had been so full of fear and disappointment.

"Yes," she said quietly.

Ward looked momentarily stunned, as though he had been bracing himself for a different answer. And then he smiled, and it was as if a light went on around them.

But then neither of them knew what to do! Did you shake hands on such an agreement? He took a tentative step toward her. Her eyes widened as his head dropped close to hers. Her heart went crazy.

But then he took both of her hands in his and bussed her lightly on the cheek, the way you might an elderly aunt you hadn't seen for a while! He let her hands go as quickly as he had taken them. Maddie felt oddly chagrined, even though she knew this was the safest way to treat their arrangement.

Though how were they going to make it seem as if they had experienced a wild, impetuous romance with kisses like that?

"I want you to know," he told her, "that though we will make a public appearance of husband and wife, you will always have your own sleeping quarters."

Don't blush, she ordered herself.

"I'll ensure your schedule is not too onerous, leaving you time to pursue your own interests and to explore the new world you will find yourself in on your own terms."

She nodded.

"I'll make sure you are generously remunerated for your time. Lancaster will work out the details with you."

"Thank you."

"And at every opportunity I will look for ways to promote Mountain Bend, and look for ways our business interests might benefit each other."

This was precisely why she had said yes. She took a deep breath.

"I'm sorry," he said. "A written contract might be complicated."

"That's fine." She stopped short of saying she trusted him. "What's next?"

"I have a private jet."

Of course he did.

"I've had Lancaster working on the logistics. We'll go to Las Vegas. No waiting period, and no difficulty marrying people who aren't citizens of the US. We can fill out an application online and be at the Clark County office to pick up a marriage license by this afternoon. An official will be lined up to conduct the proceedings."

She gulped. Had she been expecting things to unfold that quickly? *Not really.* On the other hand, it gave her less time to think, to lose her courage, to listen to that voice that was still insisting on rattling off the thousand and one reasons this was not a good idea.

"I need to talk to Kettle. And Sophie. I'll need to pack."

"Don't worry about packing too much," he said. "I can have someone come and pack for you."

She looked at him. It occurred to her he had probably not packed for himself *ever*. He had servants and staff who looked after all the mundane details of life for him.

"Why don't you see what you still need from here after I buy you a new wardrobe? We'll send someone with a list after you're settled."

She contemplated that. What did it mean? That her clothes weren't good enough? Obviously, they weren't good enough. She was wearing a cotton dress she had picked up on the sale rack.

And they'd send someone? From Havenhurst to Mountain Bend to pack her belongings for her? The easy extravagance of it took her aback. She could feel her feet getting colder by the second.

But suddenly, there was no time for second-guessing.

She quickly packed one overnight case, which Lancaster would not allow her to carry. He stowed it in the trunk of the car, and then they stopped at the Black Kettle.

"I'll go in alone," she told Ward.

"No, you won't."

"I don't know how much to tell them," she said, suddenly nervous.

"I think the fewer people who know the whole truth of it, the better."

She agreed. She set her shoulders and let Ward open the familiar door for her. She stepped in and looked around. Her home. This place had given her sanctuary from the world when she needed it most.

"You're late!" Sophie sang from the kitchen. "How unlike you. Guess who our ooh-la-la guys really are? It's all over town, and Lancaster confirmed it last night. He came to see me!"

Sophie came out the kitchen door and stopped, looking from Ward to Maddie, and then beyond them to where Lancaster was waiting outside.

"What's going on?" she asked.

"I—I—I'm going with them," Maddie said.

"I've asked Madeline to be my wife, and she's agreed," Ward said, taking her hand in his. Maddie was shaking. Was she going to be called Madeline now?

"What?" Sophie, naturally, was stunned. Her lip trembled. "Are you going to be a princess, Maddie?"

"I guess I am."

"That's fantastic," Sophie said, through tears. And then

Maddie found herself wrapped in a hug that was so tight that she could hardly breathe. That's why she was crying, wasn't it?

Kettle came out as Sophie broke away. Maddie told him her news.

Unlike Sophie, he was not prepared to see the romance of the situation. His face looked like thunder. "That's plain dumb," he told her. "You don't even know the man."

"Not that knowing the man served me that well," Maddie reminded him.

"Is that what this is about?" Kettle demanded. "Playing it safe? Taking yourself out of the game?"

Maddie hadn't thought about it like that, but was there some truth in what Kettle was saying? Love had let her down so badly, that she wasn't risking that again?

No, it was about being given an opportunity—to help her town, and those she cared about—and taking it.

Though she had a feeling if she said that to Kettle right now, he'd lock her in a closet and never let her out!

Kettle shook the spoon in his hand at Ward.

"I don't give a crap who you are—you hurt her, and I'm coming to get you. You hear?"

"Yes, sir, I hear. I won't hurt her. I promise."

Kettle limped over. He looked her up and down and then with tears in his eyes, he embraced her long and hard.

"Oh, Maddie," he said, his voice choked, "I thought you were going to be the sensible one."

"Are you and Sophie going to be able to manage? Without me?"

"We will," Kettle said firmly. "You'll step up to the plate, won't you, Sophie?"

The younger woman nodded solemnly. "Maddie, can I talk to you for a minute by yourself?"

"Of course," she said, and they went off to a table, leaving Kettle to grill Ward.

"Do you love him?" Sophie asked earnestly.

"Oh, Sophie, how could I know that? I just met him."

"But you're marrying him!"

"There are many good reasons to get married that don't necessarily involve love. Love's a funny thing, Sophie. I thought I loved Derek. And look how that ended."

"I love Lancaster," Sophie said firmly.

"Oh! You can't. Sophie, you're so young! You barely know the man!" Though given her own choice, that was a poor argument.

"Well, I do. When he came over last night, he told me something. He told me he thought I was a beautiful, smart girl, and that he didn't rebuff my affections—isn't that posh, rebuff my affections—because he didn't like me. He told me his wife and baby, a little boy, were killed in a fire. He said there's a stone where his heart used to be."

"That's very sad," Maddie said.

"It is *so* sad. But it just makes me love him more. Eventually, I'll come there, to Havenhurst."

"Of course you will!"

"And maybe he'll be ready," Sophie said, determination and wistfulness mixed.

"Maybe he will," Maddie agreed. "I'll call as soon as I'm settled. Maybe you can come in the fall, when things are slower here."

"I'm going to miss you so much," Sophie said, and then they were hugging and crying all over again.

When the hug broke, Sophie went and filled a bag with scones and a tub with cream. She handed them to Maddie, her eyes moist.

"Tell him they are a gift from me."

And then, their goodbyes finished, they were in the car

and heading down the road. Ward told her he thought it
might be best if they didn't announce their intentions at
all. Only Lancaster knew the truth of their arrangement,
and he had arranged for the news to travel for them *after*
they were married.

Before Maddie could really register what was happening, she was being ushered aboard a private jet. There was
a crest by the tail: a dragon woven around a heart, and a
crown above both of those things. The pilot and stewards
and staff were all lined up at the bottom of the stairs, in
navy blue blazers with that same crest embroidered above
their breasts. As Ward ushered her by them, they each
snapped off a crisp salute. She was pretty sure the shock
of that would have made her trip and fall on her face if
Ward did not have such a tight grip on her arm.

The inside of the jet looked more like a very fancy living room, than an airplane. Deep white leather sofas faced
each other. Beyond the sofas, was a tall counter with a
marble top. Shelves behind it showed a fully stocked bar,
coffee, tea and kitchen items.

To one side of that, there was a desk with a deep leather
chair on swivels facing it. And then there was a hallway
that Lancaster disappeared down, still hugging his sack
of scones with a look on his face that said he would protect that particular package with his life.

"Miss, my name is Glenrich, if you'll take a seat here,"
one of the uniformed attendants, a middle-aged woman
with graying hair and a pleasant smile, told her, "I'll brief
you on our takeoff procedures and see to all your needs
on the flight." Already, an engine had thrummed to life.

Her needs? What could she need on such a short flight?

Ward took the seat beside her and showed her where
the seat belts were tucked into the sofa.

Maddie only half listened to the safety talk, overwhelmed by what she was experiencing, the reality of it all around her. She wished Ward would take her hand, but he did not. In fact, he was brought a briefcase and immersed himself in papers!

The jet lifted off with such power, Maddie was sucked back into her seat. Moments later, she was being offered coffee and hot breakfast. She realized she was starving. The breakfast was superb, flaky croissants, homemade preserves, fluffy eggs. This was on an airplane!

Lancaster came back down the hall and settled in one of the chairs by the desk. He was now wearing a navy blue uniform, pressed shirt, with that same crest on the breast, tucked into crisply pleated trousers, which were tucked into black combat boots. He was clean-shaven and had an epaulette on both shoulders with three solid gold bars on each. What looked to be a beret was tucked under one shoulder bar, and there was a plain black dirk and holder on his belt. He said no to breakfast and tucked into the bag of scones, a notebook computer balanced on one knee.

He looked formidable, like a warrior, plain and simple, and had Maddie not been faintly intimidated by her surroundings she would have snapped a picture of him to send to Sophie.

"Miss Nelson," Lancaster said, appearing at her side with the small computer, "if you could fill this out, it will expedite matters substantially."

"Miss Nelson?" She didn't want Lancaster to call her Miss Nelson, but something in his face stopped her from inviting familiarity. She realized she had a whole new set of rules to learn.

The computer was open to the online application for the Clark County Marriage License Bureau.

"Your Highness, I've already filled yours out. Unfor-

tunately, you both have to appear in person at the bureau
to be issued a license."

Maddie slid Ward a glance. Was she supposed to address him as Your Highness? She was appalled at the
thought and about how little she knew about the situation
she was racing toward.

Was it unfortunate that they both had to appear because
Ward did not normally have to do things for himself—not
even fill out his own application—or unfortunate from a
security standpoint?

"We should be there by noon," Lancaster went on. "You
can marry immediately after being issued the license but
I booked an Officiant of the State of Nevada for 4:00 p.m.
I've arranged a suite at the Estate Hotel where the ceremony can be conducted. I thought it might be best if the
two of you spent the night there."

Maddie could feel a deep blush darkening her cheeks.
Good grief, the deception began. It was being made to
look as if they consummated their marriage.

Ward nodded, then leaned forward and whispered
something in Lancaster's ear.

"Yes, sir, my pleasure."

"Am I supposed to call you Your Highness?" she whispered when Lancaster had moved away and was out of
earshot.

"I'll make sure you are fully briefed on proper protocol, but for now, there's no rush. I like it when you call
me Ward."

And even though she was in a strange new world, those
simple words made Maddie feel more at ease, a faint hope
that maybe what she had agreed to wasn't complete insanity.

CHAPTER TWELVE

A REAL LIVE prince caused something of a stir, even in Vegas, where the marriage bureau saw everything and everyone from celebrities to Elvis look-alikes.

Despite an awestruck clerk, the license was issued quickly and efficiently. Then they were back in the stretch limo. Even in Vegas, where such vehicles were common, people were straining their necks trying to catch a glimpse of who might be inside.

The hotel, which looked like a Southern mansion, was an oasis of calm in the middle of that bustling, crazy city. They entered through a secluded garden and check-in was private and seamless, all handled by the Prince's unflappable staff.

The private plane should have prepared Maddie for the opulence of the hotel, but it did not. She explored the suite shamelessly. It was four thousand feet of pure luxury, and included two master suites, which given the *real* nature of their wedding night, was a relief to see. There was an indoor lap pool, a waterfall cascading down one wall and a huge fireplace, lit, even though the air-conditioning was on. There was a huge private deck.

Tables were covered with fresh flowers and pricey confections.

"I don't think I can get used to this," she confessed finally, meaning all of it—private planes and staff and VIP treatment and places like this. "Is your…er…home like this?"

"The palace is quite grand."

She gulped. His home was a palace. Her home for the next year was going to be a palace, too. It made her feel quite dizzy.

"But the palace is grand in a different way than this. This all seems quite new and glittery, the palace is more steeped in history and refinement. For instance, the table in the dining room is six hundred years old."

"I guess you wouldn't want to be spilling your red wine on that," she said.

He laughed. "I guess not. I think some of the table coverings are as old as the table."

She was beginning to feel like pressure was building up behind her eyes. On a good day, she wasn't even sure what fork to use!

Her drop into a new lifestyle was nearly immediate because the thing Ward had whispered to Lancaster about was apparently some serious pampering for her before her wedding. A whole team of professional pampering people arrived at the suite door and she was ushered into the smaller of the two master suites.

A massage table was set up, and before she knew it, modesty was cast aside, and she was under a sheet completely naked, being slathered in warm mud. The mud slathering was followed with her being wrapped in a thick white terry cloth robe and given a facial and pedicure and a manicure.

And then the door rocketed open, and a man swept in, pushing a clothes rack in front of him.

"Frederique is here," he called officiously. He abandoned the clothes rack and strode over to her. He took her chin in his hands and forced her head this way and that.

"Who are you?" she asked, pulling away from his hand.

"You don't know who I am?" he asked, aghast.

"I do not."

"Frederique, stylist to the stars." Then he smiled. "But also a long, long time ago, a young man who grew up on a little-known island called Havenhurst. Lancaster and I are childhood friends."

Somehow that was hard to imagine.

"I understand you are about to become *our* Princess." He said this with a certain frightening reverence, which, thankfully, was negated by his next words. "I see I have my work cut out for me."

"Thanks," she muttered.

"First, the hair. Did you cut it yourself?"

"Yes."

"Well, it's dreadful."

Maddie glared at him.

"So much to do, so little time." He lifted a lock of her hair and looked at it like a worm had attached itself to his fingers. "Maybe hair extensions," he muttered. "Except they take so long. A hair extension is a commitment," he told her sternly. "Are you prepared for that?"

"I think getting married is enough of a commitment for me for one day."

"Argh," he cried, throwing up his hands in frustration. But despite a rather major attitude, Frederique turned out to know what he was doing, and to be quite fun. He had "preshopped" for her and all the clothing on the rack he had wheeled in was for her to try on.

"How can you preshop for someone you know nothing about?"

"Five foot four and a half, approximately one hundred and eighteen pounds. What else would I need to know?"

Maddie gaped at him. How could he know that? Had Ward watched her that carefully? He had seen her in a bathing suit! She had seen him in one, too, but guess his weight? Accurately?

Frederique clapped his hands. "No time for lollygagging, love. Off you go. Start with underwear."

"I have my own!"

"I'm sure you do, and if it goes with that cheap little yellow dress, you will be needing new. I don't suppose you bought new for your wedding night?"

Maddie's mouth moved, but not a sound came out. See? This was where deception led you, straight into a more and more complicated web. What bride did not have new underwear for her wedding night?

"It's rather sudden," she said. "I guess I didn't think."

"Thank God for that. You would have ended up with precisely the wrong thing, I can tell by looking at you— sports bras and T-shirts. Gag me."

Happily, she thought.

"You do have potential, though. And I'd kill for the little bauble on your neck." Frederique reached out and touched her pendant, and then withdrew his hand. "Oh, how odd! It's warm."

Maddie touched it, too. The pendant was indeed warm, as if it was radiating.

"Here. Try this. And this and this." He tossed tiny pairs of lingerie at her, constructed primarily of silk thread spiderwebs. She retreated into the powder room and put on the lacy delicate items.

She stared at herself. She actually did have potential! The bra worked miracles with her modest bustline, and the scanty panties made her feel gloriously sexy. Had she ever allowed herself to feel that way before? Wasn't this bad timing? To be feeling sexy for a mock wedding night?

Still, she could not resist looking so feminine and pretty, and so she surrendered. Each outfit he passed her, she tried on. She saw the good underwear made the clothes look even more exquisite than they already were. She started to look forward to each outfit—a pretty cocktail dress, a colorful summer frock, a beautifully tailored pantsuit—and to twirling in front of Frederique's critical eye. He divided the bed into accept and reject piles and a large number of items were accumulating in both.

"That's way too many," she finally protested, surveying the growing stack of items to keep.

"Seriously, there is no such thing, but we are in a bit of a time crunch," he said, checking his watch.

Maddie was aware of feeling both exhilarated and exhausted, a thousand miles, literally and figuratively, from the girl she had been this morning.

"It's three, wedding is at four. A man could have a heart attack from this kind of pressure. Chop, chop, wedding dresses."

He opened the door and another rack awaited outside. On it were several selections of gorgeous dresses. He wheeled it in, took one off and put it aside. "I think it will be this one, but we'll try some others first."

"It's just a little private ceremony," she cried. Those dresses were something out of a dream, the kind of dress every girl longed for on her day of being a princess.

"Well, I understand there will be photos after, exclusive to three well-known media outlets. My reputation is at stake here."

Feeling trepidation, Maddie put on the first dress. Trying on wedding dresses was something every girl dreamed of. She had anticipated that day when Derek had proposed. Now, looking at herself in the floor-length white chiffon mermaid dress, she felt nothing, like an actress playing a role. Frederique walked around her, tapping his lip thoughtfully.

"No," he decided. "It doesn't work. Next."

He handed her another dress. It was a gorgeous champagne-colored ball dress. It didn't fit properly, and he had to pin the back of it. Again he circled her tapping his lip and squinting his eyes.

"No," he said. "Maybe for an evening wedding. Ach, as I thought, out of time. No more dillydallying!"

She could clearly see there was absolutely no point in addressing the fact she was not the one dillydallying!

He took the dress he'd put aside. "This one," he said.

She slipped into the washroom. The dress was white, the top fitted with laser-cut lace, dropping to a small belt, adorned with a silk bow. At the waist, the dress fanned out, an overlay of lace over an underlay of silk. The dress was tea length, and as Maddie looked at herself in the mirror, her eyes filmed over.

This was a dress for the girl she used to be: filled with hope, a believer in love. This was exactly the dress she might have once chosen for herself.

She suddenly felt sick that this was all fake, like a giant stage set. Had she really become so cynical she had accepted *this* instead of love.

Had Kettle been right? This, though it seemed crazy and bold, was really quite a *safe* choice? A fake marriage did not risk your heart, after all.

Unless you did something really dumb.

Like fall in love with him.

Meanwhile, it was a business arrangement. Help Kettle, help her town, maybe have an adventure in the process.

But all that made this perfect dress so bittersweet she wanted to weep. She took a deep breath and marched out of the bathroom. Frederique kissed his own fingertips and blew them at her. "Perfection. Now go take it off so it doesn't get rumpled." When she reemerged in the robe, he pulled out the chair at the dressing table. "Sit. Sit."

Maddie sat, sat.

And she watched the most amazing transformation happen. He started with her hair, each of the curls coaxed into good behavior until her hair was a soft wave around her face. And then he began with makeup: mascara and shadow, eyeliner, which she had never in her life used. Her eyes became astonishing: huge and green as a moss-covered forest floor. A sweep of blush here, and a sweep of blush there, and her cheekbones emerged, high and proud. He got out little pots of color, and with a look of furious concentration on his face, he painted her lips with a brush. Once, twice, three times.

She stared in disbelief as her lips became a shimmering, sensual invitation that said, without a shred of a doubt, *kiss me.*

As if in a dream, she stood and let the robe fall, while Frederique dropped the dress over her head, fussed with the bow and the hooks in the back. He knelt before her and inserted her feet into tiny white silk slippers.

And then he took a carved wooden box that she had not noticed on the bottom of the clothes rack.

"This," he said, bowing to her slightly, "is Prince Edward's wedding gift to you."

With shaking hands, she took the box from him and opened the lid. It was a tiara, encrusted in diamonds that shot blue flame into the room as the light caught in them.

"May I?" he asked softly. His own hands were shaking as he removed the tiara from the box and settled it on her curls.

She had expected it might feel heavy. Or silly. But it felt neither. It felt as if it fit her perfectly in every way.

Maddie regarded herself with astonishment. Dangerously, it suddenly did not feel as if she was playing a role at all. She felt as if, indeed, the magic wand had been waved.

She was Cinderella, turned into a princess for the night.

Frederique smiled. "May I be the first to congratulate you, Princess Madeline?" And then he bowed to her.

Without waiting for her answer, he went to the door and opened it.

Lancaster waited for her, in a full dress uniform of navy blue, resplendent with gold braiding and medals.

"I would be honored, Miss Nelson, if you would allow me to escort you."

She was so grateful for his solid strength, for his arm to slip her own through. She felt as if she was walking on air, as she and Lancaster made their way down the long hallway and into the main room, Frederique trailing them like a flower girl.

The room was empty, save for Ward and a woman in a gray business suit. They were chatting beside a desk, and Ward turned and looked at her.

Like Lancaster, he was in uniform, his jacket red with gold braiding, his pants navy and fitted. She looked into his face.

His handsome face was so familiar to her after such a short time. She remembered his shout of laughter as they hit the hot pools, and she remembered dancing with him at the concert, a man who had not been allowed to delight in small things.

But most of all, she remembered waking in his arms after she had fainted, the heat of his kiss still on her forehead, and looking into the deep blue of his eyes and seeing something there that a woman could hold on to.

That look was in his eyes now, as she walked—no, floated—toward him. He was looking at her, astounded by her transformation. He was looking at her as if he was a real groom and felt like the luckiest man in the world.

She shouldn't be feeling this way! And neither should he.

She drew up beside him. And then she turned slowly to face her future, and the man who would be her husband, Edward Alexander the Fourth, Prince of Havenhurst.

Briefly, she wondered if she would faint again, so huge was the welling of her heart. But then his fingers slipped under her wrists, and her hands were being cupped in his, and it felt as if he was coaxing every bit of strength in her to come forward.

And so Maddie heard her name and felt stronger and more certain than she had ever felt in her entire life.

"Madeline Elizabeth Nelson, please repeat after me."

She heard her voice, strong, confident, saying, "I, Madeline Elizabeth Nelson, take thee, Edward Alexander, to be my wedded husband, to have and to hold, from this day forward, for better or for worse, for richer or for poorer, in sickness and in health, to love and to cherish, till death do us part."

And then, his voice somber, made richer for the accent, he said those same words to her.

They were pronounced husband and wife, and they stood staring at each other in stunned silence.

"You may kiss the bride," the officiate said.

They stared at each other. What now? Lancaster cleared his throat when the silence dragged too long.

It was their first performance. Obviously both the official and Frederique believed this to be real. Both would probably talk about their experience.

Was that what Ward was thinking as he drew her closer? He stared at her as if asking her permission. She nodded.

He claimed her lips without hesitation, with mastery, with power, with passion.

Her first kiss from him—not counting the one on her forehead—did not disappoint. Everything faded save for the exquisite softness of his lips on hers. Everything faded save for the taste of him, which was as pure as forest dew. Everything faded save for the way she *felt*, which was on fire with life, which was as if every moment before this one had existed only to make way for this.

Connection.

Completion.

Ward broke the kiss and took a startled step back from Maddie, and she one back from him. She could tell he was as stunned by what he had just experienced as she was.

It was as if two souls intended for each other had met. The kiss had spoken in a language they, so new to each other, had not arrived at yet. *That* language was a language deeper than words, a language that shimmered along the skin, and charged the air they breathed with electrical current, and filled every space around them with the pure power and magic of possibility.

After it seemed as if they may have looked at each other with frightened wonder for way too long, she followed Ward's lead and turned to Lancaster and Frederique. The latter was wiping at tears.

Ward's hand found hers, and the *language* of his caressing her palm with his thumb was nearly as dizzying as that kiss.

Lancaster popped the cork out of a very expensive-looking bottle of champagne. Maddie felt as if she had already consumed the glass of champagne that was passed to her.

"A few members of the press have been invited," Ward said quietly, for her ears only. "They are waiting in the outer room. I thought it would be best if news of our marriage preceded our arrival in Havenhurst tomorrow. Would it be all right if they came in now?"

Maddie nodded, though she was stunned to be brought back down to earth with this reminder it was a pretense. This was what it was for: for show, for the cameras, and to save Aida, a girl Maddie did not know, a girl who was a *real* princess.

Not a fake created by Frederique.

CHAPTER THIRTEEN

WARD HAD FELT as if he was in a daze ever since he had seen Maddie walking toward him in that dress, looking gorgeous and outwardly composed. That pendant on her neck had been glowing as though it had taken on a life of its own. Though, when her eyes had met his, he'd known the outward composure was a show. She'd been nervous, and so had he.

The kiss had dissolved the nervousness and ushered in something far worse.

His desire for Maddie felt like a red-hot ember in his belly, and every time she glanced toward him, every time their hands brushed, it fanned the growing flame a little more.

When Lancaster bowed before them and offered his congratulations, Ward saw the slightly raised eyebrow, questioning the depth of the kiss.

Lancaster didn't speak it out loud, but he didn't have to.

Ward remembered their conversation all too clearly.

Just wondering, Lancaster had asked, *how do you keep it from getting real with a girl like that?*

Ward remembered how foolishly confident his reply had been.

With great effort, he had said with a certain nonchalance, as if yes, there would be effort, and no, not any temptations he could not overcome. He had known then, if she said yes, the most important part would be protecting her. He had promised Kettle she would not get hurt!

Well, she had just said *yes* and not any ordinary kind of yes, an *I do* kind of yes that felt bound up in tradition and honor and trust and faith.

But then along had come that mind-blowing life-altering kiss. Everything felt changed. His own power, which he had always been certain of, felt compromised.

Three carefully chosen members of the press waited in the outer room: coverage from one major magazine, one newspaper and one television network.

To invite the press was different for him. His whole life had been spent avoiding them, deliberately evading the spotlight.

But now he needed to use his position to get word back to his island kingdom before he arrived, so that everyone, including his father would accept this was a deal already done.

He thought of his father's great capacity for fury, and felt that need to protect Maddie grow in him.

Something cooled in her when they met the press, particularly as the television camera was set up. Lancaster read a prepared statement about how Prince Edward had been traveling in the US, incognito, with his vacation culminating in seeing his favorite band. In the small, pristine town of Mountain Bend, he had met an American girl who stole his heart, and after a whirlwind romance, they had married before his scheduled return to Havenhurst.

"How does it feel to be married to a prince?" Maddie was asked.

"Exactly like a fairy tale!" she responded, looking at Ward and smiling. He was sure only he could detect a certain tightness about her smile.

"Prince Edward, don't you have a fiancée?"

"Princess Aida Francesca has been informed of this turn of events," he said. Did Maddie flinch at the mention of Aida's name? But why would she? He'd told her the circumstances around their betrothal were less than romantic.

"And how did she take it?"

"I know my answer will disappoint you," he said. "The story would be better if there was a betrayed lover, with weeping and wailing and gnashing of teeth, but nothing could be further from the truth. Our arrangement was contractual, and Princess Aida was surprised, but very happy for me. She has always believed people should follow the dictates of their hearts."

Lancaster saw they wanted to press on the subject, and so he indicated the interview was over. The magazine and newspaper representatives took some photos, and then the cameras were shut off and they were escorted out.

Lancaster told them quietly their wedding feast had been laid in the dining room, and then took his leave also.

They were totally alone.

Maddie seemed to be avoiding his gaze, and she turned and went to the dining room. She stood in the doorway of the dining room for a moment, taking in the pheasant under the glass cloche that kept it warm, the silver serving dishes, the exquisite place settings, the flowers in the middle of the table.

"I'm not hungry," she said.

She sounded surprisingly like Belle in *Beauty and the Beast*. The theatrical performance had come to Havenhurst last year and he had attended.

The story, he realized, shocked, was not dissimilar, a girl who had exchanged her freedom for the promise of her father's well-being.

He was surprised by how much he had hoped for her company, but she brushed by him and went down the hall. He followed on her heels.

"Maddie? What's happened?"

"I just miss Mountain Bend," she said.

He considered that. She had ridden in a private plane. She'd been pampered. She had been showered with gifts of clothing and jewelry. She'd had a feast laid out before her.

And she missed Mountain Bend.

Home. He tried to imagine what that felt like—that bond with the place where you felt sheltered and loved and understood. He had a bond with his island nation, to be sure, and a deep love for it. But a sense of home? Not so much, perhaps. She took a deep, brave breath.

"I think it would be best," she said, her voice strained, "if we didn't kiss again."

"I had the same thought," he said solemnly.

"You did?" Even though she had put it to words first, now she looked wounded!

How could he possibly have thought this wouldn't get complicated? Relationships were always complicated! And one that involved marriage? On paper, but not for real? With a woman who was extraordinarily beautiful and smart and exquisitely fragile, even though life had asked her to be strong?

"Unless you wanted to," he said hastily.

"I don't," she said firmly, "unless you want me to. For the press. Or whoever else you're fooling. About loving me."

He realized now would be a very bad time to remind her that this had never been about love. He'd told her that—any union he had would not be about love.

She thrust her chin up and he saw the hurt there. And then she slipped in her bedroom door, and snapped it firmly shut in his face. He heard the lock click, as if she felt she needed protection from him.

He stood there, utterly stunned. He had already broken his promise to both Kettle and himself. He'd already hurt her.

This was so different than any man's expectation for his wedding night that he might have laughed at the absurdity.

Not that, given the circumstances, he had expected a normal wedding night. But he'd been looking forward to her company, to getting to know her better. When he had seen her coming toward him in that dress, when he had drunk in the light in her eyes, he had actually had a moment when he thought it was all going to work out even better than he planned.

Truthfully, he had cast himself in the chivalrous role of using every bit of his strength to *just* get to know her better. And that did not include tasting those delectable lips again!

Now he saw it was Maddie who had done the right thing, the wise thing.

Still, when he thought he heard muffled sobs behind the door, he had to stop himself from kicking it in. He was the cause of those tears, after all. He'd been a married man less than two hours and already his bride was in tears.

He was sure that was probably a record of some sort.

Prince Edward was not sure he had ever felt as miserable in his entire life as he did, standing helplessly outside of Maddie's door, on the night of his wedding!

Maddie awoke the next morning, by herself in the luxurious bed, still in her wedding dress, which was now a crumpled ruin. She slid out of bed and went to her bathroom and looked at herself in the mirror. The makeup Frederique had so carefully and expertly applied had made raccoon circles under her eyes, which were a little puffy from crying. If she was not mistaken, there was a splotch or two of sooty black on the dress.

She should not feel for all the world as if she had a hangover. She had had one glass of champagne.

She touched her necklace. The gold still felt warm beneath her finger tips.

"Maddie Nelson," she heard her father's voice say sternly, "that is enough."

It was a reminder of what she came from: not royalty, but good, strong stock. She was a logger's daughter raised in a part of the country that prized toughness and resiliency.

Her father would have no patience with whining and even less for self-pity.

You made your bed, he would say, *now lie in it.*

So, she regretted that she had married the Prince? She had realized, a little too late, that his world was completely different from hers, and that the adjustments would be difficult? She was shattered that theirs was a business deal? Was shaken by what had been in that meeting of their lips?

"Too bad, Princess," she told herself, in her father's voice, and then giggled shakily, because she really was a princess.

She had made a deal, and she was not going to cry about it, or drown in regrets. She was not going to try and get out of the deal she had made.

That was not how she had been raised.

So she would perform whatever tasks were required of her to the best of her ability. She would not look longingly at her husband's lips, or give in to the longing to feel his hand in hers.

It was a job. She had accepted it, and she would do it.

She stepped into the shower and let the hot water wash away all of yesterday's angst. Today was a brand-new day.

Wrapped in a towel, she went and sorted through the clothes that Frederique had chosen for her. She put on the pale cream pantsuit, she blow-dried the curls out of her hair, she put on the lightest dusting of makeup.

She regarded herself in the mirror.

She didn't look like a princess, per se, not like she had in the wedding dress. But she did look calm and confident and ready for whatever was next.

Just before she opened the door, she made a decision and turned back into the room. She made the bed so expertly it looked as if no one had been there. Then she took the towels from the bathroom and the dress off the floor. She went across to the other master suite, hesitated, then knocked once briskly and entered.

Ward was in the bathroom. The door was open. He was standing before the mirror, with a razor in his hand, in a cloud of steam. He was dressed only in a towel. How she remembered those strong, sculpted lines from their day at the hot pools.

The longing rose up in her, but she quelled it quickly. "Good morning," he said, looking at her out the door, his eyes widened in surprise.

She dropped her wedding dress on the floor beside his bed, then surveyed the bed critically and rumpled up the sheets more than they were, then marched right by him and dumped her wet towels on the floor.

His eyes met hers in the mirror. She could not quite read his expression. Pity? Sympathy? Regret? Some combination of all three of those things?

"Good morning," she said crisply. "The maids might gossip if it didn't look as if we spent the night together. I thought we should make it look normal."

"Oh," he said. "Normal."

As if he had a clue what normal was! Ward had not

bought that razor in his hand. He'd never bought a razor. Or a tube of toothpaste. Or a roll of toilet paper. Everything in his whole life had been done for him. It gave him a kind of self-confidence, even in this totally awkward situation, that Maddie found extremely irritating.

Or was it kissing her until she had nearly lost her senses that made him feel as if he had the upper hand with her?

On her way out of the bathroom, she put her hand on the knot in that towel that was knotted at his waist and tugged. Hard. She felt the towel give under her hand, heard it whisper to the floor.

She didn't dare look back, but she had a feeling that look of aggravating self-confidence had been wiped entirely from his handsome face!

And that whatever he was feeling for her right now would not be even remotely related to pity!

From the bath and bedroom, she went to the dining room. The feast was untouched, but maybe that would make it look as if they couldn't keep their hands off each other?

A soft knock came on the door, and a key turned. Glenrich had arrived with breakfast things.

"May I congratulate you on your marriage, Your Highness?"

"Er...thank you."

"I'll pack your bags now, if that's all right?" she asked.

Another thing he didn't do. He didn't pack his own bags. Or do his own laundry. He'd probably never made himself a sandwich in his entire life. And now she wouldn't be doing those things either, and she was dismayed that she missed them already!

A third staff member came in, smiled, curtsied and handed her a newspaper.

"You look lovely, Your Highness."

Maddie stared at the picture on the front page of the paper. American Girl Marries Real Prince! the headline blared. But the picture was worth a thousand words.

She and Ward were gazing at each other with the look of two people madly in love, that wedding kiss they had shared still shimmering in the air around them. They looked like just the type of couple who would take advantage of Nevada's marriage regulations to impetuously get married.

Success.

If all went according to plan, only three hundred and sixty-four days to go.

She was going to need something to help her pass time. To get her mind off things. What had rescued her from every crisis she had ever faced? Helped her get through it? Provided reprieve from a reality that had become too hard to face?

Books!

She'd just pop down to the hotel store—startled, she looked up to see Lancaster blocked her way.

"I'm just going to go get a few books. For the flight," she told him.

He shook his head, ever so slightly, but it was still no. His eyes went over her shoulder, and she turned to see Ward behind them.

He was looking very princely, now that he had his clothes on! He was in a tailored shirt and jacket, a beautifully knotted tie at his throat. The shirt was brilliantly white. Did he ever dress casually?

"Good morning, Your Highness. I was just going to explain to your lovely bride why she can't pop by the bookshop. Perhaps you could take over?" Lancaster handed Ward the newspaper and Ward scanned it.

"Come have breakfast," Ward said, taking her elbow.

"I want to go get a book," she said dangerously, keeping her tone low. She extricated her elbow from his grip.

He held up the paper. "You can't."

"Can't?" she challenged him.

"I'm sorry. You were on the front page of the paper this morning, and possibly on the television news. You'll be recognized now. Everyone will want a picture of you. And there are others who would see you, unprotected, as a target."

Her mouth fell open and her arguments dried up. Her days of going out for a book were over? She was beginning to see why Ward did not buy his own toothpaste.

"If you'll give me a list of some of the books you'd like, or favorite authors, I'll make sure it's seen to," Ward said quietly.

Only three hundred and sixty-four more days.

Of imprisonment.

Her hand went to her necklace, as it always did when she felt uncomfortable, trapped, as if there was no way out.

One day, she could hear her father's voice say. *You feel like this after one day? Imagine what he feels like?*

Looking at his face, she realized this had been Ward's whole life. No wonder he had been so carefree in Mountain Bend. No wonder every moment had seemed to shine for him. She had never seen being able to buy toothpaste as a privilege before, but now that she couldn't do it, it did seem like one.

One she had taken for granted and he had never enjoyed.

Did she actually feel a tiny bit sorry for him? She did, and what was that going to do to her resolve to keep everything strictly business? Maddie's hand was still on the pure gold of her necklace.

What if, her father's voice said, gentle but with faint recrimination, *it wasn't all about you? What if you, the girl who seems to have nothing, had something very precious to give him, the man who appears to have everything?*

It was true. Ward had exercised his power, so far, to make this a good experience for her. He had given her a spa treatment, and a whole wardrobe, and that gorgeous tiara.

On the other hand, what did she have, she asked herself. *What have I got to give a prince?*

You know.

And then she did.

CHAPTER FOURTEEN

As MADDIE HAD boarded the plane—her bags fully packed for her—Lancaster handed her a heavy sack. She peeked in.

A dozen or so books. She caught glimpses of some of her favorite authors' names.

"It's like having a magic wand," she told Lancaster. "I wave it and say, I'd like books please, and they appear. No saving money, no deciding which one you want the most, no going to the secondhand book store when cash is short."

"I'm glad you are pleased, Your Highness."

"I don't really like being called that," she said.

"Ah," he said, "you'll have to humor me."

"Watch it, or I'll wave my wand and turn you into a toad."

"Not your style," he decided with a smile. "Now if we gave Sophie a magic wand…"

They both laughed, and it felt good to laugh with him.

"Can you get me a deck of cards, too?" she asked.

"Poof," he said, as if making a deck of cards materialize would be the easiest thing in the world. If the request surprised him, it did not show in his face. If he had questions about the request, he did not ask them. If it was a problem to get her a deck of cards—as in it might delay the flight—he did not let on.

Maddie went to the same seat she had had yesterday and looked around. Already the awe factor was wearing off, already she felt less intimidated by the whole experience.

Ward boarded, acknowledged her with a faint salute and disappeared down a corridor toward the back of the plane. Did he intend to ignore her for the duration of the flight? Maybe for the duration of the marriage, except for public appearances? She frowned.

"What's back there?" she asked, when Lancaster returned.

"Prince Edward's office and private quarters."

"Hmmm."

He produced a deck of cards. "Solitaire?" he asked.

"That's a funny question to ask a newly married woman," she said. "No, I have other plans for these cards. Thank you for finding them. Which door is his office?"

Lancaster cocked his head at her. "Would you like me to ask when he can see you?"

"I'm not asking for permission to see my husband."

Lancaster regarded her thoughtfully for a moment, and then a faint smile played across his lips. "Yes, Your Highness," he said.

And she waited until he had taken his own seat some distance away from her to have a giggle at her own audacity. She could lose courage, though, and so as soon as the plane had leveled and the very subtle seat belt sign at the front of the cabin went off, she undid her seat belt, and holding her cards tight, she went down the same hallway that Ward had gone down.

She guessed at the door since Lancaster had not divulged that. Lancaster was watching her, but didn't try to stop her.

She had chosen the right door. It looked like the office of a successful executive anywhere: walnut paneling, a beautiful desk, a painting, no doubt priceless, hanging on the wall. It parted company with any executive office, because a door was slightly ajar, and through that was a bedroom, every bit as well-appointed as the bedrooms in the hotel they had just left.

Ward looked up, surprised, possibly a trifle wary.

"Hello."

She held up the cards. "Do you know what these are?"

"Playing cards?"

"Have you ever played cards?"

He frowned. "I don't believe I have."

"Well, it's going to be a long, boring flight for me, so I guess I'd better teach you."

He looked uncomfortable. As she had guessed, few people called the shots with him. "I was going to do some work, but—"

"What kind of work does a prince do?" she asked, taking the seat across from him at his desk, sliding the cards from their cardboard box and dividing the cards into two even piles, one in each hand.

"The island has many business concerns. I'm CEO of two crown corporations and a primary shareholder in several others. I also am the honorary head of several charities and the leader of our military."

She did a riffle shuffle—dovetailing the cards into a D-on-its-side shape—so that they cascaded down like a waterfall. "Military?"

"Mostly palace and personal security, but we also possess valuable resources that we protect, so we liaise and do exchange programs with other organizations, like the British SAS, Special Air Service."

She performed the same shuffle again.

"You're very good at that," he said, watching her hands on the cards.

"Yes, I am. That's what happens when you grow up a

logger's daughter in a town with long winters. You learn to play cards. Have you ever played poker?"

"I'm afraid not."

"Oh good," she said, "that improves my chances of winning."

"Isn't it a game of chance?"

"Some of it. Some of it is skill. I'll show you." She pulled her phone out of her pocket and went through her photos to a screen. "These are the hands and the values of each of the hands. So, clearly a royal flush takes all. Just like in your real life.

"So this is a simple form—I'm going to deal you five cards, and then you'll have three opportunities to discard and get new ones to build a winning hand. Here, we'll do a few dummy hands."

The Prince was intrigued, and caught on very quickly. As they played, she asked questions and found out as much as she could about Havenhurst: the population, the industry, the climate. She was learning and he was learning—and there was lots of laughter in between.

A staff member came in and put coffee and biscuits on the desk between them, then left. It made it hard to believe they were on an airplane!

"Does that happen all the time?"

"Coffee?" he asked.

"People sliding in and out, anticipating your every need."

"Oh." He looked surprised by the question. "I guess it does."

"Where will we be living?" she asked.

"I have a suite in the palace."

"Two bedrooms or one?"

"Four, actually."

"If anybody is going to believe this, Ward, there can't

be people sliding in and out all the time. They'd figure out pretty quickly that our marriage isn't a real one."

He looked perplexed. "I think I can trust my staff for discretion."

"Is that another way of saying who is going to change the toilet paper roll?"

He stared at her, and then he threw back his head and laughed. "That hadn't actually occurred to me. But I have a valet who briefs me in the morning."

"Well, he'll have to brief you somewhere else, because there isn't going to be any staff in our suite."

The laughter was still twinkling in his eyes. "Are you telling me how it's going to be?"

"I am. You can tell your staff it's a weird American thing. We don't like people hovering about, doing things for us that we are quite capable of doing for ourselves."

"The cook?" he said, hopefully.

"Your Highness, get used to scrambled eggs for dinner."

The hands went back and forth for a bit, and then she said, "Are you ready to play for real?"

"What does that mean?" he asked, a bit warily.

"Let's place a bet. Whoever wins ten hands is the winner."

"What's the bet?" he asked.

"I don't really have much of value. My necklace?"

"I couldn't take your necklace," he sputtered.

"You probably, literally, couldn't. You're not going to win."

He winced. "Still—"

"If you win it, I'll win it back from you next time we play."

It was in the air between them. Next time. This could be what their lives together were like, this casual banter, these easy conversations, this sense of building trust and friendship.

"No," he said, "if I win, I keep the cook."

"Okay."

"And what would you want from me?"

She smiled at him. "Diving lessons."

"Seriously?"

"Something wrong with that?"

Ward eyed his new wife warily. She had some surprises in store for him. The towel thing this morning had been a clear indicator of that.

"Choose something else," he told her firmly. "It's dangerous. For every dive you see that looks like the ones Lancaster and I did at the pools that day, there are a dozen or a hundred that didn't look like that. That have bruised and beat up the body. Lancaster has broken his nose and several ribs."

She looked properly frightened. He hoped that was the end of this conversation.

"Then why does he do it?" she asked. "Why do you?"

He hesitated. "I suppose there is a feeling of being alive that can't quite be replicated in other activities."

Wrong thing to say, apparently. She got that stubborn look about her that he was already beginning to recognize.

"That's *exactly* how I want to feel."

He saw he had walked himself into a trap. He had already said other activities did not quite replicate that feeling of falling through the air.

"Choose something else," he said firmly.

"Nope," she said, just as firmly. "Diving lessons. I'm sure you don't start on a ledge fifty feet above the pool."

He sighed. She could have asked for anything. The necklace she had offered him—the one that had deep sentimental value to her—also was probably worth several thousand dollars. She could have asked him for something in kind—a shopping trip, a bauble, an expensive perfume.

But she had not, and it told him a great deal about her. It also told him a great deal about her that she was not prepared to back down. People had been backing down from him for his entire life! If he said no, they acquiesced, immediately.

"Okay," he said. "Diving lessons. *But* starting very, very small."

She grinned at him, impish in her easy victory. Ward watched, fascinated, at Maddie's competence with those cards. He felt pressure to work—his in-box after his time off was overflowing—and yet he could not draw himself away from this fun time with her.

Even though she was exquisitely dressed today, and had done some awful thing to tame her hair, she was what he had seen least often in his life.

Real.

Genuine.

Normal.

And maybe most importantly, unintimidated by him. After their awful start last night, tears and slammed doors, he felt something like hope unfolding ever so softly within him.

They weren't going to be man and wife. He would not do that to her. He could not imagine any role stealing her lovely freshness, her ability to be genuine, more quickly than that one.

But maybe, just maybe they were going to be friends.

And most certainly, for a reason he did not understand, but felt grateful for nonetheless, she was going to give him little glimpses into normal, into a life he had missed and had given up hope of ever having. Though he hoped that meant his future wasn't full of toilet paper rolls, and that they were going to eat something beyond scrambled eggs.

The poker hands unfolding proved that they were both fiercely competitive. They shared laughs. He noticed how she was using this time to casually coax details about Havenhurst and his life from him.

He found out more about her growing up in Mountain Bend. They were, it would seem, getting to know each other. It was backward as could be to get to know each other *after* the wedding, but he was still enjoying it immensely.

He was not sure how, but the cards always seemed to land in her favor.

"Are you cheating?" he asked, throwing down his cards in disgust after she had taken six games in a row and there was no chance of him winning.

"Ah! The losers always ask that! When you're a little more certain around the cards, you'll be able to tell."

"You didn't answer the question," he pointed out drily.

"I can't wait to learn to dive!"

"Well, that should be a first. I've never heard of a girl diving on Havenhurst."

"Tell me about that, then. About the culture, about why a girl wouldn't dive on Havenhurst."

"It's probably because we don't have any swimming pools, and the rocky outcrops and high perches can be dangerous to dive from."

What had she let herself in for?

"Despite some changes because of the internet and television, we remain quite a traditional society," he said. "With quite traditional male and female roles. For instance, women tend to stay home with the children, while the men go out to work. The older people resist change."

"And you, are you traditional? Do you resist change?"

"I'm traditional in some ways." He didn't want her to dive, for one thing! "But in other ways, I feel it's my responsibility to shepherd Havenhurst into this century. The firstborn male son, at the moment, has more rights, say for inheriting land, than older siblings who are female. Even our monarchy is geared to a son taking the crown, not a daughter. I hope to change that in my lifetime."

"Are you that son?"

"Yes, I'll be King one day."

"It seems from another world," she said. "Like a fairy tale."

"It is another world," he agreed. "I'm not sure about the fairy-tale part."

"Is it at least charming?" she asked, leaning toward him, her chin cupped in her hands, so earnest.

"Charming. Aggravating."

"What do people do for fun?"

Fun. Not that that had been a big component in his life.

"We have a theater of sorts, and it's a big deal when we can entice the occasional live production to come in. The last one was *Beauty and the Beast.*"

"Does the theater have popcorn, like an American theater?"

"No."

"That's something I'll have to change," she said.

"Ah, your first royal proclamation."

He didn't tell her if they did get popcorn, he and she probably would not eat it, because the people had a certain expectation. And it was not to look up to the royal balcony to see a greasy-fingered prince and princess munching contentedly on popcorn.

"What else do people do for fun?"

"Well, we have hot pools literally everywhere, and so

that's a big part of island life—taking a picnic to one of the pools. But mostly entertainment is the party, the cei-lidh, gatherings of people in kitchens and pubs, where they play homemade instruments, and games. Singing and dancing and lots of imbibing."

She looked at him, hearing something he hadn't said.

"You don't do that, do you?"

"No."

"Not ever?"

"No."

"Are you a lonely man, Prince Edward?" she asked.

He stared at her. Just like that, she had cut through to the emptiness in his heart. Just like that, she had uncovered a longing in him that could not be met.

"You ache to belong, don't you?"

"It's not what I was born to," he said, deliberately hardening his voice.

This would be the problem with her: she would ask questions of him that he did not want to answer, she would stir longings in him that were best left sinking way below the surface.

Even this: playing poker, having a normal conversation, he could not give in to it. It would only lead to more wanting.

Wanting more from her than he could ever ask her to give him.

Now was the time to set limits, to remind her how it was going to be: a business arrangement between them.

He could not afford to indulge in more than that. To let his weakness out, his secret hopes, his longing.

To have a lass look at him, just the way Maddie was looking at him now.

"This has been great fun," he said, his voice firm,

"but having lost my shirt at poker, I must now get back to work. Duty calls."

She looked slighted.

She looked hurt.

It was what he had promised Kettle he would not do. But here was the question: hurt her a little now, or a lot later?

Because that's all that could come of it if he let down his guard around her, let her behind the closed doors of his world.

Yes, there would be riches. The baubles and the privileges, the jets and the yachts.

But Maddie had already shown she had little taste for those things.

And if he drew her into his world—if what they had pretended ever became real between them—every other door would be closed to her.

She would stand on the outside, as he did, listening to the laughter and the music of the ceilidh without ever being invited in to experience its warmth.

There was no sense her not knowing the absolute truth of his life: duty *always* called.

She only looked hurt for a moment. And then she touched that gold nugget necklace that never left her neck, smiled, stuck out her tongue at him and flounced from the room.

Stuck out her tongue at him.

Did she not know he was a prince?

Of course she knew. And it was so refreshing that she didn't care. But he could not allow himself the weakness of dipping into that pool of freshness that her guileless eyes offered. Really, this all would have been so much easier if Sea had not let him down.

He sighed heavily, turned to his work. As if to affirm

his decision to distance himself from Maddie, there was a scathing email from his father, who had just heard the news of his marriage and berated him soundly for his betrayal of his duty.

It was this world that Ward needed to protect Maddie from. He had promised.

Ward put his head in his hands? Who would ever invite a woman they actually liked to share this kind of life? If Aida married quickly, he would find a way to release Maddie before a year was up.

Because he felt more strongly for her with each passing moment, with each encounter. His heart sank when he thought what he might feel like after a year. He had to keep his distance or he was never going to be able to let her go.

And even having made that vow, when the jet began its descent toward Havenhurst, he found himself going to be with Maddie. Somehow, he did not want to miss her first reaction to his island home.

"It's beautiful," Maddie breathed as Ward materialized at her side and buckled himself in, in preparation for landing.

As she watched out the window, the jet circled her new home.

"I've asked them to fly low and circle, so that you can see it from this perspective," Ward told her.

From the air, the island of Havenhurst was absolutely gorgeous: lusciously green from its neat fields, to forests, to carpeted mountains. From the air, she could see it was dotted with turquoise pools and cascading waterfalls.

"The carpets of pale purple around the pools?" Ward pointed out. "Those are wild lupines."

They flew over three villages, which he named, but when she tried to repeat the names after him, they both ended up laughing. She could see thatch on the stone cottage roofs and winding cobblestoned streets.

"This is the main city, Breckenworth," Ward said. Maddie pressed her nose against the window and looked down at a place out of a fairy tale. A thick stone wall surrounded a town with soaring church spires and Gothic-style buildings, interspersed with neat pastel painted cottages and row houses and shops. The greenish slate tile roofs shone from a recent rain. Narrow streets wove, with seeming randomness, through the city.

"It's absolutely charming," Maddie said.

And then, the plane swooped upward, and she drew her eyes away from the town. On what appeared to be a rock with a sheer cliff face, overlooking the town was a magnificent Gothic-style castle. The closest she'd ever been to a castle was the Sleeping Beauty Castle at Disneyland. This one looked remarkably similar with its soaring towers and spires, its intricate maze of walls and interconnecting buildings.

"If you look closely," Ward said, "you can see a staircase carved into the stone cliff from the castle to the town below."

"Oh my gosh, I hope that's not how the groceries are brought in!"

He laughed as they flew up and over the castle, revealing stables and car parks, fields and forests, stretched out on a plateau behind it.

She could also see the airfield they were landing on. She gasped. It was surrounded by people!

"How many people did you say are on the island?" she asked.

"A million."

"Are they all here?"

"Possibly," he said, wryly. "They'll be wanting to catch a glimpse of their new Princess."

"Word traveled fast."

"For a place with little internet, you'd be amazed."

She looked down at her now-travel-rumpled suit. "I'm changing," she said, and tried to get up.

"You'll have to wait until we've landed." Ward's hand slipped into hers. She took a deep breath and felt the reassuring pressure of it.

She wasn't sure if she should feel this way, because really, what had he done to earn her trust? In fact, he had dismissed her just a short time ago!

But then she thought of all the effort he had made to make her wedding day perfect, despite the pretense, and she thought of how gamely he had played poker, and she let herself relax a tiny bit. He was a strong man; it was okay to rely on that when meeting a million people!

Maddie was shown to where her things were: an opulent bedroom across the hall from Ward's office. Her suitcases were there, and suddenly she was grateful for the quiet assistant, Glenrich, who took her choice of dress and quickly steamed the wrinkles out of it. It was a very simple burgundy dress with a matching short jacket. Even though the low heels were brand-new, Glenrich quickly swiped them with a cloth that brought out a deep shine in them.

Maddie went and stood by Ward at the door of the plane. He too had changed. And shaved. He was wearing a navy blue suit with a white shirt, that made him look powerful and calm and confident and as though he owned the earth.

But of course, he did own this earth!

"Ready?" he asked.

Lancaster was there, behind her, and spoke in her ear,

"The Prince will descend the staircase first. He'll stop at the bottom and take your hand. He will hold hands with you, and you'll go left to the fence that holds people back. Shake a few hands, one light pump and withdraw, or your hand will ache for a week. Exchange a word or two, keep moving. If you accept flowers, hand them off to Glenrich after you've admired them. Watch the Prince. When he makes his way to the car, follow."

"Is everything this choreographed?"

"It's not all eating bonbons and attending balls," Lancaster said mildly. "Glenrich will be putting together a protocol book for you, which should prevent any major gaffes. It remains to be seen if the people will take to you more or less because you're an American."

The door of the plane opened, and Ward stepped out. A roar of approval shook the ground as he raised his hand.

Maddie realized this was the last time he would feel like Ward to her. He was their Prince, and everything about him, from his stance, to his raised hand, made him Edward Alexander the Fourth, the future King of this small island.

As they went down the stairs, a chant began to build.

She was stunned to hear what it was.

"Princess Madeline! Princess Madeline!"

It was as if one huge voice called her name. It made her want to shrink behind Ward, to turn and run back up the steps to the plane. But the way was blocked with Lancaster and staff coming behind her.

Ward stepped to the right, exposing her for the first time. He took her hand.

A great, approving cheer went up from the crowd, his abandonment of Aida apparently already forgiven in favor of a love story.

The chant changed. "Kiss! Kiss! Kiss!"

He turned to her. Their eyes met. They had promised each other no more of this, but it was evident the crowd was hungry for romance. His eyes asked the question.

She nodded, her heart beating harder than it had when she had seen how large the crowds were.

He dropped his head over hers, and the crowd went wild.

The kiss was not as lingering as the wedding kiss had been, but still Maddie was so aware of how she loved the taste of him, how it filled her with a sense of a rightness in the world. And that was what she carried with her as they went forward to the crowds that pressed against a steel, waist-high fence.

She shook hands, she accepted flowers, which she buried her nose in, before handing them to Glenrich. She could not stop smiling as the love and approval washed over her. They welcomed her. They congratulated her. They wished her the best. They said how they loved their Prince and wanted a happy life for him.

She didn't really need any words, beyond thank you.

The experience was so lovely it was actually very difficult to remember this was not real: that she was not his bride in the sense any of them thought she was.

Maddie and Ward, finally, made their way to a waiting car, a beautifully restored Rolls-Royce. A uniformed driver held the door for her, saluted the Prince. They turned, as a couple, and waved one last time.

One tiny old lady was holding a baby over the fence, and Ward dropped Maddie's hand, ran over, scooped the baby from her and kissed it on the cheek. The crowd roared their approval as Ward handed the baby back.

Maddie noticed Lancaster, watchful, but relaxed as Ward came back toward them.

"I am a little overwhelmed," she confided to him, in

a quiet aside. "I don't know what to do with this kind of adoration."

"You do what he does."

"Which is?"

"You earn it, every single day."

That single statement gave her a very different perspective of the man who was walking back toward her.

They drove away from the airport, leaving the crowds behind them. Then the car was on a road, lined with mature trees that formed a canopy of green over it. At the end of that tree-lined roadway was a courtyard, a wide staircase, and the main entrance to the castle.

A spectacular fountain shot geysers of water into the air in the center of the courtyard. The car floated to a stop at the bottom of the stairs. Staff, dressed mostly in white uniforms, lined both sides of the steps, and at the top stood a man and a woman.

"Your father and mother?" Maddie asked with a gulp.

"King Edward the Third and Queen Penelope."

"I guess I don't refer to them as Mom and Dad?"

The Prince hid a smile.

Lancaster was at her ear. "When you reach the top of the stairs, drop the Prince's hand, curtsy and address them—first His Majesty the King, and then Her Majesty the Queen."

"I don't know how to curtsy," she whispered.

"Maybe poker-playing time could have been better used, Your Highness," Lancaster suggested drily.

"I'm afraid I wouldn't trade that time for anything—not even making a perfect first impression on my new in-laws."

Lancaster eyed her sternly, but she could see laughter behind his expression. "Do not offer your hand. If either of them offers theirs, you may take it."

Ward's hand tightened on hers as they walked up the steps. Unlike the warmth that had radiated from the people who had greeted the plane, there was a definite chill in the air here.

At the wide platform at the top of the steps, Maddie offered an awkward curtsy, and the acknowledgment of their titles. Neither offered their hand. Ward's mother was extraordinarily beautiful, but her eyes were remote, and her mouth had the downturn of perpetual bad humor about it. His father radiated a kind of power that was not like the kind of power Ward radiated, but his eyes seemed cold as they assessed her, and it was everything she could do to prevent herself from shivering.

Though of course they would be irritated with Edward going against their plans for him and choosing his own bride in America, Maddie found their greeting to him to be stunningly chilly.

And then the King and Queen turned their backs on them and swept away, the doors of the castle opened by two servants in matching livery, and then closed behind them.

"I take it we haven't been invited for tea?" Maddie said in a low voice. She was scanning Ward's face.

There was a look on it as remote as the look on his mother's had been, as if he had not been hurt by the remoteness of the interchange and by the total lack of welcome for his new bride.

"Come," he said, his tone crisp and level, "I'll show you our suite."

"Are they always like that?" Maddie asked, as they descended the stairs.

"Always like that? No. Usually, they're worse."

She stared at his face. It was cast in cool lines. She had hoped he was kidding, but she could see he was not.

Suddenly, unexpectedly, she ached for this man who was her husband. She had already seen that he lived a life constantly surrounded by people, who clearly worshipped the ground he walked on. And yet none of them were his friends, though obviously he was as close to Lancaster as anyone. Still, his station in life separated him from others. He'd grown up with that, accepted it, and as far as Maddie could see, had no expectation of anything else.

But somehow she had assumed that he had family who loved and supported him, who formed his clan, his safe place, his soft place to fall.

She thought of the remoteness of the couple she had just met, and she could clearly see nothing was further from the truth.

She touched the beautiful warm gold stone on her neck.

Another woman might have wondered if she had impulsively allowed herself to be dropped into a nest of rattlesnakes.

But that was not how Maddie felt. Not at all. Audacious as it was, Maddie thought perhaps she wasn't here to save her town. Or to have an adventure.

Perhaps she was here on Havenhurst to rescue a prince.

CHAPTER FIFTEEN

WARD LED HER around the side of the castle and through a lush garden. It was filled with early roses, and well-kept beds of rich, dark loam. There was a stone bench and an exquisite fountain that bubbled happily. But what was the point of a happy fountain and gloriously blooming roses—what was the point of all this beauty—if everyone was miserable?

His suite was past the gardens, and under an arch that dripped with purple-flower-laden wisteria. She craned her neck to see the plant went up over the arch and climbed the castle walls. It seemed it must be nearly as old as the castle.

He went through a door and held it for her.

"Welcome," Ward said, watching her face.

They had entered a vestibule with carved wooden wainscoting that gleamed from polishing. Beyond that was the living room, and she stepped into it as if she was a guest looking at a roped-off room in a museum.

It was gorgeous, of course, with high ceilings, a glorious chandelier, an enormous fireplace and tufted silk sofas facing each other over a low glass table that sported a huge vase of fresh flowers. All of this sat on a large square Turkish rug that was probably priceless. Everything in the entire room looked very elegant and very old.

"But where do you curl up with a book and a cup of tea?" she asked.

"I want you to do whatever you need to do to feel at home."

She wondered if there might be a garden shed somewhere she could make into a little reading spot. She could not ever imagine feeling at home in this expansive room.

Over the fireplace hung a portrait of an extremely stern-looking ancestor. He was positively glaring at her from his gilded frame.

"Good grief," she said. "Is this a relative?"

"Great-grandfather—King Edward the First."

"Is everyone in your entire family miserable?"

He laughed with surprised enjoyment. "Is it that obvious we aren't exactly—" he paused, obviously searching for a reference, and then brightened as he found it "—the Brady Bunch?"

"No one's the Brady Bunch," Maddie said. "But a family is supposed to be—how should I put this?—your safe place, in all the world. The place where it's okay to be yourself, and to make mistakes, and people get mad at each other from time to time, but underneath all that it flows like a river that will never stop."

"It?" he said quietly.

"Love," she whispered, and somehow she was afraid to even say that word in such close proximity to him.

She barely knew him. They barely knew each other. But they were going to. And love had a way of finding its path, of always breaking rules and refusing to be defined, because when she looked at him, her heart felt something.

Something sweet and pure and lovely that wanted desperately to rescue him from his loneliness. If she followed these impulses, they were going to lead her to a place where the potential for hurt was enormous.

But also to a world that felt brighter and more hopeful than it had before. A world that made her over into something different than she was now: someone more complete, more connected. More *everything*.

Ward's laugh was so world-weary it made her heart ache.

"Love?" he said cynically. "Love would be seen as a weakness in this family."

So it was true. Maybe she was here to rescue him. But at what risk to herself? The thing about love was it was so brave. So darned brave. It didn't care if you'd been wounded before. It threw itself down at the feet of possible catastrophe and it said *Stomp on me, tear me up. I don't care. It's worth it to feel this way.*

Love beckoned; it whispered *I am stronger than that imagined catastrophe. I am stronger than anything. Give me a chance and I will win.*

She turned hastily away from him. One day into her marriage of convenience and she was already in the thrall of something that felt much larger than herself.

Maddie shamelessly explored every inch of the suite. It wasn't huge, though it was obviously way more than two people needed. Besides the living room there was a formal dining room with a table that could sit sixteen, a homey kitchen with a table in it. She took a quick look in four luxurious bedrooms, but didn't explore too deeply because one of them must be his, even though they all looked equally unlived-in.

After she had finished looking around, she found Ward in a book-lined study. It was possibly her favorite room!

"Well?" Ward asked. "What do you think? Can you feel at home here?"

"Can I really do what I want?"

"Of course."

"I'd like to get rid of the grim paintings of old men glaring down. The fixture with the dragon in the entry has to go. It could give nightmares. And the curtains are awful. So dark and heavy. They cut the light dreadfully."

"And keep out drafts in the colder weather," he said. "You'd be surprised how hard it is to keep a castle warm October to March."

"Hmmm. I bet there's a lot of babies born here May to September," she said and then laughed at the surprise on his face. Was he blushing, ever so faintly? Devilishly, she liked that!

"It's obvious there's staff, but I'll have to kick them out to feel at home."

"Of course," he said, but she heard a trace of doubtfulness in his voice. "Whatever you need to do to feel comfortable."

Her eyes slid to his lips. And she could have sworn he was blushing again, but he turned away from her quickly.

"Which bedroom should I take?"

"Let me show you." He got up from his desk and led her down the hall.

"See if this room suits," he said, opening the door of one of the bedrooms she had only glanced at earlier.

The room was like something out of a movie, particularly the huge four-poster bed in the middle of it. It looked as if a family of eight could sleep comfortably. Still, there was a faint heaviness to the room. She would get rid of the dusty tapestry that lay heavily across the bed, and she'd have to put the delicate porcelain figurines away. She'd live in fear of breaking one if she didn't.

She hated the painting on the wall above the bed, a dour woman whose eyes seemed to be following her with pure malice. She shivered. "Another relative?"

"That would be a great-great-great-aunt—Mary. She's said to have been rather nasty. Ran her husband through with a sword while he slept."

"She is leaving right now!" Maddie went right over to the bed, jumped up on it and lifted the framed canvas above it off the wall.

It was heavier than she had thought it would be, and once it was in her hands she found it hard to get her footing on the soft bed.

"Drop it," Ward said, and when he saw she wasn't going to listen, he hopped on the foot of the bed and lurched toward her. The mattress bounced with his added weight and bounced more as he made his way across the bed to her.

"Oh," she said, unsteadily, "oh, dear."

She released the painting, and he went to catch it, but then realized he had to catch it or her. He chose her, but it was too late.

Her legs had collapsed under her. Her momentum pulled them both down in a hopeless tangle of limbs, him on top of her. He managed to deflect the painting from hitting them, but she heard it hit the floor with a distinctive crunch.

Maddie stared up at him and felt his weight on her, most of it being held off, but still enough that she could feel the uncompromising lines of him, be nearly overwhelmed by his gorgeous scent.

She freed an arm and touched his face. He had shaved before getting off the plane and his skin was smooth, as sensuous to touch as silk. She traced the line of his lips, the lips that had kissed her so recently, and felt a surrender sigh within her. She loved how the blue sapphire blue of his eyes deepened to the navy blue of deep seawater as he looked down at her.

"Maddie?"

"Yes?" she whispered.

"I don't think this is a good idea."

"It wasn't really an idea. More like an occurrence."

His mouth tilted up on one side. He really had a sinfully sexy smile. The expression on his face was one of amazed discovery. *Of her.* With exquisite softness, he traced the line of her mouth.

They heard a door open.

He leaped off her. "That will be the luggage. Should I send it in?"

"Tell them to leave it at the door. We don't want them in here, Ward. Or they'll know."

But know what? It certainly didn't feel like a sham at the moment! He gave her one more faintly tortured look and disappeared out of the room.

Maddie's first weeks at the palace passed in a blur. She wasn't sure if Ward had planned it like this to minimize "occurrences," or if he'd done it to keep her from feeling lonely, or if this was simply the pace of his life, but it seemed every moment of every day was highly scheduled.

She barely saw her husband, let alone had an opportunity to "rescue" him from what she had perceived as his loneliness. Now it was clear he was far too busy to experience the normal pangs of human loneliness. She was not sure she had ever seen a man who started so early in the morning and worked so late. Was he avoiding her? Or was he always like this?

But her own life was also a whirlwind. Mornings were devoted to the wedding gifts and cards that had begun to pour in from around the world. Edward's sister, Princess Abigail, sometimes dropped by to help, her precocious daughter, Anne, with her. Though Abigail was reserved, Maddie soon delighted in the visits because of Anne.

Glenrich became her lifesaver. Though much of what was sent was presorted, every gift received had to be acknowledged with a signed card. Many of the gifts were extremely valuable, and Maddie had to decide what to do with them. Some were adorable, like the one from a six-year-old girl in California who sent her a plastic tea set for hosting her princess parties! She passed that along to Anne, who treasured the plastic set above her many, many rare and expensive toys.

During those mornings, Glenrich coached her, gently and firmly. Protocol. What to wear for what occasion. How to address whom, in public and in private. When did you shake hands, and when didn't you? The proper way to hold a teacup. And a knife and fork. There was even an accepted way for her to sit, her legs never crossed, but pressed together and leaning to one side, her hands clasped neatly together in her lap.

Glenrich also taught her a few words of the ancient language of Havenhurst, particularly old greetings, and words of thanks and sympathy. She taught her the colorful history of the island and helped her sort through the mind-boggling number of invitations she received.

Maddie was so grateful to Frederique that she had a suitable outfit for every occasion, for every day held occasions. She was the Prince's wife, and people wanted to meet her. Glenrich, thankfully, slipped into the role of her secretary. Having her own staff member increased the sense of this all being a dream. In what world did Maddie Nelson from Mountain Bend have a secretary? In this world, where she desperately needed one.

Maddie's favorite events quickly became the ones she attended with Ward, since she seldom actually saw her husband and got to spend time with him. It was with growing amazement she watched his skill with people. He treated everyone—from the flour-covered baker walking down the street, to high-ranking officials—with equal respect. He made time to listen. He engaged people at a deep, deep level. The admiration of the palace guard soldiers was obvious, as was the affection of every member of the palace staff.

He was also treated with extraordinary respect and not entirely because of his station. She could tell his skill at business was extraordinary and his investment in the future of his island was all consuming.

In private he was unfailingly decent and respectful to her, winning her trust and her admiration day by day, and yet she found she was beginning to like the public occasions, because his affection came out. Maddie loved the feel of his hand resting on the small of her back, the way he teased her, the way he cocked his head to listen to her, the pride in his voice when he introduced her to someone. He made her feel special, but of course, he did that to everyone.

It was what she had signed up for, and yet she felt disappointed that the small gestures were dropped at their front door. They barely shared the suite.

The truth was her husband was winning her heart the same way he had won the hearts—the absolute devotion—of his people. But she wanted more.

She was the one who wanted a change in the rules!

And when she received a handwritten invitation, addressed to her personally, to Princess Aida's wedding, she hoped she had found a way to do that.

CHAPTER SIXTEEN

PRINCESS AIDA'S WEDDING was small, perfect and beautiful. She and her groom had invited only a few select guests. Despite that, for privacy, they had secured an entire lodge on the Island of Wynfield. Everything had been set up at a grotto around a pool, and once the ceremony and meal were finished, the tables were put away and music and dancing ensued.

Aida and her husband, Drew, were so in love, and so open in that love, that Maddie was envious.

Ward was particularly handsome tonight, in a black tuxedo, white silk shirt and bow tie. He knew all the people there and was so skilled at including Maddie in the conversations that she soon felt that she had known them all her life, too.

They had not danced together since the concert.

Now, when they did, Maddie was so aware how much her feelings for him had changed. But just like that night, she felt sexy and beautiful, and she loved it that she could tell by the look on his face that he found her sexy and beautiful, too.

They laughed and danced and talked until the wee hours of the morning. It was the most time they had ever had together.

As they were preparing to leave, Lancaster appeared and whispered something to Ward.

He turned to her. "I'm afraid there's been a small

mechanical problem with the plane. It will be fixed by morning."

It occurred to her they would be staying here! And that they couldn't very well ask for separate rooms.

Maddie was thrilled. She couldn't wait to have her gorgeous husband to herself. She could not have planned for the evening to end this well.

They entered the room, and both of them gaped. It was like a honeymoon suite: a beautiful four-poster bed at its center, draped in white gauzy fabric. There were even rose petals scattered on the cover.

"I'll sleep on the floor," Ward volunteered.

But Maddie was tired of Ward being the gentleman. Tired of the distance between them. She craved a deepening of their relationship, in every way. She took his hand and pulled him to the bed, sat down and patted the place beside her.

He hesitated, and then sat.

She spoke no words. She placed her hand on the back of his neck and drew his lips to hers.

She tasted him, well aware this was their first kiss that was not public. This was their first kiss that was not for display. It felt as if she had waited her whole life for this kiss. She felt like a flower that had waited for rain, as if her petals, dry and thirsty, were opening up in celebration of the force that gave life.

He groaned with surrender, wrapped his hands in her hair and pulled her in tighter to him. The kiss became savage with need. He pushed her gently onto the bed, and lay down over her, covering her body with his own. Her every cell felt as if it was screaming with need of him. She let her hands roam the hard surfaces of his body. She reached for the buttons on his shirt.

He rolled away from her, sat up on the edge of the bed,

and then found his feet. He ran his hand through the dark crispness of his hair. His chest was heaving. His eyes were dark with wanting.

But he looked tormented.

"I can't," he said huskily. And then he turned sharply on his heel and left the room, closing the door with a quiet snap behind him.

What? What had he seen, naked in her face, that he knew he could not—or would not—return? It was a warning, and she wished she could heed it. His family, after all, saw love as a weakness. She had thought she could knock down his barriers, but now she was not so sure that her growing feelings for him could break down the barriers he had put around his heart.

Or maybe it wasn't him, at all. Maybe it was her. It seemed every insecurity she had ever had rose to the surface. She wasn't good enough for him, just as she had not been good enough for Derek. She let the tears fall.

Edward made his way through the dark streets of Wynfield to the airport. Lancaster, with his instinct for these things, had somehow materialized and dogged his heels down the dark streets, but did not try to engage him in any conversation.

Edward decided he would stay on the plane tonight. He could not believe what had just happened. He was a man who had been raised knowing the virtues of control. He had known, practically since he was a toddler, how to control himself. As he had grown older, he had learned how to control the world around him.

And yet, just now, with Maddie's sweet curves nestled underneath him, with her eyes wide on his, with her lips moist and full, he had nearly lost control completely.

Oh, not the *me Tarzan, you Jane* kind of control,

though, yes, her lips beckoned and he had given in to the temptation to taste them. And taste them. And taste them. It was like drinking a wine you could never get enough of.

But it was a different loss of control that he feared even more than the desire that burned like a hot coal in his belly anytime he was within touching distance of her.

He had seen something in her eyes. Something to reach for. Something to believe in. Something to trust. Something to hope for.

He had seen what she was offering him: a lifeline.

The shocking truth was that he had not known he was drowning!

In terms of control, this whole marriage to Maddie was already going seriously off the rails. His goal had been to save Aida so that she could have what he had resigned himself to never having: true love. Was it the utter romance of the wedding that was making him feel the gaping wound of emptiness where love could not be?

Or was it what he had seen in Maddie's eyes right now? A chance. An opportunity to know love.

Impossible. Dancing with that particular dream could only get her seriously hurt. Nursing such fantasies couldn't be good for him, either!

What was the point of saving Aida, if he crushed another young woman's hopes and dreams and prospects in the process?

"What a mess I've made," Edward muttered out loud as he made his way to the safety of his bedroom on board the plane. Well, he could not undo what had been done. He could not take back the kisses they had shared—ones where he had actually felt as if the earth shifted under his feet.

He knew himself to be a strong man. But not strong enough to resist the invitation he had tasted on her lips, and seen in her eyes, and sensed in the soft pliability of her body underneath his when they had collapsed together on the bed just now.

He had to avoid her. In the morning, he had the plane return him to Havenhurst alone, and then sent it back to her.

And so began the most miserable period of the Prince's entire life. While he stayed away—eating in the palace dining room and making sure his business interests consumed his days—his suite underwent the most amazing metamorphosis.

When he stumbled in at night, too exhausted, thank God, to think of Maddie—her eyes, her lips, his longing for her conversation, or a hand of poker—he noticed portraits that had hung for hundreds of years had disappeared. He didn't want to know how she got them down, or what she did with them as staff were still banished from the suite.

Walls—some of them eighteen feet tall—were washed, filling his house with the clean scent of new beginnings. Then they were painted, heart-stoppingly tall ladders leaning about the place. One wall in the living room was painted a burnt orange that should have hurt the eyes, but somehow warmed the soul instead. Cheerful abstracts and art that showed things like little children in rowboats, cottages behind masses of flowers, puppies chewing on old boots, took their place.

Early, early in the morning, when he rose to avoid her, he noticed curtains had come down and light spilled in. He had paused to look at the changes, when her bedroom door squeaked open.

Her hair was a mess, and her pajamas were crumpled.

She looked adorable. And gorgeous. Somehow, impossibly, she looked sexy.

And so hopeful. As if maybe they could sit and have a coffee together. Talk. Yearning leaped in him.

"I hope you are not getting up on those ladders yourself," he told her curtly.

The sleepiness was gone in a second. She had lifted a rebellious eyebrow at him.

"I am ordering you to stay off those ladders."

She had stared at him for a moment, and then stuck out her tongue at him, flounced back into her room and slammed the door.

But underlying that show of feistiness, had there been sadness in her eyes? Despite the metamorphosis to his home, was he responsible for some new insecurity in her? He hated that. And didn't know what to do about it without getting in over his head.

Only his own room remained untouched. She never came in it, and as soon as he closed the door at night, instead of feeling safe, instead of feeling as if he had a sanctuary from her, he could feel the acute emptiness, the lack of her, somehow. Every day his bedroom seemed a little darker and a little danker and a little colder in comparison to all the places she had touched. Sometimes, it seemed to him, it was the kind of room a bitter old man would have: surrounded by his riches, his heart impoverished.

Combining with the smell of paint and cleanliness, in every room but his, was the underlying smell of good things cooking: the delicate aroma of scones, fresh-baked bread, cookies. He didn't know where she was finding the time for all this, or where all the goodies went, but they seemed to disappear as fast as she made them. When he pressed Lancaster, he found out she was baking for the whole regiment.

He also found out Maddie had taken to walking to town every day, taking the steep steps down the cliff, her shopping basket over her arm. She had accepted the security personnel, but refused to let her security detail carry her groceries. She greeted everyone she met. She stopped and exchanged pleasantries. She listened to problems. She hugged babies and old people.

She had, according to Lancaster, found a drop-in center for young people, and once a week she taught a group of young mothers how to make scones.

Of course, Ward ran into her by accident, though sometimes he wondered if she wasn't trying to catch him. He was curt rather than cordial. The invitation to come into the warmth she was creating never flagged in her eyes. He never quit resisting it with all his might, and the hurt in her eyes at his rejection always seemed brand-new.

Over time, she stopped trying so hard to engage him. She became more impersonal with him when they were together for official functions. She talked to him about the people she met. Sometimes she asked him to intercede in a problem that had been brought to her. She wanted him to look at putting a bakery in a vacant main street shop, so she could start a proper business and training program for her "girls."

He limited public engagements together, but there were several official engagements he could not avoid, and they attended as a couple.

He didn't make the mistake of touching her. He thought it would be perfect if they were the same kind of royal couple that his mother and father were.

It was at these public engagements that Prince Edward found out how much her little trips to town had been winning her favor.

People knew who she was. And they loved her with a

kind of simple devotion. Maddie, at these gatherings, performed as if she had been born to the role of princess. She was gracious, natural, good-humored and compassionate.

The fact that she was making such a good life for herself without him took away some of the guilt he was feeling that he had brought her into this.

And, if he was completely honest, made him jealous, too!

He thought he probably could have gone on this way indefinitely. Until one night he came home very late and heard the sound of quiet crying.

His head told him not to investigate.

But his heart refused to listen. He followed the sound through the darkened apartment and to Maddie's bedroom. The door was slightly ajar.

He went in, and stood for a moment, stunned by the transformation in the room. It was brightness itself, rich jewel tones on the bedding, on the new curtains that hung on the brightly painted walls. He wanted to stand here forever, breathing it—breathing her—in, as if he could never get enough.

But the sound of her muffled sobs drew him deeper into the room.

Where was she? And then he saw her. Lying on the bathroom floor. He thought his heart would stop beating at the fear he felt.

And then he raced to her.

CHAPTER SEVENTEEN

MADDIE FOUND HERSELF lifted off the floor. Ward sank down onto the edge of the tub with her cradled against his body. She felt the comforting heat of him, and drank in his scent. It was like homecoming and it made her cry harder.

"What have you done?" he asked. "I suppose you've fallen off one of your damned ladders?"

His voice was so harsh. But his touch was so tender. She turned her face into his chest and wept.

"What is it?" he insisted. "Are you hurt? Maddie, talk to me."

"Your mother invited me for tea," she finally choked out.

"If she's done something to you, I'll—"

"Done something to me? Oh no, it wasn't like that at all."

"What was it like then?"

"She served these awful things. She called them sausages, but they looked like pickles. They were even green."

"Blarneycockles," Ward said. "A local delicacy. But not for the uninitiated. Surely, you're not crying over blarneycockles, love?"

Love. She savored it. She let it wrap around her.

"Glenrich has been helping me with protocol. I knew I should just follow her lead. She took two and I took two. The smell was dreadful, but I couldn't refuse to eat what she was eating. So, I took a bite. Nowhere in the protocol book does it tell you what to do if you feel a desire to heave while lunching with the Queen."

"Over a blarneycockle? They're not that bad!"

"They are! I didn't know what to do, and then one of the horrid dogs started creating a ruckus. I put one down my skirt, and pretended to nibble away on the other and then the horrid dog attacked the little one, and while your mother was distracted by that, I disposed of the other one. The second blarneycockle."

"Down your skirt?"

"Please don't laugh. It's not a laughing matter."

"I'm sorry."

"I didn't know what to do with them. I wanted to just put them in the garbage, but I thought what if somebody notices and reports to the Queen I didn't eat them?"

"It's hardly a hanging offense, even in Havenhurst."

"I felt as if we were getting along famously."

"You and my mother?" he said incredulously.

"I understand her," she said softly. "I know I haven't been here long, but I understand her loneliness. Everyone is eager to please. Everyone does whatever you ask them to do. But nobody is honest with you. No one would tell you if you had spinach on your teeth. No one feels they can be your friend. It's kind of this awful awe and fear mixed, and you can't overcome it, no matter what you do."

"You're crying because you're lonely?" he asked, stricken.

"I guess partly. Partly because of something else your mother said."

"What?" What had his mother said?

"I asked your mother about the kind of little boy you were—"

"And she knew?" he asked, amazed.

"Of course, she knew. She talked about the time you

fell off your pony, and you were crying, and your father told you to man up, and you did. And then later they found out your arm was broken. She teared up, telling that story."

"My mother? Teared up?"

"Yes. And so did I."

He felt something clog his own throat at the thought of these two women feeling such compassion for him.

"It wasn't that big a deal," he said stiffly, staving off what the compassion in her eyes was making him feel.

She looked at him long and hard, but she must have learned her lesson about trying to connect with him, because she brushed at her tearstained face and turned her attention back to the toilet.

"I've plugged the toilet with the blasted blarneycockles, and I can't get it apart."

"You're trying to get the toilet apart?" he asked with horror.

"Well, I can't call anyone. I'd be the laughingstock of the whole palace, wouldn't I? And then word would get back to your mother, and she would think I was sneaky and deceitful, and maybe I am."

"You are not!"

"Look at our marriage, Ward," she said softly.

Apparently he would rather look at blarneycockles plugging the toilet, than at their marriage, because he set her down firmly and went and flipped open the lid.

"I don't see anything," he said.

"That's because they're caught in the trap."

"The what?"

"The trap, the curve where the pipe bends around."

"Oh."

"Do you see why I'm lonely, Ward?" she asked him softly. "I'm a logger's daughter who comes from a place where we had to be self-sufficient and self-reliant. The only people in this castle who are like that won't talk to me, at least not as a friend."

"I can fix this," he said, with determination, and when he lifted his eyes and looked at her, she saw something new in them.

And she saw he was not talking about just the toilet.

"Why don't we fix it together?" she asked. And she wasn't talking about the toilet, either.

But that was where they started, prying the rusty bolts off the bowl and lifting it off the seal and screaming with laughter as water went everywhere.

With as much bravery as she had ever seen in a man, he donned the rubber gloves and stuck his hand in there, and came up with first one and then the other blarneycockle.

"Damn slippery," he said as one slid through his hand. She chased it across the bathroom floor, but then couldn't bring herself to touch it. He picked it up and wagged his eyebrows fiendishly at her, thrusting the disgusting blarneycockle toward her.

She took off running, and shrieking with laughter, they chased each other through every room of that apartment until both of them were breathless with exertion.

Still laughing, they wrapped the horrid green sausages in newspapers, and then in plastic bags, and then put them in a box.

They cleaned up all the water and washed to the elbow at least a dozen times, when he finally admitted he still didn't feel clean.

"Me, either."

"I know a secret place," he said.

And she did, too. And she knew, finally, they were heading straight toward it, the secret guarded fortress of Prince Edward's heart.

And if they got there by way of the palace garbage dumpster, muffling their laughter in pitch blackness as they got rid of the blarneycockle box, so be it.

Ward shouldered a pack he had brought. The palace grounds were extremely dark, but he knew his way perfectly. As they circled around the dark ramparts of the castle, Maddie felt as if they were explorers embarking on a great adventure. They came to a place in the wall where there was a large, prickly hawthorne.

"Careful," he said, as he shoved it aside and protected her from the worst of the prickles. Behind the thick shrub was a hole in the wall. He paused and fished around in the pack until he found a flashlight.

He lit it and she saw a tunnel stretched before them until it dipped suddenly, steeply out of sight.

With her hand in his, ducking in places because the tunnel was so narrow, they went where it led. She could smell it before they arrived. It felt like homecoming.

"Hot springs!"

"Underground. I found them when I was a boy. I don't think anyone else knows about them. When I was a child, it felt so lovely to have a secret. I would tell my nanny I was reading in my room, and then I would slip out the window. And, for a few hours I would be free."

She felt the deep honor of his sharing this place with her.

The tunnel gave way to a cave, the ceiling dripping with stalactites. The cave was open to a sheltered bay of the sea, and stars winked through an opening in the cave ceiling. Small waterfalls cascaded down the sides of the cliff and into a deeply turquoise pool with steam rising off the water.

"Here we are," she said huskily, "back at hot pools. It's like a full circle, isn't it?"

"It's a chance to start again," he said quietly. He opened the pack and pulled two thick towels from it. He turned off the flashlight. She heard his clothes whisper to the floor. Surely he had something on? Surely he had brought suits?

"No clothes allowed," he told her, from the darkness of the pool. "For me, it was part of being free. No rules, at all. No one watching."

"But you're watching!" she whispered.

"I can't even see my hand in front of my face."

That was true. The darkness inside the cave was the pitch-black variety. She hesitated, but only for a second. And then she let her clothes fall in a puddle at her feet. Wearing only her gold chain, and the nugget that dangled from it, Maddie stepped toward the water, feeling her way along the slippery floor with her toe. There it was. She stepped in, gingerly, and felt the water close on her naked skin.

It was truly the most sensual thing she had ever felt. Until Ward reached for her in the darkness, until his hand found hers. Her eyes adjusted, slowly, to the darkness, but the water cloaked both of them. Save for his face, the drops of water on his lashes, the line of his nose, the fullness of his lower lip, the cleft of his chin, illuminated by starlight.

She leaned toward him, but he let her go, gave a gentle teasing splash and moved away from her. They played tag in the darkness, just as they had when they first met. They played tag and laughed and discovered the joy of each other. Because the water hid them, she didn't feel shy.

But then, unexpectedly, Ward hefted himself from the pool and raced for the sea. For a moment she was totally hypnotized by his perfect form, by the poetry of the faint starlight cascading off his wet body, by his sureness and his freedom. He threw himself into the cold water and his shout of pure exhilaration echoed through the cave.

Elation such as she had never felt shivered along her spine.

This magnificent man was her husband.

Maddie stood for a moment, knowing he was watching her, and then went into the sea behind him. The cold water embraced her heated flesh.

And then Ward was beside her, and his hands were in the wet tangle of her hair, and his body was hot and smooth against hers, taking the chill from the water.

His lips claimed hers. In them was everything that love was: power and freedom and something completely untamable, unconquerable, the force that was life itself.

Her lips opened to the command of his, and her heart opened to his need.

She became his wife, and she knew, gladly, with a tremulous song in her heart, that her life would never be the same again.

Losing control, Ward discovered, was like letting a dragon out of a box. It would not go back in again. It did not obey orders. It scorned efforts to dominate it.

The fire in him was a dragon that had tasted something foreign and forbidden and could now not get enough.

Ward fell in love with his wife. He fell in love with the secrets of her body and the intricacies of her mind. He fell in love with her laughter. And the way she looked sitting with her feet up on the sofa reading a book.

He fell in love with her fearlessness as he taught her to dive. He fell in love with her endless baking. He fell in love with her delight as he revealed to her all the secrets of his island—the patches of wild lupines that grew by the hot springs, and the secret paths and groves that led to old ruins, and churches and crumbling castles. To Lancaster's rather tolerant dismay they became experts at giving him the slip.

He fell in love with her quiet as he revealed all his own secrets and fears.

He fell in love with her as he watched her blossom into a true princess. She started her bakery with her girls.

His mother adored her. Even his father seemed amazed by this force of love and light that had been brought to their island.

In her, in Maddie, in his beautiful wife, he had found the place his heart had always longed for, the place he wanted so badly he feared it.

Not that he planned to jinx it by saying it out loud!

CHAPTER EIGHTEEN

MADDIE WOKE WITH a start. It was midafternoon. Why was she so tired all the time? Her stomach rolled. Not a blarneycockle in sight. In fact, she'd had a cheese sandwich for lunch. Her stomach rolled again, and she raced for the bathroom.

The flu, she thought after, as she wiped her mouth. She caught a glimpse of her reflection in the mirror above the sink.

She stared at herself. Her hair had grown quite a bit, wild curls softening into waves that framed her face. Gone were the worry lines that had looked back at her such a short time ago. Her face looked more than relaxed—it looked radiant.

"You don't look like a woman with the flu," she told herself.

And then the truth hit her.

It was not possible. They had only been unprotected that once, the first time they had gone to the secret underground pools. After that, Ward was always prepared.

And it was a good thing, too, because they seemed intent on exploring every secret of each other in every secluded enclave and hot spring on the whole island. They had become experts at ditching Lancaster, though he didn't seem to mind.

Maddie walked out of her bathroom in a daze and sank down on her bed. She counted on her fingers. And then counted again.

A baby.

The joy that rose in her was quickly overtaken by doubt. She was no more prepared to have a baby now than she had been when she had experienced that pregnancy scare in her past.

The situation even had similarities! She was besotted, and he was... What?

Not certain of his feelings, obviously, since he had never spoken of them. Maybe, just like that boy from long ago, he had taken what was offered but thought there were no strings attached. Their marriage was not supposed to be a real one.

For all the intimacy they enjoyed, Ward had never once said he wanted to change the terms of their agreement.

In fact, thinking back on it, just like that other boy, he had never once said he loved her. Didn't the fact he had always, always been prepared after that first time, speak volumes to the complication to their relationship that he did not want?

Oh, he would do the honorable thing! Of course he would. How horrible to have the man you loved so madly, whose baby you were almost certain you carried, do his duty by you.

To be the one who trapped him, exactly as he had been trapped by circumstances his entire life.

Maddie felt she was not a person who had trouble making decisions. Look how quickly she had decided to become Ward's wife!

And yet, suddenly, she did not know what to do. She was acutely aware she had no one, aside from Ward, to take into her confidence. His mother had warmed to her, but in this circumstance, how could she trust her?

Or him for that matter.

Lancaster adored her, but his first loyalty was not to her.

Carrying the royal baby was probably a very serious matter, indeed.

They would think the baby belonged to them. Her child was the heir to the island kingdom of Havenhurst.

Maddie felt such a rush of fierce protectiveness it nearly knocked her over. She needed some space. She had to figure out, and quickly—if the count she had just done on her fingers was correct—what to do. She had to figure out what to do, not just for herself, but for the ultimate good of the child.

You didn't just leave Havenhurst. There was one flight out once a week. And there were three boats every week. If she said she had to leave, questions would be asked. Though she had become accustomed to it, Maddie was not allowed to travel anywhere by herself. A guard always followed discreetly. She did not think that love of her scones would be enough for any one of them to overcome their sense of duty and smuggle her out of the country.

Duty, she thought angrily.

But she had no time to indulge her thoughts. Only action counted now. If she used a phone in the palace, they would trace it when she was missing. They would know who she had called.

Grabbing her cloak, aware as never before of the guard that dogged her, she walked quickly to town.

The bakery was bustling. The girls smiled and nodded at her, but it was very crowded. Hardly anybody noticed her slip into the back room and take the phone off its hook. She was trembling so badly it took her three times to remember how to dial an international number, even though she had been checking in with Kettle and Sophie regularly.

Thankfully, despite the differences in time, Kettle answered. He'd obviously been sleeping, but came awake with that alertness that anyone who had served active duty never quite lost.

"I need your help," she said. "Kettle, I'm in trouble."

Kettle did not say he had told her so. Every time she had talked to him since her hasty marriage to the Prince, he was no closer to forgiving her for bailing him out, and for saving the Black Kettle. In fact he was furious about it.

But this was the thing about family—about the families you were born to and the ones that you chose—the love was always there.

And that was all she heard in his gruff voice. The love.

"Tell me what you need."

She did. It seemed she was making an impossible request.

But he only said, "You did the right thing to call. I'll be there for you as quickly as I can."

She could not cry in front of her girls.

Ward had been away for three days. Maddie had not come with him on this trip, saying something was going on at the bakery that needed her.

He couldn't believe how much he missed her. He went into their suite, so eager to see her, to hold her, to talk to her, that it felt as if he was vibrating at his core.

"Maddie?" he called.

There was something about the emptiness, about the way that his voice echoed back to him that made the hair stand up on the back of his neck.

Ridiculous. She would just be at the bakery, or visiting with his mother, or perhaps delivering scones to the besotted members of the palace guard. Perhaps, she'd been invited, at the last moment, to hand out certificates at the kindergarten graduation ceremonies or trophies at the Senior's Centre Annual Lawn Bowling Tournament.

Lancaster would know where she was.

Then he saw the envelope, a white square sitting on the kitchen table. He felt his heart sink to the bottom of his toes. He picked it up with trembling hands and a shadow of premonition.

He opened it and scanned the words.

Need time. Please understand. Don't try to find me.

How was that possible? He thought back over the last few days he had spent with her. Delightful. With the underlying intensity of the freed dragon.

He wanted to believe his father had done something. Or his mother. But he knew it wasn't that. He knew it was him. Somehow he had disappointed. Hurt her. Been insensitive. She had seen what he came from—the coldness between people, the remoteness, the lack of connection—and she had decided, probably wisely, to extricate herself.

And he wondered how could he have forgotten the dragon's flames destroyed everything in their path?

But how could she have done it? How was it no one had noticed she was missing? And was she safe? She was a public figure now. Her face was known around the world. What if someone harmed her?

He called Lancaster. "Maddie is missing."

"Missing? I don't understand."

He didn't want to share his greatest failure with anyone, but her safety might be compromised. Contemplating that made Ward feel physically ill. If something happened to her, it was on him.

Within minutes Lancaster was there with a report. "She left a note on a bag of scones for her security this morning.

She said she was staying home and wouldn't go for her walk. There's no way she got off the island. There's one flight and three sailings. None of them last night. We'll watch the ones today. We'll search the island. We'll find her. I promise."

And Lancaster kept his promise.

But it was three days later, and the big man had obviously not slept or eaten. Ward had barely slept or eaten, either. So far, the fact the Princess was missing was only known by those who needed to know.

"She's not on Havenhurst," Lancaster said.

"What? How?"

"I don't have the details, yet. I pried it out of Sophie."

"Where is Maddie?"

"I don't have her exact location. Sophie didn't know that. But I know who does know."

"Kettle," he said quietly. "Let's go."

"The jet is already waiting. Sir, he's not the kind of man you're going to be able to get it out of."

Ward considered that. He knew it was true: no threat would work. Probably torture would not even work.

But there was something that might.

The truth.

CHAPTER NINETEEN

MADDIE WALKED THE long sandy shore of Cannon Beach, hugging herself against the nippy wind coming off the ocean. Somehow, the last few days seemed more of a dream than marrying Prince Edward had seemed.

Kettle had found a crew of hardened old Navy SEALs like himself. They whisked her away from Havenhurst with an ease that was matched only by their secrecy. Then, Kettle had a friend with this little cottage in Cannon Beach. She was there for now, blending in with all the tourists, in a ball cap pulled over a face mostly hidden by large sunglasses. She had taken to wearing red lipstick, which made her nearly unrecognizable to herself.

Maddie felt the oddest combination of grief and elation. She missed Ward with a physical ache. And yet the baby felt real already, filling her with a quiet sense of calm and determination. She was not bringing a baby into the world with a father who did not want it.

A long time ago, she had realized you could not wait for a man to rescue you. Not even a prince. Here was the thing: you had to rescue yourself.

And so even though she was in the worst predicament of her life—having left a man she loved with all her heart, practically hiding because of her unwanted fame, with no resources besides the love of those closest to her—she felt certain that she could do this.

She could make a safe haven and a safe life for her baby. She felt differently than she had when she'd had her previous pregnancy scare. So differently. There was no panic at all, but rather a deep sense of all being well for her and for her child. And it wasn't just that she was older. Even though her love with Ward had not been reciprocated, something about loving him had made her braver, not afraid to love and to love fiercely.

This was a gift she would give to her baby.

She saw a man coming toward her and started.

No, it could not be him. It couldn't be. And yet her heart raced as if it was, and as he drew closer, there was no doubt. For a panicky moment she wanted to run. He would see in her face her love for him, her need.

But he had probably only come because he had figured it out. He had figured out she carried the royal baby.

He couldn't make her go back against her will.

He came closer and she was taken aback. Ward looked glorious, and yet there were dark circles under his eyes, and a thinness to his face he had not had before. Finally, he drew in front of her and thrust his hands deep in his pockets. He scanned her face and then looked away to where puffins screeched off Haystack Rock.

His face looked so tormented. She wanted to touch it. But she followed his lead and put her hands in the pockets of the hooded jacket she was wearing.

"Ward," she said.

"Maddie."

"How did you find me?"

"Kettle told me."

"Kettle would never tell you."

"Not if I tortured him, I'm sure. Or threatened him. The truth was a different matter."

"The truth?" she whispered.

"Maddie, why? Why did you leave?"

"I told you in the note. I needed some time to think."

"Just so suddenly?" he asked. "I thought we were doing so well. Given the circumstances."

"The circumstances," she said. "A fake marriage, that we were both treating as if it was real."

"Maddie, I'm so sorry."

"Sorry?"

"I know it's me. I know we've had great fun, but I don't blame you for coming to your senses. I know you saw what I came from, and I know the deep love you came from, and you realized it was unworkable. That I can never be the man you want. And deserve. I'm sorry I put you through all of this. Of course, you are free to leave. I'll ask for an annulment right away. But I hope you will accept security—personal and financial—for as long as it takes for it all to fade away."

An annulment, she thought, dully. And, of course, his ever-present sense of honor. He would look after her, even though it had not worked out.

But then she looked at the torment on his face and let his words sink in.

He didn't think he was good enough? He didn't think he could give her what she deserved? That's why he was going to set her free?

He didn't know about the baby. He didn't have a clue.

"Are you here because you are trying to do what is best for me?" she breathed.

The question seemed to take him by surprise.

"Of course."

"Look, this seems strange to me. Are you, the Prince, telling me, a common girl, you are somehow unworthy of me?"

"I think you figured that out. You need a man who knows how to love you in the way you deserve to be loved. I think you realized that's not me."

"You think you don't know how to love?" Maddie asked, incredulous.

"How could I know that?" he growled, his pain raw in his voice.

"Ward, you don't think putting Aida's needs ahead of your own was a form of love?"

He tilted his head at her. "A form, I suppose."

"And what about the relationship between you and Lancaster? You don't think that's a form of love? He's like your brother!"

"Well, maybe—"

"And what about the way you treat your niece, Anne? You're playful with her, and yet it is so obvious you would lay down your life to protect her if need be."

"Of course, I would."

"That's love. How do you feel right now, this instant, standing here, telling me you'll let me go?"

"Broken," he said, his voice low and strained. "It feels as if letting you go is tearing the heart out of me."

"Ward," she asked softly, "don't you think that's love? Putting what you think are another person's needs ahead of your own? How did you find me?"

"Kettle."

"Do you think Kettle would have sent you here, if he didn't see the truth in you?"

He ducked his head. "Why make this harder? It's obvious I have feelings for you. I've decided I'm not the best person for you."

She reached up and touched his face, cupped the side of it, his chin in her palm.

"Say it," she said.

"Oh, Maddie, always telling me what to do. The only

person who orders the Prince around. But must you hear this? Must you have my heart at your feet?"

"Yes," she said.

"All right." He refused to look at her. "I love you. I love everything about you. I would give up my whole kingdom for one more day of chasing you through the hot springs. For one more hand of poker. For one more kiss. For one more opportunity to hold you.

"I've never felt this way before. I did not know it was possible to feel this way.

"And for that, I thank you. That I have been allowed the great privilege of knowing love, however briefly. It has made me a better man."

Her eyes filmed with tears and they fell.

He lifted his hand and traced the path of one down her cheek. "See? Now, I've made you cry. I'm inept at this business. I'm sorry. I'll go. I don't know why I came. I just had to see you one more time, to look at your face…"

"Ward, be quiet. Look at me."

And then he did look at her face. He looked at it long and hard, like a man who had had a drink from a cool pool of water, and knew he would never drink from it again.

But as he looked at her, something in his own expression changed. He saw it. He saw her love for him shining out of her.

"You don't have a clue, do you?" she asked him softly.

"I'm afraid—"

"Ward, I didn't leave because I don't love you. I left because I did."

"I'm not following. At all."

"You really don't know?"

He shook his head, baffled, and yet hope had risen in his eyes.

"I'm pregnant, Ward. I'm going to have our baby."

"What?"

He fell on his knees before her. He gently opened her jacket and ran his hands over the smoothness of her belly. He kissed it.

"I thought—" She was crying hard now. "I thought when you found out, you would feel an obligation to make our marriage real. I couldn't have that. I couldn't be married to you without love. Without knowing the child would be loved."

He rose to his feet and gathered her hard against him.

"How could you not know I loved you?"

"I don't know," she said, staring up at him from within the circle of his arms. "I don't know why the words seemed so important, when it is so clear to me right now that you were telling me in so many different ways all the time. I think being pregnant frightened me."

He looked stricken that anything he had done—or not done—had frightened her.

"I didn't know how to say those words," Ward admitted. "But I know how, now, and I will never stop saying them. I will never stop loving you. Or our baby. I will love you both until the end of time and beyond. This is my vow to you."

She felt it. She felt the truth, not just of his words, but the truth of his heart, to the bottom of her soul. She felt the truth of it, of the power of love.

And at last she was home.

EPILOGUE

PRINCE EDWARD ALEXANDER THE FOURTH stood with a baby
in his arms and his heart in his throat.

He looked way up, to the rock outcropping above the
top pool of Honeymoon Hot Springs.

Maddie stood there, poised, arms straight out in front
of her, on the tips of her toes.

He wanted to shout at her not to, but she was still the
only person in his world who did not listen to him.

She gathered herself, and Ward saw what all the people of Havenhurst saw in their beloved Princess: she was
of the earth.

But when she launched and soared upward, he saw
what he alone was allowed to see.

She was not just of the earth. She was also of the sky.

She was a bird who had found its wings. She spread
her arms wide, embracing the air and the sky, and Ward
saw her strength and her grace and her confidence in herself. He saw her bravery and her tenacity. And he saw that
she did not need him.

Which made the fact that she chose him all the more
remarkable.

Maddie had come into herself even more since the baby
was born. One of those women who blossomed under love.

His love. His imperfect, stumbling along, learning new
and magnificent things every day kind of love.

As he watched, she jackknifed and did a perfect, almost-
splashless entry into the water of the pool. A few seconds

later she surfaced, laughing, shaking droplets of water from her hair.

This was the first time they had been back in Mountain Bend since the mineral water bottling plant had opened here, after Havenhurst had shared its technology and marketing with the mountain village. Already the town was prospering from the work generated by that pant. Already the sales of that healing mineral water were through the roof.

But it didn't hurt that a sign hung at the entrance of the town saying it was the birthplace of Madeline, Princess of Havenhurst. People were intrigued. They came to see, out of curiosity, and stayed because there was something here that had been lost.

The town represented the purity, the innocence, the wholesomeness of times past. And because it still had those rare things, and had them in abundance, Mountain Bend was thriving—little cottages lovingly restored, shops busy, people happy.

"Great dive," he said.

Maddie lifted herself out of the water. She was wearing a two-piece, but the thrill he felt was even deeper than the first time he had seen her here, and it had nothing to do with her choice of bathing attire.

"Your turn," she said, holding out her arms for the chubby, gurgling baby. He had been named Ryan. Prince Ryan Lancaster the First. It was not a historical royal name, but honored both Maddie's father and the man who had been so much more than a protector, more like a brother to Ward. It was rare, however, for Maddie to call Ryan either of his given names. To the delight of the people of Havenhurst, who loved her so much, she mostly called the baby Prince Chunky Monkey.

Ward left her and scrambled up the rocks until he stood

high above his wife and his baby. He threw open his arms to the sky, but somehow he did not jump.

No, he stood there, in gratitude and in wonder.

A long time ago, that night that had changed everything, that night when he had asked Maddie to be his wife, Ward had not really ever considered the nature of miracles.

But now he did.

He had been a prince, one of the richest, most successful, most admired men in the world. And yet he had been impoverished.

It was love that made him who he was.

It was love that had crowned him King.

He bounced on his toes. Once. Twice. He was aware, not of the wealth of being a prince—he had found out you could be intensely poor, while the whole world admired your outward signs of riches—but of the wealth of being alive.

He tingled with recognition of the utter abundance of this moment, birdsong, the scent of the forest beyond him and the scent of the ponds beneath him. Of Maddie, watching, that wiggly baby held firmly in her arms, her upturned face alight.

It was love that made you alive.

On three, Prince Edward Alexander launched off the rock, then tucked into himself and somersaulted through the air, opened into a twist, and then cleanly cut into the calmness of the waiting water.

He surfaced, laughing joyously, aware he was still showing off for his Princess. And he hoped that would never end.

* * * * *

A FORTUNATE ARRANGEMENT

NANCY ROBARDS THOMPSON

This book is dedicated to the "Hey, Tinas,"
who are living proof that friendship can thrive
despite the miles and mountains between us.

Chapter One

Austin Fortune almost missed the plain white envelope at the bottom of the stack of papers his assistant Felicity Schafer had set on his desk. After he'd read the letter, he wished he'd never seen it and for a moment, he considered pretending as if he hadn't read it.

Maybe it would just disappear.

Instead, the reality of it danced around him like illuminated dust motes.

Felicity, his gatekeeper, his right hand, the person who kept him organized and on track ahead of the fray, had tendered her resignation.

"Is this a bad joke?" he muttered aloud, trying it on for size.

But no. Even though Felicity was good-natured, it

would've been out of character for her to kid around about something like this.

"She's leaving me." Uttering the words out loud made it sound personal. It wasn't personal—it was work, but it sure felt personal.

He looked up from the note and watched her through the glass wall of his office. She was engrossed in something on her computer. He didn't know what. He could see her in profile. Her head was bowed over her keyboard, her dark blond hair a curtain hiding her face.

What the hell was he supposed to do without her? Every morning when he got to the office, she had a daily briefing typed up and waiting for him on his desk along with his coffee and a smoothie with energy booster. She remembered birthdays, anniversaries and the minutiae of family and client particulars that elevated and solidified his business relationships and could prove costly if forgotten. She was always game for brainstorming new concepts and abstract business angles. Ultimately assisting with client presentations.

Plain and simple, Felicity made him look good and was always there to help him succeed.

It wasn't just a matter of hiring someone new. Felicity was a rare find. She had an uncanny ability to anticipate his every need—even before he knew what he needed. In all fairness, he paid her well and she seemed happy. So, why was she leaving him?

He skimmed the letter again looking for clues, but in true Felicity form, it was short and to the point:

Dear Austin,

Please accept this letter as notification that I am leaving my position with Fortune Investments at the end of the month.

I've left the date open, so I can be of assistance during the transition.

Sincerely,

Felicity Schafer

Austin reread the note twice more, making sure he'd read it right. Once he'd absorbed it, he had a good idea of how he might fix it. He pressed the button on the intercom.

"Felicity, could you come into my office, please?"

"Sure."

A moment later, she was standing in his doorway.

"What do you need?" she asked.

"If you wanted a raise," he said, "all you had to do was ask."

She wrinkled her nose. "A raise?"

"Of course, you just had your half-year review and got a bump in salary, but if it wasn't enough, if you want more money, we can talk about it."

She gave her head a quick shake. "Who said anything about a raise?"

He picked up her letter. "I thought maybe that's what this was about. I mean why else would you resign?"

Her cheeks flushed, and her mouth fell open before she snapped it shut, into a thin line and folded her arms across her chest. She looked at him as if he had insulted her.

How could offering someone more money be insulting?

He leaned back in his chair, crossing his arms, mirroring her posture.

"Austin, you've always been generous when it comes to my salary. But I'm graduating with my MBA at the end of the month. I don't need a graduate degree to be someone's personal assistant. It's time I moved on."

"Do you have another job?"

"No, not yet. I'm going to start interviewing soon. I wanted to be up-front with you about it."

"Thanks," he said.

She flinched. He realized he might have sounded sarcastic. Maybe a very small part of him had meant it that way. Was he supposed to be happy he was losing her?

He raked his hand through his hair. This was not the way he wanted to start his Friday. It certainly wasn't the way he wanted to end his week.

He gestured for her to sit down in one of the chairs on the other side of his desk.

She sat and folded her hands in her lap. "I've loved working for you and Fortune Investments, but I've worked hard to get this degree."

He didn't say anything because he was afraid what he wanted to say would sound wrong. He'd always prided himself on being fair.

"I hope you can understand that I want more than being someone's secretary for the rest of my working life," she went on. "Because that's what I am. We can dress it up and call me your assistant, but when it comes down to it, I'm your secretary. It's been a great job, but now I need more."

He held up his hand.

"I get it," he said. "I do. Congratulations on accomplishing this, Felicity. I'm happy for you. I know how hard you've worked. You're smart and you're creative and I understand that a person with an MBA is way overqualified to be a personal assistant. You'd be wasting your potential staying in this position. But that doesn't make it any easier for me because I don't want to lose you."

He held her gaze and her expression softened.

"I mean did you expect me not to be upset about the prospect of losing you?" He held up his hand again to signal that the question was rhetorical. "But that's me being selfish. This isn't about me. It's about you. What do you want to do with your degree?"

"My undergraduate degree is in advertising. I've always wanted to work in that field."

"You'd be good at it," he said. "You'd be good at anything you decided to do."

Her cheeks turned pink again. She looked down and then back up at him.

"Is there anything I can do to convince you to stay with Fortune Investments?"

"I don't know. Are there any opportunities here?"

"What if I talk to Miles and see if we can create a position for you? I'm not making any promises, but would you consider staying if we could come up with something?"

Felicity smiled. "It depends. Would it mean doing advertising work in addition to everything I do for you?"

Austin laughed. "You know me too well."

"I know I do."

"How am I supposed to get by without you, Felicity?"

She shrugged. "You did fine before I came on board. You'll survive."

No, he hadn't been fine before she came onto the scene. His life had been a mess, a big tumbleweed of mistakes and misjudgments that had cost him dearly. It had taken him five years to get himself back on track after his disastrous marriage. Sure, he'd come through it intact and he'd learned a lot about himself and life. Yes, he would be fine on his own, but he didn't want to lose her.

"If they can't create a position for me, I'd like to stay until after graduation, and as I said in my letter, I'll stay until we find my replacement."

Maybe if he didn't find someone new, she wouldn't go. It would be like waiting for tomorrow. Did tomorrow ever really come?

"I'll tell you what. I'm having dinner with Miles tonight. I'll broach the subject with him and let you know what he says. Sound good? You won't quit on me before you let me figure something out, right?"

How am I supposed to get by without you, Felicity?
If she was a silly woman, Felicity would've let herself read so much into that question. But true to form, she had already overthought it, turning it round and round in her mind, examining it from every angle until

it had completely lost its shape and she'd killed off any dreams that Austin Fortune felt anything for her that wasn't strictly platonic.

However, her heart hadn't gotten the memo from her brain, because her heart thudded in her chest like a drum in a New Orleans funeral procession.

He'd said *get by*.

He didn't say *live without you*.

There was a world of difference between the statements. Like night and day. Love and like. Get by and live without.

Even so, she couldn't shake the satisfaction she felt over his reaction to her letter of resignation. Sure, she'd known he wouldn't be happy, but she hadn't fathomed that he would react the way he did.

She stole a glance at Austin through the glass wall that separated his office from her workspace. He was wearing that blue button-down that she liked so much. It contrasted with his dark hair and those soulful brown eyes. Eyes that hypnotized her, that made her lose track of time and occasionally space out and miss what he was saying because she'd been totally transported.

Her thudding heart slowed, leaving her more breathless and full of longing.

He acted like I was breaking up with him.

As if I'd ever break up with him.

If I ever had him.

But I never will.

Why did she have to be in love with her boss?

Why did he have to dangle the potential of a promotion in front of her? She thought she wanted a clean break, so she could get on with her life and forget about him and this ridiculous crush, but the moment he'd offered to talk to his father, all fresh starts flew out the window.

Of course, the Fortunes had been so good to her. They were dream employers. The pay and benefits were top-notch. The working conditions were first class.

She stole another glance at Austin and her ridiculous heart picked up the cadence right where it had left off.

Felicity knew she shouldn't get her hopes up. Fortune Investments was a family firm. Austin's sister Georgia handled public relations for the investment firm. They'd never had to advertise in the true sense of the word—not the kind of advertising Felicity wanted to do. They'd built their business on solid reputation and word of mouth. But even from her position as support staff, she knew the business had grown.

Maybe they were ready to expand.

If she got a promotion, it was likely that she'd be in a different department with a different supervisor. Which would mean Austin wouldn't be her boss anymore—

Don't even go there.

She'd worked with him for almost five years and during that time, it had been all business all the time. What made her think anything would change if she got promoted?

Yeah, well, a girl can dream.

Just not on Fortune Investments' time.

"Did you do it?" Maia Fredericks asked after she let herself in Felicity's patio door. She didn't knock. Maia never knocked. Felicity didn't mind because her friend's hands were never empty when she came over. This evening, she was carrying a bottle of something that looked like it could be champagne.

"I did," Felicity said.

"Well, how did it go? Don't keep me waiting." Maia dislodged the cork on the bottle. Felicity winced at the loud popping sound.

"You do know you're not supposed to open champagne that way, right? Besides the possibility of damaging eardrums and putting out someone's eye, it kills the bubbles and the taste."

"This way is more fun," Maia said, helping herself to two flutes from Felicity's china cabinet. "Besides, it's not champagne. It's sparkling rosé."

"Same principle," Felicity said. "Haven't you heard the saying, *the ear's gain is the palate's loss*?"

Maia made a face and waved away her words with a flippant flick of her hand. "You gave your notice. We're celebrating, and I wanted to start the night off with a bang. How did he take the news?"

Felicity shrugged. "He took it about as well as you might expect."

Maia handed Felicity a glass of sparkling rosé.

Felicity couldn't suppress a smile thinking about how upset he'd been by the news.

How am I supposed to get by without you, Felicity?

Did she dare tell Maia what he said? One of two things would happen: her friend would either point out what Felicity already knew—it wasn't personal. It simply meant that she was good at her job. Or she would read way too much into it and try to tempt Felicity into abandoning her common sense about where she stood with Austin Fortune.

Either way, this little nugget was best kept bottled up. Because much like the sparkling wine Maia had brought over to help her celebrate, once the feeling was uncorked, it wouldn't be long before the harsh reality made it flat and unpalatable.

Actually, that was Felicity's view on romance in general. Once romance was set in motion, it was as if a clock started ticking, counting down toward the inevitable end.

Instead of letting the air out of her giddy feeling, she sipped her drink and closed her eyes, savoring the bubbles that tickled her nose.

"What exactly does that mean?" Maia asked. "The guy has his good days and he has his beastly days. Which was this? Was he Mr. Wonderful or was he the Beast?"

Maia knew way too much about Felicity's unrequited crush on her boss. The two women were next-door neighbors, each owning half of a double shotgun-style home that had been converted into two units. They had become fast friends that cool February evening when Felicity moved in and Maia, bearing a casserole of red beans and rice and a bottle of zinfandel, had knocked on Felicity's door and introduced herself.

Felicity had invited her in and amid a maze of boxes, they'd bonded as they feasted on the dinner and wine.

Four years later, they shared more than a common interior wall and communal outdoor space. Maia was so easy to talk to that Felicity constantly found herself confiding secrets that in the past she would've never entrusted to anyone. Secrets such as the big honking crush she'd had on Austin since the day he'd hired her.

"Austin was…Austin." She shrugged. "He was all business, as usual."

Maia didn't just frown, she looked outraged. "What? He just said okay and was fine with letting you walk out of his life forever?"

"I gave my notice. I didn't ask him for a divorce."

"I know that," Maia said. "Did he not show any emotion at all?"

"He didn't cry, if that's what you were expecting."

"Don't be ridiculous. Of course he wouldn't cry. Beasts don't cry. But they do bellow. Did he bellow? Please tell me at the very least he bellowed. If he didn't, I'll have to worry about him."

"You're ridiculous," Felicity said.

Truly, she was. Ridiculously good at getting Felicity to spill her guts. Because suddenly, she was brimming over with the need to tell Maia everything.

"He said he didn't want me to go." Felicity bit her bottom lip. Maia looked at her expectantly. "Actually, he said, 'How am I supposed to get by without you?'"

"Oooh, giiirl." Maia whistled.

And that was how Maia did it. It was *that* subtle, almost like sleight of hand. One minute, Felicity would be steadfast in her resolution to bury a secret deep in her heart, in a place only she knew. Then somehow Maia had diverted her attention and extracted the secret from her.

"*Get by* without you," Felicity repeated. "Not *live*

without you. There's a world of difference in *getting by* and *living*."

Maia shook her head. "Same thing, baby girl. That's simply Beast-speak. He loves you. You need to tell him how you feel."

This time Felicity was the one shaking her head.

"Then you're telling me *you're* perfectly happy *getting by* rather than *living*?" The woman was relentless. "But he let you off work early." Maia glanced at her watch. "Relatively speaking. It's 6:45. I guess that's almost normal business hours."

"He's having dinner with his parents tonight," Felicity said. "After that, he's catching a flight to Atlanta for a meeting tomorrow. I was at a good stopping point. I figured it wouldn't hurt to call it a day at a reasonable hour for a change."

"I'm surprised he didn't insist that you go to Atlanta with him. Seems like he has a hard time functioning without you there to keep everything in order."

Felicity would've loved to go to Atlanta with him. Arriving at the hotel, which would allow her to indulge in the brief illusion that they were checking in together. One room. A king-size bed. Both of them naked, spending one glorious night making love—

Felicity tried to shake the image of hot, sweaty, naked Austin. It wasn't the first time she'd thought about what he'd look like naked. She just knew that underneath his custom fit Tom Ford suits, Austin's body would be long and lean and sexy. His shoulders—oh, those shoulders, they were so perfect they made her want to weep— those broad shoulders would give way to strong, muscled arms—not too muscled, but just right so that his biceps would bulge when he pulled her into his arms and against his perfectly defined chest. Lean hips would showcase a washboard-flat stomach just above the part of his body that would rock her world.

She drew in a sharp breath. She couldn't help it. That's what he did to her. It wasn't considered objectifying a man if you were in love with him, right? She didn't think of anyone else like this. She didn't want to just sleep with him—okay, she did want to sleep with him and she'd fully imagined that experience, too. She wanted so much more than lust or a one-night stand. She wanted to love Austin and she wanted him to love her, too. But he didn't. Clearly, he didn't.

Her sexy daydreams were the consolation prize for the fact that beyond the office, Austin didn't even realize she existed.

"That's not true," Felicity said, answering her friend's comment about how Austin couldn't function without her.

Maia pinned her with a dubious look.

"Okay, maybe it's partially true," Felicity conceded. "It's called job security. I make myself indispensable and I keep getting paid."

"I think you're long past needing to worry about job security. How long has it been now?"

"Almost five years."

"Do you think he will remember your anniversary?" There was a gleam in Maia's eye that Felicity tried to ignore. "I think it's an occasion that calls for flowers and jewelry."

"Stop. He's my boss. There will be no jewelry involved. Because I'll be at my new job by then."

"But you wouldn't mind jewelry. Maybe a ring?"

"Maia, stop. Even if I was still working there, I doubt it would even cross his mind to get me a card. I'm sure in his mind my paycheck is proof of his appreciation."

Austin did pay her well. She couldn't dispute that. Once, when she'd been offered an entry-level position as an account executive with a local advertising agency, she'd given him two weeks' notice. He'd doubled her salary without blinking an eye.

He'd told her she was worth it.

For a bright and shiny moment, she'd read something deeper into his words. Something that bordered on personal. Then she'd blinked and the next thing she knew, he'd launched into what a hassle it would be to find and train someone new and what an imposition it would be to suffer through a new assistant's initial learning curve.

The explanation had dulled the luster in a hurry.

Still, the money was nice. The raise had allowed her to save up a substantial down payment for a house. A year later she'd been in position to buy one of the units in the cute little green house in New Orleans's Irish Channel neighborhood. Technically, it was half a house, but it was hers and she loved it so much she wouldn't have traded it for one of the stately mansions in the neighboring Garden District. Well, in theory, anyway.

In the years she'd worked for Austin, nothing had changed. Felicity was still single, and Austin was none the wiser to her feelings for him. Every day was the same. Except, the days had morphed into weeks and weeks into months. Now, here she was looking back at nearly half a decade that had gone by in a heartbeat and she felt like a hamster on a wheel, bored and mostly unfulfilled by the sameness of it all, but safe and comfortable hiding behind her fat bank account and feelings for him she could never reveal.

Emotionally, she couldn't afford to go on like this much longer. She'd go insane. That's why she had promised herself she would quit and get a real job after she graduated with her MBA at the end of the month.

"I don't understand why you don't just level with him and tell him how you feel," Maia said. "You might just be surprised. I mean, you're leaving soon anyway. Nothing ventured, nothing gained."

Just the thought made Felicity want to turn and run. She had no idea where she wanted to run to other than somewhere far away from the idea of confessing her secret to Austin. In fact, right now she was sorry she'd confided in Maia. It wasn't the first time her friend had suggested such nonsense. She'd been bringing it up more frequently since Felicity had told her of her plans to leave after she graduated.

"Austin said tonight at dinner he would talk to his father about creating an advertising position for me. That's all the more reason why I need to keep my feelings to myself."

"I don't know," Maia mused. "Most likely, you won't be reporting to him anymore if they do make a position for you. Might be a good time to come clean with your feelings."

"Stop." Felicity held up her hand like a traffic cop. "Please listen to me. *If* they create a job for me—and that's a big *if*—I would be one of the few non-Fortunes in a position that wasn't support staff. If I start publicly mooning over Austin, it could be career suicide or at the very least I would embarrass myself."

Maia shrugged. "You look pretty cozy over there in your comfort zone."

"Leaving the comfort of a well-paying job is hardly staying in my comfort zone."

"You know what I'm talking about," Maia said. "I'm talking about the love part. I'm talking about you not wanting to put yourself out there. It was one thing to not to want to jeopardize your job, but now that you're leaving you have no excuses."

Ah, but she did.

She hadn't shared it with Maia because her friend had never asked.

"You know what they say, a comfort zone is a very safe place, but nothing ever grows there—especially not love."

Felicity shook her head. "He has never given me any indication he feels the same way for me."

Maia sighed. "Fine. If you don't want to try to make things work with Austin, then you need to open your mind to other prospects."

"Such as?"

"Be open to dating other men."

Felicity sighed.

"I'm just saying," Maia said. "Just think about it. And since there's no use arguing with a brick wall, let's change the subject."

"Good."

"I have a huge favor to ask you," Maia said. "You know the hair show I'm doing next weekend?"

Felicity nodded.

"I've already sunk a boatload of money into this show and Jane Gordon, the girl who was going to be my model, got a paying modeling job in Paris. She had to bail on me."

"Oh, no. That's terrible. I'm sorry."

"It's good for her, but it stinks for me," Maia said. "So, I have an idea. Will you be my model?"

"Me?" Felicity laughed, unsure if Maia was joking. "I'm not a model."

Her friend set down her drink and walked over and started fluffing Felicity's hair and assessing her as if she was a horse at auction.

"If you try to pick up my leg and look at the bottom of my foot, I'm going to kick you," Felicity said. "I'm not a show pony. I don't do things like this."

"I'm not asking you to change careers." Maia smoothed Felicity's hair away from her face, shaping it into a high ponytail before she turned it loose and let it cascade around her shoulders. "Just help me out of this pickle."

Chapter Two

Austin drove through the stately iron gates that surrounded his parents' rambling eight-bedroom, Garden District mansion. Miles and Sarah Fortune still lived in the same house where Austin and his six brothers and sisters had grown up. The sprawling Victorian was way too much house for most people, but maintaining the family home was a point of pride for them, especially on nights like this, when they called everyone together for a family dinner meeting.

Austin parked his Tesla next to his brother Beau's BMW. He took care to park where no one could block him in, since he'd have to leave early to catch a flight to Atlanta tonight.

He wound his way around the other cars that lined the driveway. When the family got together, it looked like Miles and Sarah were having a party. Tonight, it appeared that Austin was the last to arrive.

As he let himself in the front door, the antique grandfather clock struck 7:15. That meant he'd missed the cocktail hour and they were probably holding dinner for him. Work had kept him late. His parents would understand since they had called the last-minute family dinner meeting just this morning. Austin already had important meetings on the books. He'd gotten away as soon as he could, given the short notice.

As he strode down the hall, he glanced in the living room and could see vestiges of what looked like predinner martinis. Something smelled good. Austin inhaled deeply, and his stomach growled in appreciation. There was nothing like a home-cooked meal. His mom employed a chef who helped her prepare for parties and family gatherings like tonight, but Sarah Fortune could hold her own in the kitchen. She made a mean beef Wellington. Judging by the delicious aroma, that beef Wellington might be on the menu tonight. Austin hoped so as he made his way toward the dining room, where he heard the sound of amicable chatter punctuated by peals of laughter. The sound warmed Austin's heart.

For a moment, he stood in the doorway of the family dining room, taking in the sight of his parents with his four siblings, Beau, Draper, Georgia and Belle. Their brother Nolan and sister Savannah got a pass on tonight's family dinner meeting because they lived in Austin, Texas. They would have to hear secondhand Miles's misgivings about attending the wedding of his half brother Gerald to his long-lost love, Deborah. That was the topic of tonight's summit.

Funny, though, Nolan and Savannah probably regretted missing an opportunity to get together with the family. That's just how they were. They were a close-knit bunch and enjoyed each other's company, respectfully listening when one of them felt it necessary to call a family meeting. To them, family was everything, which made the topic of tonight's meeting so curious. They had all been invited to Gerald and Deborah's wedding in Paseo, Texas. However, based on recent turns of events, Miles believed they should not attend.

"There he is." His mother beamed at him and motioned him inside. "Come in here and give your mama a hug." Even though Austin was thirty-two years old, he did exactly that, following it up with hugs for Belle and Georgia and solid handshakes and backslaps for his father and brothers.

His mother fussed about, offering him a martini. "It's no trouble to mix one up for you right quick." Her Louisiana accent was a bit more pronounced this side of the cocktail hour. Ever the lady, Sarah never overindulged, but she certainly did enjoy a predinner libation.

"Thanks, Mom. I'll have a glass of wine with dinner. I have to drive to airport later."

Soon dinner was served. Just as Austin had hoped, it was beef Wellington, with sides of asparagus with hollandaise sauce, baby carrots and garlic mashed potatoes. It was delicious. Austin hadn't realized how hungry he was. He'd been so busy he'd only had time to eat half the turkey sandwich that Felicity had ordered for him at lunch.

Felicity. He made a mental note to talk to his father about creating an advertising position for her. He'd planned to present it as if Felicity had approached him about advancement opportunities within Fortune Investments. He knew his dad well enough to know if he told Miles that she was quitting, he would've thought her unimaginative.

Miles might not realize how hard Felicity worked and how good she was at her job. To Austin, she wasn't just an assistant, she was his right hand. She was the person who kept him on track. She was one of the few people outside of his family that he trusted implicitly. Even though a new position meant she might not be able to do as much for him, he owed it to her. At least she'd still be with Fortune Investments. So, yes, before he left here tonight, he would plant the seed about promoting her.

In the meantime, he would enjoy his meal and this time with his family. During these family meals, food and catching up were first. Business second. They never broached family business until the coffee and dessert course was served.

True to form, after everyone had a generous helping of brandy-laced English trifle, Miles started the discussion.

"I called you here tonight because we've all been invited to Gerald and Deborah's wedding. There's been a lot of discussion about whether or not we should attend."

He sipped his coffee. "As much as I'd love to go, I don't think it's a good idea. With all that's happened lately, gathering the family in one place doesn't seem like a very smart idea. Essentially, it would make us sitting ducks. We'd be an easy target for whoever has been terrorizing the Fortunes."

Miles was talking about a series of events that had taken place over the last five months. It had started with a fire at the Robinson estate in Austin. The fire had injured Gerald's son Ben, though he had recovered. Gerald's company, Robinson Tech, had been targeted, causing the business to have to recall some of their software. The sabotage had even affected the extended family. Fortunato Real Estate, the business of Kenneth Fortunato, Miles's other half brother, had experienced a downturn after being the target of rumormongering. Most recently, events had hit closer to home when Austin's sister Savannah's apartment had been vandalized.

All signs pointed to Gerald's first wife, Charlotte Prendergast Robinson, as the perpetrator. After discovering some unsavory realities about Charlotte's true nature, Gerald divorced her and had gotten back together with Deborah, his first and one true love. They met when Gerald was on the run from his past, but they'd split and lost touch before she'd discovered she was pregnant with his triplet sons.

No one had been able to catch Charlotte in the act. The family was concerned, as she had already proven herself to be a force to be reckoned with. Now that she had been excommunicated from the family, she'd made it clear she had no compunction about wreaking havoc on anyone related to the Fortunes, even if it meant hurting people in the process.

"Maybe not, Daddy," said Belle, her pretty brow furrowed. "This is an important day for Gerald. He's marrying the love of his life. He has more money than he knows what to do with. Since this day is so important to him and Deborah, don't you think he will invest in the best security?"

"I'll bet it will be on par with the Secret Service," said Draper.

"I know," said Belle. "Call me crazy, but I want to go."

Miles looked furious as he sipped his red wine. "She burned down her own house, injuring her own son. A sociopath like that won't rest until she seeks the ultimate revenge."

Miles shook his head. Georgia, who was seated to his left, reached out and took her father's hand. He squeezed hers in return, but the anger was still apparent in his eyes.

"I'm trying hard to embrace my new extended family." Miles used his fingers to make air quotes around the word *family*. "I know you think it's nice to think that we have found this wonderful, big family and that they are welcoming us with open arms. But don't forget, I've lived all but the last six months of my life without them. You—" Miles spread his arms wide and gestured to his wife and grown children gathered around the table and then pounded his fist on his heart "—all of you, and Savannah and Nolan are my family. And you're all the family I need. If anything happened to any of you because of them, I couldn't forgive myself. I say we send Gerald and Deborah a nice gift and our best wishes for a happy life together, but we're staying away."

Miles was still trying to come to terms with the extended family. Not only was he a self-made man, he was also incredibly self-reliant. His birth father, the philandering millionaire Julius Fortune, had denied Miles at birth. Mile's mother, Marjorie Melton, had raised him on her own. When Miles, who had shared his mother's last name, turned twenty-one, Marjorie revealed his father's identity. That's when Miles took on the Fortune surname. He'd done it to prove a point. He didn't want his father's money. In fact, he set his sights on doing well in spite of his heartless father and the Fortunes.

Not only was he driven to achieve financial success, but he wanted a large family to hold close and shower with the love his own father had denied him. It was a subtle way of showing old man Fortune and the myriad others, *I don't need you. You didn't love me, but I'm going to show you how love is done. In the end, you'll be the lonely, broken one on the outside looking in.* It was a silent and dignified middle finger.

Then a strange thing happened; Miles learned that he wasn't Julius's only dirty little secret. There were others. Much like Miles, they, too, had created their own large families and successful lives. Finally, Schuyler Fortunado Mendoza, daughter of Kenneth Fortunado, decided it was time to end all the secrecy and hurt. It was time for all the Fortune family branches to come together. She arranged a family reunion for the "bastard Fortunes," inviting them all to come to the Mendoza Winery in Austin.

Her intentions were pure. She thought she was doing a good thing by bringing everyone together. However, calling the illegitimate Fortunes together actually ended up putting them in danger, which was why Miles and Sarah were having so much trepidation about attending the wedding.

"If we don't go," Belle said, "they might think we're snubbing them. Family relations are a bit tenuous right now since everything is so new. In addition to being there to support Gerald and Deborah, I think this is an important opportunity to claim our rightful place in the Fortune family."

Miles glared at his daughter. "Enough!" he bellowed. "I am the head of this family. I have decided we are not going. End of discussion." His voice was low and simmering as he bit off each word one by one in a way that had everyone holding their collective breath. Once Miles Fortune made up his mind, he didn't tolerate people challenging him like Belle was doing. "If you'll excuse me, I'll say good night."

Scowling, Miles scooted his chair back from the table and left the room. Austin knew now was not the time to broach the subject of creating a new position for Felicity. Miles was not in the mood and it might undermine the promotion. Austin would approach him after he got back from Atlanta.

Felicity had been waiting all day to ask Austin if he'd had a chance to talk to his father about a new position for her. After the talk with Maia, Felicity had a chance to mull it over a bit and the more she thought about it, the more it made sense to stay at Fortune Investments. If she could get promoted within the company she could keep her benefits and they were always so generous with compensation. It would be less like starting over and more like making a strategic career move up the ladder. Plus, she would still be around Austin, just not as close. Maybe if she wasn't always "right there," Austin might feel her absence enough to realize he missed her.

As counterintuitive as that might sound, it made sense. It was like taking the same route to work every day. You got in such a habit that you went about the drive with blinders on, missing the most important sights along the way. One day, you'd notice a house or shop or a tree that you'd driven by hundreds of times and realize it was the first time you'd really seen it.

Felicity propped her elbows on her desk and rested her chin on her fist. She wanted to be Austin's tree. She chuckled to herself. She wanted him to look up and suddenly notice her.

Notice me, Austin. See me.

She heard his voice coming from the other side of the corridor. That snapped her out of her daydreaming, and she busied herself on the computer, pretending to type away, adding notes to her to-do list for the Fortune Investments gala. She was way ahead of schedule, but she never wanted to give Austin the impression she was slacking off on the job. If she let down her guard, that would be the time he'd notice her.

Come to think of it, she would be doing herself a favor when she went in to talk to him if she told him she really was enthusiastic about the opportunity to stay on with Fortune Investments. The other day when Austin had mentioned the possibility of creating a position for her, she had been so flustered about giving him her notice that she hadn't even acted very excited about the prospect. She smiled at him as he came closer, cell phone pressed to his ear.

"Mackenzie, seriously?" His laugh was infused with a sexy flirtation that made Felicity's heart drop.

Who was Mackenzie? It certainly didn't sound like a business call. In fact, it didn't sound like any type of call she'd ever heard Austin take out in the open like this. Most of the time his calls were business. The small percentage that weren't were family.

He laughed again.

Oh, Mackenzie, you funny girl, you. Felicity stared at her computer screen, so he wouldn't know she was listening.

"Okay. Okay. If you insist. *Macks*, it is." Then he slipped into his office, closing the door behind him.

Max? Or Macks?

As in short for Mackenzie?

Either way, it proved they were on personal terms.

Through the glass wall that divided their workspaces, she watched Austin sit down at his desk and continue the conversation. She couldn't hear what he was saying now, but he was animated. More than she'd ever witnessed before.

His face transformed as he seemed to give a full-throated laugh, his eyes crinkled at the corners, lighting up and dancing. He leaned back casually in his chair, raking his hand through his hair.

She wasn't even bothering to sneak peeks at him now. She was full on staring, greedily watching him delight at whatever it was that this Macks had to say. Of course, Austin was oblivious that she was watching him.

What kind of a woman called herself Macks?

Felicity's phone chirped Maia's text tone. Reluctantly Felicity dragged her gaze off Austin to see what her friend needed.

Are we still on for tonight? Just wanted to make sure you're able to untangle yourself from the Beast.

I'll be there.

ETA?????

6 p.m. as planned

By the time Felicity put her phone in her purse and looked back at Austin, he was off the phone and on his computer.

She needed to borrow a page from this woman and start being more of a *Macks*—not a Mackenzie. Mackenzie sounded prim and proper, like a rule follower. Macks sounded like a woman in charge of her destiny.

Felicity pulled up the interoffice messaging system on her computer and typed, Do you have a moment?

She pressed Send before she could change her mind. It was twenty minutes until five o'clock.

She was going to channel her inner Macks and march in there. First, she was going to tell him she was leaving at five because she had plans. Then she would ask him if he'd talked to his dad. She was not going to sit around and wait for him to come to her. She was going to be proactive.

Austin had been out of the office all day, which meant he would be pulling a late night tonight. Usually, she stayed as late as he did. She didn't mind, as it gave her time to get a jump on future projects such as the FI charity ball. She was single-handedly organizing the ball. It was a big job and took a lot of extra time. But tonight, she had promised Maia she would come to the salon so her friend could practice for the hair show. She said she'd be there at six o'clock. That meant she needed to get a move on if she was going to go home and grab a bite to eat and change out of her work clothes and into something more comfortable before she went to the salon.

She jumped at the sound of the chime notifying her of Austin's reply.

Sure, come on in.

She looked at him, but his head was bent over his desk and he was busy writing something.

Felicity's stomach bunched, then fell as she realized in a matter of minutes, she would know whether or not Miles Fortune was on board for keeping her on board.

The sooner she knew, the better. She gathered her courage and closed the short distance to Austin's office.

"Hey, what's going on?" He leaned back in his chair, laced his fingers together and cradled the back of his head. His biceps pushed at the boundaries of his shirt sleeves. Her gaze lingered. She couldn't help it.

He motioned for her to sit on one of the chairs in front of his desk. She chose the opposite chair from where she'd sat when she'd given her notice.

"What did your father say? I'm dying to know."

His blank stare made her wish she could retract the question.

"What did he say about what?" Austin asked, leaning farther back in his chair, but not looking nearly as relaxed as he had when he was talking to Macks.

"Really, Austin? You don't remember?"

He blinked once. Twice. Then he tapped his head. "Oh, my God, right. I'm sorry. It's been a crazy day."

I'll bet. Macks must be occupying a lot of real estate up there.

"I'm sorry, Felicity. I haven't had a chance to bring it up with him. The other night when we were at dinner I intended to talk to him, but it ended up not being a good time. We had some family business to discuss and Belle was pushing his buttons. She got him a little riled up. You know how he can be."

Felicity didn't answer.

It was the stupidest thing but suddenly she felt a hot, stinging sensation behind her eyes. God, she was not going to cry. She couldn't cry. Why did she want to cry over this?

So, he hadn't remembered right off the bat. The guy had a lot on his mind. But suddenly it was crystal clear to her that she really didn't want to leave. She wanted to stay.

Obviously, Austin wasn't so devastated by the thought of her leaving. It was ridiculous, but it hurt her feelings.

Needing to get ahold of herself, she bit her bottom lip hard to keep the tears at bay. It worked.

"No problem," she heard herself saying. Maybe after he'd initially thought up the possibility of creating a position for her, he'd realized it wasn't feasible. Or maybe he had mentioned it to Miles and his father had shut down the idea. Maybe Austin was trying not to hurt her feelings.

"It's five o'clock," she said. "I need to leave. I have plans tonight. I'll call Derek and ask him to bring your dinner to the office. What time do you want him to deliver it?"

"Anytime is fine."

Derek was Austin's personal chef. Usually, Derek left Austin's dinner in the oven of Austin's condo, which was around the corner from the Fortune Investments offices, and Felicity would pick it up and bring it to the office. Tonight, Derek would have to deliver it.

If she was leaving at the end of the month, Austin would need to learn to fend for himself until he got his new assistant up to speed.

It hit her that having someone else deliver Austin's dinner wasn't exactly making him fend for himself, but it was part of the weening process for her. She enjoyed taking care of him. It was a point of pride. Moving on would be a loss for her, too.

She felt his eyes on her. "Are you okay?"

"Sure. Why wouldn't I be?"

"Something's wrong." He shook his head. "I'm sorry I haven't had a chance to talk to Miles. I will as soon as I can. I promise. Okay?"

"It's fine, Austin. Really."

She stood to leave, feeling a little better that he'd noticed that she was upset and had said he would speak to his dad. If Miles had already shot down the idea, Austin wouldn't have said that. She knew him well enough to know that.

"Don't leave me, Felicity. Okay?"

Her mouth went dry at his words.

Dear God, if you only knew.

But he didn't. This was strictly business. It would always be about business when it came to them. That was the problem. Her *taking care of* Austin was so personal, sometimes her heart crossed the line. She needed to make sure her mind and better judgment stayed in complete control. Because her heart could only lead her astray.

Still, it didn't help that the look on his face was so earnest it made tears sting the back of her eyes again. God, she was a mess. Her emotions were up and down like a roller coaster. One minute she was ready to walk out the door, and the next minute his *don't leave me* had her wanting to withdraw her resignation and dedicate her life to him... Well, to being his personal assistant. And that was no kind of life. Especially when she felt like this for him.

"Before you leave for the day, would you do me a huge favor? Will you call a courier to deliver this?"

She nodded and reached out, taking the large white envelope he held.

It was addressed to Mackenzie Cole. Felicity recognized the lower Garden District zip code. The name Mackenzie was crossed through on the package. Austin had rewritten *Macks* above it in that script that was so achingly familiar to Felicity. For some stupid reason, seeing Macks's name written by Austin's hand felt so personal. It was a punch to Felicity's gut.

No. She would not call a courier to deliver this package.

Felicity would deliver it herself.

Chapter Three

Macks Cole was Felicity's worst nightmare.

Felicity knew it had been a mistake to deliver the package herself the moment the tall, willowy Margot Robbie lookalike answered the door. She was exactly the kind of beautiful, worldly woman who would call herself Macks.

Scratch that.

Her old-monied parents had probably called her Macks since birth. She'd probably been named Mackenzie after the great-great grandmother with the money. Her brothers would be Digby and Shep. They probably spent hours on the golf course and drank too much with their Mardi Gras krewe. Of course, there would be a baby sister. Her name would be Margaux, but they'd call her Go, because she was cute and sweet, and they'd already determined Macks was the strong, efficacious girl child.

"May I help you?" Clad in impeccable Eileen Fisher white linen, barefoot with wide stacks of thin gold bangle bracelets on her tanned arms, Macks managed to look both effortlessly sexy and sophisticated.

"Are you Mackenzie Cole?"

She regarded Felicity with the assurance of a woman who was comfortable in her own skin. If Felicity had to guess, she'd peg Macks for midthirties, which meant the woman was probably seven or eight years her senior.

"I am." Her expression was bemused but patient, as if she'd opened the door to find a Girl Scout selling cookies.

Why did you come here, you idiot? Curiosity killed the cat.

Or at least it killed the fantasy that she, Felicity, was secretly Austin's type. That there had been a chance for them.

She had been utterly wrong.

"I have a package for you."

She pictured Macks talking on the phone with Austin, alternately reclining on a red velvet chaise longue—she'd pronounce it the French way because she'd know things like that—and sitting in lotus position on the polished cherry mahogany floor in a perfect patch of sunshine. All the while, her white linen would stay as pressed and pristine as the moment she'd removed it from the dry-cleaning bag.

Macks took the envelope and examined the writing. Her eyes flashed, and she smiled a smug, knowing smile. She turned sparkling green eyes on Felicity as if she expected her to deliver a singing telegram that sounded like this:

Austin says he loves you.
Soon you'll be his wife.
You're absolutely perfect.
You'll have a lovely life.

"Come in, come in." Macks motioned Felicity inside.

Felicity blinked and balled her hands into fists. For a split second, she wasn't one hundred percent certain she hadn't inadvertently been making jazz hands as she sang the telegram in her head.

Apparently, she hadn't because her arms were rigidly at her sides, and Macks wasn't looking at her like she was a spontaneous performing weirdo.

She should have said no to Macks's invitation to come inside. She was going to be late meeting Maia, but the need to see Macks in her natural habitat overpowered Felicity's preference for punctuality.

Macks closed the leaded stained-glass front door and disappeared down the cherry mahogany hallway. The flooring was the only thing Felicity's imagination had gotten right. The living room, which was to the left, was furnished with expensive-looking pieces that were surprisingly minimalist and modern. Except for the dark wooden floor, the room was done in monochromatic white and punctuated with pops of color from artwork on the wall. Clearly expensive fine art. A freeform sculpture that looked like Chihuly glass was lit in one corner. On the opposite wall was a life-size roughhewn stone sculpture of a man's naked torso showcased from throat to muscular midthigh. It was very lifelike and... um...erect. Felicity felt her cheeks warm.

Now, that was a conversation starter if she'd ever seen one. Did Mr. Erectus have a first name? Was Macks personally acquainted? No? Would she like to be? He looked like a strapping young man. Maybe Macks could date him instead of Austin?

Just an idea.

Felicity sighed. She should've called the courier. Because meeting perfect Macks and standing here inside her perfect home was akin to watching a disturbing scene in a movie. She knew she should've closed her eyes, looked the other way. But she didn't. Now she couldn't unsee the reality.

No wonder Austin had been flirting like a schoolboy.

"Here you go." Macks's melodic voice echoed as she approached, one bangle-clad arm outstretched, dangling a twenty-dollar bill from her perfectly French-manicured fingers. "This is for you—what did you say your name was?"

I didn't.

"I'm Felicity. I'm Austin's assistant. I was in the area on my way to another appointment. I told him I'd drop off the package. So, I can't accept that." She gestured to the money. "Thank you, though."

Felicity flashed her best smile.

Macks was looking at her in a different, more appraising way. "Austin didn't mention that his assistant was so pretty."

Austin had mentioned her?

Maybe in passing. *I'll make sure my assistant puts our first date on the books.*

But he hadn't asked her to reserve a date or make a reservation or—

"Thank you, Felicity." Macks's voice had regained its self-assured, slightly superior tone. She gracefully reached around and opened the front door. Felicity's cue to leave.

"It was *lovely* meeting you," Macks said. "I'm sure this won't be the last time we'll see each other."

"This makeover was a great idea," Felicity said. "I'm glad you roped me into this hair show."

"I didn't intend to rope you into anything," Maia said as she swiped the blending brush over Felicity's face before stepping back and admiring her work like a master artist.

"Roped or not, I probably wouldn't be sitting here tonight if not for the hair show." Felicity stared at herself in the mirror, turning her head this way and that. "Even if it was a ploy, it's okay."

The makeover was subtle. The cut made her hair bouncy. The modest highlights made it shiny. Maia had applied just enough makeup so that Felicity looked polished and put together. This new, more professional look would come in handy when she started interviewing for jobs at the end of the month. Because if Austin had a girlfriend, she did not want to watch it unfold from the front row seat of Fortune Investments.

Even if the money was good, mooning over her boss

and his new girlfriend wasn't. She'd been at Austin's beck and call since she'd started working for him. Her job had dominated her life. She hadn't even dated anyone seriously since college. Sure, she'd told herself that she didn't have time to date. And to what end?

Even if Macks had called her pretty, ultimately, she'd sized Felicity up and decided she wasn't a threat. Of course she wasn't. Austin Fortune dated women like Macks Cole, not Felicity Schafer.

She ran her fingers through her honey blond hair, letting the locks fall through her fingers and cascade onto her shoulders. The highlights were understated. They looked natural, as if her hair had been kissed by the sun.

The FI charity ball was two weeks before her graduation. She would focus on getting through the ball and then put her energy into finding a new job and hiring her replacement.

She nodded as if confirming the plan to herself.

"So, you like?" Maia asked, handing Felicity a mirror and turning her around so she could view the back of her head.

"I love it. I have to admit, I was a little bit skeptical. I didn't know what to expect. I thought you might do something a little more extreme for the show tomorrow."

It was a relief compared to what she'd feared as she'd watched Maia cover her head in foil rectangles that fanned out in all directions, making her feel like some kind of a space-age creature that could transmit radio waves.

Maia smiled at her approvingly. "Didn't I tell you? This show is about everyday, polished looks. There are some shows where they want looks that are pretty out there. But this is you, only better. Right?"

"What? Like Felicity 6.0?"

"More like Felicity 10.0." Maia laughed. "Don't get me wrong. You were perfect exactly the way you were. You're lucky, you can pull off the no-makeup, girl-next-door look, but it doesn't hurt to change things up every once in a while. Who knows, maybe this will make the Beast finally notice you."

Heat flooded Felicity cheeks.

"Maia, shhhh." Felicity pressed her index finger to her lips and looked around to see if anyone in the bustling salon was listening. As if anyone knew who *the Beast* was or would be interested in a twenty-seven-year-old woman's secret crush. Her cheeks warmed again at the ridiculous thought.

Still, she didn't want to talk about him in the busy salon. The last thing she needed was for someone to recognize her as his assistant and put two and two together and report back that she'd been talking about him. Stranger things could happen.

Austin was a prominent New Orleans business figure. More than one magazine had named him one of New Orleans's most eligible bachelors. During the time she'd been his assistant, one woman had befriended her with the ulterior motive of getting closer to Austin. Another woman had been more up-front about her purpose. She'd approached Felicity in a restaurant bathroom and said, "You're Austin Fortune's assistant, aren't you?" It was more than a little creepy since she'd never met the woman. She'd handed Felicity her card. "Will you please have him call me?"

The card had her name, Beverly Sands, and a phone number. Nothing else. "Is this a business matter?" Felicity had asked because she didn't want to take a chance of offending a potential client.

"Oh, no, this isn't about business. I'm a florist. I want to meet him since I'm going to marry him." She'd laughed and for a minute, Felicity thought she was joking and was about to hand back the card. But there was something in the petite brunette's eyes that was a little crazed. *Crazy eyes*, that was the way Felicity had described her to Austin. Big, round blue eyes that didn't blink as she continuously nodded her head while she talked.

They were alone in the restroom. Deciding it was better to be safe than sorry, Felicity said she would relay the message. That afternoon, a big bouquet of flowers arrived for Felicity. The card said, *Thanks for hooking me up. Love, your friend, Bev.*

She'd showed the flowers to Austin. Since they knew Beverly's name and place of employment from the envelope that came with the card attached to the flowers, they were able to find her photo on social media. Austin had supplied the information to security and had insisted on walking Felicity to her car for a solid month. They'd never heard from Bev again, but it had been a good lesson that people may know more than you realize.

Austin was a smart man. Even if a good portion

of New Orleans's female population was in love with him, if word got back to him that someone of Felicity's description was mooning over him in Maia's salon, it wouldn't take long for him to connect the dots back to her.

She'd worked for him all this time without divulging her secret. Why would she want to spill the beans now?

A little voice in the back of her head screamed, *Because when you quit, you're not going to be working for him anymore. You'll be free to make your move. If you don't, Macks will get him. Go for it!*

But that was the thing. She didn't want to be the one to make the move. Was it so wrong to be old-fashioned? To want him to make the first move? Even if he hadn't even given the slightest hint of interest. Even if he didn't see her that way. Plain and simple. She'd humiliate herself if she told him her feelings.

During the time that she'd been his personal assistant, he hadn't been serious about anyone. And she would know because she kept his calendar and scheduled practically every detail of his life, even the occasional first date that never led to a second.

Most wives didn't know their husbands as well as she knew Austin.

She knew that his favorite music was jazz. His childhood pet was a yellow Lab named Bandit. He liked his coffee strong and black. She had it ready for him every morning. He wasn't very talkative in the morning. Even though he got to the office at the crack of dawn, he needed a moment to read the *Times-Picayune* and drink his strong, black coffee, letting the caffeine get into his bloodstream before he was fit to see any-one. His family was the only thing that ever came be-fore work. He had a sweet tooth, which he indulged in moderation, and she blocked off time for him to have daily workouts, which allowed him to enjoy his treats and stay healthy.

Austin Fortune had said it himself. She was his right hand. She anticipated his every mood. She knew him better than he knew himself sometimes, understanding what made him happy and how to preempt the things that didn't. She was his gatekeeper. If anyone wanted to get to him, they had to go through her. Yet, some-how Macks had managed to infiltrate.

Since Austin didn't seem to mind, it was out of her hands.

"There's my best girl." A blond guy walked over and hugged Maia.

"Hey, handsome," she said in her flirty voice.

Who was this? Did Maia have a guy in her life? Why hadn't she mentioned him?

"Thanks for fitting me in on such short notice."

Okay. Maybe he was a client.

Maia prided herself on forming strong bonds with her clients. That's why her business was booming.

But his hair was very short. He didn't look like a haircut emergency. Then again, Felicity was not an expert in this arena. Maybe it was a special cut that needed to be meticulously maintained?

"Yeah, hon, have a seat right there. I've just finished up with Felicity. Have you met Felicity?"

"I haven't had the pleasure. Kevin Clooney." He offered his hand and Felicity pulled hers out from under the cape she'd been wearing while Maia cut her hair. Kevin held her hand a little too long, his eyes sweeping over her face and his mouth widening into a broad smile.

"Felicity Schafer," she said. "I'm Maia's neighbor."

"Maia, babe, you've been holding out on me," said Kevin. "I can't believe you haven't introduced us before now. I'm in love."

Okay, bring it down a notch or two, bud. People are staring.

They were. The woman in the station next to Maia's was alternately exchanging glances with Mark, her burly, bald, tattooed hairdresser, and grinning at Felicity and Kevin.

"Felicity is my model for a show tomorrow night," Maia said, as she wet Kevin's hair with water from a spray bottle and combed it through.

Kevin nodded. "You look gorgeous."

Was he flirting with her? "Maia does good work."

"It's easy to do good work when you start with such a good canvas," he said.

"True," said Maia.

As much as Felicity hated it, she felt heat bloom in her cheeks. Doing her best to channel her inner Macks, she pushed her shoulders back, lifted her chin and looked him directly in the eyes. "You're a flirt, aren't you, Kevin?"

Maia snorted. Kevin laughed and so did Felicity.

"He might have been called that once or twice," Maia said.

Kevin held up his hands in a show of surrender. "All I'm saying is that you two are going to own that hair show."

"Yeah, we are," Maia said, her scissors flying as she sheared fractions of an inch off Kevin's hair.

Felicity was just about to say goodbye when Kevin asked, "Is this hair show industry only or is it open to the public?"

"Why?" Maia asked. "Do you want to go? I can get you a ticket if you do."

He slanted a glance at Felicity. "I'd love to. Maybe the three of us could go out for drinks afterward."

"It's a date," said Maia.

A date, huh? Felicity had a suspicious feeling she'd just been set up. Maia knew she'd be in the salon. She just happened to fit in Kevin for a haircut he didn't really need.

But Kevin was cute, and he seemed fun. She could give him a chance. She didn't have to marry the guy. If Austin was seeing Macks, maybe having drinks with a cute, fun guy was exactly what she needed.

Austin got to the office at a quarter to seven Monday morning. Felicity was already sitting at her desk working at her computer, as usual. As he walked by and grabbed the cup of coffee she had waiting for him on the corner of her desk, something made him do a double take and stop.

"May I help you?" She kept typing and didn't look away from her computer. She had used her smart-alecky voice. The tone she took when she was about

to point out the obvious after he'd been painfully obtuse about something. The voice that would soften later
and allow them to laugh at whatever it was that needed
correcting.

"Something's different," he said, studying her.

She lifted her brows at him and that's when he realized she was wearing makeup. Or at least more makeup
than she usually wore. Did she wear makeup? Was it
politically correct to tell her he'd noticed?

"You cut your hair." It was a statement. Not a judgment.

"I did." She ran her fingers through the silky-
looking strands.

Silky-looking. Now, admitting that might get him
into trouble.

"What do you think?" she asked.

"If I say it looks nice, it won't offend you or make
you feel compromised or objectified, will it?"

Her eyes flashed and there was the briefest second
before she burst out laughing.

"Austin, I asked you what you thought. I'm certainly not going to run and file a harassment charge
with Human Resources."

"Okay, then. I like your haircut. It looks nice. You
look nice."

She smiled and did that fingers-through-the-hair
thing again. This time he noticed that her hair was
shiny and that pieces that caught the light were the
color of honey.

"Thank you, Austin. You, on the other hand, could

use a haircut. You're looking a little untamed there. Do you want me to schedule one for you?"

Now it was his turn to run his fingers through his mop. She was right; it was a little long. "Sure, that would be great. Thanks."

He turned to go, but Felicity said, "Oh, hey, listen. I need to leave at five o'clock again."

She had every right to leave at five. But when he worked late, it was always nice to know she was there, too. Often, it would just be the two of them in the office until late and she'd buzz him and say, "Austin, go home. The work will be here tomorrow."

It's not that he needed her to remind him—well, maybe he did. He liked the office better than home. What was he going to do if she left?

"Do you have something with school going on?" he asked, and added before she could answer, "Be sure to let me know the date of your graduation so I get it on my calendar."

"I've already put it on your calendar. And no, tonight is not about school. I have a date."

A date? Felicity dates?

That was another one of those obtuse questions that would send her into smart-aleck mode. Why wouldn't Felicity date? She was beautiful and smart and she had a smokin' hot bod, curves in all the right places. Okay, that was definitely the kind of comment that would send her down the hall to HR faster than he could tell her he hadn't meant anything offensive by it. It was just a fact—like the honey-gold highlights in her hair and the pink stain on her bee-stung lips.

Why was he thinking about this now? And when did Felicity have time to date when she was always working late with him?

"Who's the lucky guy?" he asked, trying not to look at her lips.

"It's a guy named Kevin Clooney. My friend Maia introduced us. We hung out on Saturday."

"Kevin Clooney?" he asked. "Why does that name sound familiar?"

"You're probably thinking George Clooney, the actor. No relation."

No. That wasn't what he was thinking, but—

"You'll get to meet him because he's picking me up at the office."

"Don't you think you should meet him out the first few dates? You don't know this guy. He could be some kind of sociopath."

She squinted at him. "Austin, I thought him picking me up from work was gentlemanly. He's not a sociopath. He's been a client of my neighbor Maia's for years."

"Yeah, but you never know. You can't be too careful these days."

He should've been more careful when his ex-wife Kelly swooped into his life. He'd been duped. Such an easy mark. He didn't want Felicity to rush into anything and find herself in a bad situation.

She was smiling at him now. "Thank you for caring."

He grunted. "Of course."

I care about you. I'll rip the SOB's head off if he doesn't treat you right.

Felicity bit her bottom lip, which made him look at her mouth again. Thank God she was studying her computer screen, so she didn't see him looking.

Kevin Clooney.

What a dumb name.

So that's why she was all dressed up and wearing that pink lip stuff today.

"Hey, listen. Can you stay late tomorrow night and maybe Wednesday, too? We need to talk about the charity ball."

"Sure. That's not a problem."

"Good. Thanks."

Maybe they'd need to work through the weekend, too.

He turned away on a jerky motion that made his coffee slosh and splash onto his crisp white button-down.

He growled and muttered a string of expletives under his breath.

"I heard that, potty mouth," Felicity said. "What did you do?"

"I spilled my damn coffee down the front of my shirt and I don't have a spare in my office. I used the last one Thursday before the McCutcheon meeting."

Cursing again, he frowned down at the stain. He should've put his suit coat on when he got out of his car.

What a great way to start the day.

"Now, I have to have to go home and change. I have a meeting at nine and I look like a freaking bum."

"No, you don't," Felicity said. "I'll go pick up your

dry cleaning when they open at eight. You have some white shirts in that order."

"I do?" he said, the edges of his bad mood lifting. "Thanks. So, uh—you're not going to let this guy take you home, are you?"

Felicity's cheeks flushed. "And you were worried that complimenting me on my haircut was inappropriate? That's none of your business, Austin. Who I go home with is kind of private. Don't you think?"

"What? No. That's— No, wait," Austin sputtered. "That's not what I meant. I meant it's not a good idea for you to let a guy you've just met know where you live. Letting him know where you work is bad enough. Take an Uber home. Don't tell him your home address."

Felicity looked a little embarrassed. "Oh. I misunderstood. If it makes you feel any better, he has to drop me off here because my car will be here."

Austin ran a hand over his face. "Yeah, I guess so. Are you in the parking garage?"

She nodded.

"Text me about five minutes before you get here, and I'll come down and meet you."

She scrunched up her nose. "Um, thanks, Dad, but I think I'll be okay. I've been on dates before. This isn't my first rodeo."

He tried to say something, but the words got stuck in his throat and it came out sounding like something between a grunt and a growl. He turned around to go brood in his office.

"Austin, wait a second."

He turned back to her.

"Now you have me second-guessing everything. You're right. I don't know Kevin. I mean, Maia does, but she hasn't dated him. She cuts his hair. I'll call him and tell him I'll meet him at the restaurant. It'll be easier that way."

"Good."

Austin nodded and went into his office. He should've felt better, but he didn't.

What the hell was wrong with him? Why did learning that Felicity had a date throw him into such a tailspin? This was *Felicity*, for God's sake. His assistant. Maybe this date thing and her leaving earlier than usual were underscoring the fact that he really was going to lose her—that Fortune Investments was going to lose her—if he didn't talk to his father soon. He made a mental note to do that today.

He sat down at his desk and stole a glance at her through the glass wall.

Was this the first time he'd been aware of her going out with someone? Until now, it seemed as if he'd never had to share her with another man because he'd always kept her so busy. If he was completely honest with himself, he didn't want to start sharing her now.

God, but not like that. Not in an intimate way. He blinked and shook away the strange feeling lurking in his solar plexus.

What the hell was that all about? Where had it come from? Sure, Felicity was a smart, beautiful woman, but Fortune Investments had a strict no-fraternizing policy. He couldn't allow himself to think about her in any other context than platonic.

He reframed his thoughts.

What he'd meant was he didn't want to share her because he'd grown accustomed to being the sole beneficiary of her efficient capability. She kept him organized and on track. She made him look good. And made it seem so effortless, though he knew damn well it was hard work.

That's why it wasn't fair to her to expect that she would spend the rest of her working life wasting her talent fetching his coffee and picking up his dry cleaning. But what the hell was he going to do without her?

Chapter Four

The next morning, Felicity sat at her desk, sipping her morning tea, mulling over last night's date with Kevin. He was a good guy, but she wasn't interested in seeing him again.

She was more eager to get back to her desk and resume life as usual.

Early morning was her favorite time in the office. She and Austin occupied the northeast corner of the Fortune Investments building. Since Felicity always arrived at the crack of dawn, it meant the office was still quiet and she could collect her thoughts as she sipped her tea and watched the sun rise over the New Orleans Central Business District.

It put her in a good place, started her day off right. Since Austin had to drink his coffee before he was fit for the world, it sort of felt like they were waking up together. If you didn't count the inconvenience of separate beds, in separate houses.

But even the most serene morning couldn't prepare her for the flowers.

Felicity was on the phone when Carla from the reception desk personally walked the huge arrangement back to Felicity's desk. Carla waited for her to get off the phone before she thrust the stunning bouquet of white lilies, peonies and roses at her, and proclaimed in a sing-song voice, "Someone got flowers. Who are they from and most important, what did you do to deserve them?"

"I have no idea," Felicity said. She was surprised that Carla hadn't opened the envelope herself and peeked at the sender. Clearly, Carla wasn't budging until she got the scoop.

Felicity accepted the fragrant bundle and took the card off the holder. With a sinking feeling, she took her time opening the envelope and pulling out the card.

Actually, she had a pretty good idea who'd sent them—and she wished he hadn't. It just felt wrong. All wrong. Then again, they could've come from a vendor she'd been working with for the charity ball. Another perk of being Austin's assistant was that sometimes companies sent incentives and samples, trying to entice her into using their goods and services. There had been a cashmere scarf from the office cleaning service; Belgian chocolates from the paper dealer; a leather day planner embossed with her name from the temp agency they sometimes called on when they needed extra help. In fact, that's how Felicity had found her job at FI. Austin had brought her in as a temp and when she'd had his coffee and newspaper waiting for him without his asking, he'd offered her the job permanently.

So, the flowers could've been from someone else. But no, her first inclination right.

You're still the most gorgeous model in the show.
Last night was fun. When can I see you again?
Kevin

No. No. No. No. No.

But, yeah, Kevin had sent her the flowers. Gorgeous flowers. They must've cost a fortune. If she'd been able to send them back, she would have, because looking at them and reading his candid note produced in her that particular brand of dread that happened when a guy was interested in you but you didn't return his feelings.

She didn't want to hurt his feelings. But she just wasn't into him. Not like *that*. Sure, the date had been…pleasant. He was easy to talk to. He hadn't made her feel bad when she'd turned her head, offering a cheek when he'd leaned in for a good-night kiss.

Yeah… Kevin was a nice guy, she supposed, but he wasn't doing it for her. Something felt off.

She cast a quick glance at Austin, who was concentrating on something on his computer, and her heart hurt for a completely different reason. That caused a host of mixed emotions to flood through her. Why didn't she like Kevin? Why had her heart sentenced her to a lost cause? Sure, Kevin was laying it on kind of thick, but maybe if she let down her guard, maybe if she faced facts, she'd realize it was nice and a lot healthier to open her heart to someone who cared for her. Reflexively, her gaze tracked back to Austin's office. This time he was looking at her.

Her heart leaped into her throat. After it lodged back into place, it thudded in her chest.

"Well? Who are they from?" Carla asked. "Don't leave me hanging."

Felicity shoved the card back in the envelope. "Just a friend."

Out of the corner of her eye she saw Austin stand up from his desk.

"Austin's coming out here. I need to get back to work, and you better get back to the front desk so he doesn't get annoyed with us."

Carla flinched and did a quickstep down the hallway that led to the reception area.

"Don't tell me Bev is back," Austin said.

He looked good today in his charcoal gray suit and white button-down. Of course, he always looked good. Felicity particularly loved that suit on him. It made his shoulders look a mile wide. He was wearing the green paisley tie she liked. It brought out the subtle hazel flecks in his eyes.

Damn him for making her want him when she couldn't have him.

"What are you talking about?"

"Beverly Sands. The flower stalker." Austin gestured to the bouquet.

For some reason the smug look on his handsome face pushed every button she possessed. Everybody knew he could have any woman he wanted—the Macks of the world…the Beverly Sandses…the Felicity Schafers— but did he have to act so self-satisfied?

"These are not from Beverly Sands. Not everything is about you, Austin."

He flinched. Blinked.

"Gaaaa!"

Did she really just say that out loud? She'd certainly been thinking it, but she hadn't intended to say it.

A goofy smile spread over his face. "Someone's in a mood."

She bit her bottom lip to keep from pointing out that *he* was usually the one in a mood, but at least *she* had the good grace not to mention it. On those occasions, she tried to lighten the air, not poke the bear.

"These are from Kevin. My date last night."

She held her breath. If Austin made one off-color smirk, one *wink-wink, nudge-nudge, what did you do to merit flowers after a date*, she was going to quit on the spot. Let him book his own restaurant for the first date with Macks.

The silly grin that had previously been on Austin's handsome face darkened. "Kevin Clooney?" He spat out the words like they tasted foul.

"Of course. Who else?"

"Looks like Kevin Clooney wants another date."

Felicity shrugged.

"Tell me you're not going out with him again—uh, never mind. I shouldn't have said that. Who you date is none of my business. I hope he treats you like you deserve to be treated. Don't settle for anything less."

Profound words coming from the man who didn't even realize she was a woman.

Scowling, Austin said, "I need to make a call." He turned around and walked away, mumbling something that sounded like, "You could do better than Kevin Clooney," leaving Felicity more confused than ever.

He stepped inside his office, then he leaned out of the doorway and said, "We're still on for tonight, right?"

"Yes, of course."

He gave her a curt nod and ducked back inside.

You could do better than Kevin Clooney.

If she was a complete idiot, she might let herself believe his sudden mood change meant he cared. But, of course, he cared. It was more than that. This went deeper. She was picking up a vibe that suggested his mood stemmed from...jealousy?

White-hot currents of electricity coursed through her. She glanced at Austin, but he was on the phone, scowling up at the ceiling, looking impatient.

How had a beautiful bouquet of flowers sent everyone's morning south?

She knew she'd be setting herself up for a world of hurt if she tried to read anything into this other than what it was: Austin was afraid that if she started dating, she wouldn't be as available as usual for the remainder of time she was there.

What was wrong with her? Why was she being such a masochist? Kevin was making all the right gestures. He wasn't playing the "wait three days to call" game, which was refreshingly candid.

Felicity sighed. Maybe she should follow Kevin's

example? Platonically, she could tease and throw innocent barbs at Austin. She could pull him back into line when he needed a reality check, but when it came to matters of the heart, she couldn't tell him how she really felt about him.

Her own reality check was she probably never would tell him how she felt—especially now that Macks was in the picture.

Maybe she should give Kevin a chance. It didn't mean she had to marry him, and at least she'd be investing in someone who treated her the way she should be treated.

Austin stared at the bottom line on the statement he'd been analyzing for the better part of an hour, and realized he had no idea what he'd just read.

He hadn't been able to focus on work since his exchange with Felicity this morning. What the hell was wrong with him? Work was always his escape. When the outside world felt like it was closing in, he'd bury himself in work, which was easy to do at Fortune Investments.

Usually.

Until now.

Felicity was free to see whomever she wanted. Even if it was this Kevin Clooney.

Austin scrubbed his hand over his eyes. He knew it was unfair to form a judgment like this without even meeting the guy, but something didn't feel right. That name was familiar—and not in a good way. But he couldn't place the guy. After discovering how his ex-wife, Kelly, had played him for a fool when she'd set her sights on marrying a Fortune, he'd become exceedingly good at sizing up people and situations. Sometimes only based on a feeling.

Why the hell was Clooney sending Felicity such elaborate flowers after just one date? Austin had been plagued by the question since he'd seen the flowers and Felicity had gotten a little snippy over his questions about Kevin.

What was even crazier and harder to come to terms with was his dread over the reality that he was losing Felicity. In more ways than one. She wanted to move on and leave him behind, and the damnedest thing was it felt more like a breakup than simply losing his assistant. He knew that was unfair and ridiculous and not right on so many levels. She had every right to move on, to find a better situation for herself. He understood.

Part of the problem that he'd realized with the delivery of those damn flowers was that if she left, he might not see her again. For nearly five years, she was usually the first person he saw in the morning and often the last face he saw in the evening. And since it wasn't unusual for him to phone her about business after hours, she was often the last voice he heard before retiring for the night.

He watched her as she wrote something on a legal pad. Probably notes about the ball that she wanted to discuss at their dinner meeting tonight. Or maybe she was mapping out her résumé.

The light coming in from the windows picked out the honey highlights in her hair. She was wearing a black tank and a black pencil skirt that hugged her curves. He'd noticed that this morning. She was wearing that pink lipstick again and she'd styled her hair in the new way she'd been wearing it.

He raked his hands through his hair, fisting them at the nape of his neck.

He needed to give her a reason to stay, even if she would be working in a different department and he'd have to hire a new assistant. That's the only thing that quelled the near panic he felt at the thought of never seeing her again.

The first order of business would be to get his father excited about creating an advertising position for her. He'd left a message for his dad yesterday, asking if they could meet to talk about something important. When Miles's assistant called back, she had informed Austin that his father was out of town this week. She offered to schedule a phone meeting, but knowing Miles the way he did, this was a conversation best done in person.

Felicity just needed to hang on a bit longer. He'd tell her as much at dinner tonight.

In the meantime, it would do him good to be a little less gruff toward her. He knew he wasn't always the easiest person to deal with. Nobody liked working with a bear. But she had always been so good about pulling him out of his dark moods.

It suddenly dawned on him how badly he'd taken her for granted.

It would behoove him to slow his roll and soften his approach.

"How was your day?" Austin stopped when he reached Felicity. He leaned a hip against the corner of her desk and looked at her expectantly. Like he was interested.

This is weird.

When was the last time he'd asked her about her day? Um, never. For that matter, when was the last time he stopped to talk about something personal? Well, other than to harangue her about Kevin. And the flowers.

When they talked, they talked about him. Or about work. He usually didn't get into her business. Not that she minded.

She could see the bouquet in her peripheral vision. Austin was on her left side. The flowers sat on the right side of her desk, as if standing in proxy for Kevin.

"It's going well," she said cautiously, her hands poised on her computer keyboard, her heart thumping in her chest.

Please don't hassle me about Kevin and ruin it.

"Good." He nodded enthusiastically. "Good."

There was an awkward pause as she waited for him to get to the point.

Oh! Maybe he'd talked to Miles. He would've called her into his office if it was bad news or maybe he would've waited to broach it tonight at dinner. He was smiling at her. Maybe this was his way of delivering good news.

She pushed in her computer keyboard drawer and put her hands in her lap. "Did you talk to your dad?"

Austin's smile faltered. "No. But I did call him yesterday to set up a meeting. He's out of town. I figured it would be best if I talked to him about this in person. Peggy is not sure how long he'll be gone. It could be a week. It could be less. I'll get something on the books as soon as he gets back. I've been meaning to ask you... how is school going?"

Felicity blinked at the non sequitur.

"Fine. I'm all set for graduation. All I have to do is pass the finals."

He was nodding again, maintaining eye contact.

Those eyes. She could get lost in those eyes and happily never find her way back to reality.

"Felicity?"

Oh, God, had he asked her a question?

"I'm sorry, what?"

"I asked if your family was coming in for your graduation?"

"Well, my mom lives in New Orleans. So, she'll be there."

"I didn't realize your mom was local. What about your dad?"

Ugh. She should've seen that question coming. She should've headed it off before he'd had a chance to ask. She didn't like to talk about her dad.

"No, just my mom. And Maia. You know, my friend who owns the salon." She flipped her hair with her right hand and felt dumb for doing that. "She's the one who did this." She raked her hand through her hair and let it fall back into place. "For that hair show last week."

Those eyes were still on her. She didn't want to love it, because that's how she got hurt. But dammit, she did.

"Have you ever been to the restaurant R'evolution?"

"Is that the one over on Bienville Street?"

"That's the one. I made reservations for us."

Shut the front door. What?

First, he'd made a reservation for their dinner rather than just showing up somewhere and working his magic in person—or having *her* make the reservation. All she had to do was call any restaurant in town and say Austin Fortune would like a table. It didn't matter how far in advance the average person had to reserve a table, they would make room for Austin at a moment's notice, because he was Austin Fortune.

The fact that he'd made the reservation himself... Okay, she was not going to read anything more into that than...

Than what?

R'evolution was in the French Quarter, across Canal Street and down some ways from the Roosevelt Hotel. While it was in the general area of the hotel where they were having the ball, it was still a surprise. They could have easily just grabbed tapas in the hotel's Fountain Lounge. Or if Austin wanted to be fancy, they could've popped into Domenica, the Roosevelt's Italian restaurant.

She certainly wasn't complaining. She was too off-kilter for that.

"Is R'evolution okay?" he asked. "We can go somewhere else if you like."

"It's fabulous. I've always wanted to try it."

"It's a date, then."

Felicity bit the insides of her cheeks. Clearly, he had no idea what he just said. It wasn't a date. It was a business meeting...for which he'd made a reservation for two at a fabulous restaurant. But she wasn't going to point that out and embarrass him.

"I have a meeting," he was saying, "but I should be ready to go by 6:30. I thought we could leave the office and go to the Roosevelt and check out the space first. We should have plenty of time to make our 7:45 reservation."

"Oh, you were going to come back to the office?" she asked. "I'm looking after Maia's dogs while she's out of town this week. I need to go home and let them out. Should I meet you at the Roosevelt?"

"There's no sense trying to park two cars downtown," he said. "I'll swing by and pick you up at 6:30. Does that give you enough time to take care of the animals?"

She paused, waiting for him to say, *Just kidding.* But it wasn't like Austin to joke like that.

"Sure. 6:30, it is. I'll text you my address."

As he walked down the hall, Felicity watched him, feeling like she'd just entered the twilight zone.

Fifteen minutes later, she was jotting down questions for the rep at the Roosevelt and pondering the new dilemma—should she change clothes or wear the skirt and blouse she'd worn to work?—when her desk phone buzzed. It was Carla at the front desk.

"Hey, 'Liss, there's someone here for Austin. Her name is Macks Cole. She says she doesn't have an appointment, but she'd like to talk to him."

Felicity could hear her pulse in her ears. Macks was here? Her antenna had probably pricked up, warning her that another female was encroaching on her man.

"Tell her to have a seat. I'll be right there."

So, this time Macks had come to Felicity's door. Or actually, Austin's door was probably more accurate.

Felicity checked her posture and took a deep breath before she turned the corner into the reception area.

"Ms. Cole, hello. How may I help you?"

Macks pinned her with the same bemused expression she'd worn the other day when Felicity had shown up at her door. As if Felicity had greeted her speaking some sort of goo-goo-ga-ga baby-talk gibberish. Today she was wearing an all-black ensemble: skinny jeans, a fitted shell and an oversize, long-sleeve maxi cardigan that fell all the way to her ankles and looked butter-soft. Her feet were clad in patent leather platform sandals. Her makeup was minimal, except for black winged eyeliner and shiny, candy-apple red lip gloss coloring her perfect cupid's bow mouth.

She looked as if she'd just stepped off the runway of a Calvin Klein show at fashion week.

"Hello again, Felicity. I'm here to see Austin, please."

As if his sole purpose was to sit around the office, waiting for her to grace him with her presence.

"I'm sorry, he's in a meeting." Felicity eyed the white envelope in Macks's hands. "May I give him a message for you?"

Macks frowned. Her gaze darted around the reception area as if she didn't believe Felicity and expected to see him hiding behind a plant along the far wall.

"Will he be long? I'll wait."

"I'm afraid he'll be tied up for the rest of the afternoon. Is that for him?"

Felicity nodded at the envelope Macks was holding with both hands, as if reluctant to give it up.

"It is. It's an invitation to the opening of an art exhibition at my gallery."

Oh, so she owns a gallery. Okay. That explains the art in her apartment—and Mr. Erectus.

Felicity reached out to take the envelope. Macks didn't give it up.

With her outstretched hand, Felicity gestured to the invite. "I'll see that he gets it."

For a moment Felicity feared that Macks might decide to take the invitation with her and attempt delivery another time. Finally, she relinquished it.

"Thank you, Felicity." Macks's red lips tilted up in a tight-lipped smile. "Tell Austin I'm sorry I missed him."

As she watched the woman walk away, she couldn't help but wonder if Austin had taken it upon himself to book dinner reservations for himself and Macks, the same way he'd booked their dinner at R'evolution. She would never know. She'd better get used it, because once she left Fortune Investments, he'd likely be out of her life forever.

Chapter Five

Austin arrived at Felicity's house a few minutes earlier than he'd promised. He parked on the street and took a minute to take in the neat green double shotgun-style home with its symmetrical front porch decorated with darker green gingerbread embellishments, potted topiaries and hanging ferns.

Before tonight, he'd never really pictured where Felicity lived, but if he had, this would be the place. It was perfectly her. He let himself out of his red Tesla and in through the gate of the waist-high wrought iron fence that surrounded the tidy little front yard, then made his way up the brick path toward her front door. Hers was the left half, with the corresponding address in brass numbers above the threshold.

He glanced at his watch before knocking on the

door. He was a full ten minutes early. But her car was in the driveway and surely it couldn't take very long to do what she needed to do for Maia's dogs. If she wasn't ready to go, he could wait.

Tonight, patience and kindness were the key words.

"You're early," she said when she answered the door. Austin noticed she'd traded in her sleek black pencil skirt and pumps for a blue dress and strappy sandals.

"Sorry," he said, glancing around, taking in the nicely furnished living room. Its hardwood floors and brightly colored furniture added a feminine touch to the otherwise traditional room. It was on the tip of his tongue to tell her how nice she looked, but he reeled the words back in the nick of time. "We have time. Go ahead and finish whatever you were doing."

Although, he couldn't imagine that she needed to do anything else to herself because she looked gorgeous.

"No problem, but here." She handed him a pretty gold necklace. "Will you help me with this? It's difficult to put on by myself."

"Sure." As he put the necklace around the front of her, she held her hair up, allowing him a better look at the fine clasp on the piece of jewelry. He could also see the delicate curve of her neck, which was just long enough to be graceful, and the gentle sweep of her jawline. He leaned closer, trying with clumsy fingers to hook the necklace into place—it really would be difficult to manage alone. Not that he thought Felicity had ulterior motives.

Okay, maybe it had crossed his mind.

But then he got a whiff of her perfume, a delicate floral scent. It not only made him want to lean in closer and nuzzle her neck, claim that recess where neck flowed into collarbone, but for a split second, his mind blanked on all the reasons he shouldn't do it and his most primal urges took over.

Thank God he checked himself just in time.

What the hell was going on with him? What were these feelings? And what the hell was he supposed to do with them? As Felicity's boss, he could hardly put the moves on her to test them out.

He finally hooked the blasted necklace together and took a safe step back.

"Thanks." She let her hair loose and it cascaded down around her shoulders. His groin tightened, and he shifted his weight from one foot to another hoping to lessen the tension. "I just need to bring the dogs in. They're out in the backyard taking care of business. Do you want a drink? I have wine and beer in the fridge."

"Thanks, but I'm fine," he said as he followed her out the back door and down three steps to a bricked patio. The plants and flowers were lush and made him think of the book *The Secret Garden*, which his mom had read aloud to him and his siblings when they were younger. "Did you plant all this?"

Felicity beamed and stood up a little straighter, as if it were a point of pride. "I sure did. I love plants and flowers. Gardening is my therapy."

At the sound of her voice, three corgis bounded onto the patio from the yard. With their tongues lolling out the side of their mouths and the playful way they barked and bounced around each other, they reminded

Austin of a trio of tumbling court jesters. Exactly what he needed to lighted the mood.

"Someday, I'd love to put a greenhouse right over there." She pointed to a small section of yard past the patio. "That would be my idea of heaven." She bit her bottom lip. "And that probably makes me seem like I lead a very dull life."

"No, it doesn't," he said. "It makes you seem like you know what you like, like you're very connected to your home and the earth around it."

Her lips curved into a slight smile and her cheeks colored. Felicity of the sharp wit and no-nonsense demeanor suddenly looked vulnerable. He realized that she was very good at taking care of others—at taking care of him—but she wasn't used to being the focus.

"And that's a compliment, in case you were wondering," he added.

"Thank you. Taken as such."

This first glimpse inside her world only made him curious to know more.

Austin had been a good sport listening to her talk about her garden dreams. She felt a little foolish going on about it. The Fortunes had a staff of workers who tended the gardens of their beautiful Garden District mansion. A woman who liked to get her hands dirty was probably about as unattractive to Austin as it got. But he had been a good sport about it, complimentary and indulgent, actually.

At least she always made sure her fingernails were scrubbed clean. Maybe that was why he was so surprised to learn gardening was her hobby. Macks of the immaculate French manicure probably would think such an interest quite plebeian. Oh, well, it was her loss.

One thing Felicity never had trouble with was being herself. Even after being on the outside looking in to the glamorous world of Austin Fortune, she had never forgotten her place. Tonight, as she and Austin had walked the gorgeous, gilded ballroom of the Roosevelt Hotel checking and double-checking the details for the ball, she had never been more aware of her role as facilitator. She would attend the party, but she would be working. She would not be there to have fun or donate money to the cause or have any opportunity to forget exactly who she was and where she came from.

After the walkthrough, she reminded herself of that as she and Austin sat at a lovely table for two in a cozy corner of R'evolution.

It was a banquette-style table, a built-in semicircle covered in soft, tufted white leather, just big enough to make a cozy space for two people. The good part about the bench seating was it forced them to sit next to each other, which meant eye contact was optional and she might not completely give away her feelings for him. The bad part was it forced them to sit next to each other, which meant she could smell his cologne, an intoxicating scent that smelled expensive, with hints of cedar, coffee and leather.

She'd caught whiffs of his scent before as he passed by her desk or leaned in to hand her paperwork to process. But tonight, Austin sat with his body angled toward hers, first, talking business—about the final details they needed to firm up for the charity event, then venturing into the personal realm—asking her questions about herself, her past, her future.

Felicity was not used to having so much of his attention focused on her, which was a little uncomfortable. He was talking to her, learning about her like she'd hope a guy would if they were out on a date.

This is not a date.

After the server took their order, Felicity turned the tables on Austin, asking him questions that she would ask a date. Though she knew most of the answers, tonight he seemed different, an open book, his mood lighter, and she fully intended to mine him for what she could get. She was pleasantly surprised by how he opened right up and answered candidly.

"My sister Savannah—have you met her?"

"I did at one of the company picnics. She's the one who's going to school in Texas, right?"

"Yes, in Austin. She and her boyfriend are in town. I'm eager to see her. They're staying with my parents and they'll be here for the ball."

"It will be nice to see her again," Felicity said.

Felicity started to ask Austin if she should seat Savannah and her beau at his table or at their parents' table, but she stopped herself. If she turned the conversation back to work, it might break this delicate spell that seemed to be cast over the evening. Instead, she made a mental note to talk about seating charts when they were back in the office, which would happen soon enough. Too soon for her liking, in fact.

Why can't this night last forever?

That way, she wouldn't have to remind him about Macks's invitation, which she'd left on his desk to make sure that he saw it and didn't somehow push it aside.

As if he read her mind, he said, "Did Mackenzie Cole stop by this afternoon?"

A curse word that wasn't usually part of Felicity's vocabulary popped in her brain. They really were on the same wavelength tonight. But why did he have to pick up on her thoughts of Macks? Then again, maybe it was better that it was the Macks train of thought rather than the other, more private tidbits she'd been pondering.

Plus, this provided the perfect opportunity to do a little digging.

And he called her Mackenzie. Not Macks. Hmm... is that good or bad? Or does he only call her Macks in private? When it's just the two of them.

"Yes, she came by with an invitation for an art show opening. I put it on your desk."

"I saw it."

"Are you going? I mean, should I put it on your calendar?"

Her heart thudded in her chest as she waited for the moment of truth.

He shrugged, as if he hadn't even considered it. "It's a show at her gallery. I've never heard of the artist. So, I don't know if I'll go."

Inwardly, she cheered.

Felicity one. Macks zero.

"Yeah, maybe I will. It would be nice to support her."

Why does she need your support? She's the kind of woman who gets everything.

Felicity zero. Macks one million.

"She's pretty." Felicity figured she might as well go for broke and get to the heart of the matter.

"Is she?"

"Hello? Have you not met her? She's gorgeous."

Calm down. You're not trying to sell Austin on her.

"I have, but—"

"She seems like your type."

Is she your type, Austin?

Stepping this close to the edge and looking down on the truth gave her a strange sense of vertigo that made her feel vaguely dizzy and queasy.

The observation seemed to catch him off guard.

"My type? I'm not sure I have a type."

"I mean she's pretty and seems sophisticated and…"

He shrugged. "Yeah, well, even if she was my type, as you say, she's a prospective client. It might get weird."

Momentarily bolstered by Austin's seeming lack of interest in Macks, Felicity let herself daydream a moment, pretending that the people who were dining around them looked at Austin and her, sitting cozy in the corner and deep in conversation, and thought they were on a date. Or that they were a couple.

She tried to shut out the dissident voice in the back of her mind, warning herself not to get her hopes up, because it would be a long, hard fall if she was mistaken.

"Finally! It's about time I get to see my big brother." Standing just inside the foyer, where the elevator

opened into Austin's Central Business District pent-
house condo, Savannah Fortune threw her arms around
Austin. "You'd better have a good reason for not being
at Mom and Dad's last night and it better have to do
with a woman."

"Yeah, well, not everyone is as lucky as you two
lovebirds." Austin turned to Savannah's boyfriend,
Chaz Mendoza, and offered a handshake.

"Chaz, good to see you, man."

Chaz gripped Austin's hand and clapped him on the
back. Then he moved back to Savannah's side, putting
an arm around her waist. The two of them appeared so
happily in love they were virtually glowing.

Austin ushered them inside, went to the kitchen and
brought back three IPAs.

"Does anyone want a beer stein? I have some in
the freezer."

"No, I'm good," the couple said in unison. They sat
on the couch so close to each other, legs touching, pos-
sessive hands on each other's thighs, that they almost
seemed to have morphed into one being.

Austin was glad to see his sister so happy.

As the trio sipped their beers, they chatted about
life, catching up on the small things that mattered: how
school was going for Savannah; what was new at the
Mendoza Winery, where Chaz worked as their security specialist in addition to doing independent security
work; the latest happenings at Fortune Investments;
and what was happening in the search for the person
or people that had been terrorizing the extended Fortune family.

"I'm glad you're living with Chaz." Austin held up a hand to stop his sister from going on a tirade about how she was perfectly capable of taking care of herself. "Not that you can't handle yourself, but I can't help but worry about you after what happened."

Savannah shrugged. Much to Austin's surprise, she looked resigned to not putting up a fight. It was amazing how she'd mellowed after the break-in and her subsequent move-in with Chaz.

"I feel safer living with him," she said. "That way, I don't have to worry about either of us. After all, the Mendozas have been longtime friends of the Fortunes and several members of the Mendoza family have married Fortunes. Who says their family won't be next? But anyway, all signs still point to Charlotte Prendergast Robinson being the culprit." Savannah shook her head. "Have you heard the latest developments in the search for her?"

"No, what's going on?" Austin sipped his beer and leaned forward, eager to hear the update.

"From what we've heard—and this is from a reliable source—Kate Fortune is calling in all her favors and has used her influence to track down Charlotte. Kate is being merciless." As the matriarch of the Fortune family, Kate Fortune had a vested interest in protecting her relatives and she had the resources to do it. "Everyone is expecting Charlotte to be brought in for questioning any day now."

"Any day now?" Austin asked. "That means she's still out there. Why hasn't she been found yet?"

"It's not that easy," Chaz said. "She's pretty slippery.

From what I hear she knows we're on to her, which sent her deeper into hiding."

"Good," Austin said. "Maybe she'll stay in her cave and leave us the hell alone."

"We hope so, too," Chaz said. "Unfortunately, she seems to pride herself on catching us off guard. She lulls us into a state of complacency and then she strikes again. Savannah and I are not getting complacent. Not after what she did to Savannah's apartment. We're lucky Savannah wasn't there when she broke in. If she had been, who knows how it would've turned out."

"You're not considering going back to your apartment, are you?"

"Nope. Not unless he kicks me out." She smiled up at Chaz, who pulled her in closer.

"Not if I have anything to say about it," he said. "Not even after that woman is behind bars where she belongs."

They played kissy face for a minute, cooing at each other and giving pecks on the lips.

"God, you two. Get a room, will you?"

Inexplicably, Austin's mind flashed back to last night with Felicity. He had as easy a rapport with her as Savannah had with Chaz. Only things seemed so much less complicated for his sister and her boyfriend. Why did the situation have to be so damn difficult with Felicity? If not, last night when he'd walked her to up to the door, he would've leaned in and sampled those lips to see if they were as delicious as they looked. But he'd managed to shove his hands in his pockets and keep a respectable amount of space between them. All in the name of propriety. And not making her uncomfortable.

And, of course, because he was her boss, there was the issue of sexual harassment. But would it be so if they were both willing participants? The trickiest part about it was not to assume he knew how she felt about it. To not let himself get so carried away with the moment that he totally read all her signals wrong. Of course, the easiest way would just be to ask. But "do you mind if I kiss you?" would be just about the most unromantic way that he could think of to profess his feelings.

And what were his feelings? Other than suddenly being overcome with the knowledge that he didn't want her out of his life, he didn't know what else he was feeling.

That was why it wouldn't be fair to Felicity to open that Pandora's box.

And, of course, that meant no kissing her just to see what it was like.

"So, where were you last night?" Savannah asked. "You never answered my question."

"You never asked," Austin said.

"I did so. I said, 'You'd better have a good reason for not being at Mom and Dad's last night and it better have to do with a woman.'"

For a fleeting second, Austin thought about saying he'd been with Felicity, but Savannah knew Felicity and since Felicity was a beautiful woman, his sister would take that and run all kinds of ways with it.

"I had a business dinner."

"Well, that sounds boring."

Austin shrugged as he took a sip of his beer.

Actually, it was one of the more enjoyable business meetings I've had in a while. One of the more enjoyable evenings, in fact.

Thrown off the scent, Savannah changed the subject. "This is such a great condo, Austin. Who decorated it for you? Surely, you didn't do it yourself."

"No, I hired that designer Mom uses every once in a while."

For the most part, their mother, Sarah, decorated the family home herself. She had great taste, a generous budget and the time to shop for just the right pieces to achieve the desired look. If she couldn't find it herself, that's when she called in a professional.

"It hardly looks lived in. Does that mean you're spending most of your time at the office?"

He glanced around at the stark beige and chrome furniture and fixtures. He'd been meaning to frame some family photos to add a more personal touch to the space, but he hadn't gotten around to it. He'd bought the place because of the proximity to work and the million-dollar view of Lafayette Square. Given the fact that he really did only sleep there, it wasn't surprising that it didn't look lived in. Austin shrugged. "Duty calls."

"All work and no play will make Austin a very dull boy," Savannah said. "You know you're not getting any younger. When are you going to settle down?"

"Gee, thanks for the reminder, sis."

On one hand, she was right. At thirty-two, he wasn't getting any younger. However, he was in the prime of his business life. Besides, he'd already tried married life and it hadn't worked out.

"Been there, done that, not going back again," he said. "I learned the hard way that I'm just not cut out for marriage."

"Do I need to stage an intervention? Or a round of speed dating to get you out there in the dating world? I really think you just haven't met the right woman yet."

"Even if I did meet *the one*," Austin said, "it wouldn't be fair to get involved with someone who was looking for something as serious as marriage, because I'm married to Fortune Investments."

Which is why Felicity and I work so well. She understands my career. She's like my work wife.

As if the grace of God had staged an intervention, Austin's door buzzer sounded, indicating someone was downstairs. He had no idea who it was, but he was grateful to them for providing an interruption.

He excused himself and went to the intercom on the wall by the elevator. "Yes?"

"Hey, Austin, it's Felicity. I'm so sorry to bother you. I know you're spending time with your sister, but I have some papers that need your signature. They're time sensitive and need to be in today. Do you want me to come up or will you come down and sign them?"

Felicity hated to intrude. Austin and his sister were close, and Felicity knew he didn't get to see her as often as he liked. That's why when she visited, he took a rare day off. The last thing he needed was for Felicity to barge in, distracting him with work-related issues. She wouldn't have bothered him if this hadn't been time sensitive.

In the elevator on the way to the top floor of Austin's building, Felicity took a deep breath and checked her posture. She was glad she'd worn a simple, black, sleeveless dress and black slide sandals. She anchored the file folder with the papers under her arm and smoothed the skirt with her palms. It was a comfortable outfit but still looked pulled together enough to feel good about this impromptu visit and seeing Austin's sister again.

It wasn't the first time she had been in his condo. In fact, she stopped by several times a week, on the evenings when Austin worked through dinner, to pick up the meals Derek, his personal chef, prepared for him and left in the kitchen's warming drawer. But it was the first time she had been in the condo with him at home.

The elevator doors opened, and Felicity gripped the folder with both hands and stepped into the foyer.

"We're in the living room," Austin called. "Come on in."

Austin, Savannah and a good-looking guy she hadn't yet met all looked up expectantly as she entered the room. They were all holding beer bottles and looking quite content.

Austin stood.

"Felicity!" Savannah handed her beer to the guy she was sitting next to and jumped up to greet her with a warm hug that made her feel as if she was her long-lost best friend. "I'm so glad I got to see you on this trip. It's been too long. Chaz, this is Felicity Schafer. Aus-

tin would be lost without her. Seriously, he wouldn't
know his next move without her. Felicity, this is my
boyfriend, Chaz Mendoza."

After she and Chaz exchanged pleasantries, Savannah took Felicity by the hand and led her over to the
space on the couch next to Austin. "Sit down and join
us. Can I get you a beer?"

"Thank you, but I'm just here for Austin to sign papers. I wouldn't have bothered him with it, but I have to
scan them and send them off before the end of the day."

Felicity glanced at Austin to gage his reaction. She
wanted to stay—even if it was only for a minute, but
she didn't want to intrude.

"Join us," he said. "Please."

His invitation spawned a crop of goose bumps on her
arms. She ran her hands, envelope and all, over them.

"Savannah, get her a beer," he said. "You do like
beer, don't you?"

Savannah and Chaz disappeared into the kitchen
before she could decline.

"Is that okay?" she asked. "I don't want to be rude
to your sister by refusing, but I hate to intrude on your
time together." She held her breath. In a way, it felt as
if she was testing the vibes she'd felt last night at dinner, but everything felt a little off-kilter.

"Sit down," Austin said. "It's fine."

Discreetly, she inhaled a deep breath. Right now, a
beer and some time with Austin sounded exactly like
what she was craving.

She lowered herself onto the edge of the couch.
Austin was sitting on the middle cushion. She sat next

to him, leaving a respectable amount of space between them.

"Do you want to sign these now?" She held out the file. "It would be just like me to have a beer and go off without you signing them."

He smiled at her in that way that made her wonder what he was thinking. "Then you'd have to come back and have another beer and you probably wouldn't make it back to the office." He smiled, and her heart melted a little more.

"Great, thanks for reminding me," she said. "If anyone at the office smells beer on my breath, I'll need you to tell them it was okay."

"If anyone questions you, just send them to me."

"Even your dad?"

"He's out of town, remember?" Austin said with a grin.

Felicity's stomach knotted, but that's when Savannah and Chaz came back into the room. As Savannah stood in front of her offering her the beer, she looked back and forth between Felicity and Austin with a knowing expression on her face.

"Thank you," Felicity said. She accepted the beverage that Savannah had poured into a frosty mug.

"Maybe it would be a good idea for me to sign the papers now," Austin said, seemingly oblivious to his sister's smile. He took the file and used the pen Felicity had clipped to the front of the folder, wanting to be prepared in case he had wanted to meet her down in the lobby to sign. "Do you have the email address where they need to go?"

"Yes, it's on a sticky note on the inside of the cover."

Austin checked and tapped it with his finger. "Be right back."

"Are you sure you don't want me to do that for you?" Felicity asked. She knew there was a scanner in his home office. It was the same model they used in the FI office. "I'd be happy to."

Austin waved away her offer. "I've got this. Relax and enjoy your beer."

After Austin was out of the room, Savannah asked, "How long have you been with Fortune Investments now, Felicity?"

"It's been almost five years."

"Has it really been that long? I remember when you started. Seems like yesterday."

"Seems that way to me, too."

"Does that brother of mine treat you all right?"

"Austin's a great boss," Felicity said. "How many bosses take their assistants to dinner at a place like R'evolution? Are you familiar with that restaurant?"

Savannah's eyes widened as she nodded. "Of course. It's a great place. Very romantic."

Yes, it was. Very.

But she didn't admit that to Savannah. "Well, I don't know about that."

"When were you there?"

"Last night."

Savannah's eyes lit up and Felicity got the feeling that she'd just revealed something she shouldn't have. Suddenly, she felt like she was swimming in water way beyond her depth.

"When were you where?" Austin asked, returning to the living room.

Felicity turned and saw him standing behind her holding the folder of documents he'd scanned and emailed. Her cheeks warmed. She hadn't heard him enter the room. How much of the conversation had he overheard and what did he think of her talking to Savannah about their dinner last night?

That Savannah was a wily one. She seemed to have a talent for getting people to talk about things they shouldn't. Felicity didn't believe Savannah was doing this out of malice, but the air in the room had definitely changed.

"I was just asking Felicity if she'd like to join us for family dinner tonight."

Felicity's heart leaped into her throat. Then, when she saw the look of utter horror on Austin's face, it plunged into her stomach.

"You did what?" he said.

"You heard me. Dad's out of town. Things will be a little more casual tonight. Why not bring her to dinner? Mom would love to have her join us."

He turned to Felicity and before she even heard what he had to say, one thought flew into her head: *Oh, dear God, just kill me now.*

"Felicity, please allow me to apologize on behalf of my sister. I know you have much more important things to do than to endure a Fortune family dinner." He pinned Savannah with a pointed look. "Believe me, if I had the choice, I wouldn't go tonight."

Felicity was usually pretty good at reading a situation and knowing what to do. But this felt weird, as if she was looking at it as she swam under water with her eyes open. The best thing she could do right now would be to leave. She didn't understand what was happening between Austin and his sister, but he was clearly not happy about Savannah issuing an invitation to dinner. And why had she done that? She hadn't even brought it up until Austin entered the room. Clearly, the invitation was meant to rankle him.

And it had.

This was Felicity's cue to bow out gracefully before things got more awkward. She needed to excuse herself and leave.

"Thank you for thinking of me, Savannah, but I have plans this evening." She glanced at her watch. "In fact, I should leave now so I can get back to the office and button up a few things before I call it a day. Chaz, it was so nice to meet you. I'll probably see both of you at the ball."

Savannah made disappointed noises, but she didn't try to convince her to stay.

Felicity dared a glance at Austin, who was still holding the folder with the signed documents and frowning at a spot somewhere over Felicity's left shoulder.

"If you're finished with that, I'll take it back to the office," she said. It seemed to snap him out of his trance. He handed her the folder.

"All right, you all have a good night."

As she walked to the door, Austin walked with her. She had the feeling he had something to say, and she wasn't sure she wanted to hear it, especially if he was going to take issue with her telling Savannah about their dinner at R'evolution.

It was a business dinner. I get it. Even if Savannah was waxing on about it being oh so romantic, I didn't join in. Besides, you chose the restaurant.

"I hope Kevin knows how lucky he is," Austin said in a low voice, his left hand braced on the frame around the elevator.

Wait. What?

"I know I've already said this, but it bears repeating. He'd better not mistreat you."

Did he think when she said she had plans tonight that she had a date with Kevin?

She bit her bottom lip as she racked her brain for a way to tell him her plans were actually with Maia, who had just gotten back from her trip and wanted to take her to dinner in appreciation for her taking care of the corgis.

But there was that vibe again. That slight hint of… what? Jealousy?

Maybe she was way off base, but why else would he have such a bad reaction to a guy he'd never met? Yet, the minute his sister suggested he bring her to the family dinner tonight, he acted as if Savannah had suggested he elope with Felicity.

Clearly, Austin didn't want her, but he had a real problem with the thought of Kevin having her.

Maybe it would be good for Austin to stew a little bit.

Let him think I'm seeing Kevin tonight. It might give him pause and make him take stock of what he wants.

Chapter Six

"What the hell is wrong with you, Savannah?" Austin fumed after he walked back into the living room after showing Felicity to the door.

"No, Austin, what the hell is wrong with you?" Savannah countered. "Felicity is a beautiful woman. I was just trying to make it easier on you to ask her out."

Austin gave his head a sharp shake. "You can't just invite someone to Mom and Dad's on a whim like that," he said. "Especially if it's to further this matchmaking game of yours. For your information, I have eyes. I can see that Felicity is a beautiful woman. She's also my assistant. You're barking up the wrong tree. I can't even act remotely interested in her because I'm her boss. Having a little fun with my assistant is a fast track to a sexual harassment lawsuit. Are you trying to bankrupt the family business? Because it sure seems that way."

Savannah shook her head. "I'm not buying it. I think the whole boss-employee thing is a convenient excuse. Because it's not the fact that you aren't interested in her, you're not interested in *anybody* or *anything* except work, and if you're not careful, you're going to work yourself into an early grave. I love you too much to stand by and watch you do that to yourself. You have to stop being such a grump and loosen up. At least allow yourself to have a little fun."

He crossed his arms over his chest, a protective armor. "Are you finished?"

Savannah blinked at him. "No, I'm not finished. Are you kidding?"

"Well, I'm not either," Austin said. "Your 'have fun' prescription is good in theory, but not everyone has the same idea of *fun*."

"Fair enough," Savannah conceded. "What is your idea of fun, then?"

"Well, it's certainly not taking the afternoon off work to fight with my sister. Talk about someone needing to loosen up. Are you playing the role of pot or kettle today?"

Savannah smirked and waved away his question with a flick of her wrist. "Okay, here's my idea of fun: I want to take Chaz to Bourbon Street. He's never seen it. Why don't you come with us and ask Felicity to join you?"

"Did you hear a word I said?" Austin asked.

"I did. And did you hear me say I'm not buying it?

You get this look on your face when you're with her. The chemistry between you is so strong, it should have its own element on the periodic table."

"I think you're mistaking a good working relationship with something romantic. As I said, I can hardly have 'a little fun' with my personal assistant. I'll be real with you—she is the best thing that's ever happened to me, but not in the way you think. It's purely platonic. Besides, she's seeing someone."

He thought of her going out with Kevin Clooney again tonight. What was this, their third or fourth date? Not that he'd been counting. He couldn't help but notice because something seemed to remind him of it every time he turned around.

And he hated it.

Savannah was watching him again, sizing him up. "Do you realize you were in such a good mood until Felicity mentioned that she has plans tonight?"

"No, I was in a good mood until you took it upon yourself to invite her to dinner tonight. You put me in the middle of a very embarrassing situation."

Savannah started to protest again. Austin held up his hand. There was no use in rehashing the same argument again, which was what was about to happen unless he circumnavigated it.

"Would you get off my back and drop this Felicity crusade if I agree to go on a date?"

Savannah's face lit up and her mouth dropped open.

"Not with Felicity," he hastened to add. "I can see what you were thinking. I'll ask someone to go to Bourbon Street with me, you and Chaz. Someone who is not Felicity."

He was going to ask Macks Cole. Why not? He wasn't serious about dating Macks, but essentially, it would serve two purposes: It would allow him to get his sister off his back, and it would be good for client relations.

It was a total win-win.

Why did he feel so empty?

"Your father sends his best wishes." Sarah Fortune glanced around her dining room table, smiling at her children, Austin, Georgia, Belle, Beau, Draper and Savannah. All of her kids were present, except for Nolan, who was in Texas. "Your dad wishes he could be here tonight. Savannah and Chaz, he specifically asked me to reiterate that he is looking forward to spending time with you in a few days when he gets home. This merger he's working on has taken a lot out of him. That and the Charlotte Robinson incidents have him so stressed out, he's wound tighter than a clock."

"He shouldn't worry so much." Savannah said, as she pushed a bite of roast chicken into her peas, sending them tumbling into the untouched mountain of mashed potatoes. "He especially shouldn't worry about the wedding. It will be fine."

"I'm sure it will be beautiful," Sarah said. "I hope Gerald and Deborah will share photos."

"Why photos?" Savannah asked. "You're going, aren't you?"

Austin tried to catch his sister's eye, but she was

transfixed on their mother. He wanted to kick himself for not preparing his sister for this when she came over that afternoon.

Sarah shook her head. "Your father is adamantly opposed to our attending the wedding. Because of everything that's happened, it's just not safe. We decided this at last week's family dinner. I suppose I should've told you sooner, but I knew you were coming for a visit and I thought I'd tell you in person."

Savannah and Chaz exchanged a look.

"What?" asked Sarah. "What was that look about?"

Savannah cleared her throat. "Chaz and I have already RSVP'd that we will be there. It would be rude to back out this close to the wedding, since it's only a month away."

Sarah frowned. "It's six weeks away. There's still plenty of time to send your regrets if you do it soon."

Savannah's mouth pinched into a pucker, a sure sign she was about to deliver news that wouldn't please their mother. "I understand your concern, but if I can live through my apartment being vandalized and still feel brave enough to go, I'd hope my immediate family could be courageous enough to come with me and support our extended family."

Sarah flinched, and Austin knew it was time to step in.

"Savannah," Austin said, "we understand where you're coming from, but I hope you'll listen to what we have to say. It's important."

"So, our family has sides now? All of you against Chaz and me?"

"Don't be that way," Austin said. "Charlotte Robinson has proven herself to be a dangerous woman who will stop at nothing to get revenge on the Fortunes. The divorce from Gerald and his upcoming wedding to Deborah have no doubt set her off and made her bitter toward our entire family. I think we haven't heard the last from her. I believe she's not going to stop until she makes a big statement, and what better place to do that than at her ex-husband's wedding?"

Savannah made a dubious sound. "Well, I believe they're going to catch her before the wedding. We've already talked about this, Austin. I don't understand why you're doing an about-face now."

"Talked about what?" Sarah asked.

Savannah turned back to her mother. "I forgot to tell you this last night, but I mentioned it to Austin earlier today. Kate Fortune is sick of Charlotte's shenanigans and she has made it her mission to put an end to all the craziness. She is determined to find the woman and see her arrested and locked up. I'll bet that Charlotte will be in jail by the time the wedding rolls around. I mean with Kate on it, you know it's bound to happen. And you know Gerald isn't just huddled in a corner quaking with fear. Not when his wedding is on the line. You know he's got to be doing everything he can to make sure his wedding day isn't ruined."

"She's not behind bars yet," Sarah said. "I wouldn't be surprised if she laid low until the wedding, so she could go out with a bang."

"Okay, I'll make a deal with you," Savannah said.

"If Charlotte is still on the loose by the time the wedding happens next month, I won't go."

"What are you going to do?" Beau asked. "Just not show up? That's worse than canceling now. If you bowed out now, at least you'd give them a chance to notify the caterer and they won't get stuck paying for your meal."

Belle narrowed her eyes. "I think Savannah has a point. Do you really think Gerald will go through with the wedding if Charlotte is still on the loose?"

No one answered. Even though Gerald was their half uncle, they really didn't know him very well. What they did know had come from news stories about how he had grown his garage-based computer company in to a billion-dollar empire. Though Gerald was a self-made man like their dad, Miles Fortune preferred to keep a more private profile. Another way the half brothers differed was that Gerald appeared to be a cutthroat business mogul who looked out for only himself, or, at least, that's the way the media had painted him.

It was difficult to know whether or not the guy would look out for the greater good and postpone his wedding if Charlotte was still at large.

"Have you ever considered that Charlotte is terrorizing us right now?" Savannah countered. "She has us living scared, ready to give up something we want to do because we are frightened of her. If we don't go, we're playing right into her hands. She will have won."

"Sounds like we're damned if we do and damned if we don't," said Draper. "If we don't go, she'll win by keeping us away. If we do go and she manages to blow us all up, she'll win and we will die."

Sarah shoved her chair back from the table. The sound of the wood scraping the floor echoed in the dining room as she stood. "I don't want to talk about this anymore," she demanded. "It's far too upsetting. It's not often that I have most of my children together. I am not going to let that crazy woman rob me of this night. So, I'm going into the kitchen to get dessert. When I come back, let's please talk about something more pleasant. While I'm gone, would someone clear the table and make room for the next course?"

After their mother left the room, Draper and Georgia stood and started moving the dinner plates to a tray on a stand positioned next to the sideboard. The other siblings sat in stunned silence amid the sound of clinking china and flatware.

Finally, Beau brought his hands together in a single clap. "Well, that was fun."

Austin shot his brother a look. "Mom and Dad have decided that the family is going to sit this one out," he said.

Savannah pounded her flat palms on the table. "What makes them think they can speak for us?" she asked. "The last time I checked, we were adults. I'm sorry that they'll be disappointed, but Chaz and I are going to the wedding whether they like it or not. We are adults—as are each and every one of you. Mom and Dad need to understand that they don't get to make decisions for us anymore."

Austin's mind bounced back to Felicity and his tan-

gled feelings that were wrapped around Fortune Investments' no-fraternizing policy and the debacle of all
that had happened with his marriage and subsequent
divorce. He wasn't letting his parents decide whether
or not he could explore a more personal relationship
with Felicity.

He had weighed both sides. On the one side, Fortune
Investment could lose a good employee and potentially
get slapped with a harassment suit, though that didn't
seem like Felicity's style. On the other side were all
these strange feelings that had suddenly stirred in his
heart after all these years. With Kelly, he had jumped
before he weighed all the dangers. Not anymore. This
time the negatives weighed heavier than the positives,
warning him that getting involved with Felicity would
end badly for everyone.

Sarah returned with a mile-high chocolate cake.
"Will someone help me, please, and get the coffee
while I serve the cake?"

Savannah and Austin both stood. Without another
word, they walked into the kitchen. "I can't wait to get
out of here and go to the French Quarter before I say or
do irreparable damage to my relationship with Mom.
She is so freaked out about this. But the parents and I
are going to have to agree to disagree on this because
I'm going to the wedding."

"So, you're set on going, then?" Austin asked.

It wasn't optimal, but he was confident enough in
the strength of their family bond to know that even if
Savannah did break rank and attend the wedding, her
relationship with their parents might be strained for a

while but the family bond wouldn't be broken. In fact, there was very little any of them could do to cause that kind of damage. Their bond was that strong.

Savannah nodded. "We can't live scared, Austin. Otherwise, it's not much of a life. You could apply the same philosophy to your dating life. You can't let Kelly keep you from finding love. Otherwise, she wins in a big way. Even though you say you have no feelings for her, essentially, she's holding your heart hostage. You need to adopt my credo and refuse to negotiate with terrorists, which essentially describes Kelly, and absolutely describes Charlotte."

"Yeah, well, let's leave my dating life out of this," he said. "Kelly is not holding my heart hostage. Just as you draw boundaries with Mom, I've drawn them with Kelly. And now I'm drawing them with you."

He smiled at her in a way that showed he meant business but that he wasn't mad at her. Savannah had always been a feisty one. Austin resisted the urge to ask her how often she'd been in the position to negotiate with terrorists, as she'd put it. He also curbed the urge to ask her why she was so hell-bent on attending the wedding of this newfound family member at the risk of upsetting her immediate family, but that would only get her more riled up and make her more determined to go.

"We'll see how it goes," Austin said, realizing the generalization could apply to both the Charlotte situation and his dating life. "In the meantime, let's eat dessert in peace, so we can leave things on good terms with mom. Then you can blow off some steam on Bourbon Street. I can't stay long because I have a long day tomorrow."

"But you're still bringing a date tonight, right?" Savannah asked, as she poured coffee into cups on a tray. "I'm not pressuring you. But you did say you would."

"I don't know that I'd call her a *date*. She's more of a business acquaintance, but that's one of the reasons I came into the kitchen. I am going to call her now."

Savannah's eyes lit up. "If calling her a business acquaintance makes you feel better, go for it. I'm proud of you for putting yourself out there. Though, if I'm completely honest, I wish you would've asked Felicity. I just like you two together. Your chemistry lights up a room."

Austin shrugged. Even if he wanted to ask Felicity to join them, he couldn't. "Felicity has plans tonight."

"That's too bad." Savannah lifted the tray. "It just goes to show you. If you snooze, you lose. But I'll get out of here, so you can make your call."

She bumped open the kitchen door with her backside, leaving him alone to phone Macks. He dialed her number before he could change his mind. She answered on the fourth ring, just as Austin had begun to anticipate the call sailing over to voice mail.

"This is Macks." Her tone was brusque.

"Hello, Macks. It's Austin Fortune."

"Well, hello there, Austin Fortune. To what do I owe this wonderful surprise?"

Her tone had changed. Where it had been all business and efficiency when she'd answered the phone, now she was virtually purring warmth and enthusiasm. Maybe this wasn't such a good idea after all. But it was too late to change his mind now.

"I know this is last-minute, but my sister and her boyfriend are in town. Chaz has never seen Bourbon Street. We are heading down there this evening for a drink, and I wanted to invite you to join us."

The silence on the other end of the line lasted so long, he wondered if they'd lost their connection.

"Bourbon Street? Thank you for thinking of me, but no. I don't think so, Austin. That's not really my scene."

Not her scene? He bit back a laugh. As if it was anyone's *scene*. Bourbon Street was a rite of passage, a been-there-done-that sort of thing you checked off the list, or something you endured when visitors came to town and they wanted to see it, which was the case with Chaz. For a split second, Austin was tempted to tell her as much, but it just felt exhausting. Bourbon Street certainly wasn't his scene, and, he realized, someone as seemingly high maintenance as Macks wasn't either.

Since his divorce, he'd found dating in general to take too much time and energy. But, he reminded himself, he wasn't trying to date Macks. She was a business acquaintance, and that alone helped him keep his retort to himself.

"I completely understand. Have a nice evening, Macks."

"Oh, Austin," she said before she could disconnect the call. "Did you get a chance to consider the invitation I gave to Felicity for you? It's to the opening of a show for one of my clients."

"Felicity mentioned it, but I was out of the office and

didn't get a chance to look at the details. I will when I am at my desk tomorrow, and I will let you know."

"That sounds wonderful, darling," she purred. "I do hope you can make it. I'd love to see you. Just not on Bourbon Street."

As Maia drained the pasta, Felicity refilled their wineglasses waiting atop the kitchen island. Maia's three corgis, Honey, Buddy and Jasmine, played in the living room, which was visible from the kitchen of the open concept house.

"Start from the beginning and tell me everything," Maia insisted.

Felicity did a quick rundown of everything that had happened since Kevin had sent her flowers.

"To me, it sounds like Austin is jealous," Maia said. "That means you either need to tell him how you feel, or you need to put him in the past."

As if it were that easy. She would've forgotten about Austin a long time ago if she could.

"Let me back up," Maia said. "Do you like Kevin? Because it sure sounds like he likes you."

Kevin was fine. But did she like him? That was a loaded question. She certainly didn't have anything against him. Although, at times he came across a little pushy. He kept saying he wanted to pick her up at the office and take her somewhere. She didn't want him to come to the office because if he did, judging by the way Austin had been acting, Austin might not like it very much.

On one hand, why shouldn't she be able to have

dates pick her up at the office? As long as it was after hours and didn't interfere with her work. Austin had no business telling her what she could and couldn't do with her own time. And Macks had brought that invitation to the office for him. Granted, he wasn't there, and Felicity had no idea what was going on between the two of them—

"Hello! Felicity, where did you go?"

"I'm here. I have a lot on my mind."

"Stay present, girlfriend. You spend too much time in your head. *Kevin.* I asked you if you like Kevin. Because if you like him, you are going to lose him if you keep mooning over the Beast, who I don't think is nearly good enough for you."

Felicity rolled her eyes. Of course Maia would think that. To say she wasn't fond of Austin was an understatement.

"You are acting as if this is my final answer. As if I have to commit or lose out on love for the rest of my life. I am not ready to choose right now. I like Kevin— as in he is a perfectly nice guy. I am not in love with Kevin, and I'm certainly not at a place where I am going to forsake all others for him."

"I didn't say you had to do that. I just don't want him to get frustrated with you."

"Did you ever consider that if Kevin is that impatient, maybe he's not the guy for me?"

Maia offered Felicity a conceding one-shoulder shrug.

"All I can say is I'm not in a place to commit to anyone and I don't know if or when I will be."

Felicity's thoughts drifted back to the evening at R'evolution and the easy conversation with Austin. She wasn't ready to share that with Maia. Because for all of her friend's good intentions, she did tend to take things out of context and run with them. In Maia's world, a romantic dinner could only mean that Austin was interested and therefore Felicity should bear her soul. But if she tacked on Macks Cole and included what happened this afternoon at Austin's condo, when Savannah's invitation had pushed Austin back into his shell, Maia's cut-and-dried interpretation would be that she should forget him.

Felicity only wished she could. Because life would be so much easier.

Chapter Seven

Felicity sensed Austin approaching before he got to her desk. It was funny how she could do that. It was as if she had a sixth sense and could feel his energy before she even saw him or heard him approaching.

This morning he was walking with a white envelope or card in his hands. It was the same size and shape of the one Macks had dropped off. A sense of dread lodged in her stomach.

"Sorry to interrupt. Would you please put the art show that Macks Cole invited me to on my calendar?"

He handed her the card.

"Sure. Happy to." *Liar.* "Would you like me to make a dinner reservation for two before the show?"

He squinted at her as if she had asked him a question in a foreign language. "A dinner reservation? No.

That's not necessary. Most likely, I'm just going to drop in as a courtesy."

A courtesy? That was very encouraging. She would take him being courteous to Macks over him having a date with her anytime.

As she called up Austin's calendar to add the date, the dread that had weighed down her insides a moment ago changed to something much lighter that she couldn't quite identify, but it wasn't bad.

"When I talked to her last night, I told her I'd stop by. The show is at her gallery. She wouldn't have time to go to dinner."

And just like that, the not-so-bad feeling was smashed by the wrecking ball that swung through her middle.

So, they talked last night. *How cozy.*

She took care to keep a neutral expression on her face. She certainly didn't need to give herself away now, even if she was feeling crushed by disappointment. She didn't know why she felt the need to test the waters further. But she did.

"I don't recall Macks's name being on the invitation list for the gala. Should I send her an invitation?"

Austin seemed to consider her question for a moment.

"No, don't send her an invitation. That seems too formal. I'll ask her myself."

Austin had no idea why he'd said he would ask Macks to the ball when he had no intention of doing so. Actually, that was a lie. He had wanted to see if Felicity would react.

As he sat down at his desk, he scrubbed his eyes with his palms. She'd offered no reaction. Sure, he was going to stop by the gallery, but he had never even been on a date with Macks. The one time he'd asked her to get together, she had made it clear that she liked things on her own terms. The last thing he needed to worry about at something as important as the FI charity gala was a high-maintenance date. For a moment he regretted not having Felicity send Macks an invitation to attend on her own. The woman had money and he would be remiss in turning down her donation for their charity, much less the cost of a ticket. Maybe he would hand deliver the invitation himself, just as Macks had delivered the invitation to the art opening. She could bring her own date, just not him.

When Kevin called, he'd caught Felicity at a weak moment. He'd texted her about an hour after she'd put Macks's art event on Austin's calendar and had been stewing on the thought of Austin taking Macks to the ball. It was one thing to think, in abstract, of Austin dating Macks, but to have to watch them together at an event she had to attend… Well, that sounded like cruel and unusual punishment. Utter torture.

That's why when Kevin asked her to go to dinner that evening she said yes. On any other night she would've declined. But tonight, she had absolutely nothing going on, except plans to brood over Austin's interest in Macks. And how next to gorgeous, willowy, sophisticated Macks, Felicity felt like a hairy chimp—despite having every waxable region of her body serviced.

So, in a split second, she'd weighed the pros and cons of seeing Kevin tonight. And now he was picking her up at the office at 6:30.

She stole a surreptitious glance at Austin and her heart melted a little. She couldn't help it. His hair was a little longer than it should be because a meeting had preempted the hair appointment she'd made for him and he'd said he was too busy this week. But his hair was exactly the length she liked because after he raked his hands through it, as was his habit when he was focusing on something important, it got mussed and she'd decided that's exactly what he would look like when he woke up first thing in the morning. Felicity blinked away the thought, smiling secretly to herself. He was wearing a blue shirt and a navy tie. It was a great color on him. But, come to think of it, had she really seen him in a color that didn't look good?

Your sister approves of me, even if you don't think of me as anything more than an employee.

That's when he suddenly looked up and caught her in a full-on mooning daydream. She was too deep in her trance to look away quickly before he caught her. So, he caught her staring at him, with her elbow on her desk and her cheek resting on her hand. The only thing missing from the picture was her doodling his name on a notebook while cartoon hearts and flowers danced over her head.

He gave her a little wave, which was humiliating, and, of course, meant to convey that he had caught her daydreaming. The thing about Austin, though, was that he would never call her out for slacking off. Even if it appeared that she was coasting for a moment or two, she knew he knew her work ethic and respected the fact that she worked long, hard hours and was dedicated to her job. Still, it didn't quell the embarrassment of being caught in the act of staring at him. She figured it was the perfect time to go to the restroom and fix her makeup. Kevin would be there to pick her up in about twenty minutes.

Austin was still watching her when she stood up from her desk. She grabbed her purse and gave him a little wave that echoed the one he'd offered a moment ago. He smiled at her and laughed a little in a way that seemed an awful lot like flirting. With the exception of his mild freak-out yesterday when Savannah had invited her to their family dinner, Austin's mood had seemed lighter lately.

Probably because he's in love...even if he doesn't know it.

Because wasn't that what happened to a person when they fell in love? It transformed the way they looked at the world, the way they treated others. No wonder he didn't want her to come to the dinner last night. How in the world would he explain her presence at an intimate family gathering to Macks? Or maybe he'd invited her to the dinner. He'd said he'd talked to her last night. Maybe he was taking her home to meet the family? But his father was out of town. It seemed like he might wait...unless Miles had already met her.

She was a prospective client of Fortune Investments, after all.

Felicity sighed. Her heart felt heavy as she made her way down the silent hallway to the ladies room. Since it was creeping up on 6:30, most of the employees had already gone home. She and Austin were two of the only people in the office.

She studied her reflection in the mirror. Her cheeks were flushed—probably from the lingering embarrassment caused by Austin catching her staring. She smoothed her cream-colored top down over her black pants. It wasn't what she would've chosen to wear if she'd had advance notice of a date, but it was good enough for tonight.

She pulled her cosmetics bag out of her purse. Before the makeover Maia had given her, she hadn't worried about touching up her makeup and hadn't carried a cosmetics bag in her purse. But since Austin had noticed her haircut, and of course, since Macks had waltzed onto the scene, it had become her armor.

Now she was glad she'd taken Maia up on the offer to find her a dress to wear for the ball. Maia did hair and makeup for beauty pageant contestants, and she was certain one of her pageant girls would be willing to lend a dress. Maia was like a dog with a tug toy when she set her mind to something like this. There would be no putting her off, no talking her out of it. Frankly, Felicity wasn't about to ask her to stand down. She wanted the brightest, shiniest, most pageant-y gown Maia could find. She wanted Austin to look at her and think, there she is, Miss Fricking America.

Or at least in theory that's what she wanted. She wanted him, despite the fact that she was too paralyzed to let herself take steps to make that a reality. Or maybe she fancied herself in love with him because he was unavailable—or at least not available to her.

She owed her love-related post-traumatic stress to her parents and their nasty divorce, a debacle that had left her mother alone and broken after the love of her life had walked out and left her high and dry for a woman fifteen years his junior.

Watching her mother suffer had left such a scar on Felicity that she would rather pine over a guy who was unattainable than give herself a chance with a guy like Kevin, who was interested enough in her that he was willing to look past her tepid reception of his attention and keep pursuing her.

The thing was, Felicity believed in love. She believed in love in a big way. She felt it every day, every time she looked at or thought of Austin. The problem was, she also knew that love that intense never lasted. It was like a match. In its purest, unused form, it held all the possibility in the world. However, once struck and ignited, it was only a matter of time until it burned itself out to a worthless nothing.

As she powdered her nose, touched up her bronzer and reapplied her lipstick, she made a promise to herself that she was going to give Kevin a chance tonight. She would force herself to give him her attention and not let her mind wander to Austin. She wouldn't ponder the coincidental timing of Austin's interest in Macks—after the flowers from Kevin had arrived for Felicity.

She wouldn't let herself sit there with Kevin and wonder if it been a huge mistake to let Austin know she was playing the dating game. That would assume Austin had feelings for her, too, because why else would he get jealous? She wouldn't ponder what might happen if she went for broke and confessed her feelings to Austin since she was leaving Fortune Investments after graduation. No. Dinner the other night would've been the perfect time to do that.

It seemed pretty clear that ship had sailed.

As Felicity was putting away her makeup, her phone sounded a text message. It was from Kevin saying he'd be there in five minutes and asking if he could come in and visit the restroom. He'd tacked on a comment that it would be a good chance to see where she spent so much of her time.

I want to see if it matches the mental picture I have when I think of you at work.

Since Austin was still here, Felicity hesitated. She knew it wasn't a good idea to let Kevin come up, but it wouldn't be very nice to deny him the restroom.

Austin caught the movement out of the corner of his eye. When he looked up, he saw a guy who looked vaguely familiar standing at Felicity's desk. All of a sudden, everything snapped into place.

Kevin Clooney.

That's why the guy's name sounded so familiar. He'd met Kevin Clooney before. About a year ago, one of the New Orleans television stations had sponsored a hometown version of the show *Shark Tank* to match up local entrepreneurs with possible venture capitalists. Austin had been one of the financiers. He had been flattered to be invited to be part of a panel that would hear pitches and possibly strike deals with the budding business creatives. He was jazzed at the thought of possibly having a hand in making someone's dreams come true.

Of course, it had to be the right project.

He'd heard Kevin Clooney's pitch. Sadly, it hadn't been a very good one. He might have thought his idea for the *Skin to Win* burlesque food truck had sounded titillating, but it wasn't viable for many reasons. The biggest reason was, even in New Orleans, the type of show Kevin wanted to produce alongside his food truck didn't comply with city ordinances.

When Austin had questioned him on what elements of burlesque he was thinking of—the exaggerated comedic angle or the striptease version—Kevin had indicated "all of the above." When Austin told him it wouldn't fly, the guy proceeded to argue with Austin, saying that it would be in the same vein as the antics that happen during Mardi Gras, to which Austin replied, that despite its bawdy reputation, the city was trying tried very hard to keep Mardi Gras as clean as possible.

Austin finally shut him down by saying he wasn't interested in investing. It wasn't the type of business the Fortunes wanted associated with their name. Period. Kevin Clooney had called Austin a prude. As if insulting him was going to make him reconsider and fund the guy's unworthy project.

Did Felicity know about Kevin's striptease food truck idea?

Of course, a lot could change in a year. Maybe the guy had learned some manners, even though Austin didn't believe it.

When Kevin Clooney saw Austin watching him, he waved. If Austin hadn't been pissed off before, he was now. But this was his moment to let the guy know he remembered him and he still wasn't impressed with what he saw.

Why was Felicity even talking to this dude?

Austin walked out to Felicity's desk, where she appeared to be hurrying Kevin out of the office. Purse on her arm, she looked a little sheepish when Austin approached them.

"Austin Fortune." He extended a hand.

Felicity should've stuck to her guns and met Kevin downstairs, despite his need for the bathroom.

She knew that now.

"We've met," Kevin said in his overly enthusiastic wheeler-dealer tone as he accepted Austin's hand and clapped him on the back. "Austin, my man, don't crush me and say you don't remember me. I'm Kevin Clooney."

"I remember you, Kevin. You're hard to forget."

Kevin laughed, obviously taking Austin's words as a compliment. Felicity, however, could read her boss and could sense the waves of irritation rippling off him.

Austin glanced at Felicity and furrowed his brow. She frowned and bit her bottom lip, trying to telepath an apology.

"It's good to see you again, man," Kevin said, as if he was Austin's long lost best friend.

Austin didn't reply to him. Instead he turned to her. "Felicity, don't forget we have the final walk through at the Roosevelt Hotel tomorrow evening."

This time Felicity was the one to arch a brow at him. She knew he'd just come up with this fieldtrip because it wasn't on the calendar. "Of course," she said. "How could I forget?"

"We are preparing for the Fortune Investment charity gala, Kevin," Austin said. "This is an important event for our family foundation. Felicity has been instrumental in organizing the event for the past several years. It keeps her very busy."

This was obviously for Kevin's benefit. Austin was blocking off her schedule and making sure Kevin knew it. She wasn't sure which irritated her more, Kevin's aggressive approach or Austin's passive aggressiveness. Either way, she hated being stuck in the middle.

"Cool. So, Austin, I have another business proposition I want to run by you. Can I get on your schedule this week?"

Felicity fumed. The guy really was obtuse.

"Kevin, we need to go," she said.

"As I just said," Austin interjected, "I'm slammed until after the gala and even after that I'm pretty sure I'm booked."

"It'll only take a minute. It's an opportunity I know

you won't want to miss. I'm sure Felicity could fit me in. Let me buy you breakfast. Ya gotta eat."

"Actually, I have to make a call." Austin pinned Felicity with a pointed look and turned around and walked away.

"But, hey, if you're busy, I get it," Kevin called out. "I'll be in touch. Talk soon."

Felicity was silent as Kevin talked nonstop in the elevators down to the first floor. Once they were outside, she stopped in front of the doors.

"Kevin, did you come inside so you could pitch your business idea to Austin?"

"I came inside to pick you up for our date, like any gentleman would do." He was being prickly. Maybe he wasn't as obtuse as Felicity had thought. "I had no idea that he would be in the office. But he was, so I took the opportunity. Don't tell me you're mad. How can you be mad at that?"

She wasn't mad. She was furious. She had to take a minute to collect herself so she didn't go off on him.

Kevin filled the silence. In what she was beginning to recognize as true Kevin Clooney fashion, his reaction was dramatic and completely unapologetic. "Not everyone is as fortunate as the almighty Fortunes. I won't apologize for being ambitious. I bet if you went back to the days before Miles Fortune made his money, he probably had to stick his neck out and take opportunities when he could get them, too. And then you have Austin Fortune—"

Don't say it. Do not talk about Austin. Do not even hint that he was handed everything.

"The guy was born holding the silver spoon—"

Felicity snapped. "Do not talk about Austin. I have seen few people work as hard as he does. So, don't even go there. The guy hardly has a life outside of this building."

"Look, don't get salty. I am not doubting that the guy works hard. What I was going to say was, you'd think a guy who was born into privilege—" Kevin held out his hand like a traffic cop, effectively stopping Felicity from interrupting "—because he was born into it—good, bad, or whatever, you can't dispute that fact. I'd think that if he had any decency, he would want to pay his good fortune forward. Any decent person would."

"Look—" Felicity started, but Kevin's hand went out again and it was starting to annoy her.

"All I'm saying is the best way he could pay it forward would be to help an ambitious, hardworking businessperson like me."

Felicity put her hands on her hips. "I am going to ask you one thing, Kevin, and I want you to tell me the truth. And then we are not going to mention Austin again tonight, or I am going to turn around and walk away. Do you understand me?"

Kevin nodded and looked slightly annoyed. "What's your question?"

"Why didn't you tell me you'd met Austin before?"

Kevin's brows knit. "Because you never asked?"

Tired of his patronizing tone, she turned around and walked away.

"Felicity, come back. I'm sorry. It's a good thing I

didn't mention it since it seems to piss you off when I do talk about him."

Felicity whirled around. "Let's get a couple of things straight, Kevin. First, Austin Fortune—or any of the Fortunes, for that matter—do not owe you anything. They are decent people who give back more than their fair share to their community. And the other thing is, you will not use me to get to my boss. That's what pisses me off."

Kevin gave her the big-eyed innocent look, which made Felicity even more mad. Body Language 101.

"I think it's best for us to call it a night," she said.

She turned to walk to her car.

"You really want to know why I didn't tell you?"

Felicity kept walking.

"Let's go get some dinner and I'll tell you why I didn't mention I knew your boss."

When Felicity hesitated, he said, "If it makes you feel better, you can drive yourself and leave whenever you want. But please hear me out."

Chapter Eight

The next morning, Austin got into the office earlier than usual, even before Felicity, which had happened maybe three or four times since she had been working for him. Last night, he hadn't been able to sleep thinking about what had transpired in the office right before Felicity had left for the day.

He had tossed and turned, debating whether or not he should sit Felicity down and tell her exactly what Kevin Clooney was all about, or at least Austin's perception of the guy. And in all fairness, being ambitious wasn't a crime. Austin knew that.

However, he wanted to make sure Felicity knew Kevin's game so she could make sure the guy wasn't just using her as an entrée into Fortune Investments. But that sounded smug, even to his own ears. God, it even sounded disrespectful. She was a beautiful woman. Clearly, access to Fortune Investments financing wasn't the only reason Kevin was interested in her. And that was a problem. If Felicity was dating the guy, it meant that she was taken. Austin would never know if his feelings for her were real or if they had sprung from the very real fact that he couldn't have her.

He wanted her to be happy.

She was the best thing that had ever happened to him. Felicity had been working for a temp agency and had come to Fortune Investments to help him out on a temporary basis. He'd been a wreck. His life had been a mess after things had fallen apart with Kelly. He needed someone to help him get his act together, because he couldn't even think straight after the divorce.

The minute Felicity walked in, not only did she have an instant calming effect on him, but she had also been damn good at what she did: untangling his life and freeing up his mind so that he could focus on what he did best—make money for Fortune Investments. God knew he had no choice but to work his ass off because he'd had to pay back his father for the financial hole that Kelly had left him in. Which brought him full circle.

Since Kelly, Felicity had been the only person outside of his family he had allowed himself to trust. He trusted her without a doubt. So, he was certain when it came to Kevin Clooney, she would protect the interests of Fortune Investments.

But when it came to matters of the heart...that was a little unclear.

About a half hour later, Felicity arrived. Austin stood. He had already decided that it would be best just to rip the bandage off and go out and talk to her, rather than letting things sit and fester. "Good morning," he said.

"Good morning." She looked like she'd had about the same quality of sleep as he had. "Austin, I'm so sorry about yesterday." Her voice shook, and his heart clenched at the sound of it. He hated to see her look so torn up, but he also needed to make sure she understood why he'd acted toward Kevin the way he had.

"Do you want to come into my office and talk?" he offered.

"I do." Her voice was soft, and she looked subdued as she twisted in her chair, then stood.

Today, she was wearing a pale yellow dress that made him think of sunshine. He wished this dark cloud would pass and the sun would come out again. In due time.

"Austin, I didn't know that Kevin had met you before, and I certainly didn't know he had pitched you a business idea in the past. If I had known, I wouldn't have let him pick me up at work. He was the one who suggested it, because I told him I needed to work late. But I told him that going forward, any talk about business would have to go through you. There will be no suggesting that I slide him onto your schedule, unless you tell me to slide him on."

"Does that mean you're going to keep seeing him?" Austin knew he had no right to ask.

He was edging into dangerous territory, but at the moment, he didn't give a damn.

Felicity blinked. "I don't know."

Austin blinked. "Either you are or you aren't going to see him. It's a simple question." *Dammit.* He could hear his tone, but the feelings inside him were like a living beast trying to get out.

She stared at him with wide brown eyes. So much for showing her the softer side of himself.

"Why do you need to know that, Austin?" she asked. "Is there a reason? Is there something you want to say to me?"

He scrubbed his hand over his face. There was so much he wanted to say to her. So much he wanted to do. He wanted to pull her up from the chair, straight into his arms and taste those lips that were going to be the death of him if he didn't get to taste them soon.

But he couldn't do that anymore than he could demand to know if she intended to keep seeing Kevin Clooney or forbid her from seeing him again.

"What is there to say?" he asked.

She shook her head. "I have no idea. You are confusing me, Austin."

That's because he was confused. He had no idea what these feelings were or where they came from. The best thing he could do was change the subject.

"Look, I know you well enough to know you would never do anything that would put Fortune Investments in jeopardy. I have to be judicious with the investment proposals that I bring to the board. I don't want Kevin pressuring you to get to me, when I don't even know if I can help him. That's why I need to know if you're going to continue seeing him."

Felicity nodded, and Austin thought he glimpsed disappointment in her eyes. He couldn't make sense of it. She didn't even seem to like the guy.

"Kevin is purchasing a table at the foundation gala."

"Why?" Austin asked.

Felicity frowned at him. "Why does anyone buy a table at a charity event like this, Austin? He's doing it to support your family's foundation. You can't very well turn him away. Besides, I'm the one who will be making the biggest sacrifice. His stipulation for buying the table was that I would be his date to the gala."

"You should've said no."

"Well, I didn't. And you can at least act decent and grateful about it."

Her words were a punch to the gut. Austin regarded her for a moment. Then he straightened, pulling himself together. "You're right. If he wants to contribute to the cause, we'll gladly take his check. But you do not have to be his date. That's a slimy stipulation to attach to a charity donation."

Felicity shrugged. "Of course, I told him that I would be up and down from the table because I'll be working that night."

Austin's eyes widened, and he smiled conspiratorially. "Yeah, unfortunately, I think you're going to be pretty darn busy that night."

"You realize it means you'll have to be nice to him, right?" She smiled, but her words were one hundred percent the truth.

"Of course, I'll be on my best behavior." He smiled,

too, but he wasn't sure it reached his eyes. She looked at him for a moment, as if she wanted to say something.

"What's on your mind?" he asked.

She shook her head.

"No, tell me. After all these years one of the best things about you and me is that we can be real with each other."

"All right, you really want to know?"

He nodded.

"I was thinking that you can be a real piece of work."

"Well, you know me better than most people. So, it's probably true."

She laughed, and it sounded like music.

Another good thing about them was that even when they disagreed, they always tried to leave things in a good place. Married couples could borrow that page from their playbook. For a moment, his future flashed before his eyes. The two of them, married, with the kids, the dog, the house with the white picket fence. Felicity in his bed every night. Her face would be the last thing he saw when he went to sleep at night and the first thing he saw when he opened his eyes in the morning. Kevin was not part of that picture—

"Don't forget, you have Macks Cole's art show opening tonight."

"Right, but first I have an appointment with my father to talk about creating an advertising position. Do you know anyone who might be interested?"

It had been a long day and Felicity was glad to be home. After the date with Kevin, she had barely slept

because she'd been afraid Austin would tell her Fortune Investments no longer needed her services. He
couldn't fire her because she'd already given her notice,
but he could've made her notice effective immediately.

Instead, he'd caught her off guard and shared the
news that he was talking to Miles about her promotion. The guy was full of surprises. Especially when
he'd said the part about *the best thing about you and
me…* Her breath caught again, the same way it had
when he'd said the words. She reveled in the idea that
he thought in terms of *you and me.* That in his mind,
there was an *Austin and Felicity* category.

That's why her heart belonged to him, because, well,
he was Austin. Despite his quirky ways and his dark
moods, she knew his heart was in the right place—if
not exactly in the place she wanted it.

Kevin, on the other hand, was a strange puzzle. Just
when she thought she was ready to write him off, he
surprised her. When she'd pressed him, he told her he
had met Austin before and that Austin had turned down
his business proposal. Everything he said matched up
with what Austin said, but Felicity found it trouble-
some that she'd had to ask.

He hadn't volunteered the information. Felicity's
gut was telling her that he wouldn't have told her if she
hadn't asked. But he had to know that she would find
out when he finally came face-to-face with Austin.

Still, even though she realized the connection when
Kevin spoke to Austin, he had managed to get in front
of him again—for what it was worth. If he'd told Felicity
about the connection, she would've never let him come up.

It cast a pall on the evening. Felicity had considered calling it off even before the date started. Then Kevin played the FI charity ball card. He would buy a table if Felicity went out with him and would be his fate to the gala. So, she took one for the team and tried her hardest to make the most of the evening.

The gala was right around the corner. She didn't have to see him again after that. And she shouldn't because her heart just wasn't in it.

How could it be when it belonged to someone else?

Someone else who had a date with another woman this evening. The thought of Austin with beautiful Macks made her stomach queasy. The best thing she could do would be to keep busy.

Felicity looked out the window and saw Maia's car in the driveway. She let herself out the back of her duplex and knocked on Maia's door. Through the French door, she could see Maia wave her in. The phone was pressed to her ear and she appeared to be talking to someone about hair color.

"Candice, I'm sorry you aren't happy with the color," Maia said. "When you asked me to blend your gray with the rest of your hair, I thought you meant you wanted an overall gray look. You know that's very trendy right now. We could even put a lavender tint on it and you'd look very chic."

Maia flinched and held the phone away from her ear. "Candice—Candice—" She rolled her eyes and motioned for Felicity to sit down.

Felicity had the urge to grab the phone and tell Candice to be quiet and let Maia make it right. She would, which was exactly the reason Felicity was there to talk to her.

"Candice, listen to me, please. If you're unhappy. I'm happy to fix it. No charge. I want you to be happy, Candice. I was just offering you options by suggesting the lavender—I understand. Yes. Right. I hear you. Why don't you come in tomorrow at nine o'clock and I'll get you all fixed up?"

Maia could be pushy and act like a mother hen, but she didn't have a mean bone in her body. Even before Felicity had a chance to ask her what she came to ask, she knew the answer. Still, she needed to ask. After she got the answer she knew she'd get, she needed to vent.

"Do you remember mentioning to Kevin that I work for Fortune Investments?"

Maia frowned. "Why?"

Felicity relayed last night's happenings to her friend.

Maia closed her eyes and for a moment she looked as if she might implode.

"Don't hate me. We did talk about you working for the Fortunes. It was only in the name of me trying to fix the two of you up. I wanted him to know you had a good job, that you're successful. I had no idea that he was working an angle. That's just not right and I'm going to tell him that the next time I see him. Unless you want me to call him right now."

Maia punched her pass code into her phone.

"No, Maia, don't. I'm not mad at you. I just needed to know if it was some kind of a crazy coincidence or if Kevin purposely targeted me. I'd say it's kind of half and half. You wanted to fix us up—that's the coincidence half. He got interested in getting to know me after he found out I worked for the Fortunes." Felicity shrugged.

"That little—" Maia called him a colorful word. "I don't appreciate being used. I don't fix up people very often, because when I do and it doesn't work out or if it does work out and they have a breakup—or if something weird like this happens—" She threw her hands in the air. "I feel bad."

"You shouldn't feel bad," Felicity insisted. "This isn't your fault. I shouldn't have told you, but I wanted to get to the bottom of it. Make sure I had the full story."

Felicity followed Maia into the kitchen.

"How did the Beast take it?" Maia asked. "Was he mad at you?"

Felicity shrugged. "He wasn't happy, but in true Austin form after he went off about Kevin, he surprised me by saying that he'd finally pinned down a time to talk to his father about creating that advertising position for me."

Maia's mouth gaped. "And?"

"I don't know. I mean, it's not definite. I didn't see him after the meeting. That probably means that he doesn't have any news for me. I'd think Miles would want to interview me before he offered me the position. But it's way early for that. Austin just broached the conversation today."

Maia laughed the sort of dry, humorless laugh she usually saved for conversations about Austin. She had busied herself in the kitchen, measuring water into a pan and setting it on the stove to boil.

"What's funny?" Felicity asked.

"I just think it's ironic that you say you're leaving, and he tries to create a position to make you stay. He finds out you're dating someone, and he starts acting even more beastly than usual."

Ugh. And he found himself someone else to date. The thought made Felicity's heart hurt.

"Just sayin'." Maia measured rice from a storage container and added it to the boiling water.

"Yeah, well, don't start reading too much into anything. He has a date tonight with Macks. I'd think if he was interested in me, he would ask me out. And not on a work date. Besides, I think he's taking her to the ball. So…there ya go."

"Then you go sit with Kevin at his table," Maia said. She used tongs to pick up the chicken breasts that were on a plate on the counter and place them into a skillet to sauté.

"Well, I did tell Kevin I'd be his date." Felicity watched her friend season the cooking poultry. "I'll have to work some that night, but I'm sure he's expecting me to sit with him when I can. But as far as Kevin goes, this is it, Maia. I'm not going to see him anymore. The only reason I said I'd be his date is so he'd buy the table and support the foundation. I feel kind of weird about that."

Maia shook her head. "If Kevin can use you for business, then there's no harm in you using him to get a hefty donation for the foundation. Or to get Austin's attention. It's good that you'll have a date. That way you won't have to sit there and watch him dance with that woman all night long."

"I'm not exactly attending the ball as a guest. I'll be busy." Her stomach rumbled. She put her hand on her middle, unsure if it was hunger or envy that he would be holding Macks on the dance floor. "That smells delicious. What are you making for dinner?"

"Chicken and rice. Want to stay and eat with me?"

Maia's cooking was always good and tonight Felicity needed company, so she wouldn't sit in her silent house and brood over Austin being with Macks at her art opening, wondering if they'd go out for drinks or dinner afterward. If he'd stay at her place…or bring her back to his.

"I'd love to," Felicity said. "I have a bottle of sauvignon blanc in the refrigerator. I'll go get it."

With the help of a good friend and a little liquid courage, she would make it through this night without being tempted to do a drive-by of the art show.

Felicity smiled to herself. Or she could forego the wine and take a little after-dinner drive to see what she could see.

After she'd added the date to Austin's calendar, she'd done a little research and discovered Macks owned the Chanson de Vache gallery, where the show would take place. It was located in the artsy Warehouse District. Pictures on the website showed that the front of the gallery was floor-to-ceiling glass. She'd get a glimpse of what was going on by simply driving by.

Back at Maia's house, she stowed the wine in the refrigerator. "Want to do something a little outrageous?"

Maia's eyes lit up. "Always. What do you have in mind?"

Fifteen minutes later, they were in Maia's car heading up Tchoupitoulas Street toward the gallery on Julia Street. Claiming she wasn't hungry yet, Maia had gladly put aside her chicken and rice dinner to join Felicity on the adventure.

The reception was from seven o'clock to nine. There was a little less than an hour left.

"I didn't realize it was so late," Felicity said as they turned onto Julia Street. "We may have missed him."

"Let's drive by and see," Maia said. "You know, Austin and I have never seen each other face-to-face. If you want, I could go in and scope out the scene for you, get a barometer reading of the situation."

"Oh, there it is," Felicity said as they pulled up to a stop sign at the corner. The car was directly in front of the gallery. There was no one behind them, so it gave them both a chance to look inside the windows. That's when Felicity saw him. Austin was holding a glass of wine, standing by himself frowning at what looked like a giant red papier-mâché dress that might have come from the closet of *Alice in Wonderland*'s Queen of Hearts. To the left, was a similar dress in black and white.

From the looks of it, Felicity just knew that this wasn't Austin's favorite type of gig. Yet, he was still there—

A car horn sounded behind them. Before Felicity could look away, Austin looked toward the street and their gazes locked.

* * *

Felicity?

Austin blinked and the woman in the car was gone.

He gave his head a quick shake, blinked again. He was worse off than he thought if he was seeing her face when she wasn't even there. It was ridiculous.

He pulled out his phone to text her and ask her if she was anywhere in the Warehouse District vicinity, but even if she said yes, what then? He couldn't very well invite her to join him here at Macks's gallery. However, he could ask her if she was busy, if she could meet him for a drink.

Right.

With a glass of wine in hand, he glanced around the gallery, trying to find something to distract himself so that he didn't do something that he regretted. He took in the white walls that were dotted with framed art that was not part of this art opening. Beta Perez, the artist that Macks was featuring this evening, was the creator of gigantic paper dress sculptures. There were five of them perched on the gray slate floors. Each one nearly grazed the fifteen-foot ceilings. Though Austin had made his rounds through the gallery, looking at everything, even the paintings and etchings on the walls, he marveled again at the sheer scale of the dresses.

He didn't know anyone besides Macks and Beta, the artist, whom he'd met when Macks had introduced him after he'd arrived. Macks and Beta were both talking to people, as they should.

While sculptures weren't Austin's style, and he couldn't imagine where someone would put a piece of art that big, someone was bound to fall in love with them. Wouldn't they? Why else would Macks have offered Beta a showing? He hoped she sold everything they were showing tonight and others that were specially commissioned.

And dammit, he was still thinking about Felicity and how he could be in the middle of a crowd like this and she still felt like his safe place. What would be the harm in seeing if she wanted to meet for a drink?

He drained the rest of his wine, took his phone out of his pocket and started to compose a text to her when Macks walked up.

"I'm sorry I haven't been able to talk to you much tonight, but I am the host."

"No apology necessary, I understand. Duty calls and you seem to be very good at what you do."

She batted her eyelashes at him. He noticed they were unnaturally long and sweeping. Macks was a beautiful woman, but Felicity wore just enough makeup to look pretty and pulled together. Austin couldn't help but think about how he preferred Felicity's natural beauty to Macks's worldly glamour.

"Why, thank you, kind sir," Macks said.

"I'm almost ready to kick out the stragglers who are only here for the food and wine. After I lock up, we're moving this party to Masquerade so we can dance. I'm driving. You can ride with me. Just the two of us."

Something he was learning about Macks was that she did love to be in the driver's seat. For that matter, so did Felicity, but she had a way of making him feel as if he was along for the ride, whereas sometimes,

Macks made it feel as if she'd tied him to the back bumper and was dragging him.

"Where is Masquerade?" he asked.

"It's in Harrah's." Macks laughed. "Oh, dear, don't tell me you've never been dancing at Masquerade."

Austin chuckled. Okay, he wouldn't tell her. He also wouldn't mention that Harrah's was near the river, not too far from the French Quarter, at which she had turned up her nose the other night when he'd invited her out for a drink with his sister and Chaz.

In all fairness, Harrah's was a nice hotel where she wouldn't have to risk sullying her expensive heels as she might on Bourbon Street, but just as she hadn't been up for going out the other night, tonight he just wanted to go home.

"Austin Fortune, you do live a sheltered life." She reached out and toyed with his tie, keeping her gaze trained on it as she spoke. "That's one of the many reasons I will be so good for you." She kept her head angled down but glanced up at him through her eyelashes.

He wanted to take a step back, but she had him cornered. If he did, he'd bump one of the gigantic paper dresses.

"Sounds like fun, but I'm going to call it a night. I have a long day tomorrow."

Macks stuck out her bottom lip and she continued to tug on his tie. "I wish you would come." Her voice was uncharacteristically childlike. "All work and no play make Austin Fortune a very dull boy."

Austin snorted.

Macks flinched and dropped his tie. She took a step back. "What was that about?"

"I'm sorry," he said. "My sister said the exact thing a few days ago."

"Well, there seems to be a theme happening here. However, make no mistake, I'm definitely not your sister." Once again, she looked up at him through her lashes in that coquettish way that seemed to be her signature flirt move. "Come out and play with me tonight, Austin. I promise you'll have lots of fun."

His mind flashed back to Kelly and how she'd been so damn persistent, not taking no for an answer until she'd managed to get him exactly where she wanted him. He'd rather be a boring guy than get duped again.

Fool me once, shame on Kelly and her lies and manipulation. Fool me twice, shame on me. Thanks, but no thanks, I'm not playing.

While Macks came from a good family that had been in New Orleans even longer than his family had, there was something about her slightly overbearing ways that triggered his relationship post-traumatic stress. Macks was a sexy woman and he had a pretty good idea where they'd end up if he went dancing with her tonight.

While he found her attractive, there was no danger that he would fall for her. She simply wasn't his type. She was too pushy, too spoiled and high maintenance. A one-night stand would only complicate future business matters.

Since he had no intention of them being anything

more than friends, he needed to leave before things got more awkward.

"Good to see you tonight," he said. "But I really do need to leave now."

Macks leaned in for a good-night kiss, but Austin stepped to the left, taking care not to knock into the huge red dress sculpture. He set his wineglass on a tray the caterer had set against the wall. The two of them were not going anywhere. No sense in leading her on.

Macks seemed to understand that because she was suddenly all business.

"Thanks for coming tonight, Austin. Please let me know if I can help you or Fortune Investments with any art needs in the future."

After Austin stepped out into the balmy night, he pulled up Felicity's number and texted, Are you up for a drink?

Before he reached the car, she had replied, Sure.

Chapter Nine

When Felicity walked into the Sazerac Bar in the Roosevelt Hotel, Austin was already waiting for her. When he saw her, he smiled and lifted a glass of amber-colored liquid in greeting. If he'd realized she was the woman in the car outside of Chanson de Vache gallery, he certainly didn't look irritated about it. If he was, surely, he wouldn't have invited her for a drink.

Their gazes were locked as she walked toward him, taking her time, happy that she'd put on a dress and let Maia mess with her hair, making it look stylishly uncoiffed in a way that Felicity would've never been able to accomplish if she'd been left to her own devices.

Of course, there was another matter that she couldn't overlook. Austin had gone to Macks's art show earlier that evening, but now he was sitting in the back corner of a cozy hotel bar waiting for her.

The thought was empowering.

When she reached the table, Austin stood.

"Thanks for coming out on such short notice," he said as he helped her settle herself on the plush chair that was next to his.

"Everything okay?" She held her breath, plunging into the question without second-guessing herself. If he had realized she'd been in the car and he had an issue or a question about it, it was best to get it out of the way straight away.

"Everything is fine." He knocked back the rest of his drink.

"How was the art show?"

He grimaced, shrugged. "It was great, if oversize paper dresses are your thing."

He motioned to the server and explained the show's concept to Felicity as he waited for the server to come over and take Felicity's drink order. She ordered a Sazerac, since the famous rye whiskey libation was the drink of the house as well as its namesake. Austin ordered another one, too.

"The art show sounds very *Alice in Wonderland*–esque."

Austin chuckled. "I definitely felt as if I'd drunk the shrinking potion and fallen down the rabbit hole, which, according to the artist's statement, is exactly what she intended, but I don't want to talk about that right now."

She loved the feel of his gaze on her. In a split second, she tamped down the temptation to ask him where Macks was and why he wasn't with her, but why invite the woman to wedge herself between them if she wasn't there?

Okay. If this was her chance, she was not going to blow it by talking about Macks or suddenly becoming awkward and difficult to talk to. The two of them had never had trouble making conversation. Why was her mind going blank now?

"This is a nice little spot." Even if she had to grab onto the obvious, it was better than talking about the weather. "You know, despite the number of times I've been to the Roosevelt Hotel on errands for the ball, I've never been in here."

"I'm glad we're here tonight," he said, and it made her heart thud a steady cadence that sounded an awful lot like *me too me too me too* in her own ears. "So, how are you?"

"I'm fine. Fine." She glanced around the room at the huge mirror behind the bar that reflected the moody lighting, the elegant woodwork and art deco murals. She felt suddenly shy, again at a loss for words. Not really knowing how to navigate the intimacy of the situation, should she dive into business discussion, which was comfortable territory? It wasn't very conducive for relaying the vibe that she was open for less business-y talk, or no talk at all…because she wouldn't mind one bit if he wanted to maybe, say…lean in and kiss her.

The thought made her breath hitch and Austin must've noticed because he squinted at her as if trying to assess if he should ask her what she was thinking. But he didn't. Instead, he surprised her with something totally unexpected.

"Good," he said. "And I'm about to make your night even better."

"Oh?" The word squeaked out. Because, again, she lost her breath at the thought of him leaning in and tasting her lips right here in front of everyone in the Sazerac Bar, in the Roosevelt Hotel, where next weekend they would host one of New Orleans's most exclusive charity balls.

Austin cleared his throat. "On my way over here, my father called. He wants to interview you about your ideas for advertising Fortune Investments."

"What? Are you serious?"

Austin smiled. "Believe me, I wouldn't kid about something like that. I think we need to celebrate."

He signaled to the server and ordered a bottle of Chandon Brut before Felicity could object. And she really didn't want to object because opportunities to sip bubbly with Austin didn't come along every night.

"Thanks, but aren't we a little premature celebrating at this point?" she said.

Austin smiled that smile that turned her inside out every single time. "I'm a firm believer that you need to celebrate every step along the way, no matter how small."

She laughed. "I like your style, Fortune."

He laughed, too, leaning on the arm of his chair. She mirrored him, angling toward him. When the laughter trailed off, their gazes snared, and they were looking at each other in a way that made Felicity's stomach do a double loop.

"What does this mean?" she asked, realizing too late how personal it sounded. "I mean, what will Miles expect in the interview?"

Austin sat back in his chair and seemed to seriously consider her question from the business angle, which left her with mixed emotions. "I can find out more, but from what I gather, he wants you to outline how advertising will benefit the company. You know Miles. He is driven by the bottom line. If you can show him in black and white how you, as director of advertising, will help Fortune Investments make money, he'll hire you in a heartbeat."

Felicity blinked. The only problem was she hadn't yet worked in advertising. Her experience was all academic. She stopped herself midthought. This was the opportunity of a lifetime—or at least for this moment in her lifetime. It wasn't the time to weigh herself down with negative thoughts. She had resources through her professors. She would ask them for help—

"When does Miles want to talk to me? I need time to put together a presentation."

"It won't be until after the gala. He knows you have enough on your plate with that, but, Felicity, he has also recognizes your hard work. He thinks you're a real asset to the company and he doesn't want to lose you. So, basically the position is yours. You just have to go in there and claim it."

Austin raised his lowball glass to her and smiled, but somehow the sentiment wasn't in his eyes.

"Are you okay with this?" she asked.

"Of course. I am behind you one hundred percent. I want what's best for you, even though we both know that the gain of the future Fortune Investments advertising department is my loss. I just have to rethink the way I was going to approach some things."

Felicity blinked at his choice of words. His last sentence came out as more of an afterthought. She wondered if he'd meant to say the words aloud. *Rethink his approach?* To what? Her heart did a quickstep as she mentally relived the moment they'd shared earlier. And the way he'd looked at her when she'd walked in. Or had she imagined it? Maybe the vibe she was sensing now was because a change for her would mean a big change for him, too.

She'd spoiled him. That was the part of her job she loved the most. Now that she thought about it, that little pang she was feeling when she should've been over-the-moon excited about the opportunity he'd just laid in her lap was the thought of someone else being that close to him. When she wouldn't be anymore. She and Austin were about as intimate as two people could be without being...intimate.

"If I do get the advertising position, you know I'll be there to help whomever you hire to be your new assistant."

At the thought, a pang pierced her. If she stayed at Fortune Investments, what would become of the two of them? Would they drift apart, or would they finally get the chance to explore this *thing* she felt pulsing between them? If they did get the chance, it wouldn't be anytime soon because she just couldn't see Miles smiling on her having a personal relationship with his son when Miles was taking the chance on her to break ground in a brand-new position.

"I know, but that's not what I…" He trailed off without completing his thought.

What, Austin? Say it. She had to bite the insides of her cheeks to keep from blurting it out. But why shouldn't she? He started it. He obviously had more to say. He'd called her to meet him tonight. He'd said he got the call from Miles as he was on his way here. That meant he'd wanted to meet for a drink before he'd had the news.

"What, Austin? Say it."

He opened his mouth. Shut it. She reached out and put her hand on his. He turned his hand over so that they were palm to palm. Then he shifted and laced his fingers through hers, taking possession of her hand. His thumb caressed small circles up her index finger in a way that told her more than anything he could've said. She melted on the inside and her lady parts sang an intimate version of the "Hallelujah" chorus because finally, *finally*, after all these years—

"Felicity. I want you—" He choked on the words and cleared his throat. "I want you to get this job."

Oh.

His thumb stopped the circles and she withdrew her hand, placing it in her lap as she comprehended what he was trying to say. But what could she say, besides—

"Thanks?" She shifted away from him and picked up her drink that was on the low cocktail table in front of them. She took a long pull, draining the glass. The dry, spicy shock of the rye helped her gather herself and regroup. She was just about to say she had to go when the server delivered the sparkling wine.

She considered bowing out and leaving him with the bottle that the woman had just opened with a flourish and a subtle *pop-pffft*. But she didn't want to go. It had been another herky-jerky night full of mixed signals and contradictions. So, what was new?

Actually, there was something new. Something had shifted between them. It was subtle, but it was something. Only right now, she didn't know what to do about it, other than get things back on track.

Austin handed her a flute of bubbly. "Here's to what comes next."

Gaaa! There it was again.

What's next, Austin? A chance for us? Is there a chance for us?

"Cheers." She touched her glass to his and sipped the effervescent liquid.

"Are your sister and her boyfriend still here?" Felicity knew they were was since Savannah had mentioned she was staying in New Orleans until after the ball, but the question was a sure path to get them back on solid ground. Solid ground that wasn't business.

"They are," Austin said. "But I don't know how long they'll stay."

"Why? What's going on?"

And just like that, the murky vibe that had clouded emotions moments ago had dissipated and they were back on track. Austin gave her the rundown on Gerald's wedding and the safety concerns caused by the other incidents. "Savannah and Chaz are hell-bent on attending even though my parents are against it. My sister has seized on the aspect that Gerald is family and family supports each other in good times and bad. My parents are of the mind that we just learned that Gerald is family. So, it's not worth the risk."

"So, you're related to *those* Fortunes?" Since he brought it up, Felicity figured there was no harm in asking.

Austin sipped his wine, looking thoughtful. "We are. My dad was raised by my grandmother. She was never very forthcoming about the identity of his father. Until he turned twenty-one and learned that his father was Julius Fortune. You know Miles. So, you can imagine how unimpressed he was about being related to the Fortunes. To prove it, he legally changed his name, but he didn't seek any connection to his father or his other relatives. It was a point of pride to prove that he could make it on his own. And he did.

"Miles built Fortune Investment from the ground up. He still doesn't want anything from anybody. I think even without the weird things that have been happening to his extended family, he'd still be reluctant about embracing them. That may be a large part of the reason he doesn't want to attend his half brother's wedding. The safety issue is a convenient excuse. I think he just doesn't want to get that close."

Austin shook his head and took another sip of his drink. Felicity didn't speak for fear of breaking the spell.

"You should be proud of yourself that Miles has embraced you the way he has," he went on. "You're the first person who isn't part of his immediate family that he's ever considered for upper management."

Austin gave her a pointed look that she couldn't quite read. Then he looked away, frowning at a spot somewhere in the distance. "My divorce left my dad pretty jaded."

"What do you mean, it made *him* jaded? It was your relationship."

Austin scoffed. "It's a long, sordid story. Are you sure you're up for this?"

"Of course I am." She held out her flute and Austin refilled it.

"When I was twenty-five, *Town & Country* magazine published an article about the south's most eligible bachelors," Austin said. "Yours truly was one of the men they spotlighted. I didn't know it at the time, but, Kelly, my ex-wife, saw the article and decided she was going to marry me. She didn't know me. We'd never met, but she knew I was her future husband."

"That's frightening."

"You haven't heard the half of it," he said. "Little did I know, but she started keeping tabs on me and followed me to New York City, where I was in town on business for a few weeks. During that time, she orchestrated a serendipitous meeting. She lied and passed herself off as an heiress who was spending time in the city before wintering in Europe, and she wooed me into believing it was love at first sight. I was such an idiot."

Austin blew out a breath, knocked back the rest of

his drink, topped off Felicity's glass and poured more for himself.

"After a two-week, whirlwind courtship we eloped without telling anyone." He shook his head at the memory. "She was *that* persuasive. And at the same time, she had this damsel-in-distress way about her that made me feel fiercely protective of her.

"When I brought my new wife home to New Orleans, my family was stunned and angry to learn that I had gotten married without telling anyone. My mom was crushed that her first child to the altar had eloped and cheated her out of her mother-of-the-groom honor.

"Miles was angry for a different reason. He did a background check and discovered that Kelly had misrepresented herself. She'd claimed to be an only child. She'd said her parents were dead and she'd inherited their wealth. When we decided to get married, she'd said that a traditional wedding would make her too sad since her father wouldn't be able to walk her down the aisle and her mother wouldn't be there to help her plan it. I believed her. In reality, she was divorced and financially strapped. She had maxed-out about a dozen credit cards trying to pull off her rich orphan charade. And the coup de grâce? Her parents weren't dead. They were in jail—convicted con artists."

Felicity's jaw fell open. She couldn't help it.

"Wait, there's more. She promised me that she was nothing like her family. She begged and pleaded for me to believe her. She said she couldn't tell me the truth because she was afraid that I wouldn't give her a chance, much less be able to love her, because of her family's wrongdoings. She said that my family's anger was case in point. She swore she loved me with all her heart and wanted our marriage more than anything in the world.

"Miles cut me off financially. I realized that would be the true test as to whether she wanted me or my family's money. And I wanted to prove my parents wrong. I wanted to believe Kelly and show them that we could make the marriage work. Plus, I was really pissed off at my father for taking it upon himself to dig into Kelly's background.

"So, to make a long story short, we managed to hold the marriage together for two years before other parts of Kelly's past began to catch up with her. I learned that I wasn't her first mark when a man that she'd stolen money from turned up, threatening to press charges and expose her. Miles bailed her out, for fear of what the scandal would do to our family and the business. No one wants to work with an investment company that has ties to swindlers, especially when they're trusting you with their money. But I had to pay back my father the money he'd spent to get the guy off our backs. Things went from tight to lean.

"Kelly grew restless. A few months later, I discovered she was having an affair and divorced her. After that, I learned that being married to my job was a whole hell of a lot safer than investing in a relationship."

It was a lot to digest. She knew he was divorced and judging by the way no one ever talked about it, she figured it had been a very unhappy marriage, but she never dreamed he'd been through something so horrific.

"I'm sorry that happened to you. Kelly really did a number on you, didn't she?"

"Yeah, I was pretty stupid to fall right into her trap."

"You know it's not your fault, Austin. She's the one who's to blame. You cannot blame yourself or let her make you jaded about love."

He shrugged. "Love? I don't believe in love. I don't think there's such a thing."

"How can you not, Austin? I'm one hundred percent sure love exists."

"But?" he countered.

"But what?" she asked.

"I heard an implied *but* at the end of your declaration."

"No, you didn't."

Oh, my God. He could read her like a book. Or read her thoughts, which was an even scarier prospect.

Austin, if you can read my thoughts, it's okay for you to kiss me. Right here. Right now. Just do it.

She discreetly moistened her lips, just in case. But he didn't lean in.

"It's okay," he said. "You don't have to tell me. I know how hard it is to talk about things like that. You're the first person outside of my family that I've told the full story of what happened with Kelly."

He'd trusted her with something so intimate, which made it even more crucial to not ruin his trust by doing something stupid like overstepping boundaries.

"I know love exists because I feel it—*err*—I've felt it. But I believe it never lasts. Once those feelings are pulled forth from behind the veil, it's as if there's a countdown to the end." She pointed to the bottle of Chandon that the server had left in the standing silver ice bucket.

"It's like that sparkling wine. Once you pop the cork, it's a countdown to when the bubbles go flat."

"Unless you drink the wine before it has a chance to lose all of its fizz."

Felicity arched a brow. "Oh, so you're admitting there is fizz."

"I was speaking hypothetically."

She smiled. "Sure you were. I think you're still letting Kelly hold a lot of power over you if you've let her rob you of your ability to ever love again."

Let me love you, Austin. Let me show what real love is. I would never hurt you.

It was on the tip of her alcohol-loosened tongue. But she closed her mouth, catching her lips between her teeth for extra assurance. She may have already revealed too much of herself without even saying how she felt.

Her heart hitched. Maybe their clock had already started—even before their love story had begun.

"If love does exist, but it doesn't last, then what's the point? Why subject yourself?"

"I ask myself that question every day."

His eyes widened.

Oh, schizer. She wanted to reel back the words, but it was too late.

"You do?"

"Hypothetically speaking," she said.

"Okay, but what made you feel this way? Did someone break your heart?"

She bowed her head for a moment and let the curtain of her hair hide her face while she gathered her thoughts.

"The other day when we were talking about my graduation," she said, looking up at him, "you asked me if my dad was coming to the ceremony."

Austin nodded.

"He's not, because my parents don't get along. They had a very bitter divorce when I was thirteen. Even all these years later, my mom just can't bring herself to be around him. The two of them had such a passionate relationship. When things were good, I remember it being so good. There was this time right before I turned ten that things were so good. It felt like it was the three of us against the world and nothing could touch us. It was such a happy moment in my life, I didn't realize that the clock was ticking down. When things started to fall apart, it got so ugly.

"My mom never remarried. She used to always say it was because anything that good, anything with that much power over you, can't last. In the end, it will hurt ten times more than the good it once brought. I'm not going to lie—I know I let their experience affect my feelings. I mean, a father is the first guy a little girl loves. He's supposed to be the one man who will always love you and protect you, and if he breaks your heart, how can you believe anything like love will ever last?"

The next morning as Austin walked to work, he replayed last night's events over in his mind. He hadn't been drunk, but he hadn't exactly been sober either. He had been nicely relaxed, and his tongue had been loose enough that he had confessed his life story to Felicity.

She'd been equally forthcoming in giving him a glimpse into her past, a peek at what had shaped her to be the woman he knew and cared for so damn much it was almost a physical ache.

How was it that they had worked together so long and so closely and he'd never known that about her? The most sobering part about it was, this morning, in the light of day, he didn't regret baring his soul. Or at least that's what he was telling himself. Because there was no taking it back. What was done was done. He only hoped he hadn't overwhelmed her.

If it took opening up to her to make her open up to him, it was well worth the risk. He was finding it more and more difficult to deny the feelings that had surfaced since he'd been faced with the possibility of her walking out of his life forever.

If it hadn't been for Miles's ill-timed call about a meeting today, last night may have ended in a very different way. He'd wanted her, and he'd finally decided it was time to stop fighting it. His father's call, which came just as they were at the end of the wine, had been an intervention that might have saved him from making a colossal mistake.

Felicity's promotion was important. Austin knew he needed to put her future over these confusing feelings that were clouding his judgment. She would probably get the advertising job, but Miles would probably end up firing them both if they broke the cardinal rule of not fraternizing. Blood be damned, Miles would have no compunction about sacking one of his own children if they didn't follow the rules.

Reliving the story about what happened with Kelly was a good reminder of that. Miles had cut him off in heartbeat and it had taken Austin a solid five years to work himself back into his father's good graces. He couldn't jeopardize that for these strange feelings that had suddenly materialized.

He hadn't been in his right mind last night. Actually thinking he'd seen Felicity in a car parked outside the gallery. In retrospect, the woman in the car hadn't looked anything like her. The woman's eyes had been large and haunted, not at all like Felicity's. While she wasn't the blind eternal optimist, she had a way of holding herself that was so steadfast. Even in his darkest times, even being near her gave Austin hope. But if he knew what was best for everyone, he needed to keep a professional distance between Felicity and himself. At least until he could sort out these feelings and get them under control.

As Austin exited the elevator and navigated the long corridor to their little corner of the Fortune Investments world, he contemplated whether he should invite Macks to the ball. Felicity would be there as Kevin's date. The thought sent pinpricks of irritation coursing through him. Even though she'd said she wasn't interested in Kevin and was only going to the gala with him because that had been a stipulation of his donation. Austin had driven home the point that she didn't have to do that, but she had still insisted on going with him. Maybe that meant she wanted to?

Even if it would be difficult to watch her with the guy, he wasn't going to invite Macks. He didn't want to make her think he was interested in her in any way that wasn't platonic. Maybe seeing Kevin with Felicity, as painful as it would be, was exactly what he needed to get over her and on with his life. As he rounded the corner, he heard her on the phone. She was using her all-business voice. He hoped she wasn't upset about last night.

"I'm sorry, Ms. Cole, I can't give you Mr. Fortune's personal cell number. I'm happy to take yours and give it to him."

Felicity thought Austin had called Macks from his personal phone. He must've used his work cell phone. He had two, and he guarded his personal line jealously.

"Felicity, isn't it?" Macks asked.

"Yes."

"Felicity, I thought we were friends. Friends take care of friends."

Good grief, the woman was persistent. She was probably the type who wasn't used to people telling her no.

"I'm sure they do. But I still can't give you Mr. Fortune's personal number."

Macks growled. She actually growled. Low and guttural. "When will he be in?"

"I don't know."

"You don't know?" Now she'd switched into superiority mode. Her words were clipped and crisp. So much for being friends. "Aren't you the one who keeps his calendar? Isn't it your job to know?"

Felicity looked up and saw Austin standing there. She made a face and pointed to the phone. He mouthed, *Who is that?*

On her notepad, she wrote, *Macks Cole. Shall I tell her you're in?*

He shook his head and waved her off. Then he took the pen from her hand. His hand brushed hers and she flashed back to last night when he'd held her hand.

He wrote on her notepad, *Coffee before Macks. I'll call her back.* The way he smiled at her put her completely at ease. He wasn't acting differently toward her after sharing such a big part of himself with her last night. In fact, it felt as if the two of them shared a secret—a few secrets, actually. The intimacies they'd shared last night and the fact that Macks wanted to talk to him, but he didn't seem very eager.

"I'll have Mr. Fortune call you at his earliest convenience," Felicity said into the phone.

Austin reached over her and pushed the speaker phone button in time to hear Macks say, "I certainly hope you do, because after I talk to Austin and tell him how unaccommodating you were, it could mean your job."

Their gazes locked. Austin frowned, and Felicity simply raised her brows at him.

"I will relay your message, Ms. Cole. Have a nice day."

Felicity heard a click and the line went dead.

"Good morning," she said.

Austin shook his head. "What a nightmare way for you to start the day. I'm sorry. You don't have to put up with that."

Felicity shrugged. "I couldn't very well hang up on her."

"Oh, I don't know. I hear the phone lines in this office can be temperamental. Sometimes people get disconnected. Especially when they act like jackasses. What set her off?"

"She wanted me to give her your personal cell phone number. I figured if you hadn't already given it to her, you might not want her to have it."

"Good call," Austin said. "I don't want her to have it, especially after hearing that much of the conversation. Forget her."

There had never been two words that made Felicity happier. "Aren't you taking her to the gala?"

Austin grimaced. "No. I never got around to asking her." He looked at her in a way that made Felicity's pulse kick up. "Now I'm glad I didn't. But speaking of the gala, do you have moment?"

"Of course."

"Good. Grab your coffee and come into my office. Our conversation last night made me realize something."

In the back of Felicity's mind, a wild daydream played out. Austin was asking her to be his date to the ball. But before she could close the distance between her desk and his office, she had grounded herself with the absurdity of the thought and reminded herself that it was a good thing that he couldn't read her thoughts.

"Talking about my family's wedding dilemma last night made me realize that our gala might be at risk, too. I think we need to hire security to make sure Charlotte Prendergast Robinson doesn't try to pull anything. She's been too quiet for too long. I don't know if it's because she's lying low, knowing she's being watched... After all, Savannah says the authorities are on to her. Then again, it's possible that they have the wrong person and Charlotte isn't the perpetrator. What if someone else has been targeting the Fortunes all this time and the authorities have been after the wrong person? It's all a big question mark. I know it's a lot to ask this close to the event, but I think we need to make sure we have a strong but discreet security presence at the charity ball. Because the reality is at a gathering like this, we could be in serious trouble."

Chapter Ten

Felicity did a twirl in front of the mirror in her suite at the Roosevelt. The fitted red ball gown hugged her curves like it was made for her. The strapless corset top nipped in her waist, making it look tiny, before it flared into a chiffon, A-line skirt that made her feel like a princess.

Maia had come by and had done her makeup and hair, leaving it to fall in soft curls around her shoulders.

Felicity did one more twirl, wistfully taking it all in, before she grabbed her clutch purse that contained her hotel room key, lipstick and compact for touch-up. There wouldn't be time to run up to the room once the ball got started. But she could if she needed to. That's part of the reason why the suite was such a nice gift from Austin.

Austin had surprised her with the key card yesterday. He'd arranged for early check-in. She'd arrived with her dress, shoes and accessories for the gala and a suitcase for the night. That had made it possible for her to spend the morning supervising the transformation of the ballroom from ordinary beautiful to gala extraordinary. Then she'd taken the elevator back up to her room, showered and let Maia help her get ready for the big event.

The other part of why it was so wonderful was tonight, when all was said and done, all she had to do was ride the elevator back to the tenth floor and she was home for the night. She'd worked hard this week, verifying last-minute details and lining up the security that would unobtrusively blend into the background. It had been a good call on Austin's part. Due to all the disturbances that had been swirling around the Fortunes, both near and far, it was better to be safe than sorry. However, it had taken some doing on her part to find the security personnel at this late date. She'd been forced to jump through several hoops to pull it off, but she had.

As she walked into the ballroom, she looked around at the gold-and-white wonderland. Stunning arrangements of white flowers displayed in towering gold vases offset by pearlescent linens and gold Chiavari chairs. Flickering white-and-gold candles rested atop mirrored bases that reflected the light. Elegant china, crystal and fine flatware set the stage for the sumptuous meal to come, which was detailed on the engraved gold-and-white menu cards placed atop the plates. The silent auction items were lined up on tables around the perimeter of the room. The band was doing a final sound check.

Felicity glanced at her phone, checking the time and making sure there were no SOS calls from the league of foundation volunteers who had agreed to help out tonight. There were still fifteen minutes until the doors would open and the guests would spill in. Before she'd let herself into the ballroom, she'd checked on the early volunteers who were seated at tables in the atrium near the ballroom, ready to check in the guests as they arrived.

Everything was in place and it all looked absolutely perfect. She took a minute to close her eyes, take a deep breath and savor the calm before the party started. When she opened her eyes, Austin was walking toward her, looking stunning in his Armani tux. She knew it was Armani, because she'd gone with him to render an opinion when he'd purchased it. Like something out of a dream, he floated toward her, smiling. The sight of him made her lips curve upward, too.

"Would it violate a human resources rule or make you feel uncomfortable if I said you look absolutely gorgeous tonight?"

"Not at all, because so do you," she returned, basking in the glow of his compliment and feeling just this side of giddy because of how all her hard work had come together. "You clean up well, Fortune."

Actually, he wore a suit to work every day and looked gorgeous. But this tux was above and beyond.

"Yeah, well, I try," he said. "I met with the security

team. I have all but four stationed by the check-in tables. I have one in the lobby, one at valet and two are in this room." Austin pointed to two well-built men dressed in tuxedos, one stationed at each door. Felicity had thought they were part of the waitstaff.

"They look great. They'll blend right in."

"They all have a photo of Charlotte and if they notice anything suspicious, I've instructed them to call the police right away."

"Looks like we're covered," Felicity said. She opened her handbag and pulled out a piece of paper with the evening's schedule, which she went over with Austin one more time. It was nice to stand so close to him. She could smell his shampoo and aftershave. The combination that smelled like cedar, coffee and leather was so uniquely him, it made her long to lean in closer and breathe in deeper. But, Lisa, their contact from the hotel, approached with a walkie-talkie and the list detailing the order of events.

Lisa had agreed to work with Felicity to help ensure that the program stayed on track. Austin would be the emcee for the evening, but Felicity would be close by to cue him if he needed to know what came next.

Felicity started to review a few points. "After the doors open, we'll give people about an hour to get drinks and bid on the items in the silent auction—"

Her phone buzzed. It was a text from Kevin telling her he was at the hotel.

Come have a drink with me. I want to introduce you to my entourage.

Quickly Felicity texted back. Sorry, going over the final details of the gala. See you when the doors open.

Let me in now. I'll bring you a drink.

She didn't answer because she knew he would continue to argue the point. He and his *entourage*—who even said something like that?—would just have to entertain themselves.

When the doors opened, Kevin and his buddies—five guys and a woman—found her straight away. Unfortunately, Felicity was in the middle of trying to locate a missing basketball that had been signed by the New Orleans Pelicans. It had been there before the doors opened because she and Lisa had double-checked all the silent auction items.

Kevin made quick introductions and then she had to scurry off to locate the missing ball, which, it turned out had rolled off its stand and under the table skirt.

The next time Kevin found her, she was with Austin in one of the hallways off the ballroom that led to the kitchen, coaching him on his welcome remarks.

"Sorry to interrupt." Kevin seemed a little miffed and looked at them like he'd stumbled upon a secret liaison. "Your dinner is still on the table. The servers keep trying to take it away. Do you want it?"

"Kevin, I'm so sorry," she said. "After the opening remarks and the first dance, things should slow down a little. Thanks for bearing with me until then."

He grunted something she didn't quite catch and then disappeared out the way he'd come.

Austin's welcome speech went off perfectly. The only small hitch to the program came right before he was supposed to take the dance floor with his sister, when Savannah's shoe broke. The first dance was traditionally danced by a couple of the Fortunes and it was meant to get the party started. This year, the honor was Austin and Savannah's.

"Felicity, I can't go out there in bare feet. I'll step on my dress." Savannah held up a pair of five-inch heels.

"Do you want to wear my shoes?" Felicity offered, noticing too late how tiny Savannah's feet were compared to Felicity's own size nines.

"Thanks for offering, but I don't think that will work," she said as the band played another riff of the song that preceded the first dance. Lisa had scurried over to let the bandleader know what was holding up the show and now, the singer was trying to stretch out the song until they were ready.

"Will you dance with Austin, Felicity?" Savannah suggested.

Felicity glanced around the room looking for Belle or Georgia or even Sarah, but they all seemed to be well hidden. She really didn't have a choice.

There was something in Savannah's smile that hinted that her shoe malfunction might not have been an accident. And then it hit Felicity—she would get to dance with Austin.

"Are you okay with this?" she asked him.

"Sure," he returned, his expression unreadable.

Savannah signaled to Lisa and pointed to Felicity. Lisa seemed to get the message because she told the bandleader and he announced, "Mr. Austin Fortune, dancing with Miss Felicity Schafer."

When Austin took her into his arms, she felt like she'd finally found her home. They swayed together, his hand on the small of her back, their bodies moving in time to the music. For a few short minutes the rest of the world melted away and it was just her in the arms of the man she loved.

All too soon, the music changed from the slow, romantic song to something more upbeat. The singer was inviting the rest of the guests to join them on the dance floor, and Felicity felt a hand on her shoulder.

She looked up to see Kevin ask Austin, "May I cut in, please?"

"Sure," Austin said. "You kids have fun."

No! Don't go.

But he did. He walked off as Kevin tried to pull her into slow dance form despite the up-tempo song. Felicity resisted by taking her hand and spinning herself out in a modified swing dancing move. At the end of the song, which seemed to go on forever, she told him she was thirsty and needed something to drink. Like a good date, Kevin was off to the bar to get her something.

By the time he returned, about ten minutes later, it was time for Felicity to help facilitate the silent auction results. She thanked him for the drink and explained what she needed to do. But before she could get away, he asked, "How long do you think you'll be? My friends left after dinner. They had another party."

Felicity felt a little sorry for him for spending all that money only to share his table with people who would ditch him? And she knew she was being a lousy date, but she had warned him that she had to work the event.

"Why don't you ask someone to dance?" Felicity suggested. "I'm sure there are plenty of women who would love to." Even though most of the women were there with dates. Still, she had no choice but to excuse herself and get to work, leaving Kevin with a glass of scotch and a long face.

As Austin passed by Kevin Clooney's table, Kevin stood and blocked his way.

"If I didn't know better," Kevin slurred, "I'd think you were purposely trying to keep Felicity and me apart tonight. What the hell, Fortune? What's your problem?"

Clooney had a glass of what looked like scotch, straight up, in his hand. Judging by the way he was slurring his words, it wasn't his first drink of the evening. Probably not his third either. He had pulled his tie loose and unbuttoned the first button at the collar. Austin glanced around for one of the security personnel they'd hired, but they were surveilling the entrances and exits.

"I don't have a problem, Clooney," Austin said. "But I think you've had a little too much to drink. You either need to settle down or I'll call you a car and get someone to help you down to the lobby."

"I don't need your help, Fortune." As a waiter walked by, Clooney held up his half-full glass and motioned for a refill. In the process, some of the amber liquid sloshed over the side. As Clooney transferred his glass to his other hand and clumsily wiped the liquor on the leg of his tuxedo pants, Austin caught the waiter's eye and gave a subtle shake of the head. He mouthed the word *water.* The waiter nodded and mouthed back, *Security?* Austin gave a subtle nod.

"Look, I get it," said Kevin. "You don't like me. Honestly, I don't like you either, but business is business and I need to get someone to bankroll my restaurant. But you—" He jabbed his index finger in the middle of Austin's chest.

Austin caught his hand and held it in midair before dropping it with a firm flick of his wrist. The movement caused the guy to stagger back a few steps.

He really wanted to walk away, but he needed to stay until security arrived and stopped Kevin from making an even bigger scene.

"Yeah, you. You're just a big, fat waste of my time," Kevin slurred. "But I guess that doesn't matter to you, does it? You're a Fortune. You don't care about the little people. Except for Felicity. I think you like her. And the real kicker is I think she likes you, too. But the only reason a chick like her would be interested in a loser like you is because of your money."

That was rich, coming from a guy who'd spent twenty-five hundred dollars on a table and the so-called friends he'd invited to share it with him had apparently deserted him. Austin almost felt sorry for the guy. But it was kind of difficult to muster the empathy between the insults the guy was hurling at him. The only reason Austin hadn't walked away was because as host, it was his responsibility to make sure the guy didn't provoke someone else.

"You're not the only game in town, Fortune." He bellowed the words and people were starting to stare. "I can walk out of here and have the money I need by the end of the month."

"There's the door," Austin said, gesturing with a wide sweep. "No one is stopping you. In fact, it would probably be a good idea if you left. Let me call you a car. You're in no shape to drive."

"I can drive if I want to," Kevin slurred and slurped what was left of his drink.

"Good luck getting your keys from the valet."

Kevin smirked. "This isn't even about business, is it? It's about Felicity. You take and take and take from the little guy. You probably don't even want her, but you can't stand to see her with someone like me. Yeah, her and me, we're just disposable goods to guys like you."

Austin's blood started to boil at Clooney's mention of Felicity. But he wasn't going to let himself be baited by a drunk who would probably regret his foul attack as much as he regretted the hangover that was sure to hammer his thick head tomorrow morning.

"You might have all the money in the world, but you didn't have to work for one cent of it. I don't think you even know what it's like to work hard to get a woman like Felicity."

Now he wasn't even making sense.

"You kept her busy all night to keep her away from me. Didn't you?"

"That's her job. That's what I pay her to do."

"You get her to do all the hard work, so you can sit on your candy ass because you've never had to work hard for anything in your life. You don't have the character. You ain't got nothin', Fortune."

Where the hell was security? If Clooney got any more agitated, Austin was prepared to walk him outside himself. But he hated to create any more of a spectacle than had already been made.

"She deserves someone a whole hell of a lot better than you." Clooney shoved Austin's shoulder, but Clooney was the one who staggered backward. In the process, his arm knocked over a glass of champagne that was still sitting on Kevin's empty table.

Finally, security arrived. The guy put a hand on Kevin's shoulder. "Come on, buddy. I'm going to help you get home."

As security walked Clooney toward the door, Kevin said a few choice words as he tried to pull out of the guard's grasp. "I can find my own way out."

Then Felicity walked into his path. "Fortune wants you," he told her. "I think you want him, too." He twisted around, and his legs got tangled up as the security guard continued his forward motion. He would've fallen, if not for the guard holding him upright. Sadly, it didn't silence him. "Go for it. You two deserve each other."

With a horrified expression on her face, Felicity joined Austin and they watched Clooney stagger out the door.

"What in the world was that about?" she said.

"Your date had a little too much to drink. He's kind of an angry drunk."

"Well, there goes my ride," she joked. "It's a good thing I'm staying here at the hotel and don't need a driver."

"I'll walk you home," Austin said. "It's probably my fault he got so drunk. He said I worked you too hard tonight and kept you from him. Did I?"

Felicity laughed. "Are you kidding? He knew I had to work tonight. It didn't help matters when he got a little handsy out there on the dance floor."

"It's a good thing I didn't see that," Austin said. "I would've thrown him out a long time ago."

It was later than he realized, and soon the band announced their last number, a soulful rendition of *Can't Help Falling in Love.*

"Dance with me," Austin said.

He offered his hand. She took it, and he pulled her into his arms. They swayed together to the music. When they'd danced earlier, it had been such a surprise, what with Savannah's sudden shoe malfunction. Austin chuckled to himself.

"What is it?" Felicity asked, her words hot in his ear.

"I was just thinking about the timing of my sister's broken shoe earlier this evening."

"Yes, that was unfortunate, wasn't it? Or fortunate, actually. Yes, I think it was fortunate." She rested her head on his shoulder, nestling into him.

He pulled her closer, marveling at how good she felt, at the way his hand felt on the small of her back, at how she fit so perfectly against him, her curves magically tucking into the dips in his body. Her hair smelled of flowers and sunshine and everything that was good and right in the world. He could get used to this. God, he wanted to get used to this and from the way she was leaning into him he got the feeling Felicity could, too.

Chapter Eleven

After the ballroom emptied out, Austin and Felicity returned to the Sazerac Bar in the hotel. They had an hour before the place closed and both of them were too wound up to call it a night. They decided to have a casual debriefing over a bottle of well-deserved champagne since they didn't have to drive. As Austin said, they'd earned it after the event being a smashing success.

"This is the second week in a row that we're sipping champagne in the Sazerac," Felicity said. "Is this a new thing? Because, I could get used to it."

They clinked glasses. "All in all, I'd say the gala went off without a hitch," Austin said.

Felicity shrugged. "Except for the missing basketball and Kevin's drunken performance."

She started to add Savannah's broken shoe, but that hadn't been a hardship. Felicity noticed later that Savannah had been wearing a pair of shoes. Felicity didn't know whether she was able to fix hers or she had a spare pair up in her hotel room, but it didn't matter. If Savannah had orchestrated the shoe malfunction, she wanted to hug her. If she did, did it mean that she was quietly advocating for Felicity and Austin to be together? At least that was one Fortune in her corner.

"But the gala was sold out, thanks to Kevin grabbing the last available table," Austin offered. "And Charlotte was a no-show."

And I got to dance with you, feel what it's like to be in your arms. "That is true. We found the basketball and security discreetly handled Kevin. So, for all the important reasons, it was a pretty darn successful gala."

The bar was empty, except for the two of them and another couple, who looked so wrapped up in each other that they seemed oblivious to Austin and Felicity's presence. So, essentially, they were alone. The place felt like a cozy cocoon. Kevin, Macks, Charlotte and other inconveniences of the outside world seemed far away.

"Did you always want to go into advertising?" Austin asked as he refilled her glass.

"No, getting an undergrad degree in advertising and an MBA seemed like the most practical degrees for me. The most marketable."

"What would you have studied if practicality didn't matter?"

"Something that had to do with flowers."

"What? Like being a florist?"

Felicity laughed. "I've never heard of a florist degree. I think that's mostly on-the-job training."

Austin smiled. "Of course. I'll blame it on mental exhaustion and champagne. So, what would you have studied?"

"Something really nerdy like botany."

His brows lifted. "Really?"

"I wanted to be a botanist. I love flowers—especially roses. I wanted to experiment with creating new rose species."

"You seem to know a lot about roses already. Could you still do it as a hobby?"

Felicity scoffed. "Yeah, in all my spare time."

"You have to make time for the things you love," Austin said.

"This coming from the man who proudly proclaims he's married to his job."

"Touché."

Felicity shrugged. "You're right, though. Someday I'm going to get that greenhouse for my backyard. Then I'll do it. I'm weird like that. I don't want a fancy car, expensive shoes or a designer purse. I want a greenhouse."

"I don't think it's weird at all. It's kind of refreshing, actually."

Felicity wondered if he was thinking of Macks.

"Did you ever call Macks Cole back? We've been so busy with the gala that I didn't have a chance to ask you."

"I did."

Of course, if Macks hadn't talked to Austin, no doubt, she would've kept hounding Felicity until she did. But Felicity wanted to hear it from Austin.

"Did you give her your personal cell phone number like she wanted?"

"I did not."

"Why not?"

Austin smiled, and his right brow shot up, a look that Felicity could've inferred as *none of your business* or that Austin just didn't want to talk about it. But she wanted to know.

"I know it's none of my business, but I'll play the mental exhaustion and champagne card, too, and ask you anyway. I'll blame it on that and double down. Why not, Austin?"

"Because I didn't want to."

Ugh, how did that go over? Macks didn't like the word *no.*

"Good to know," Felicity said. "So, I guess that means you're not dating her anymore."

She'd already pushed this far, why stop now?

"I never was dating her. But while we're on the subject of dating, are you still seeing Kevin?"

"I'm not."

Austin's smile smoldered. "Very good to know."

After the champagne was finished and Austin had paid the bill, he offered to walk Felicity to her room. As fate—or booking a block of rooms would have it—both of their rooms were on the hotel's tenth floor, but hers was farther down the hall than his. Still, it didn't seem right to say good-night and let her walk the rest of the way alone.

So, they walked past his.

"This is me," she said and stopped in front of her door. "Thanks for the champagne." She pulled her card key out of her purse, but instead of opening the door, she leaned against it, gazing up at him.

She looked so damn gorgeous and her lips were so inviting. He wanted to lean in and kiss her, so they wouldn't have to talk anymore. He wanted to lose himself in the taste of her, bury his face in her silky, long hair and stay there until he forgot about the very real fact that she was leaving him, one way or another.

"What are we going to do next year without you to organize the gala?" he asked, because it was a legit question and because even though talking was the last thing he wanted to do right now, it was his last option and he was grasping at straws since he wasn't ready to say good-night. He was testing the waters to see if she wanted to call it a night. It was two o'clock in the morning. It was too late to suggest they go out somewhere else, and even though propriety wouldn't allow him to ask her into his suite for another drink, he was still stalling for time.

"No matter where I end up, your new assistant can always call me with any questions, and I've kept good notes over the years."

He rested his shoulder on the wall so that they were both leaning toward each other. "Just stay," he said. "Don't leave me. I know that's not fair, but—"

"I don't want to leave you. I may not work for you much longer, but if I can help it, I won't leave you."

He reached out and touched a strand of her hair, needing to know if it was as soft as it looked. It was. He twirled it around his finger.

Then the next thing he knew, her lips were brushing his. It was a feather-soft kiss. One that could've stopped there, if she'd wanted it to, if she'd turned around and let herself into her room.

But she didn't.

He rested his forehead on hers. Her lips were a fraction of an inch from his. "Felicity, I don't want you to regret this. I don't want you to think I took advantage of you—"

"I know exactly what I'm doing, exactly what we're about to do. I've wanted this for so long. I think you want me, too, Austin. Don't you?"

If you only knew.

She leaned in and those lips were teasing his neck, her hot, delicious breath was in his ear.

"Austin, I don't mind if you kiss me. I want you to kiss me and we don't have to stop there."

Every inch of his body responded as his arms fell around her waist and he pulled her into his body. She slid her hands down to his butt, closing the distance so that his body was perfectly aligned with hers.

He didn't give her the chance to say anything else. Their lips found each other, and he showed her exactly how much he wanted her. As her mouth opened under his, passion consumed him. That moment, if he'd had the key to her room, he would've opened the door and walked her backward right into the bedroom and made love to her. Instead, he deepened the kiss and pulled her even tighter against him.

He wasn't sure how long they stayed like that, but when they came up for air, Felicity looked dazed. Her hand flew up to her kiss-swollen lips.

That's when Austin realized someone was walking toward them. He turned and saw his father letting himself into one of the hotel rooms four doors down.

Felicity flinched away.

"Austin. Felicity."

"Dad."

Miles pinned them with a steely glare. His mouth was drawn into a tight, thin line. "It was a nice party. Let's…uh…talk about everything first thing Monday morning. My office."

The moment Felicity disappeared inside her hotel room, Austin's cell phone rang. He muted the volume, so it wouldn't disturb the other guests as he made his way down the hallway to his own room.

He let himself inside his room and answered. "Hello."

"You are damn lucky you took my call." Miles sounded as if he was spitting fire. Austin almost hung up on him.

"Yeah? And what if I hadn't? What would you have done?"

Miles didn't answer his question. Instead, he jumped right into the tirade that Austin knew was coming.

"What the hell is wrong with you, Austin? Fooling around with your personal assistant? Are you trying to get Fortune Investments slapped with a sexual harassment lawsuit? How stupid can you be?"

"It's not like that, Dad." Austin flung his tux jacket onto a chair and toed out of his patent leather loafers.

"Yeah, well, I have eyes. I know what I saw. I know exactly what was going on. So does everyone else who saw you dancing with her at the gala tonight. You just provided all the corroborating witnesses she will need when she gets pissed off at you and decides to sue our asses."

"All we did was dance." It was taking every ounce of strength Austin possessed to keep his voice low and level. The soft champagne buzz had evaporated. In its place, the start of a headache was beginning to pound. Austin scrubbed his free hand over his eyes and then raked his fingers through his hair.

"It didn't look like you were dancing in the hallway. Or maybe you were saving the dance for after you got inside the room."

"Go to hell, Miles. What we were doing is none of your business. I'm not sixteen years old. What makes you think you have the right to tell me how to live my life?"

"I don't care how old you are. When you work for me, I have the final say on things that will affect my business. Your fooling around with your assistant could come back to bite me in the ass."

"She's not going to be my assistant for much longer. I have feelings for her. Besides, I know Felicity. I've known her for almost five years. She's not like that. She wouldn't turn around and try to take us for a ride."

"That's what you said about Kelly and look at how things ended up. Look what it cost us. I had to bail out your ass."

"Really? Are you really going to keep bringing that up? Because if you are, I'm going to hang up on you right now. I paid you back every penny of what I owed you. So, I made a mistake with her. Felicity is not Kelly. I am not going to stand here at nearly three o'clock in the morning trying to justify my feelings. You do not get to dictate who I see."

"I do if the two of you work for Fortune Investments. You are not above the rules, Austin. And the rules state that there is no fraternizing. Especially when it comes to an executive fooling around with a subordinate."

Austin started to object, but Miles cut him off.

"I was seriously considering promoting her. But I think you just killed that for her. Monday morning, you need to accept her notice and then keep your distance from her."

"That's not fair, Dad. Felicity has worked hard for us and deserves to be recognized for her hard work. You're an idiot if you let her go."

And so am I.

"I don't know—" Miles started to say.

"Well, you'd better think about it, because if you deny her this promotion based on what you saw tonight, then you're giving her every reason to sue your ass."

"I guess that means you have some decisions to make, doesn't it?" Miles said. "You have to choose, Austin. Do you want her to have the promotion? Or do you want to have your little fling? Because if you insist on fooling around with her, as far as I'm concerned, the promotion is off the table. In fact, she doesn't even need to come in Monday morning. It's your choice."

At eight o'clock the next morning, Felicity rang Austin's room. She hadn't slept much after Miles had stumbled upon their late-night kiss. Instead, she'd stayed up all night contemplating what to say to him the next time they talked.

She'd considered texting him—actually, she wanted to text him the minute she'd closed the door between them, wondering if Miles had called or texted or walked across the hall and pounded on Austin's door. Knowing Miles, it wasn't so far-fetched.

If Miles had started the inquisition, the last thing Austin needed was her texts pinging his phone. If Miles had been uncharacteristically silent, she didn't want to crowd Austin.

So, she'd forced herself to wait until the respectable hour of eight o'clock to ring his room phone. When he didn't answer, she called the front desk and discovered that he had already checked out.

She could've kicked herself for not texting last night. Because even if she hadn't wanted to seem desperate, she was feeling that way more and more with each hour that ticked on without word from him.

Checkout was at eleven o'clock. Felicity decided she wouldn't leave a minute earlier. She took a hot bath in the suite's garden tub. Then she took her time applying moisturizer from head to toe, styling her hair, putting on her makeup and getting dressed. She ordered room service and leisurely enjoyed the fruit plate, pastry basket and the entire pot of strong hot coffee.

She called the bellhop to assist her with her luggage and getting her car from the valet. She would not allow herself to check her phone until she was parked in her own driveway. Because by that time it was a quarter past noon. Surely, Austin would've made time to get in touch.

But there were no new texts waiting for her after she got home.

She had also imposed another moratorium on herself. Until she got home, she would not let herself fret over the fact that she had been the one who had initiated the kiss. Oh, sure, Austin had kissed her back, but what was he supposed to do?

No. She wasn't going there. Austin had definitely been into the kiss. And he had been the one who had asked her to dance the second time, the one who had suggested the drink at Sazerac and had purchased the champagne and had walked past his own room to escort her to hers. Those were not mixed signals. Those were *beacons*. Spotlight-strong beacons. And that's why she had leaned in and kissed him.

Felicity shored up her confidence. She let herself out of the car, hitched her handbag up onto her shoulder, grabbed her suitcase and the garment bag that contained the red dress that Maia had lent her for the gala. She carted her belongings onto the porch.

She had just put the key into the lock when she heard a car turn into her driveway. In the split second between hearing the sound and turning around, her heart leaped in her chest and possibility bloomed like the roses she loved.

But it was short-lived, because when she turned around, she saw that it was not Austin. It was a courier lugging a huge box up the walk.

"Felicity Schafer?" he asked.

"Yes."

"This is for you. Please sign here."

She did, and he set the large brown box inside her front door.

Who in the world would be sending her a package? Maybe it was something for graduation. That's when her heart took a second leap of faith and imagined it was from her father.

But it wasn't.

When she opened the box, there was a card, which she didn't open right away. It took a moment to figure it out, but the pieces in the box were for a greenhouse. Inside the larger note there was a piece of paper with a number for her to call to make an appointment for someone to assemble it for her.

It should've been the most wonderful moment. It should've made her happier than receiving the most fabulous piece of jewelry or the most coveted designer bag. But it didn't. Written on the note card in Austin's own handwriting was a message that broke her heart.

I'm sorry, Felicity. I crossed the line. It will never happen again. I hope Monday we can carry on as before.

This proved her theory that love was definitely real, but once acknowledged, a clock started counting down to the end. She never dreamed it would end before it had a chance to begin with Austin.

Chapter Twelve

Austin had contemplated calling Felicity Sunday night, but he decided it would have made things worse. It would've felt too personal. As it stood, things were already personal enough. So, it was for the best that he waited to talk to her again Monday morning at the office.

He didn't like it. Not one bit, but that's the way things had to be. For her sake.

After his early-morning conversation with his dad, Austin had needed time to think and get his head together. Miles might be able to keep them apart by threatening Felicity's promotion, but his mandate wouldn't change the way he felt about her.

For the first time in a long time, he was falling in love.

He was in love with Felicity, but for her sake, there

was nothing he could do about it. He couldn't get in the way of her promotion. He had to let her have this opportunity.

He stepped off the elevator at Fortune Investments and into the hallway that led to their office. He was arriving at his usual time and he planned to act like it was any other day. If he sensed she wanted to talk about things, they could do that in his office—just as they would talk about anything on any given day.

His heart thudded as he rounded the corner and saw her sitting at her desk, typing on her computer. It thudded, then it settled into a dull ache.

"Good morning," he said.

"Good morning." She didn't look up from what she was doing.

Okay. Apparently, this was going to be more difficult than he'd anticipated. On both of their parts. She was wearing a red dress that managed to look sexy and all business at the same time. His need for her was a visceral ache.

And he needed to stop noticing what she was wearing. How had he done that before? Back before everything went haywire and he realized that she was the best thing that had ever happened to him. Was it any wonder that he was in love with her?

There had to be a way to work this out and the only way to do that was to level with her. Even though his father had acted like a jackass about the situation, tossing around ultimatums and mandates, Austin wouldn't betray him by telling Felicity point-blank what Miles had said after he'd found them together. He'd have to keep the conversation more general. He'd have to tell her that due to company policy, it wasn't possible for them to work together and be together.

"Do you have a moment to talk?" he asked.

She kept typing, her gaze glued to the computer monitor. For a moment, he thought she wasn't going to answer him. But then she stopped and looked up, her eyes focused on a point somewhere over his shoulder.

"Yes. I'll be in in a moment." Her tone was strictly business. He didn't blame her.

He went into his office, which was darker than usual. Normally, Felicity turned on his lights and computer before he arrived. This morning, he had to do it himself. When he did, he realized she hadn't gotten his coffee as she usually did. He didn't blame her for that either.

Austin had never expected these little niceties, but he appreciated them. It was also quite possible that he'd taken them for granted. Just like he'd taken her for granted, even though he hadn't done it on purpose. He'd been inadvertently careless.

Just like he'd been with her heart after the gala… and all the times that had led them to that moment.

After he turned on his computer, he set out for the break room. Felicity wasn't at her desk when he passed by, but she was there when he returned with two cups of coffee in hand. One for her and one for himself.

The selection of mugs in the break room was eclectic. He handed her the mug that said You Are My Sunshine and kept the one with Snoopy lying atop his red doghouse. It would've been more appropriate if he'd been in the doghouse, but close enough.

"I made the coffee myself," he said, striving for a light tone. "It may not be as good as yours."

"Thanks, Austin," she said. "I'll show you and whoever replaces me how I make it before I leave. That way you'll both know. But in the meantime, we need to talk about other things."

Austin watched her pick up her coffee cup and a piece of paper off her desk. Then they walked silently to his office together.

She sat in the same chair that she'd sat in that first day that she'd given him her letter of resignation. He'd barely had time to sit down in his chair before she handed him the paper she held.

"This is my official two weeks' notice. The first letter I gave you was a little vague. It didn't have a date for my last day, but this one does. Now that the charity ball is behind us, I can start wrapping up other projects and you can start interviewing for my replacement. Though it might have been a good idea if we had done that earlier so he or she could've shadowed me at the gala. But it is what it is." She shrugged. "I'm graduating in two weeks and one day. Which means my last day at Fortune Investments will be the day before the ceremony."

Austin frowned at the paper, reading everything she had just told him. "You're still planning on interviewing with Miles for the advertising position, aren't you?"

She took a deep breath and shook her head. "No, Austin. I don't think so. It's probably best for me to make a clean break. For us to make a clean break."

"Felicity, please don't feel like you have to bow out just because of what happened last night."

"Last night was a mistake, Austin. You as much as said so in your note. By the way, thank you for the greenhouse, but I can't keep it. I do hope you can return it. In fact, if you'll let me know where you got it, I'm happy to see that it's returned and your account is credited."

"Felicity, please don't—"

"No, Austin. I'm afraid I'm the one who needs to say *please don't*. You made your feelings perfectly clear in the note. Let's agree not to talk about it while I serve out my two weeks. I'm sure everyone will be much better off for it."

After sorting through hundreds of résumés, narrowing the field and interviewing a dozen candidates, Felicity presented the final slate to Austin, allowing him to make the ultimate choice.

Austin chose a guy named George Daughtry.

A guy.

Not that gender mattered. Though, it was strangely gratifying that Austin had selected a guy. It felt less like she'd been replaced and more like he'd chosen the right candidate for the job. Because George had the strongest credentials.

Today was George's first full day of work. It also happened to be Felicity's last day.

While George had to work out a notice at his former job, he had come by after work so that Felicity could train him. Starting Monday, he would be on his own.

Felicity was graduating tomorrow and after the party her coworkers were throwing for her at four o'clock, she would be a free woman. She'd been so busy tying up loose ends at Fortune Investments— including writing a letter to Miles Fortune. She explained that while she appreciated his being willing to consider her for an advertising position, she thought it best if she moved on.

She hadn't yet had the opportunity to send out résumés. She would have plenty of time, though, because she had plenty of savings to allow her to take several months off if she needed to. Fortune Investments had paid well enough and she had saved diligently to afford her this privilege. This was the rainy day for which she had been saving. She spent the morning cleaning out her desk, and as each minute ticked away the hours of her last day, her heart grew heavier and heavier.

She was really doing this.

This was it. When she walked out the door tonight, it would likely be the last time she entered this building that had been her home away from home for nearly half a decade.

Ever since she'd given her notice, Austin had made himself scarce. The first week he'd been legitimately out of town on a business trip to New York City that had been on the books long before they'd known Felicity would be working out her notice. This week, he'd just been spotty.

So far, her last day was no different. Austin had not been around much today, except to meet with George for a few minutes in the morning, presumably to go over next week's schedule. Felicity had left them to meet by themselves. Aside from the fact that she hadn't been invited to sit in, it was for the best. After today, she wouldn't be around to interpret for George or clarify matters for Austin.

After she carried the last box down to her car and she had returned to her desk, her intercom buzzed. It was Carla from the front desk.

"Hey, baby girl, are you ready to party?" she asked. "We have cake." She sang the words and then lowered her voice. "God, you're so lucky you're getting out of this place. Take me with you."

"I'll see you in the conference room," Felicity said, and she hung up the phone.

She glanced at Austin's dark, empty office and felt the tears well in her eyes. She blinked them away. If he wasn't even going to show up to say goodbye, she wasn't going to waste her tears on him.

She turned off her computer for the last time, stood up from her desk, pushed in her chair, hitched her purse strap up onto her shoulder and walked toward the conference room without looking back.

The conference room was crowded with what looked like all of her Fortune Investments coworkers. Even Miles and Georgia were there. When she walked in, everyone clapped. Felicity's eyes scanned the room, but she didn't see Austin.

She hated herself for it, but her heart twisted and sank. A stinging, salty, burning sense of sorrow stung the back of her throat. She could barely swallow past the lump that had lodged there. Which made it all the more important for her to keep in place the smile she'd carefully affixed on her lips. If it slipped, the rest of the facade might, too, and fall like an avalanche. That was the last thing she needed right now. At least she still had her dignity the respect of her coworkers.

Since it hadn't been a secret that she'd given Austin her notice at the beginning of the month, no one had questioned her final date of resignation. Since none of Fortune Investments' rank and file had attended the foundation charity gala, none had been the wiser to her dances with Austin and hadn't put two and two together.

So, here she was, leaving with her reputation as Ms. Together and Efficient firmly intact.

Ha! Little did they know.

She was a hot mess on the inside.

Because despite how hard she was trying not to, all she could think about now was how fast her time with Austin had run out. She'd kissed him because she loved him and she wanted to believe that maybe, as in all the fairy tales she'd read as a child, true love would break the spell. That love would last. Like in *Beauty and the Beast*.

Did that mean he was doomed to remain a beast for the rest of his life? Probably not. He'd find love eventually.

What if she hadn't kissed him…

No. She couldn't change what was already done. She had arrived at this juncture in her life for a reason. Even if she hadn't kissed him after the gala, it would've happened eventually. And it would've ended up like this. It was time she moved on.

Carla shoved a plate of cake in Felicity's hands. It

was chocolate with white icing, her favorite. Was that a coincidence or had someone known?

The only person she could think of who knew that was Austin. Because every year on her birthday, he would buy her favorite cake and bring it into the office.

That wasn't so beastly. One of his better qualities, Felicity guessed.

She ate her cake and tried to make her way around the room to speak to as many of her colleagues as she could—even Miles Fortune, who was remarkably civil and complimentary, thanking her for her hard work and dedication to Fortune Investments. He mentioned not a word about the kiss with Austin in the hallway of the Roosevelt Hotel, but neither did he offer the standard *if you want to come back, there will always be a place for you.*

Felicity's sixth sense told her that after witnessing the kiss, ol' Miles considered her a liability, and, despite her hard work and dedication, he was happy to see her go.

And it was time.

The more she thought about it, the more she realized Austin had never really been interested in her. He'd kissed her back, but that had been the alcohol talking. Then Miles had interrupted, and the rest was history.

She disposed of her cake plate and started making her way to the door when he walked in—Austin, with his sister Savannah in tow.

Her heart leaped into her throat.

"Oh, Felicity, I'm so happy to see you." Savannah

pulled her into a hug. "Austin is taking me to the airport. We wanted to stop by before we left."

"Where's Chaz?" Felicity asked.

"He went home right after the ball. I stayed and helped Mom with some things, but now it's time for me to get back. I'm so sad that you're leaving FI. Where are you going?"

"I'm graduating tomorrow, and then I'm going to take some time off."

Even though her gaze was trained on Savannah, in Felicity's peripheral vision, she could see Austin standing behind his sister. Even more, she could feel his gaze on her. She resisted for as long as she could, but finally, she glanced up at him.

He looked as bereft as she felt. If it wouldn't have caused such a scene, she would've screamed at him. *What? Dammit! What do you want from me? You're not the one who gets to stand there looking all sad. You're the one who wanted things this way.*

"Well, I hate it that you're leaving, but the time off is well deserved. I know that workaholic brother of mine thinks that working is everyone's favorite pastime." Savannah turned to include Austin in the conversation. "Someday he'll learn."

Felicity forced her smile back into place, because it felt as if it was slipping. "I don't know. I think it's his nature. But I need to go. It was great to see you, Savannah. I'm bad at goodbyes. So I'm going to walk out of here like it's any other day."

Only, if it was any other day, she would've stayed

until after everyone else was gone, rather than being the first one to leave. But this was a new beginning.

"Could you stay for just a few more minutes?" Austin asked.

Felicity blinked. She really didn't want to, but if she said no in front of Savannah, his sister would know something was wrong.

"Sure, Austin." Her voice shook a little and she hated herself for it. She took a deep breath to steady her nerves.

Thank goodness, Austin had already begun calling the room to order.

"May I have everyone's attention, please?"

The room quieted in an instant, all eyes on Austin.

"I'm not going to lie," Austin said. "I am pretty torn up today. Because what does one do when they are losing their right-hand person? No offense to you, George, but Felicity and I go way back. Sometimes I think she knows me better than I know myself."

Oh, God, Austin, please don't do this.

Despite the way she'd been able to hold herself together, she felt her composure starting to slip. She tried to remind herself, again, that this was all his doing. Well, not all his doing. She had been the one to initiate the kiss. But if he had wanted her to stay, he would've told her so, and things could've been quite different right now. But it was what it was, and she was not going to cry.

She didn't even hear the rest of what Austin said, but the next thing she knew, he was gesturing toward a potted rosebush that was sitting on a nearby table.

"This is for the greenhouse that I had installed in your backyard today."

"What?" Maia was supposed to let a courier into Felicity's house today, so he could pick up the greenhouse to return it. Apparently, Maia had been working with Austin behind the scenes.

There was no need to make a scene. She would assess the situation when she got home, but in her gut, she knew that if the greenhouse had already been installed, there was probably no sending it back. The only thing she could do was be gracious as Austin gestured toward the rosebush and leaned in for a kiss on the cheek.

"I don't know what I'm going to do without you," he whispered as everyone else in the room applauded.

"I'm sure you will be fine, Austin. You'll be just fine."

"What's going on?" Savannah asked after she and Austin were in the car and on the way to the airport.

"Do you mean right in this moment, or with life in general?" Austin asked her, though he knew exactly what she meant.

"Don't be a smart-ass. You know what I'm talking about."

Austin slanted a glance at his sister, trying to figure out the best way to skirt the subject. He did not want to talk about it right now.

"Eyes on the road, buddy. Drive and talk."

He was silent for a few beats too long.

"Why is Felicity quitting? Tell me the real reason."

"She is graduating with her MBA tomorrow. She's

overqualified to be my handmaiden. It's time she moved on."

Savannah was quiet in that way people were when they weren't buying what you were trying to sell.

"I mean, think about it," he tried, desperately needing to fill the skeptical silence. "It would be a colossal waste of her time, talent and energy if she used that expensive education working as anybody's assistant. Even mine. Especially mine."

"And what happened to the advertising director position Dad was supposedly creating for her? It sounded like a dream job for someone in her position. It sounded like Miles was pretty gung ho about it. He was going to have her work with Georgia and between the two of them—"

"I know that. It didn't work out." He didn't mean to growl.

"It didn't work out for who?"

"I don't know. You'll have to ask Dad. No. Don't ask Dad."

"Well, I am going to ask Dad. In fact, I'll call him right now, if you don't tell me what's really going on."

Austin stared ahead at the ribbon of highway that stretched out in front of him. There was remarkably light traffic for a Friday evening. His heart felt very heavy as he relayed everything that had transpired between Felicity and him to his sister.

When he finished, she sat there for a moment without saying anything. Then he wished she would've remained silent because all she said was, "You're an idiot. I love you, but you're still an idiot."

"Yeah, I suppose I am. But that's not going to change anything. It's a whole hell of a lot more complicated than that."

"What are you talking about? You are in complete control of the situation. You are the one who is keeping the two of you apart. My God, Austin, sometimes you are your own worst enemy. Don't you see it?"

"Obviously not." His voice was monotone, because if he didn't keep it calm and level, he really felt like he was going to lose it. Not on his sister, but just on life in general.

The past two weeks he had been mad at the world because of the catch-22 he had found himself in. "If I would've defied company policy and continued to pursue the relationship, she not only would've lost the advertising job, but Miles probably would've fired us both. Then irony of ironies, she ended up turning the job down anyway."

"So…" Savannah dragged out the word. "I don't get it. What's keeping you apart now? The minute Felicity walked out that door, she was no longer a Fortune Investments employee. What's stopping you now?"

Nothing.

Everything.

Austin's head swam, and his aching heart thudded in his chest.

"She doesn't even want to talk to me. I screwed it up as I always do with things like this. It's over. It's done."

"It never even started, Austin, because you didn't give it a chance. Felicity is not Kelly. And you're letting Kelly rob you of a whole lot more than money if you let the ghost of your relationship come between you and Felicity."

Essentially, Felicity had said the same thing.

"Anyone who knows the two of you can see as plain as day that she is in love with you. And I know you and I can see that you are in love with her. You're just too big of an idiot to get out of your own way.

"Actually, let me rephrase that—you're too scared because of how things went down with your ex-wife to let things bloom with Felicity. You *will* be an idiot if you don't go after her and let her walk away. Austin, don't let her walk away. You have used work as an excuse for too long. You've been hiding behind the one mistake you made when you were twenty-five years old. It's time that you forgive yourself, quit punishing yourself. Put the past behind you and start living the life you deserve."

Sometimes it just took somebody you loved and trusted to hold up a mirror in front of your face, so you could see exactly how big of a dolt you were being and how much you stood to lose. Tonight, Savannah had held up that mirror.

Austin could feel the feelings she was talking about. He knew they were there living inside him, trapped in his heart, but he couldn't identify them to save his life. Not until his little sister had shone the spotlight on everything and made him realize he had to face his fears.

Thank God, Austin thought. Thank God he had snapped out of it before it was too late. If it wasn't too late already. He'd never know unless he tried.

On the drive home, after he'd dropped Savannah off at the airport, everything crystallized. Why was he willing to watch the best thing that had ever happened to him walk out of his life forever, without at least trying to save the relationship?

Felicity was worth it.

The two of them together—they were worth it.

They deserved a fighting chance. He didn't know if she felt the same way, but he would be an idiot if he didn't at least do what he could to let her know how he felt. The best way to start was by telling her exactly how he felt about her. He was in love with her. This wasn't just a passing whim. These feelings had been building for nearly five years. He owed it to himself and to her and to their future to let her know how he felt, even if it meant risking her rejecting him and telling him she didn't feel the same way.

On the drive home, an idea brewed. A big gesture. It might very well backfire in his face. Felicity might look at him and tell him to go to hell. But he had to do it. He had to chance it. Because she was the love of his life.

Felicity woke the morning of her graduation feeling empty and overcome by a sense of gray ennui. Maybe it was mental exhaustion after everything she had endured the past two weeks. Actually, going back even further than that—the whole buildup to the charity gala, the buildup and eventual letdown with Austin. The final two weeks at Fortune Investments spent avoiding each other in an awkward dance of pretending. Or, at least, pretending on her part. Then, the grand finale when she thought Austin would be a no-show at her going away party, and true to form, then Austin had changed everything, coming through the door at the very last minute.

But now, she was free. She wouldn't have to ride that roller coaster any longer. The messed-up thing about it was she was sad. She had worked so damn hard to get to this day, to get her MBA, which was supposed to set her free, but now more than ever she felt as if it had been the instrument of her demise.

She got out of bed, shuffled into the kitchen and poured herself a cup of coffee that had autobrewed, knowing that she was being overly dramatic. The MBA hadn't been the cause of her demise. What happened between her and Austin had been inevitable—and so had their parting of ways. This was like the day after an accident where she had been banged up. She didn't realize how badly her pride had been wounded until now; it had suffered a beating. Every day from here on out, she would get stronger and feel better. The first thing she had to do was make sure she held her head high and kept a positive outlook.

She had just finished showering and getting dressed when Maia knocked on her door. Her arms were loaded down with makeup and hair implements.

"Good morning, graduation girl. On a special day like this, I come to you. Is Beauty ready for the royal treatment?"

Ahh, Maia. What would she do without her friend? Even if she did sometimes take matters into her own hands, like she did with the greenhouse. Last night, when she had gotten home, she had scolded Maia for being in cahoots with Austin about the greenhouse, but all Mira had said was, "It's a nice present. Just be gracious. Or if you don't want it, I'll take it. I don't know what I'll do with it, because you're the woman with the green thumb, but you can't give it back now."

She was right. After mulling it over for a couple of hours, Felicity decided there was a lesson in it. In these new days of freedom, she needed to free her mind of the structure and the worry that had gotten her nowhere.

So, she relaxed with a mimosa from the pitcher that Maia had mixed. The friends chatted away about everything and nothing as Maia fixed Felicity's hair and makeup for her big day.

Three hours later, Felicity had her diploma cover in hand and she walked out into the audience of the auditorium to meet her mother and Maia who had come to cheer her on.

Her mother stood there with Maia, who held a bunch of sunflowers bound by a beautiful green ribbon in one arm like a runner-up in a beauty pageant and a bouquet of balloons in the other. She looked as if she might float away if a big gust of wind happened to blow through. Alas, they were indoors so there was no chance of that.

By this time, the auditorium had started to empty out. The people who lingered were gathered in small knots, congratulating their graduates with high fives, hugs and gifts. As her mother held out her arms and gathered Felicity to her, murmuring about how proud she was of her, Felicity reminded herself of how lucky she was to have the love and support of these two wonderful women. That love was guaranteed to last. It wouldn't float away like balloons on a storm. She had so much to be grateful for, and soon this empty feeling would dissipate. She would fill it with new adventures and she would feel like herself again. Eventually.

No, not like herself, maybe a better version of herself? Actually, right now, she would settle for feeling like herself again, because when she put everything else aside, that wasn't a bad thing.

Then she saw him. He was standing a few rows back holding a bouquet of roses. At first, she thought her mind had conjured the vision, that her eyes were playing tricks on her. Because ever since the kiss—the kiss that had changed her from the inside out—Austin Fortune had been living in the back of her mind. He had taken up residence in the hollowed-out place in her heart that felt like it would never again be whole because he held her heart in his hands.

But Felicity blinked, shook her head, and he was still there. He lifted his hand, tentatively as she pulled out of her mother's embrace. Almost in unison, Maia and her mom turned to see who she was looking at.

"Oh!" the two women said.

"Maia, is that who I think it is?" Mom asked in a stage whisper.

"Yes, it is. You know, I need to visit the ladies room. Who wants to come with me?"

Felicity's mother raised her hand. "I do."

The women hadn't taken two steps before Felicity saw them motion to Austin to approach, and then, as they walked away, they were chattering on about how good-looking he was and what a gorgeous couple he and Felicity made. If Felicity had been in her right mind, she might have turned and walked away with her mom and Maia, but she was rooted to the spot.

"Congratulations," Austin said. He handed her the blood red roses. There had to be at least five dozen. The bouquet was almost unwieldy, but it was breathtakingly beautiful. Austin shoved his hands in his back pockets. "I hope you don't mind me being here, but your graduation was on my calendar and…and I had some things to tell you. Don't worry, I'm not here to try to convince you to come back to work. If you want to get a new job, I just want you to be happy."

He pulled one hand out of his pocket and raked it through his hair and muttered a choice word under his breath. "And I am making the biggest mess out of this. It's so damn hard for me to admit my feelings, because for the longest time I didn't believe in true love. I was convinced it was a myth.

"But then you came along, and you made me a believer. Not that love was a myth. You made me believe in love. What I'm trying to say in my clumsy way is I'm in love with you, Felicity. I've probably been in love with you since the moment I first saw you. There's a dozen roses for every year we've known each other. And if you'll give me a chance, I'd like the opportunity to give you many more dozen roses in the years to come. Can we start over, or better yet, pick up where we left off in the hallway of the Roosevelt and—?"

Felicity didn't let him finish. She shifted the bouquet to one arm and threw her other arm around him, planting a kiss on his lips that left no doubt where she wanted them to go next.

When they finally came up for air, she said, "Austin Fortune, you're still a piece of work, but you're my piece of work and I wouldn't have it any other way. I love you so much."

At the sound of clapping and Maia's whoops, Felicity turned around to see her mother and her friend beaming at them. As Austin put his arm around her, Felicity shifted the bouquet of roses from one arm to another. A few petals floated to the ground.

Beauty had finally tamed the Beast.

Afterward, Austin took Felicity, her mother and Maia to Commander's Palace for a celebratory dinner. It was important for Felicity to bask in her accomplishments, surrounded by the people who loved her. Austin was so happy to be part of the celebration, but he would've been lying if he didn't admit, the entire time, all he wanted was for the two of them to be alone.

He'd waited years for her—even if he hadn't been fully cognizant of that fact until a few weeks ago.

Now, they sat in his living room. The only question was, where did they go from here? He handed her a glass of champagne. As he lowered himself onto the couch next to her, she smiled and gave her head a quick shake.

"What's wrong?" he asked.

"Nothing." She squeezed her eyes shut and smiled. "This is dumb, but I just realized this is the first time that I've been to your home and it hasn't been about business."

Austin searched her eyes, looking for a clue as to how she felt about being there. Was it too much? Was she putting on the breaks? He knew what he wanted. He wanted Felicity and not just for the short-term. But he needed to make sure she wanted the same thing.

"I don't want you to be uncomfortable?" he asked. "If you are, we can take things slowly—"

Suddenly, her lips were on his and her arms were around his neck. She claimed his lips in a kiss that seared his soul. She slid her hands into in his hair, pulling him closer. He responded by taking the champagne flute from her hand and setting it on the table. He wrapped his arms around her and pulled her in tight, as if he'd never let her go. Every inch of her body was pressed against his. He lost himself in the heated tenderness of that kiss.

Once, the mere thought of caring for someone that much scared him, but no more. He'd already passed the point of no return. There was no denying the truth. He'd fallen. And hard.

He was in love with Felicity.

He pulled back and placed his hands on either side of her cheeks. "I love you," he whispered, looking into her eyes, savoring the depth of their connection.

"I love you, too."

Those perfect words passed over her perfect lips and wrapped around his heart, touching him in places where he thought he would never be able to feel anything again. Places he once thought were dead, he now knew were very much alive.

Desire grew as he held her and tasted her. In response his own body swelled and hardened. He loved the feel of her curves, sexy and supple to his touch. When he dropped his hands to her hips and pulled her onto his lap, she arched against him fueling his desire.

"I want you," she murmured breathlessly.

He wanted to show her exactly how much he ached for her. Instead of using words, he stood and picked her up, carrying her to the bedroom.

The anticipation of their lovemaking sent a shudder wracking his whole body. He needed her naked so that he could bury himself inside of her. She wanted the same thing, because when he set her on the bed, she began to unbuckle the button on his pants, slid down the zipper and freed them of one of the barriers that stood between them. He shrugged off his shirt, unashamed of his nakedness.

Wanting to permanently imprint her on his senses, he deliberately slowed down, undoing each button of her blouse. Pushing it away, he unhooked the front clasp on her bra. As he freed her breasts, she lay back on the bed, and he lowered himself next to her. In turn, his mouth worshipped each one until she cried out in pleasure. Then, when he was sure she was ready, he stripped off her trousers and panties.

As they lay together—skin to skin, soul to soul—once again, he purposely slowed down, taking a moment to savor the way she looked and commit to memory the beauty of her body.

This was the Felicity he loved.

And then they were reaching for each other and touching everywhere, a tangle of arms and legs. He kissed her deeply—tongues thrusting, hands exploring, teeth nipping, bodies moving together in the most sensual pas de deux. Austin wasn't cognizant of space or time, he was only aware of her—the smell of her, the taste of her, the feel of her and the realization that he could not bear to spend another day—or night—in this world without her.

His heart, body and soul belonged to her.

He needed to make her his.

"Now," she whispered, her breath hot on his neck. And he buried himself deep inside her.

As they lay together, spent and glowing, Felicity snuggled deeper into the crook of Austin's arm—a place where she fit so perfectly it felt as if it had been made for her. She turned her cheek and nuzzled his chest, breathing in the scent of him—that delicious smell of cedar, coffee and leather. She breathed in deeply and melted a little more with the heat of his body.

But he moved, propping himself up on his elbow. He smoothed an errant lock of hair off her forehead, kissed the skin he'd just uncovered.

"I could get used to this," he said.

She smiled up at him. "I already have."

He pulled her into his arms and kissed her. Then he held her so close she could hear his heart beat. For the first time in ages, she felt safe and things felt right. She knew she was exactly where she belonged. Together, they completed each other.

Together, they were whole.

Epilogue

Thanksgiving at Miles and Sarah's was almost overwhelming, in the very best, most thrilling way. The whole family was there—all of Austin's siblings along with their spouses and significant others.

Miles and Sarah had graciously welcomed Felicity's mother and Maia to the festivities. Over the months, Felicity had grown quite fond of Miles and Sarah and Austin's huge, boisterous family.

After Miles offered Felicity the advertising director position, he had made a special exception to the Fortune Investments' no fraternizing policy, allowing Austin and Felicity to have the best of both worlds. Because of that, she was regularly included in the family's infamous dinners. Sometimes those could get a little lively with all of the big Fortune opinions.

After all the years of growing up as an only child, with it just being Felicity and her mother, the Fortunes were the big, warm family she never knew she had always wanted.

This Thanksgiving Day also held another special meaning. Felicity and Austin had officially been together for six months. Six months and they were getting stronger every day. Finally, she had let go of the notion that love had an expiration date. Crushes and flights of fancy might expire, but true love knew no end.

Today, as the family sat around the big dining room table, the waitstaff that Sarah had hired effortlessly facilitated the holiday meal, including serving the delicious-looking desserts on display on the antique buffet.

The server had poured champagne to go with the pumpkin pie. It was a combination that Felicity and her mother had never enjoyed during their small celebrations—they usually paired coffee with pie—but she was constantly learning new things from this family.

The servers were still plating slices of pie when Austin stood and began gently pinging the side of his crystal champagne flute with a sterling silver knife.

"I am so happy we could all be together this holiday. As I look around the table, I realize how much we have to be thankful for. We are truly blessed. Our family is happy and healthy and we're all together. That's why I couldn't think of a better time to do this."

Felicity saw Austin exchange knowing glances with his father and then her mother.

"Six months ago today, I finally came to my senses and took a chance on confessing my love to Felicity. Ever since that day, I've never looked back. That was, without a doubt, the smartest move I've ever made in my life. Until today."

Little pinpricks of dawning skittered up and down Felicity's body. The subsequent events unfolded in a surreal sort of slow motion: Austin turned toward her; he took her hand; he lowered himself down on one knee; he reached into his pocket with his free hand and pulled out a small light blue jewelry box. Somehow, he managed to open it with one hand, revealing a stunning sparkler of an oval diamond.

"Felicity Schafer, you are the woman who finally made me believe in love. Will you make me the happiest man in the world and be my wife?"

The events may have happened in slow motion, but Austin's words were crystal clear and so was her instantaneous response. "Yes!"

The room erupted into raucous applause. Miles Fortune raised his glass. "To Austin and Felicity. To family, old and new. Happy Thanksgiving and many, many years of love and happiness."

* * * * *

MILLS & BOON

Coming next month

SUMMER ESCAPE WITH THE TYCOON
Donna Alward

"This is a great spot," Molly said, leaning back to look at the stars that had popped out overhead. "I mean, I know this is supposed to be some great adventure tour, but I feel as if I'm in the lap of luxury. Wineries and great food and a massage and a soak in a hot tub. It's positively indulgent."

"Enjoy it now. In a few days we'll be roughing it."

The mood had changed a bit, and Molly felt a bit off-balance. She hadn't really been tested so far on this trip, and now she was afraid of looking silly in front of Eric as the more challenging aspects were just ahead. He seemed so…capable. Of anything.

"Just think, though," he said softly. "We'll be out there surrounded by nature, seeing orcas and sea lions and who knows what else? It's pretty amazing."

"I'm trying not to be intimidated."

"But you are?"

She nodded, deciding to confide a little. What would it hurt? That was the whole purpose of the trip, wasn't it? To stretch her boundaries a little? Besides, after this trip was over, she'd never see him again. There was some safety in that.

"I'm good at what I do, but I've lived a pretty sheltered life." Especially since Jack's death, and she was left an only child. "I'm not used to feeling vulnerable. So while kayaking with killer whales sounds amazing and exciting, it's also way out of my comfort zone. I mean…" She gestured down at herself. "I'm this size. And an orca is…"

"Much, much bigger."

"I have this fear that one will swim under my kayak and flip me over."

"We'll stay close to shore. I don't think you have to worry about that."

"Probably not. But…it is what it is." She smiled weakly. "Please don't use that against me."

"I won't." He studied her with a somber expression. "I don't believe in using people's fears against them."

She thought about that for a moment. "Really? Because I'd think that might be a strategy for someone in acquisitions. A negotiating tactic."

He tilted his head as he thought for a minute. "No," he answered. "I might exploit a weakness, but not a fear. And yes, there's a difference."

He removed one arm from the edge of the hot tub and turned to face her, only inches away. Her pulse hammered at her throat as his gaze captured hers. "What you just said? That's a fear." He moved an inch closer. "But the way I'm feeling right now, this close to you? That's a weakness."

Her breath caught. "Are you asking me to exploit it?"

His gaze dropped to her lips, then back up to her eyes. "Oh, it's tempting. Very tempting."

Continue reading
SUMMER ESCAPE WITH THE TYCOON
Donna Alward

Available next month
www.millsandboon.co.uk